# IRRESISTIBLY RISKY

## J. SAMAN

# 1

## ASHER

**M**y forehead lands with a muted thud, smashing against my forearm that's pressed into the tile wall of the bathroom. Everything spins and I need a second to get my bearings as the room slows a little, bringing a buzzed, tingly warm smile to my lips. I can't remember the last time I got drunk, and I wonder if I shouldn't have taken the second muscle relaxant after taking that last shot.

Inhaling a deep breath, I force myself to stand upright, unzip my jeans, and do my thing, humming a song that's been going through my head on repeat all night. My best friend, Greyson Monroe, a world-famous rock star, wrote it for our team when we made it to the playoffs. It's been our anthem since, and tonight, I like to think it helped lead us to a Super Bowl victory.

It's also one of those songs you can't get out of your head no matter what you do.

Absently, the fingers not wrapped around my favorite guy tap out the rhythm against my thigh. My head joins in, moving along to a mixture of the song and the heavy house beat just outside the bathroom door. Once I'm done, I zip myself back up, unlock the stall door, and head to the sink, groaning when I get a look at myself in the mirror against the blue-tinted light of the bathroom.

My hair is scraggly and long, and my beard is itchy as fuck. I can't wait to get rid of both of them tomorrow. Then again, they represent the weeks and months that got me here, and I practically whoop into the air as a total shit-eating grin spreads across my face.

I won the fucking Super Bowl tonight.

Me. The guy who everyone counted out because instead of living, breathing, and dying football for all four years of college, I toured the world with my best friends as part of the hugely successful rock band, Central Square. I didn't make it to in-person college until my junior year, and then I had to go as a walk-on at the University of Alabama despite my family legacy both there and on the field.

But fuck all the assholes who bet against me and said it could never be done. Drafted in the sixth round, I showed them all.

I snicker a bit drunkenly to myself and then wash my hands. Just as I dry off on the cloth napkins they have in this club, a woman comes stumbling into the bathroom. Her eyes catch mine, first in the reflection in the mirror, and then snap over to face me directly.

And once I get a good look at her...

*Hell.*

I'm shocked my tongue isn't hanging out of my mouth.

She's tall, with *long*, toned legs on full display beneath the short hem of her dress. Her large tits, curvy hips, and ass I can't fully see but can already tell would fill up my hands perfectly, have me doing a double and then a triple blink. Her short, white, tight-as-all-sin dress has a few spots of something pink trickling down it. Could be her drink, could be part of the couture—no way to know for sure. Her ink-black hair flows down her back in thick, bouncy waves, and her eyes are a vibrant green that only appears to be accentuated by the pink of her pillowy lips.

She looks like that hot Victoria's Secret model whose name is eluding me because, who cares when this woman is standing before me?

"H-hi," I stutter, amused that she has me tripping over my words. Well, that's a new one.

"Hi," she squawks, startled to find me here. "Um—" She shifts to her other foot. Looks around. And when she realizes we're completely alone in here, she says, "I thought this was the ladies' room."

I grin, tossing the used towel in the bin but making no move to leave. "It is. The men's room had a line."

She snorts, shuffling three steps in my direction in her five-inch black platform heels that nearly put her at eye level with me. "That's a first."

"I have no doubt it is. Your bathrooms are nicer than ours."

"That I definitely believe." She cocks her head playfully. "First time in the ladies' room then?"

"First time. I'm a ladies' room virgin."

She emits a breathy laugh. "Glad I could be here for your cherry popping. I did notice it was mostly a sausage fest up here." She holds up a hand, redirecting herself. "Not that I'm complaining. The only men I see are the ones I work with, and no thank you there. Is this some sort of work or corporate event?"

"Something like that." I don't bother following up that this floor is filled with Boston Rebels' team members only. That means players, coaches, trainers, staff, their families, and my friends. That's it, and about eighty-five percent of us are dudes, hence the line for the men's room and none for the ladies.

It's also a private event, which means if she doesn't know that, she snuck up here, which makes me curious if she's trying to play me or if she truly doesn't know what's going on.

"Do you plan to stay in here while I pee?" she challenges, folding her arms and giving me a raised eyebrow.

I wipe my smirk with my fingertips. "Someone has to make sure you're safe in here. It's an empty bathroom in a club. That has risky written all over it."

Another step and her eyes do that slow, sexy sweep thing women do when they're interested. My cock gives a languid jerk in my jeans.

"Risky?" She tests the word on her tongue. "I don't know about that. If anything, I think a solo guy in a ladies' room while I pee is far sketchier."

She might have a point. Except this is my party. Something I don't think she's aware of. In fact, judging by the lack of recognition in her eyes, I'd say she has no clue who I am.

"How'd you get up onto this floor, beautiful?"

She laughs, the sound genuine and sweet, as she passes right by me, entering the stall and locking the door behind her. "Are you the club police?"

I grin, glad that she's not uncomfortable that I'm still here and relieved that she didn't ask me to leave. "Definitely not. I like you up here and think you should stay. I was simply curious since I hadn't seen you earlier."

"It's my birthday," she declares as I hear clothes being shifted this way and that, and I can't stop the mental image that comes with that. "Are you still with me, muscles, or did you flee?" she asks when I don't immediately respond.

I lean against the counter. "I'm still here."

"Good stuff. Cover your ears for a minute, would ya?"

I can't fight my laughter. "Sure. You need privacy."

"You're the one in the wrong room, but I kind of like talking with you, so give me a minute."

"Done." I cover my ears and even close my eyes, ignoring how that makes the room spin ever so slightly. A minute or so later, I hear the automatic toilet flush and drop my hands, shoving them into the pockets of my jeans.

"I'm done. You can listen now," she calls out. "So, it's my birthday, as I said," she continues without waiting on me. "But it's also my goodbye party. I'm leaving Miami tomorrow."

"Funny. I am too."

"How adorable. We both have something in common." A moment later, she's out of the stall, stumbling and staggering a bit until she's beside me at the sink, washing her hands. I spin around, and my eyes meet hers in the mirror. "My work friend dared me to sneak onto the

VIP floor, so I did it. *After* I had a few drinks and a birthday shot or two. I'm never daring, but she pushed me a bit by reminding me you only live once—"

"So live every day to the fullest," I finish for her, and her face lights up.

She blinks at me, dumbfounded. "Yes. Exactly that. How did you know?"

I chuckle lightly. She's adorable. And sexy. And a bit quirky, which I like in my women.

I fall in behind her, and my hands somehow decide to make their way to her hips over her dress. I pause. I wait. Her gaze snags on my hands on her body, and she drags in a heavy breath before her gaze meets mine once more.

"Because that's precisely how I live my life," I tell her. "This okay?" I check, my eyes flickering down to my hands and then back up to hers.

"I... um. Yes. I think so." She licks her lips nervously and then laughs in a self-deprecating way. "Yes, it's fine. I like it." She flushes lightly. "It's new for me. The most adventurous thing I've ever done is..." She pauses and scrunches up her face as she thinks about it. Then she sighs. A deep, heavy one. "You're going to think I'm so lame."

"Not even a little. Try me." My hands slide forward and then up a little into the dip of her waist, and I can't believe she's letting me touch her like this, but I can't stop it either. I can't remember a time when I've been so instantly and consumingly attracted to someone as I am to her.

"Okay. This. Sneaking up here tonight."

"That's..." I trail off.

"Lame, right? Totally, pathetically lame."

I laugh at her horrified expression. "Maybe a bit, yeah. But hell, you're here. You did the crazy thing. So let's keep it going."

She smiles a sassy, taunting smile that makes my heart smash against my ribcage and my cock ache in my jeans. "Keep it going, how?"

Oh, I can think of at least a hundred ways, and all of them involve her being naked. Leaning in, my lips meet the soft skin beneath her ear, inhaling her intoxicating fragrance. She trembles, her breath catching in her lungs, and I smirk, feeling like Hades stealing sweet Persephone or the serpent tempting a curious Eve to eat the apple.

"Wanna go out there and dance with me?"

She twists in my arms and peers up at me through her lashes. Her hands plant themselves on my chest, the warmth of her touch seeping through the cotton of my shirt. "I love to dance, but I'll break an ankle in these shoes. I don't even know why I wore them here. They're terrible."

I'm not the least bit disappointed by that. Every muscle in my body aches, and I'm covered in bruises from all the rough hits I took tonight. "Your shoes aren't terrible. They're sexy as fuck. But if it makes you feel better, I'm a terrible Scrabble player."

She laughs. "Oh yeah? That's hot. Tell me what else you're bad at."

I grin, dragging my hands to her back and pressing her into me. Her soft tits squish against my chest, the scent of her perfume hitting me on my next inhale. I want to touch this woman. I want to see what she looks like when I make her come. I want to strip her down and take in every inch of her pale skin.

I hold her against me, swaying us ever so gently to the beat that filters in through the door. "Playing guitar." I smirk since I was the backup guitarist for Central Square. "Now you."

"Elizabethan English." She feigns a shudder. "I sucked at Shake-speare. I'm a math and science nerd. Let's switch this up. What are you good at?"

Maybe it's the alcohol or the muscle relaxants, or maybe it's the way she asks—with layers of innuendo barely veiled beneath the surface—that has me pulling out all the stops and blowing past pretenses. "Making women come. Hard."

She shudders against me, and I feel her body move in on mine, her hip now rubbing my lower abdomen. I don't know what's happening, and I don't care. She's easily the hottest woman I've ever seen, and she clearly doesn't know who I am. It only makes her, and *this*, hotter.

"That's a pretty cocky statement."

I raise an eyebrow at her choice of words. "I'd say so. Then again, I'm known for being cocky."

She giggles, falling back against the counter and covering her face with her hands. "I can't believe I'm in a bathroom in a club having this type of conversation and acting this way with a total stranger. And he just delivered a line like that."

"Too cheesy?"

"*So* cheesy, but I started it. Still… this isn't me."

"Why?" I press as I pry her hands from her face, only to lace them with mine. "You said you wanted a bit of adventure. What's more adventurous than meeting a random stranger in a bathroom and seeing where it takes you?"

She stares up at me, her pale eyes hooded, her cheeks flushing a stunning shade of rose. In my next breath, she's on me. Her lips slam against mine, her body coming along for the ride and knocking me back a step with the shock of it. She stumbles forward in her towering heels, our momentum carrying us, until her feet tangle with mine, tripping us till we go tumbling. I smash into the wall, hitting my head and already sore back with a hard oomph that drags a laugh out of both of us.

"How much have you had to drink tonight?" I question, the sudden movement making me dizzier than I was a few minutes ago.

She smiles up at me, her eyes a little glazed but wild and alive. So pretty that she robs the breath from my lungs. "Enough to have sex with a hot stranger in a bathroom."

"Uh—"

Her hand slams over my mouth, literally cutting off my protest. "Shut up. Stop thinking, or I'll start thinking, and that's not what I want to do right now. I've never had random sex with anyone, and I want to—with you. It's my birthday, and generally, I don't like my birthday, but I'd love to change that. You told me you're good at making women come hard. Prove it. Give me a night I'll never forget."

I stare into her eyes for a moment, at the way her dark pupils eclipse all the green, and then I knock her hand out of the way, cup her face, and kiss her. Hard. So hard it makes me groan because I haven't kissed a woman in far too long, and her lips are like my own personal form of catnip. I can't get enough of them.

My lips explore—playing, moving, sliding, nipping. That only manages to last a moment because I need to taste her. Her lips part with mine, and my tongue takes full advantage, diving in and finding hers.

She tastes sweet and fruity, like whatever she's been drinking all night, and it sears yet another groan from the back of my throat. It's a groan of desperation. A groan of frustration. Because here we are in an unlocked bathroom in a club, and any second, someone could walk in. I don't have the luxury of time. I can't undress her, I can't lick every inch of her skin, and I can't explore her body the way I'm dying to.

This has to be fast, which makes it dirty—and that's hot, but not fully what I'm after with her. Maybe after this, I can convince her to come to my hotel for the rest of the night.

It's with that thought in mind that I tear my mouth from hers and spin her around to face the mirror. Hazy, lust-drunk eyes reflect mine, and I watch them as my hand slides up the back of her thighs. Her skin is so soft, almost delicate against my palm as I drag the hem of her short, tight dress up and over her luscious ass.

Unable to stop it, my gaze snaps down, and I take her in from this position. "Sweet Jesus," I murmur, almost absently, as I start caressing the globes of each cheek. "Your body..." I shake my head. "Every inch of you makes me hard."

Only... well...

Shaking that off, I shift her thong to the side and slide two fingers inside her. She's wet and warm and so goddamn tight. She moans, her back arching, as I start to pump my fingers in and out of her. I twist my wrist and my thumb finds her clit. I want to make her come. I want to make her come while I stare at her pretty face in the mirror.

I want her to watch as I do that because it's hot and only seems to add to the risky adventure of what we're doing.

"Hurry," she whines as if reading my thoughts. "Someone could walk in any second."

I continue to play with her pussy even as I reach into my back pocket with my free hand, searching for my wallet. I flip it open and reluctantly pull my fingers from her, licking them clean so I can taste more of her and then fishing for a condom.

"We're doing this fast, but that's not what I want," I tell her as I catch the condom wrapper in my teeth and unzip myself.

"It's not?" she questions, and I shake my head, but I lose my train of thought as I pull my guy out and find him... inactive. Well, maybe that's not the best way to describe him. He's active. He's just not *fully* active. Certainly not anywhere near my regular size and a wave of panic hits me and hits me hard.

I've *never* had this problem before.

I give him a few quick jerks, mentally egging him on. I keep rubbing her, touching her, using her wetness to coat my dick, and still, he's half-mast.

"Come on," she clips out nervously, her gaze casting over to the door, reminding me that I'm on the clock, and that's not helping anything. "What's wrong?"

My eyes jump up to hers. "Nothing," I sputter quickly, forcing a smile as sweat starts to coat my brow.

"You sure?"

No. I'm not fucking sure.

Because why in the motherfuck am I not hard? The hottest woman I've ever seen is bent over a bathroom sink with her sweet ass and wet, wanting pussy in the air, and I'm having... performance issues. No. This is not who I am. Something like that doesn't happen to guys like me. I'm twenty-seven, not eighty-seven.

*This is not the time for whiskey dick, brother. Come on. Harden up for me.*

"Please. I want this. I want you. Now."

I shake my head and, without thinking, plunge my semi straight into her. And holy hell, she feels unbelievable. I don't know if it's her or if it's the situation, but I'd swear, nothing has ever felt better. This is it. This is what I need. Her hot, tight pussy around me. I'll be hard in no time.

I start to pump into her in earnest, thrusting like a madman, convinced that the harder I fuck her, the harder my cock will grow.

My mouth opens as I suck in a ragged breath, absently noting something flashing from the corner of my eye as it falls. I don't linger on it as I'm too busy giving her everything I have. Harder. Faster. But to no avail.

All I can think about is, *Why the hell am I not hard?*

Her pussy is gripping me, sucking me in, wanting every inch I can give her.

She's moaning and pushing back against me, wiggling her hips, and searching for me as she says things that I'm hardly listening to because I'm too focused on this.

This... nothing. *Fuck!*

"Good?" I somehow question, already knowing it's not good for her. How could it be?

"Uh. Hmm. Yeah. Um. Can you... go deeper, maybe? Harder?"

*I can try.*

I'm losing my mind right now, and that's only seeming to make this worse. I do my best. I give it my full focus, as I pound into her like a madman. I reach around and find her clit, anything to make it better for her. Anything to give her the orgasm I promised.

She's not going to come, and I feel like garbage for it.

But then something happens. Something out of nowhere. "Fuck!" Because with all my pumping and thrusting and fucking and focus on my dick, *I* start to come. It slams into me like a tsunami, abrupt and utterly devastating. It happens so fast that I can't stop it. Hell, it doesn't even make sense. Can you come without being fully erect?

Evidently, the answer is yes, because that's what's happening right now.

"Did you just..."

"I did." Shit. *Fuck.* "I'm so sorry. That's never happened before." I stare down at where I'm still inside her and then up to her face. She's not happy with me, and I can't blame her. "I swear, that's never happened to me. There has to be some sort of medical explanation. Give me five minutes. My best friend is a doctor. He'll figure this out."

Without waiting for her to say anything, I pull out and tuck my former best man back into my jeans.

In my desperation, I start spewing words a mile a minute. "Just don't go, okay? I'm sorry. I know this is messed up and not what you were looking for. Please stay and wait for me. I... I want to make this so good for you and I want you, so just stay." I flee the bathroom, thoroughly mortified and panicked in a way I've never been before.

Adrenaline races through my veins, and I shoot around the loud VIP club floor, squinting past the stupid strobe lights and multicolored bullshit, anxious to find Callan. Callan can help. Callan can fix this.

He's over by the bar talking to our friends Zax, Greyson, and Lenox, and I bolt straight for them. My hand latches onto Callan's arm, and I shake him. "I need Viagra. Now, dude."

"What?" Callan blinks fifty thousand times at me and who has time for that shit.

"Viagra, bro. Now. I was just with this incredible woman in the bathroom, and my guy not only wasn't fully hard, he prematurely shot his load. Something is wrong with me, and I need Viagra to fix it now."

He coughs out a laugh, as do our friends, but I ignore that and them. "Does it look like I carry a pharmacy on me? Besides, I'm not writing you a prescription for Viagra. You had alcohol and muscle relaxants, not to mention you are likely a bit dehydrated after playing football for hours. Viagra will tank your blood pressure."

"Fuck!" I yell and then race back for the bathroom. This can't be happening. I plow through the ladies' room door, only I already know before I enter what I'm going to find. She's gone. The room is empty, and my mystery woman ran off on me.

Not that I can blame her.

I can't even chase after her, because what would I say? Worst performance of my life, and it had to happen tonight. With her.

My hands scrub up my face and through my hair as I fall against the wall, staring at the space where I just undoubtedly gave her the lousiest sex of her life. Only it gets worse.

Lying on the floor is the condom, still in its wrapper. Because I never opened it and put it on. Double fuck.

# 2

---

## WYNTER

A year and a half later

"ALEXA, STOP," I call out to the device we have in the corner of the OR, and immediately Taylor Swift shuts off.

Half the room groans in protest. "Ah, come on. That was the best part," one of the nurses complains.

I grin behind my mask. "No, it wasn't. This is. We're done. You can close," I tell Jequai, the resident beside me, all business, though my heart hasn't stopped hammering like a jackrabbit's since I stepped foot in this OR with my first patient this morning. Three surgeries later, it still hasn't slowed. The rush never gets old, but it's also my first surgical day as an attending with this practice, so nerves are to be expected. "But I want those stitches to be tight with perfect approximation. The last thing we need is for this patient to return with any sort of abscess or wound infection. We'll glue the top layer."

Jequai does this blinky owl-eyed thing to me and then does the same to the surgical field before us. "Really? You're sure? Dr. Limpdick never lets us do that."

I choke into my mask. "Who?"

The intern across from the resident clears his throat, as do two nurses.

"What am I missing?" I question, searching the eyes of everyone in here since that's all I can see over their masks. I'm too new to know if this is some sort of initiation or gag.

"Dr. Limbick."

I snort out a laugh, my eyebrows at my hairline. "Does he know you call him Limpdick?" I hold up my gloved hand. "And wait, how did you get Limpdick of all names?" Then I think better of it and hold up my hand a second time. "Never mind, I get it now. Evidently, I'm a little slow on the uptake. Let's get back to the patient and away from Limbick's limp dick—a mental image I could have gone my entire life without, so thanks for that."

"I know right?" Jequai laughs. "I keep picturing it old and saggy—"

"Enough," I cut in sharply. "For real, I can't take anymore. Do you feel comfortable closing without me?"

"Yes," Jequai promises earnestly. "We study in lab all the time. He just never lets us touch a patient and feeds us lines about how this hospital is number three in the country, and our sports medicine program is number one, and we're here to learn."

I scowl at that. "You're also here to *do*. See one, do one, teach one. I'm letting you do one Jequai. Next time you'll teach one to Ross over there."

Jequai bobs his head at the intern across from us. "See? I knew she was cool when she let us both scrub in and stand patient-side. And then put on music."

Jesus. What are the attendings doing here?

Maybe I'm in the wrong, but when I was a resident in Miami and then doing a fellowship in the UK, it was entirely hands-on with no holding back. How else do you learn? That said...

"I'm not cool. I might be the least cool person you've ever met. I'm boring and annoyingly type-A, and my idea of a good time is sleeping."

"But you won a gold medal. I heard Limpdick bragging to a patient about how you were barely even fifteen when you won it for figure skating. That was you, right?"

"Yes. That was me."

"That's cool."

I smirk beneath my mask at his awed tone. "Okay, I agree, that was cool, but I'm far from cool now. Back to the patient. Show me your stuff and prove to me that you deserve to be the resident on my team."

Jequai gets to work on suturing and gluing our patient closed. And he does a damn fine job of it. By the time we scrub out, it's late, and after I speak to the family of the patient and crack my back about fifty different times in fifty different ways, I'm more than ready for this day to be over.

I wasn't lying about the sleeping. It's become my favorite sport, and I've learned to get it wherever and whenever I can. Probably because I haven't stopped moving since I was three. But the last year and a half of my life has been trial by fire.

I spent six months in London working with an ortho team there, and then I came back to Miami to, well, deliver my son and finish up my residency. Then I hung around the ortho floor at my hospital in Miami until I was offered the position here in Boston.

I wasn't about to give up on my dream of becoming a sports medicine orthopedic surgeon, certainly not when I was that close to the finish line. Nine years—including medical school—of struggling and toiling were not going to be overthrown simply because I had an epically horrendous drunken one-night stand and got pregnant.

But now Mason is almost one, and when the sports medicine orthopedic surgeons at Mass General Hospital offered me a position as a new surgeon on their team, I didn't hesitate. For one, it's the premiere sports orthopedic surgery practice in the country—I mean, hello, Boston sports. And for another, my mother and stepfather moved up here about five years ago after my stepfather retired from the NHL to become the head coach of Boston College's hockey program.

I now have help with Mason and a place to stay until I figure out a better alternative for us.

Stretching my arms over my head, I head back toward the locker room to grab my stuff so I can get out of here. If I rush, I can make it home before my little man goes to sleep. Maybe he'll stay up so I can read him a story or at least snuggle him a little.

"There you are. I've been looking for you," Dr. Limpdick—er, I mean Limbick—says to me. "I was hoping to catch you before you left for the night. Do you have a minute?"

No. The word snags on my tongue. The very tip of it. But it's my first week and he's my new boss, so I can't say no. I plaster on a saccharine-sweet smile and force out, "Sure."

"Great. My office?" He checks but doesn't wait for my response as he heads in that direction.

Two minutes later, I'm shutting the door behind us and taking a seat as I covertly text my mom to let her know I might not make it home for bedtime. My heart plummets when she tells me he's had his bath and seems sleepy. Fuck. I'm the worst mother in the world.

"Wynter?"

My gaze snaps up, clearly having missed whatever he said before that. "Yes. Sorry. I was just letting my mother know I might be a bit late to say goodnight to my son." Hint, hint, nudge, nudge.

"Right. Sure. I remember those days. My boys are all out of the house, living their own lives now, and no longer have any need for their old man other than my wallet."

Ha, ha, ha, yes, how funny and awesome for you that you're not a single parent with an infant and can stay at work as late as you'd like.

"Did you want to speak to me about something?" I ask, trying to temper my tone.

He sits up, clearly remembering his focus. "Yes, I did. I know you had mentioned how you wanted hockey and basketball to be your sports focus, but it's been requested that you take on the Boston Rebels."

I do my best not to glare or find a random sharp implement to stab his carotid with. "Football?" The word hisses past my lips with more venom than any curse word ever could, and I clear my throat, hoping it wasn't as obvious as I'm sure it was.

"Not your favorite sport then?" He surmises with a conspiratorial grin.

*Understatement of the century there, Limpdick.* "Uh. No. It's not. Who made this request?"

A gleeful light hits his eyes. "Joe Cardone."

Just like that, my world stops along with my breathing. The now necrotic part of my heart that he used to own burns, giving me chest pain. "I'm s-sorry," I stutter through. "Joe Cardone?" His name on my tongue causes a wave of nausea.

"Yes! Can you believe it? I didn't know you knew him."

"I, um. I don't. Not really. I thought he was still coaching in LA." It's why I stayed on the freaking East Coast all these years.

"He was just named as the new coach for the Boston Rebels last month after they fired their last coach in the offseason."

My insides freeze over. "Oh." That's all I can manage because I had no clue my biological father was living in Boston, let alone the new coach for the Boston Rebels. That's a massive oversight on my part.

More shocking than that, how on earth did he know I was here? Hell, I had no clue he was aware I was an orthopedic surgeon. The last time I saw him was on my fifth birthday when I fell out of the tree in our front yard and gave myself a lovely compound fracture of my radius. I screamed for him, but he never came, and when I finally managed to get myself inside the house, I found him in my parents' bed naked with my mother's best friend.

She wasn't his first mistress—just the one he was caught with.

After that, he divorced my mother and got himself transferred to another team across the country since he was still playing profession-ally then.

I didn't see him or speak to him again. Not once.

Not even when I would call him and call him as a child desperate to talk to her father.

He never bothered with any of my skating events and wasn't there when I won a fucking Olympic gold medal or when I subsequently blew out my knee less than two years later and my career ended. He didn't care to learn that I got early acceptance to Yale for college or that I went on to Princeton for medical school. He had no knowledge that I was placed in a top-tier residency program. He definitely has no clue that I got pregnant and had a kid—he likely doesn't know Mason even exists.

As far as I was concerned, my father had completely written me off when he told me he was moving away and wouldn't see me again for a very long time.

The best thing to come out of that birthday was the orthopedic surgeon who fixed my arm and made me fall in love with this profession. Then there's the man who later became my stepfather, a professional hockey player who renewed my faith in mankind—literally. It's his last name that I bear. It's him I call Dad.

Certainly not Joe Cardone.

"I have to tell you," Limbick continues, oblivious to my inner panic and turmoil, "not many get this sort of opportunity. One of their players is having a hush-hush shoulder issue, and Joe specifically requested that you be the doctor to take over not only for Asher Reyes's care but for the team."

I shake my head, still lost in this. "Asher Reyes?"

He chuckles. "You really know nothing about football, do you?"

"No," I admit. "Nothing." Not if I can help it. I have spent my life avoiding all things football, the one thing my father loved. Anything that had to do with him, I shunned. I couldn't tell you one single football player on any team. I've never watched a game—collegiate or professional.

I'd rather watch fucking paint dry than football.

"Asher Reyes comes from a long line of football greats. He nearly blew his shot at making the pros because he was part of some rock band during his first two years of college. He was the backup in

Alabama and then started his senior year. After that, he was drafted in the sixth round. Anyway, just last year the starting QB got hurt, and he stepped in and led the team to a Super Bowl victory. Now he's our guy. A guy the team can't afford to have hurt."

"That would be tragic, I'm sure," I deadpan, knowing he's missing my sarcasm completely. "I'm assuming that's where I come in."

He points at me. "Exactly. The team wants you to go to the stadium and meet with him tomorrow."

I shake my head in confusion. "Why isn't he coming here?"

"Because, as I said, this is hush-hush. The team doesn't want it getting out, and if he's seen walking into an orthopedic surgeon's office—"

"I get it," I interrupt, licking my lips nervously. "Isn't there anyone else who would be better suited for such a high-profile person? Someone who actually *likes* football, perhaps. Someone who's at least been doing this longer than I have."

I've only been an attending for a year.

"I offered my services, but Joe's assistant was adamant it be you."

That slimy motherfucker. What game is he trying to play with me? And why now? "I see." It's all I can force out.

"So, how do you know Joe?" He continues conspiratorially as if I'm about to impart him with some great state secret. "His office wouldn't say anything other than he wanted you."

I haven't been here very long, and this is the practice all other sports medicine practices try to be. I should tell Dr. Limbick that Joe Cardone is my biological father.

But just as I never wanted anything to do with him or his sport after he left me, I don't want anyone to know he's technically related to me. I've worked so hard and come so far to get here. An uphill battle few would have been able to reach the summit of.

But I did.

On my own. As a newly single mom too.

I can't let my asshole father be the one to take me down. Not now. Not ever.

"I knew him a long time ago."

His eyebrows rise, impressed when he should be anything but. "He's clearly kept track of you to know you now work here. In any event, I'm going to shuffle your cases to other providers. That shouldn't be difficult since you're so new here. You're going to be solely with the Rebels for now."

I grit my teeth. "For how long?"

He shrugs. "Likely through the season if that's what Joe wants."

I need to say no to this. I can't... I can't see Joe. I can't. I won't know how to be an adult or a professional around him. I work with surgical implements and power tools for a living. The man will be lucky if he's still able to stand or walk when I'm done with him. But... it's my first week here, and I can already tell that I don't have a choice if I want to keep this job.

He's too excited over the prospect of me knowing Joe and working with this player.

"Fine," I clip out, no longer caring if I sound pissed off. "I'll go meet with this Asher Reyes tomorrow." But I won't be happy about it.

By the time I walk into my parents' house, I'm exhausted, and it's late. I already know Mason is in bed, and my heart sinks to the bottom of my feet when I crack his door open and find him fast asleep. Being a mom is harder and sweeter than I thought it would be. I was so goal-oriented for so long, and then when I found out I was pregnant with him, everything had to be adjusted.

I was alone, living in a foreign country, working my ass off on my fellowship. I had dreams—big freaking dreams—and a baby didn't enter into them. It wasn't the first time my life had taken a drastic detour. I knew how to weather storms like that better than most.

But I also knew this was infinitely bigger than a blown-out knee and the end of my skating career.

My life was never going to be the same again.

It wasn't just about me anymore, and some days, like today, that's a harder burden to bear. I want my son to see me as a strong, capable woman who can do it all, but most of the time I feel like I'm drowning in an endless sea with no land in sight.

I don't yet know how to balance this new job and be the mother I want to be.

I had him in Miami, literally working to finish my residency, right up until my water broke in the hospital. My mother flew down, and after my C-section, I took a grand total of six weeks off to heal and be with my son. I had to get back to work. I had boards to take and a program to complete.

It was hell, and I think I cried every damn day, and I still don't know how we made it through. But we did, and now we're here, and I'll do whatever I have to do to make his life the best I can for him.

He deserves that from me. He deserves the world.

I lean over the edge of his crib and run my hand along his soft, reddish-brown hair, a trait he must have gotten from his father—whoever the hell he is. I don't remember much about that night. That was the most alcohol I had ever consumed in one sitting, and I'm not sure I could pick the guy out of a lineup.

I never even got his name.

After the bad sex and him running out of the bathroom, spewing crap about how that's never happened to him before, I fled, went downstairs, drank two more shots—straight vodka that time—and then left the club. I was embarrassed and angry. I had put myself out there for the first time ever, done something so risky and out of my comfort zone, and it backfired on me.

The bastard didn't even put on the condom. I knew it had all been a ploy, and that he had likely done the exact same thing with a hundred other women.

I felt used and dirty and miserable.

The next day, I woke up hungover, the details of the night before more than a little fuzzy. I left it all behind, flying to London to work with their national soccer—or football—team and the sports medicine orthopedic surgeons they have there. It was the shot of a lifetime, and I had beaten out hundreds of other surgeons for that fellowship.

I dove straight in, pushed aside that awful night, and was so busy that I didn't realize I didn't get my period, or that my breasts were a little tender, or that I had some nausea here or there. I didn't discover I was pregnant until I was about ten weeks along and finally took a breath long enough to put it all together.

I kiss my fingertips and press them to his forehead. "Good night, baby boy. I love you."

Closing the door to his room, I go downstairs and find my mother and stepfather in the kitchen, each having a cup of decaf coffee and splitting a piece of coffee cake along with their secret smiles. My mother met him when I was eight and married him two years later. Gary Hathaway didn't hesitate to step into the role of my father, to the point where we both competed in the same Olympic games, cheering each other on as father and daughter and teammates.

We made national news for it.

Those were the best two weeks of my life.

"I tried to keep him up as long as I could," my mother offers.

I wave her away and slice myself a piece of cake, taking a seat beside them. My fork impales the flaky pastry, and then I ask the question that's been burning me since I left Limbick's office. "Did you know Joe was in town?"

My mother's hand freezes, fork in midair on the way to her mouth, and her gaze slingshots over to my stepfather's. Gary clears his throat and then sits back in his chair as my mother lowers the fork back to the plate.

"Yes," she says contritely with a slight wince. "We knew."

The air leaves my lungs. "And you didn't think to tell me?" I can't contain my incredulous ire.

My mother gives me a troubled look and places her hand over mine. "We didn't want you to turn down the opportunity simply because he's living in the same city as you. We missed you and self-ishly wanted you and Mason here with us. Plus,"—she shrugs—"we figured you'd never see him, even if you learned he was here."

"How *did* you learn Joe was here?" Gary asks, giving me a sheepish grin, and I feel bad about snapping at them. I understand why they didn't tell me, but I wish I had known so I wouldn't have been blindsided by it either.

"He requested me," I tell them both, still sickened as I say the words. "One of his players is having a shoulder issue, and Joe requested me to be the team physician."

My mother worries her lip between her teeth and gives my hand a squeeze. "Did you say yes?"

"I didn't exactly have a choice," I defend. "The asshole was adamant it be me. Have you spoken with him?"

She shakes her head.

"Then how does he know about me, Mom? How could he possibly know?"

"I'm sorry." She sighs, her features lined with regret. "I don't know what to say because I don't have any real answers for you. The last time I spoke to him was through an attorney after I married Gary because he stopped paying child support for you then. It was a fight. Anyway, I'm not sure what his motive is for reaching out to you now after all this time. What are you going to do?"

I didn't know about the child support thing. He really is a piece of work.

"The only thing I can do. Go to the stadium and meet him and his player tomorrow."

## 3

### WYNTER

The only good thing about today is that training camp doesn't start before 10:00 a.m., which means I was able to wake up and spend my morning playing with Mason. I made him eggs—his new favorite food—and watched a baby sign language video, and then we played with the color stacking toy he can't get enough of.

It was absolute heaven. Heaven for a solid hour and a half until I had to leave him.

I keep telling myself that when I can get him into the daycare at the hospital, I'll see him more during the day. He's on the waitlist, but they were hopeful it wouldn't be too much longer before he got in. Once that happens, I'll find us a place to live closer to the hospital, and then things will finally settle down and we'll get into a more stable groove.

And hopefully, I'll be done with football and Joe freaking Cardone by then.

Last night, I laid awake for hours trying to work this all out in my head.

At the end of the day, he's simply a case of biology and nothing more. He doesn't deserve my reaction or my time. He hasn't earned anything from me, and by the time I fell asleep, I had convinced myself I would go into today equipped with a solid battle plan of indifference.

But now as I walk into the stadium, giving my name to the security guard positioned by the player's entrance, my heart in my throat and blood thrashing through my ears, I'm not sure I can do this. My pace slows and my steps falter as a burst of adrenaline hits my veins, making my muscles antsy for me to flee.

*Don't let him win. You're not a quitter. You're a fighter. You're a winner.*

Only my stomach doesn't agree as it roils and revolts. Instead of fleeing for the exit, I'm racing into the first bathroom I see, straight for the stall, as eggs fight their way up my esophagus. I throw up violently, ejecting everything in my stomach, and even after that's done, I continue with dry heaves until there's nothing left in me.

With a groan, I flush the toilet and drag myself to the sink, washing my mouth out with cold water and patting my forehead with the excess on my hands before pressing them into the counter. I haven't thrown up since before I took the ice at my first world championship. I haven't even seen him yet, and it's like I'm a kid all over again.

The door flings open, and in walks a tall, broad man wearing red track shorts, a white Dri-FIT shirt, and bright blue sneakers. He's probably one of the players.

"Are you in the wrong room or am I?" He has the grace to ask, even though it's pretty damn obvious from the urinals on my right that I'm clearly the one in the wrong room.

"Sorry," I murmur, grabbing some towels from the dispenser to wipe my hands and mouth with. "My mistake."

"Not a problem." He takes another step toward me, but I haven't dared look up at him yet. "Take all the time you need. Are you okay? You look a little... pale."

I scowl, glancing up at my reflection through my lashes. He's right. I do look pale.

"Sorry," he rushes on. "If that was rude or insulting, I didn't mean—"

"No," I cut him off quickly. "It's fine. I am pale. My breakfast didn't agree with me."

Just as I go to throw out the paper towels, I peek up at him, but the moment our eyes meet, his grow comically wide, and he sucks in a giant breath. "It's you," he says breathily on the exhale.

I scrunch my brow at the way he says that. Before I can respond, he's taking another step until he's right before me, large and muscular and filling up my entire field of vision.

He laughs, almost disbelieving, a huge smile erupting across his face, showing off his pearly white teeth and making his gray eyes sparkle silver. *Not just a nice body but a pretty face too*, I absently muse, only to mentally smack myself. Though there is something about him that strikes me as familiar in a way I can't place.

"I can't believe I'm running into you like this," he rushes on. "What are the odds? Are you here for me?" he asks, his voice rising, and I stare up at him, bewildered, unable to make sense of his words or reaction. "You must be, right?"

"That depends if you're Asher Reyes, since I know you're not Joe Cardone," I answer without thinking.

That seems to pull him up short. "Is that a joke?"

"Is what a joke?" I throw back at him, my mind still frazzled and my stomach still lurching. I need to pull myself back together, and this guy isn't helping. "Listen, I'm sorry I was in the wrong bathroom, but I really should go. I'm expected upstairs and likely already running a little late now."

"You can't go." He grabs my arm as I try to move around him, and I immediately jerk myself free of his grasp.

"Don't touch me," I snap.

His hands shoot up in surrender. "Sorry. It's just..." He cuts himself off there, staring at me, squinting in a way that makes me shift my position, a little uncomfortable with his blatant scrutiny. "You don't recognize me, do you?" Disappointment leaches from his lips.

I give him a quick once-over, and in doing so, my skin heats and my nipples tighten. An unexpected response, but Christ, this man is big and strong and insanely fucking gorgeous. Silver-gray eyes, dimpled chin, straight nose, full lips, and short, brown hair with hints of copper in it.

He's hot.

That's an obvious one, but I'd rather die than admit that to him.

Yes, there is definitely something familiar about him. *Maybe*. Probably because he's a professional athlete and I've seen his face somewhere in passing. But still, I come up empty, having no clue who he is.

"No, I don't." Then I think better of it because the way he's acting, it's almost as if *he* knows *me*. "Should I?"

His mouth twists into a hard line, and his hands go to his hips. He blows out a heavy breath, an unhappy one possibly. For a moment, he just continues to stare down at me, working something through, until finally, in a rough tone, he says, "I guess not."

"Uh. Okay." This is getting awkward. Really awkward. "Now that we've cleared that up, I'm going to go." He shifts in front of me again as I attempt to leave, and my heart rate spikes. "Move," I demand, about ready to punch him in the balls if necessary. I don't need this right now. My thoughts are swirling with what's waiting for me, and this guy is the last thing I want to deal with.

He shakes his head at me, irritated almost, but at least now he's keeping his distance. "You just said you're here to meet with Asher Reyes?"

I fold my arms and refuse to answer, unsure if I should have said that.

"Well, that's me, sweetheart." He thrusts his hand out at me. "Asher Reyes, quarterback for the Boston Rebels. And you are?"

Oh, shit. Reluctantly, I reach out my hand. "Dr. Wynter Hathaway. Your new team and personal orthopedic surgeon."

He grips my hand, and the moment we make contact, something funny happens. I can't even describe what it is. It's subtle, yet it's not. It's fire, yet my hands are ice-cold. It raises the hairs on my arm and sends a tingle up my spine. Both the good and the bad kind. Immediately, I release him.

He steps in a bit closer to me, his eyes doing a slow drag along my face feature by feature as if he's trying to memorize every line and color I'm comprised of. "It's a pleasure to officially meet you, Dr. Hathaway. Coach Cardone mentioned you to me and spoke quite highly of you."

It takes everything in me not to scoff and roll my eyes. I don't dare touch that because I won't have anything kind to say in return.

"I didn't recognize you as the player I'm here to meet with," I admit. "Football is my least favorite sport, and I don't follow it."

Now I understand why he was upset. He must have known I was coming to meet with him and since I'm in the football stadium, literally on his turf, and no doubt everyone in this town knows who he is, he must be annoyed I didn't.

He emits an amused chuckle. "Wow. Most people never confess things like that to me."

I quirk an eyebrow. "You mean most people kiss your ass."

He smirks, rubbing at his chiseled jawline, which looks sharp enough to cut glass. "Something like that. I'll admit, I could die a happy man if you were at least the slightest bit impressed by me."

My fingers clasp in front of me, and I meet his steady gaze head-on, ignoring how my body suddenly grows hot under the intensity of his eyes. "I'm here to help fix whatever orthopedic issue you're having. That's it."

"So that's a no on you being impressed by me?"

I hold in my smile at his charming, cocky, sure-fire grin. "That's a no. A solid no at that."

"Shame. You have no idea how rough on my ego it is that you don't recognize me, but I suppose it's no less than what I deserve given the circumstances. Hell, maybe it's even a bit of a relief."

"Pardon?"

He waves me off. "Nothing. I'm going to use the bathroom, but I look forward to our meeting. And to you putting your hands on me. Even if I can't put mine on you."

My jaw drops. What an egomaniac—the beautiful, talented ones always are—and now that I've met him, I can honestly say I like this assignment even less than I did before. If he's anything like my father —who was also a quarterback—then I want as little to do with him as possible.

"I wouldn't get too excited about me touching you. I know all the best ways to make you hurt. Trust me, you won't enjoy it." I hate football. I hate football players. I hate everything about this goddamn sport. "Later, player." I saunter out of the bathroom as if he hadn't come in and found me post-projectile vomiting.

The door slams behind me, and I blow out a breath as I stumble back into the cool, brightly lit hallways of the player area. I glance left and then right, and when I see that the coast is clear, I press my palm to my racing heart.

The man made my heart race.

Then again, no one's ever spoken to me that way before. A sly grin curls up my lips. I just threatened the quarterback for the Boston Rebels, who also happens to be my new patient.

And I think he liked it.

One down, one to go. On a tremulous breath and wobbly legs, I push myself on, clenching and unclenching my fists as I find my way closer and closer to Joe's office. I need to face him if I'm ever going to do my job. That was also part of the plan I conjured in the wee hours of the morning. I won't hide from him, and I won't run.

I'll show him just how little he means to me.

But when I approach his door and see the placard with his name imprinted in bold black letters, I realize all my bravado is a joke. Part of me—a hateful part of me—is still that vulnerable little girl who stole her mother's phone so she could call her dad with the hope and the prayer that he'd pick up and talk to me. Something he never did. Even when I'd leave voice messages, he'd never call back.

He meant so much to me—I worshipped him—and I meant nothing to him.

And now he's doing this, and I don't understand why.

With a shaky hand—*my hands never shake, I'm a goddamn surgeon!* —I tap on his office door.

"Come in," he grumbles, and that voice. It's the same voice he had when I cried out his name as I found him in bed with that woman. The same voice that echoed through my head when I'd cry myself to sleep for months and months after he left us.

Armed with an artillery of bitter and pissed off to go into battle with, I snap the doorknob and fling open the door, practically kicking it with the tip of my black, somewhat classy, yet badass bitch heels.

His perturbed gaze flashes up to mine, and the moment he realizes it's me, he falls back in his seat as his hand covers his mouth and his green eyes hold mine.

"Wyn."

I shake my head. "No nicknames. I need answers from you this very second, or I'm walking out of this building, and I will never return."

He nods slowly, sitting up straight in his chair, clearing his throat, and waving me into his office. "Come sit down then."

"I want to stab you in multiple places, not sit down."

He grins, and it makes me hate him more. Something he must read because it quickly slips from his lips.

"Start talking, Joe. Why am I here?"

"I have a player who needs you," he says simply, and I can't stand that answer.

"Elaborate. Why me specifically? How'd you know I was in Boston? Hell, how'd you know I was a surgeon?"

He stands and rounds his desk, only to sit on the edge of it, cutting the space between us by half. He looks a lot older than I remember. Older than a typical man in his mid-fifties. Brown hair that's streaked with heavy swaths of gray, and lines on his forehead and the sides of his eyes indenting his tanned face. The only thing we have in common feature-wise is our eyes, only it doesn't soften me toward him.

Not even a little.

His hands press into the edge of his desk. "I kept track of you. I watched you in nationals and world championships, and I watched every second of you in the Olympics. Then I followed your career in medicine after."

I turn for the door, unable to listen for another second. "I'm done here."

"He needs his nonthrowing shoulder fixed," he calls out, stopping me at the door. "It's complicated. He's torn things in there for years that were never fixed, but he needs the force and the momentum of his non-dominant shoulder to deliver."

My hand finds the frame of his doorway. "Why should I care? There are hundreds of other surgeons who could do this."

"The last orthopedic surgeon who was considered the best in the country saw the films and said it'll never heal right, and he'll never play again. I don't believe them. I think they're cowards. You graduated top of your class first at Yale and then in medical school at Princeton. Got selected for a top residency program in Miami. Beat out how many other surgeons for that fellowship in London?"

Motherfucker. I had no clue he knew any of this about me. Bastard knows I'm competitive and is using it against me.

"So?"

"So, I also heard shoulders, in addition to knees, were your specialty."

I grit my teeth because now I want to see the MRI. Now I want to know why the others passed and said it would never heal right. Now I want to prove that I can fix it when those other hotshots chose not to try.

I flip back aground. "Limbick would have done it. You turned him down. Said you only wanted me."

"He's not my daughter."

My fists clench, and my vision grows hazy with rage. "Neither am I."

He glances away for a moment, nods slowly, and then looks back at me. "You don't owe me anything, but he's a great player and deserves another shot at a ring."

"I don't give a shit if you win another championship. In fact, I hope you don't. I hope you sink like the fucking Titanic without being nearly as cool or dramatic."

"You hate me."

I laugh caustically. "That's more than putting it mildly, but the truth is, you aren't even worth the energy to hate. Hating you requires emotion. It requires thought. I stopped thinking about you when I was barely seven. You are nothing to me now."

He shifts on his large desk and glances out his window at the base of the stadium beyond. "Football—"

"Shut. Up!" I scream, and I'm not even sure where it comes from. "I don't care. I don't care!" My hands fly out. "I don't want to be here, and I don't want to help you, and I don't care about your player, and I sure as hell don't give a shit about football. You pulled strings with my boss and are fucking with my job. You had no right."

"Wynter." He sighs and stands. "I requested you because you're hungry, and not complacent or afraid. You are the most confident, smart, dedicated, ruthless, and talented person I know."

"You don't know me."

"Fine. You're right. I don't know you. But I know the stock you're built from. Will you please look at his MRI? That's all I ask. I'll stay away. I'll keep my distance. Just look at his damn MRI and tell me if I need to cut him or trade him."

"So much for he deserves another shot at a ring. Real fucking loyal there, Joe."

"It's business."

I smirk viciously. "Don't I know it. Loyalty was never your strong suit anyway. Give me one real reason other than your precious game."

"He's a good guy. He goes into hospitals and sits with sick kids without ever sharing a second of it on social media. He wants everyone to succeed and motivates his teammates and this town. But more than that, he's a patient, and he needs your help."

*Dammit.*

# 4

---

## ASHER

After she called me player, and the door slammed shut, I spent a solid five minutes staring at my reflection in the mirror, a million things running through my head at a dead sprint. I shouldn't have mentioned her touching me. She was right to fire back at me about that one. It was inappropriate, to say the least.

But at that moment, I had become irrationally angry. I couldn't stand that she didn't recognize me when I hadn't thought of any other woman for a year and a half.

A year and a half of *her*.

Of wanting to know who she is. Of wanting to see her again and set the record straight, and hell, apologize for how it all went down.

And. She. Didn't. Fucking. Recognize. Me.

I stood there, staring at myself, trying to swallow the pill that it was for the best that she didn't. That it could be a clean slate. A do-over. But I couldn't stop that voice. The one that told me that makes me a liar and a bit of a bastard. That's not the sort of guy I am, and now as I walk down the hall toward the trainer's room, I feel like shit.

Still, what am I supposed to do if she doesn't remember me?

Be like, "Hey, you remember the night when I was so worked up that my dick wasn't hard that I forgot to put on a condom, gave you shitty sex, and then prematurely jizzed inside of you?" Yeah, that'll get her crawling back into my bed in no time.

This woman. Wynter Hathaway. How many nights have I spent wondering about her? Curious about her name, and where she was from, and what she was up to. Dreaming of finding her again and what I would do when I did. It was as if she left her fingerprints on my skin. The imprint of her is indelible, though my memory didn't do her nearly the justice she deserves.

Damn, my future wife is fucking hot.

I chuckle to myself at that thought and then breeze into the empty trainer's room and hop up on the cushioned table they have in here. The facility is empty save for me, Joe, one of the trainers who is somewhere else right now, and Wynter. My new doctor.

Shit. That probably means I can't touch her, right? Isn't there a thing against that? I'll have to ask Callan about it. He'd know.

Looking around the empty room, I hate that I'm having to be here and go through this. I feel like Coach is making a bigger deal out of this shoulder issue than necessary. Day one of training camp, and I took a hard hit. Not the first one, and certainly not the last. It took me a bit to get up, and then it took me a bit to work it out, but I eventually did. Sorta.

My speed is off a little.

I know it is.

The first time I took a hit like that, I was in my senior year of college, and it was my first game as a starter. They could have broken every bone in my body, and I would have gotten back up and continued to play. That was finally my shot, and I wouldn't let them X-ray, let alone MRI anything on me because no way was I taking that chance. I could still throw. I could still play ball. As the youngest son of Dominic Reyes, younger brother to Jude Reyes, I couldn't let the legacy die with me.

I had already dicked around for too long—that's what my father called it—when I was with Central Square, touring the world and living out rock star glory with my best friends. But now...

I roll my left shoulder, trying to work it out, only... I feel it. The twinge. The creak of something not right inside me. Truth? It scares me. What am I if I'm not Asher Reyes, quarterback for the Boston Rebels? The team I grew up loving with my life's blood. The team I would do anything for.

Now I have to sit through an exam with the woman I did wrong one drunken night in a bathroom. She is going to touch me. That's part of her job. And my shirt will have to be off during it. If this were porn, I'd have her blouse off and my mouth on her cunt in a hot second.

Only, it's not.

I'm stuck in some paradigm where I'm a bit obsessed with the girl things didn't go well with, and suddenly she's back in my life, only she doesn't know who I am.

Do I want her to remember me? Hell if I know.

The door swings open and in walks Wynter—how adorable is that name for my ice queen?—and behind her is Coach and one of the trainers. She's pissed. Not the least bit happy to be here or checking me out.

And then she leads with...

"How many times have you been hit in that shoulder where you knew it was more than a basic hit?"

I refrain from shifting. She's so damn cute and studious, and I wonder if she's aware that I can see the outline of her lace bra—and a peek of her nipples—through her thin white blouse.

"Honestly?"

She rolls her eyes, already done with me. "No, please lie to me. That's always so helpful."

"Wyn—" Coach starts, only she holds her hand up behind her, in his face, and... holy shit, the man shuts up. Who is this magical woman? What powers does she wield over this hard-nosed man?

"Three times," I answer honestly. "Once in college. Once the night I won the Super Bowl." *Remember that night,* I want to ask but rightfully don't. "And once three days ago."

A noise clears the back of her throat. "May I see the MRI?"

Johnny Scott—one of the trainers—runs over to her like a golden retriever, ready with a tablet and the films already pulled up. She stands here for a solid five minutes, staring at the screen while I stare at her.

"Take off your shirt, Mr. Reyes."

"Yes, ma'am." And fuck. That totally came out sounding all sexy and seductive, and *you may own my ass this second, but I plan to dominate yours later.* Not good.

She blinks up at me. Raises an unamused eyebrow. And then returns to the screen. Her all-business doctor thing is so hot, my dick is impossibly hard for her. *Finally!* If only this were the moment for her to appreciate this level of devotion.

"That's Doctor, Mr. Reyes. Don't forget how this works."

And *shwing*, I jerk in my shorts. Her confidence is sexy as fuck. I don't think a woman has ever given me this level of shit before. Well, a woman who wasn't Suzie, our manager for Central Square, but she was my best friend Zax's woman, so it was different.

Women never talk back to me. They're always too eager to please. Too hopeful, like simply being with a football player and a former rock star is all they need in this world, and everything I am on the inside is superfluous.

This woman doesn't care either way, and it's unbelievably sexy.

"My apologies, Doctor. I meant no disrespect." I reach behind and pull my white Boston Rebels Dri-FIT shirt over my head without removing my eyes from her face for more than a millisecond. *Look, sweetheart, I dare you. We both know you want to.*

She does too. She totally twitched, and her eyes jerked in my direction when I did that. Plus, her cheeks flush ever so slightly. It's so fucking cute. I forgot about the secret innocence she radiates. Like beneath all this smart, powerful exterior lies a vulnerability that begs not to be jerked around.

Until she says...

"Mr. Reyes, are you aware that you have a *severe*—and I'm not saying that word lightly—AC joint separation *and* labrum tear?" Her fingers play with the sizing on the screen, scrolling this way and that, looking over the smallest detail of my MRI.

"I'm not entirely sure—"

Her lips purse and then twist. "This will require extensive surgical intervention. It's ligament repairs, definitely for both the AC and CC joints at least." She stops. Squints. Hisses between her teeth. "Jesus, you've ripped apart your shoulder, and some of this is not new. There's a lot scarring in there."

My heart starts to pound a merciless rhythm, and my skin grows cold and clammy.

"It doesn't feel that bad. How can I have that level of damage when it doesn't feel that bad?" It doesn't make sense to me. I mean, I know I've been hit, and I know I've sustained some injuries over the years to that shoulder but...

"The MRI doesn't lie. I don't know what else to tell you."

I drag my hand across my face. "Can it be repaired?" I ask, losing all pretenses and bravado. It's not for money, fame, or glory. I have all of those. I was part of the world's biggest rock band for four years. I've turned all the odds in my favor and won a Super Bowl. I have nothing to prove. But that doesn't mean I want my game to be done.

Not by a long shot.

She shakes her head, her eyes still on the screen. "I... I don't know." She glances up at me. "I don't know," she repeats. "There is a ton of damage in this shoulder."

"Wynter, this is exactly why I brought you here."

She glares vitriol over her shoulder at Coach. "In this room, I am Dr. Hathaway. And though you may have brought me in here specifically to wave my magic wand and fix this, that's not how the human body works."

I squint, wondering what exactly her relationship with Coach is. They clearly know each other. But how?

"What's my recovery time like if you do surgery and it's successful?" I swallow my fear, wishing I had at least Callan with me so he'd understand this better than I would.

She turns back to me. "Typically, a full recovery takes a minimum of four to six months. *If* the surgery is successful and you do well with physical therapy. You're at least out for this entire season. I can't guarantee you'll regain full range of motion or strength either. I also can't guarantee I can repair everything or fix what's already scarred over."

Fuck. Just... *fuck!*

"How soon can you operate?"

"Next week," she answers. "I'll have my nurse review the OR schedule and let you know for sure."

I glance over her shoulder at Joe. He gives me a firm nod, but I don't know him all that well. My last coach had been here since I came to the team right out of college and won the Super Bowl with me. We had trust. We had a rapport. I've known this guy for less than a month, and from guys I loosely know who played with him in LA, he's a love-the-one-you're-with sort of man.

We have a backup QB. A kid who was drafted in the first round this year. A kid who is itching to replace me. But he doesn't hold this city in the palm of his hand the way I do. But how long does that level of devotion last when you're unable to perform?

Or play since now it looks as though I'll be out for the entire season.

For the first time in my life, I'm scared and questioning everything.

"Okay." I swallow. Hard. "Tell me the truth. Do you feel you can do this successfully?"

The tablet falls to her side, and her green eyes—the prettiest fucking eyes I've ever seen—meet mine. "I think I'm your best shot at ever playing again and being the type of player you want to continue to be."

"Then put your hands on me, Doctor, and let's get this started."

And she does. The tablet gets set on the table, and then she's standing before me. Her hands fall to my shoulder, and she manipulates me this way and that. Testing my range of motion and my strength—even limits of my pain—as she said she would.

Despite my worry over my shoulder and how generally what she's doing isn't the most pleasant, the feel of her hands on my skin isn't lost on me. Neither is her proximity, or the way she smells like heaven —if heaven were sexy and smelled sinfully delicious. She's focused on my shoulder, but I can't drag myself away from looking at her. At how her bottom lip is slightly plumper than her top one and how she has a freckle just to the left of her mouth. Her skin is so creamy white, and I can't get enough of how it almost glows in contrast with her dark hair.

She rakes her teeth along her bottom lip as she presses in on a particular tender spot, making me wince ever so slightly. My pretty minx presses again, just to the side of the spot, and gauges my reaction.

"Is that tender too?" Her voice comes out airy, and I wonder if she's feeling this the way I am. I hope she is.

"Not as bad as the first spot."

She nods, and then she's done, her hands are gone, and her expression is stoic.

"Your strength and range of motion are better than I would have anticipated given what the films show. That's good news for you. I'll need you to come to my office on Monday for a presurgical interview."

"No," Joe cuts in sharply. "That has to be done here."

She is not happy about that, and her expression lets him know it. "You do understand I can't do his surgery here. He *will* have to come to the hospital."

"Yes, but Limbick already promised me the earliest surgery time possible, an empty floor, and a private entrance," he counters. "I want to minimize possible exposure to the press as much as possible."

She grits her teeth and then turns back to me. "Fine. I'll be back here Monday morning. Now, I'd like a private moment with my patient."

Joe leaves the room, and so does the trainer, and suddenly it's just us again. This is *not* the time to tell her how we've already met. Especially while she's planning to cut into my shoulder. I sit here, my shirt still off, my eyes totally, completely, irrevocably on her.

"You can get dressed now," she instructs me, but I don't because she's looking at my chest. At my shoulders and biceps. At my abs as I sit up straight and they naturally flex.

"You should come back tomorrow," I offer instead, because Monday feels too far away, and I want to see her again.

Her head tilts. "Why should I do that?"

"So you can see how I throw the ball. So you can watch me play and figure out how best to fix me." Makes total sense to me.

She scowls, shifting her weight. "I don't want to be here anymore than I have to."

"Then consider it part of your job, Doctor. From my understanding, you're not just my doctor; you're the team doctor now."

Her eyes narrow into tight slits as anger visibly takes over her body. She doesn't like that. Not one bit. "Fine," she clips out. "I'll be here tomorrow to see how you throw the ball and understand better where your deficits are."

"Can the surgery wait until the end of the season?"

"You tell me, player," she tosses back at me. "From what I saw, your MRI is a nightmare. From what I just examined, you've managed to compensate quite well for your injuries."

I grit my teeth and turn away from her. I'm stuck in a tough spot. If I don't have the surgery and I suck because I'm not in top form, Coach will bench me and put in the kid. If I have the surgery, then the season belongs to the kid.

I have a serious decision to make.

I turn back to her. "Will you watch me play and give me your honest thoughts?"

She shrugs. "I have no frame of reference when it comes to football. That's a decision for you and your coach to make. Not me. I just give you the medical facts as I see them."

"I don't want you to cut into my body when you hate me."

She emits a resigned sigh, or a heavy breath, or whatever that is. All I know is this is the first she's softened since I found her in the bathroom earlier today. "I don't hate you."

"Then what is this to you? Because to me, it's my career."

She drops onto the stool and peers up at me. "This is a nightmare.

It's not something I want to be a part of. That said, I'd never cut into anyone without the intention of fixing them completely and giving my full focus to their case. My anger with your coach or even with you will not interfere with your surgery."

"Why do you hate Coach?"

"Personal business that's none of yours. The reason I wanted you alone is because I'm curious why you never had surgery on this shoulder before."

I lean forward, my hands dangling between my parted thighs. Close enough that our faces are only inches apart, and it makes her breath catch. Yet she doesn't pull back, and she doesn't break eye contact.

"I don't like doctors, other than my best friend, of course. But anytime someone I know has gone to see one of you, they're either cut open, diagnosed with some seriously scary shit, or something vital is missed and they die."

"Well, I'm here to cut you open, and it might not be pretty when I do."

"Everything about you is pretty." My eyes skate across her face, and when I land on the bottom of her neck, I reach out and gently place my fingers over her racing pulse point. "Is this for me?"

A blush rises up her cheeks and her pupils expand. "I thought you said the only one of us who would be doing any touching is me."

"I lied." My fingers trickle up her neck and then back down toward her pulse and the sexy dip just beneath it. I watch as goosebumps erupt across her skin, and she shudders ever so slightly.

Oh, I affect her all right.

"I don't like flirts or football players, and I definitely don't like it when my patients touch me inappropriately." She shoves my hand away, and I sit up, smirking as I do.

"That all may be true, but it won't stop me from trying to change your mind about that." I hop off the table, throw my shirt back on, and head for the door. "See you tomorrow, Doctor."

# 5

## WYNTER

"There's something about that football player," I muse to myself for at least the tenth time since I left here yesterday afternoon. It niggled at me until I finally gave in and looked him up. I didn't scroll through the pictures—I didn't need more visuals of him—but I did read his Wikipedia page as well as a few celebrity tabloids.

He was the backup guitarist for Central Square, and while I never listened much to their music—other than what was played on the radio—I think that must be where I recognize him from. His face was plastered across posters and magazines and was everywhere it could be when he was with the band. I remember that.

I remember thinking those guys were hot because they were.

Or maybe it's the fact that he affects me, and that has his voice, his face, and his words slicing through my brain.

I haven't had sex since that night in the club, and before that, I wasn't exactly rolling in men. So suffice it to say, I haven't had good sex in a *very* long time, and when hard-pressed, I'll admit I don't think I've ever had great sex. My vagina is a sad, cold, lonely old woman who spends her days in a rocking chair knitting herself a sweater. Even my vibrator is tired of seeing her. It's only natural that a good-looking man who seems physically attracted to me would wake the old lady up.

But Asher Reyes is not the man to hop back in the saddle with.

Mixed metaphors or not, the point is the same. He's trouble, and I don't have any time or space in my life for it.

Then there's Joe, who is watching me with deliberate eyes as I walk out of the cool, dark tunnel into the bright August sunshine and over to the sideline of the field where the team is practicing. My mom and I talked about him for a long time last night. I don't like knowing he's followed my career—both on the ice and in medicine. It only infuriates me more because I don't know why.

Why would he bother doing that with a child he abandoned?

Asher is on the field, talking with a few of the players, the ball in his hand that he gesticulates with as he speaks. He's tall, and his presence is commanding, both on and off the field. I've never seen him play before, but I can tell he's passionate about what he does, and he's not even in game form. The first day of training camp was Monday, and that's when he took the hit.

Movement on my right has my head flipping in that direction and immediately locking onto another player wearing the same red jersey Asher is wearing whereas every other player is wearing white. I'm going to assume that makes him another quarterback, but I don't know for sure. He's giving me the "I'm a stud" smirk, and inwardly I roll my eyes in derision.

Football players. They're all the freaking same.

"I haven't seen you here before," he says by way of a greeting. "Girlfriend or wife?"

"Pardon?"

"Are you someone's girlfriend or wife? Since I know you're not press."

I raise an eyebrow. "How do you know that?"

His brown eyes drop to my stomach. "Wrong badge. Yours just says, Visitor."

"If you already knew that, why did you feel the need to take another look?"

He breaks out into a huge smile in a way that tells me he's not the least bit embarrassed. "Leo Dodd. QB2, but soon to be QB1. But you never answered my question. Are you single?"

"Yes. I'm a single mother."

He laughs. "That doesn't scare me off the way it does other guys. I love kids. I'm the oldest of six."

"Congratulations to you, but I don't date ball players."

"You should," he continues, stepping in closer to me. "We're a lot of fun. In fact, I bet if I took you out tonight, we could have a lot of fun together."

"You can't be serious with that line."

"Actually, it's the truth. Not a line. But if you're not into ball players, then what are you doing here, visitor?"

I point toward the field. "Watching your QB1 so he can stay QB1, since I'm your new team orthopedic surgeon."

"Beauty and brains. I like it."

"Hey, Rookie!" Asher calls out just as something zips like a bullet through the air in our direction. The ball nails Leo right in the stomach, making him hunch over with a loud groan and an audible wheeze. The impact causes me to jump for how close that was. "Stop flirting with my doctor and get your ass back on the field where you belong."

I blink about ten thousand times, my heart up in my throat. My head snaps in Asher's direction, but he's not paying me any attention. He's too busy breathing fire at his backup. He could have hit me. I was no more than two feet from where he threw that ball.

The kid grumbles something out to me about how he'll see me later, and then he slinks onto the field, being teased and jostled by other players along the way. Asher stares me down, and I fold my arms over my chest, anything but amused.

He jogs over to me, smacking the rookie on the back of the head as he goes by.

Before I can react, he's on me. His arm swoops around my back, and his sweaty body presses into mine. His mouth dips by my ear, and his hot breath fans my neck. "I'd never have hit you, ice queen. Ever. My shoulder might be messed up, but I'm accurate as fuck."

"Ice queen?"

I can feel him smile. "I had that name in my head for you before I looked you up. Pretty fantastic coincidence, right? Actually, I watched the video of you skating in the Olympics. You were amazing. Why did you stop?"

I push at his hard chest, trying to move the wall of muscle back. He smells good. How can a hulk of a sweaty man smell good? But he also... feels familiar like this. Pressed against me. Like we've done this before when I know that to be impossible.

"You're touching me again, player."

He doesn't go far, but his hand unwinds itself from my back. "I'm staking my claim. That kid might steal my spot on the team, but I won't let him steal my doctor."

"Is that jealousy or just obnoxious male ego?"

"One hundred percent jealousy *and* male ego." His tongue snakes out and licks my neck.

"The hell?" I shove him off me.

He takes a step back, all cocky smiles as he walks backward toward the field.

I wipe my neck. "Gross. If you don't want someone who hates you cutting into you, don't do things to make me hate you."

"Don't pretend you didn't like me tasting you. But now that I've officially licked you, you're mine, ice queen. So hot and yet so cold."

I shake my head, anger building within me, and I snap out, "I can't believe you—"

"Watch me play, Dr. Hathaway." He cuts me off. "I'm about to show off just for you." He winks at me and then jogs off back onto the field.

That son of a bitch. I can't believe he just did that. He *licked* me in front of everyone, right here on the field. Players. All of them. The conquest, and the easy pussy, and whatever it takes to get a woman in bed are all they care about.

I let him put his arm around me. My attempt to push him away was meager at best.

I can't allow the fact that he's the first man to show me any real attention in far too long to overshadow what I'm here to do. Ice queen is what he called me, so it's the ice queen I shall be.

Hot. Arrogant. Good with his hands. A woman could succumb to all of that. Especially when he pins her with those magnetic eyes and sexy smirk. But the truth is, he's a risk I'm not willing to take.

And I have far too much at stake to play his games.

For all I know, he treats every woman he meets this way. Like an object to claim and then destroy. Disposable when the next one comes along. Only useful until he gets what he needs from them. I refuse to be his discarded trash.

For the next hour, I watch him throw a ball around the field. I watch as he commands his players' focus and compels them into action. I watch as he makes most of his passes and misses a few. The ones he misses are when a defensive player is heading for him. Which tells me he's skittish about getting hit again. It also tells me he's already hurt. I might not know football, but I know athletes, and I know sports medicine.

"Hell of a game you've got here, Joe," I deadpan as he comes over to stand beside me. "Looks like the running of the bulls, only instead of chasing terrified tourists stupid enough to wear red, they're chasing a ball like a dog chases a frisbee. I can see why it held you so captive that nothing and no one else mattered."

He ignores my sarcasm as he says, "He needs surgery," in that stern, self-important voice he likes to use to prove he's in charge when all it does is make him sound like an asshole.

"Isn't that why I'm here? To cut into your top bull and try not to turn him into ground chuck?"

"You're here so that he has a chance to come back next season. With any hope, we can finish on top even without him."

"I'm not a coach, nor do I care about whether or not you finish on top. I'm here for his injury and nothing more."

"Fix him up then, Wynter, so I can get him off my roster. I want to trade him at the end of the season, and if he keeps throwing the ball like that, he's useless to me."

I grit my teeth. I might not like the player, but I hate the coach. "Does he know this is your plan?"

"If he's healthy and can prove himself, I'll let him fight for his spot. Maybe. Depends on what he's worth for a trade before that. Right now, I want to see what the kid can do. This is a football team, not a charity. Winning is all that matters."

I keep my focus on the field even though I'm no longer watching. His words stick to that cursed soft spot that still hides in the hollows of my chest. "As it's always been for you."

"I'm not as evil as you think I am."

I scoff at that. Hard. "I don't think you're *evil*, Joe. I think you're morally and emotionally apathetic. Possibly sociopathic, but psychiatry isn't my field of expertise. I'm about 99.8 percent positive you don't have a heart, and I'm not exaggerating with that assessment." I force myself to turn and look at him, only to find his gaze on the field and not on me. That should be no surprise, and it shouldn't hurt, but I still feel the twinge. "I don't know why I'm here. I sent the films to Limbick last night, and he agreed with me. It can be done, but it'll be tough and without any guarantees of outcome given how bad things look. He'd do the surgery. He told me he would."

"He's not who I want."

I roll my eyes. "Why? Because having a newbie attending operating on your star quarterback is in his best interest? Or is this some misplaced nostalgia you got from a Hallmark film where you think this will somehow reunite father and daughter? Because I can tell you, that won't happen. I've gone twenty-six years without you, and I sure as hell don't want you in my life now."

*Or in my son's life.*

"I could explain—"

"Don't make me throat punch you in front of your players," I sharply interject. "The idiotic notion that you could try and explain away abandoning your five-year-old child makes me go postal. There is no excuse for you, Joe. None. I don't know why I'm here or what made you reach out now, but I'm not interested. I owe you nothing."

He releases a heavy breath. "Did it ever occur to you, Wyn, that I'm doing this because I'm the one who owes you?"

With that, he walks off, back onto the field, blowing his whistle and yelling at two of the players who missed a route or something inconsequential.

"Dickface."

"Tough morning?"

I groan. Asher's short, reddish-brown hair is wet, sticking up all over the place. His face is flushed, and his body is covered in sweat. Sweat that's rolling down his sculpted arms. He smiles, and something hits me. Something... strange. A memory almost, but it's fuzzy, and I can't make sense of it.

"You men are like cockroaches. Just when you get rid of one, another shows up." I spin to Asher. "If women ruled this world instead of men, everything would be efficient, clean, and smell good. There would be no sexual assault or wars. We'd handle everything over cocktails and dinner and actually talk things out instead of blowing shit up because that's how we get things done. You men are the bane of our existence. Once we learn how to synthetically engineer your sperm, we can render you obsolete."

"You know I'm a lover, not a fighter, right?" He quips, smirking at me in a way that should be infuriating but somehow flips the tables on me and reluctantly makes me laugh. "Ah, there it is. That smile. That sound." He's way too pleased with himself. "I can die a happy man now. But don't get any ideas when I'm on your table. Euthanizing me won't save you because I'll come back and haunt you for eternity."

"You are going to be on my table," I tell him, growing serious.

"I know," he says simply, wiping at the back of his neck with a towel. "I just don't like it, and I work better with denial and humor as my defense mechanisms. Want to go get a sports drink with me so we can talk a bit more?"

"A sports drink?" I snort. "That's a hell of an invitation."

"I'd invite you to dinner if I thought you'd accept."

"You're my patient, and I don't—"

"Date football players. I know. I just want you to get to know me away from the field, so you realize I'm not the monster of your preconceived notions."

He looks so earnest when he says that, and I realize I have been rough on him. I mean, he's pushed boundaries and done things he shouldn't, but I'm not sure I ever gave him a fair shot before that.

"Is there coffee where you keep your sports drinks?"

"I'm sure there is, but I don't drink coffee during the season, so I don't know if it's any good."

I squint up at him, shielding my eyes with my hand to block the sun as I do. "Why don't you drink coffee during the season?"

"It's a diuretic, and I don't want to dehydrate. No caffeine, no junk food, very little sugar and alcohol."

"Sounds like a great time."

He reaches out and tugs on a piece of my hair before tucking it behind my ear and dragging his thumb along the shell. "I am if you give me the chance."

"Stop flirting, player."

His hand moves away, and his expression grows sincere. "I'm sorry. I am. It's just that you're easily the most beautiful woman I've ever seen. You have the kind of beauty that fucks with a man's head and self-control. My natural instinct is to flirt, so I can try to win your attention. But you're right. I'm being inappropriate and likely making you uncomfortable. I'll behave."

I blink up at him, my mouth agape as my heart flutters in my chest. "You're serious? That wasn't a line?"

He looks surprised by my shock. "No. I meant every word."

"Uh." I have no idea what to do with that. All I know is that it's making me flustered and feels like I have ants crawling on my skin. I'm itchy, and my body simultaneously tickles and burns like it's on fire.

"Coffee?" he offers, and I nod numbly. He waves his hand over his shoulder as he starts to head toward the tunnel, and I follow after him. "I told Coach I was going to talk to you more, so it should just be us for a while since the rest of the team has another forty minutes or so of practice."

"Okay." I'm still stuck on that most beautiful woman I've ever seen thing.

He leads me into the locker room that, well, smells like a locker room. Like men and sweat and rubber and gym equipment.

"Sit tight."

He points to the bench and asks me how I take my coffee. I tell him, and he walks off only to return a few minutes later with a steaming cup for me and a sports drink for himself.

He removes his cleats one by one, and then my face scrunches up when he starts pulling off his red jersey and pads, tossing them toward a dirty laundry hamper.

"What are you doing?" I screech.

"Going to shower while we talk," he says simply as if he isn't stripping in front of me and will be naked and wet and smelling like soap in another minute.

I stand. "Um, no. We can talk on Monday when I do your pre-op."

"This isn't sexual," he promises in earnest. "You won't see anything you don't want to see."

Except I'm already seeing things I, unfortunately, *do* want to see. Like his incredible chest and abs, and hell, his shoulders. I have a thing for shoulders, and I'm not simply talking about the mechanics inside of them. His are perfect.

"Give me five minutes, please, and then we'll talk. Drink your coffee, just stay. Don't go."

*Stay. Don't go.*

I'm getting another flash of a memory and I close my eyes, trying to capture it, but it's gone just as quickly as it was there.

He turns and heads toward the showers in the next room, unlacing the strings on his pants as he goes.

I spin around, my hand over my racing heart. What the hell? I can't be in here while he's showering. Only I don't want to seem like that woman. The one who is skittish and immature. He isn't bothered by it, and he already said it isn't sexual, so why am I making a thing out of this?

*Because a hot man who thinks you're the most beautiful woman he's ever seen is naked not even twenty feet from you.*

Just because attraction is there doesn't mean we act.

I sit back down and cross my legs, my knee jumpy as I take my first sip, and of course, I burn my tongue because that's how everything is going for me lately. Five minutes later, as promised, he returns wearing nothing but a towel. Water runs down every inch of him, over every muscular ridge and valley before getting absorbed in the white cotton.

I'm staring. I know I am. But it can't be helped. My face is flushed, and it's like watching live-action porn, only better because this man is chiseled from stone and built with more muscles than I remember learning about in med school.

He goes for his locker and starts digging through it, and I take in the lines of his back with equal fascination and appreciation as I did the front of him. The man is a work of art. Sculpted and muscular—I might have already mentioned that, but *damn*—yet still somehow long and lean. He's not overly bulky, but I doubt there's an inch of fat on him. He has those twin indents right above his ass that mimic the twin indents on the other side of him, and I swear, I never cared or noticed any such thing on any other athlete I've worked with in the past, but I'm a living, breathing, drooling, pathetic mess of a woman right now.

"Are you with me, Doctor?" he questions, and my gaze snaps away from his back and up to his face that's turned over his shoulder and angled right at me. He's been talking to me this entire time, and I was too busy drooling over his body to notice any of it.

He gives me his favorite cocky smirk when he realizes this. "Should I start again?"

I open my mouth to say something when my phone rings in my bag. Setting down the coffee, I pull it out and see it's my mother, and she never calls unless it's a big deal.

I hold up my hand to Asher and immediately answer. "Mom?"

"He said, Mama!" She cries into the phone, and instantly tears spring to my eyes.

"He did?!" My hand covers my mouth. "When?"

"Just now, Wyn. He was looking at a picture of you on my phone and said, Mama. Clear as day. He's only ten months old. Such a smart baby. Just like you were. What did those doctors know when they said his speech might be delayed."

I hiccup out a sob. I missed my son's first word. A first word that is especially epic given his slight hearing impairment. "I'm on my way home now."

I stand up, shoving my phone back in my bag. "I have to go," I tell Asher.

"Is everything okay?" he asks, concern all over his face as he reaches for me, almost as if he wants to comfort me.

"It's... fine. Good. Amazing almost, but also..." Not. Because I wasn't there to hear it. "I'm sorry. We'll talk on Monday." With that, I fly out of the room, away from Asher Reyes, and back toward the man in my life. The only one who deserves my attention. Certainly not the hot quarterback who seems to effortlessly steal it every chance he gets.

# 6

## ASHER

When I was sixteen years old, I left home with my four best friends and Suzie to tour the world as a rock star. It was the best time of my life. I didn't care about the music—that was always Greyson and Suzie. I wanted the adventure. The high that came with it. But little by little, as I started college online and not in person and spoke to my older brother, who had just won his first Super Bowl, I felt a shift inside me.

I didn't want to play music anymore. I wanted to play football.

I knew I had the talent, but with every passing day, I was watching the opportunity slip away. When Suzie died of a stroke in the shower and our band fell apart, I was even more of a mess. I was relieved the band was over—how fucked-up is that?

We lost Suzie. The best and coolest girl I knew.

So I always wondered if I was tempting fate or Karma with that relief.

It's why I never went to the doctor when I got hit. I was afraid they'd tell me it would require surgery because that's what happened to every ball player I knew who ever went to the doctor. They had surgery. I knew I was potentially putting off something important, but I wasn't ready for that level of risk.

Now I don't have a choice. It's surgery or my game is over.

My father retired at thirty-six. My brother still plays, but he's laid up with a torn ACL—I wasn't lying when I told pretty Wynter Hathaway that anytime someone has gone to see a doctor, it's never been good news—so I don't want to bother him with my woes while he's going through his own and is at the end of his career.

We're not that close anyway.

He and my father never liked that I went with Central Square instead of football from the get-go.

Besides, any time I've ever needed advice or simply to talk, I went to my guys. My best friends. Which is what I'm doing now because as luck would have it, tonight is our monthly Friday poker night at Zax's. Even Lenox comes in for it, and that dude hates leaving his cabin in the wilderness of Maine. He was Suzie's twin, and where he wasn't much of a talker before she died, now if he strings more than five words together, it's a lot.

I ring the bell for Zax's penthouse, and the door opens a moment later. "Hey, doll," I say to Aurelia, Zax's fiancée. "You're looking beautiful as always." Aurelia, or Lia Sage, as she's known in the fashion world, is a model turned designer. She's also Grey's and Zax's ex-stepsister who now works for Zax's fashion company, Monroe Fashions. The two of them reunited and had a lot of drama, but Zax finally stopped being such a grump, and they fell in love.

"Hey yourself. You look... kind of like shit."

I snicker. "Thanks, babe. I love how you always set it straight for me."

She gives me a hug but then cups my jaw and stares into my eyes. "For real, Ash. Your smile is fake as hell. Are you okay?"

"Come with me." I drop my arm around her shoulder, and we walk through their mammoth place toward the game room. The guys, Fallon, who is Grey's woman, and Layla, who is Callan's, are all here. I hug and handshake everyone, and then turn to Callan. "Where's Katy?" Katy is his niece, but he recently became her guardian when his brother and sister-in-law died in a tragic car accident.

"At a sleepover," he tells me, helping himself to a huge plate of bar food—everything from nachos to sliders to buffalo wings. Great. Junk I can't eat. Awesome.

"Good stuff." I lick my lips and then force myself over to the bar, pouring myself a small drink. I don't normally drink much in season, but I'm not sure how much in season I am right now considering I'm likely having surgery next week. Everyone is watching me do it, quiet and curious, so I decide to cut to the chase. "I had a day. Well, more like a couple of days."

"We can tell," Grey muses. "What happened?"

I swivel around as I bring my bourbon up to my lips, taking a long sip and savoring the smooth, sweet flavor of it. "A lot actually. Do you all remember my bathroom lady?"

"Your bathroom lady?" Zax parrots. "You mean the one you gave lousy sex to in the bathroom of the club and have been obsessed with ever since?"

I point my finger at him. "That's the one." See, I told you she's all I've thought about for a year and a half. "Well, as irony would have it, I ran into her again yesterday... in a bathroom. The men's room this time. At the stadium."

I get a lot of blinking eyes. "And..." Callan drags out the word.

"And her name is Wynter Hathaway. She's my new orthopedic surgeon, and she doesn't remember me. At all." I drop into one of the chairs at the card table, feeling shitty and defeated all over again. How can she not remember me? Was she that drunk? I mean, I was messed up six ways to Sunday, but I didn't forget anything about her.

Or that night.

Then again, I had just won the Super Bowl, and she was the hottest woman I had ever seen—and still is—and my dick didn't work. All very memorable events.

"I know Wynter Hathaway," Fallon announces, and I think my eyes do that cartoon flying out of my skull thing.

"You do?" I practically shout the words. "How? Where? When? Tell me everything."

Fallon shrugs and comes over to sit beside me. "She's two years older than us. I knew her at Yale since we were both premed. In fact"

—she turns to Grey—"she did her residency in Miami and is the reason I told you that's where I was doing mine when I lied to you about it."

Grey frowns but leans in and kisses her forehead. Christ, is love ever easy for anyone? I swear, each of my friends who are now with their women never had an easy time getting where they are.

"Anyway," Fallon continues, "I didn't know she was up here in Boston. Last I heard she was in London or something. We haven't kept in touch much over the last couple of years."

I scrub my hands up and down my face and then finish off the last of my one and a half fingers of bourbon. "She hates me," I admit and then start to ramble. "Or maybe doesn't hate me yet since she doesn't remember me, but she doesn't like me because I'm a football player and evidently have a bit of an ego and cockiness about me and I like to inappropriately touch and lick her." I hold up a hand. "Don't ask about that last one. I know I shouldn't have, but I was in the moment, and jealousy had me by the balls. Anyway, she knows my coach somehow and won't tell me about it, but she hates him too. Even more than she hates me, I think, since she called him a dickface today. As it is, sometime next week she is going to open my shoulder up with the hope she can fix it so I can play ball next season— because I might officially be out for the rest of this one, which I haven't even begun to process or mourn—and I don't know how to tell her who I am without making her hate me more, because how could she not?"

I fall forward and faceplant into my forearms.

It's silent. Too silent.

"I was going to drop hints like timebombs today when I brought her into the locker room, but she had some sort of emergency and had to leave before I could."

More silence. *Argh.*

"If you have any words of wisdom, now is the time to start laying them on me. I've touched her and teased her and smiled at her and she has no clue that I've had my dick inside of her."

"You have to tell her," Layla says adamantly. "I mean, maybe add a bit of polish instead of saying, hey, I've had my dick inside of you." She makes a noise in the back of her throat. "God, why are guys so freaking crass?"

"Right?" Aurelia chimes in.

"Sorry," I grumble. "It's just how we think, and I didn't mean it disrespectfully or misogynistically."

"Fine. Whatever," Layla continues. "But bad sex notwithstanding, she should hear it from you before she figures it out."

"Agreed," both Aurelia and Fallon say in unison.

"The women are right," Lenox comments, and damn him, he knows we all listen when he speaks because he does so infrequently.

"Thank you for hitting the final nail in my coffin, silent warrior, but how do I do that without her hating me more?" I sit up and then decide eating a slider might be a better way to occupy myself while my friends help me work this out. Evidently, booze and junk food are my things tonight.

Lenox gives me a *fuck if I know* shrug.

"Thanks, brother. Always so helpful. Ladies, you're back on the clock." I suck a dollop of ketchup off my thumb and then take a bite of the burger, talking through a mouthful. "Seriously, though, it was an awful night, and I don't think telling her who I am will turn the tide of her liking me in my favor."

"When do you see her next?"

"Monday," I tell Callan. "Oh, and she works at your hospital." I wiggle my finger back and forth between him and Fallon.

"She does?!" Fallon exalts, doing an excited little jump. "That's fantastic. I'm going to text her now. Maybe I'll see if she's free for lunch this week."

I groan. "Fall, if you become besties with her—"

"That helps you," Layla announces, walking over and shaking my arm as if she's just had an epiphany. Thankfully it wasn't my bad arm, since that's the hand holding my slider.

"How?" I challenge.

"We throw a party," she declares. "Tomorrow. Totally last minute, but who cares. I'll get all my Fritz people to attend, and you'll all come, and we can even invite some other doctors from the hospital if you want. That way she'll meet people, and she'll see the people you're friends with and might think you're not so awful after all. After that, you can tell her who you are, so it's not done in a professional setting."

"That's actually... brilliant," I admit, thinking deeper on that. The idea is like a massive storm cloud, kicking up lightning in my head. Because Layla is a Fritz—her sister, who was her guardian, married Oliver Fritz, and so Layla took his name when she was a kid and he adopted her—and the Fritzes are a family of famous billionaires, but they all work in the medical field. Some even work at MGH where Fallon and Callan work.

Where Wynter now works.

So she'll meet people she works with in the hospital, which is great because she's new in town, and then I can show her I'm not a total douche and tell her the truth. Before she cuts me open. Gulp.

"Okay. Text her," I tell Fallon while Layla and Aurelia start to dig in with gusto and plan an impromptu party. I even volunteer my place because it's big, and well, it's the least I can do since I started this circus.

A few minutes later, as we settle in to finally play some poker, Fallon's phone chimes with a text. She reads it and then hits me with a huge, dazzling smile. "She's in."

My heart jumps in my chest. I'm going to see Wynter tomorrow. And I have no clue how this will go.

Doctors are boring. Or at least they're very different to party with than football players or rock stars. Or maybe I'm just antsy while I wait for Wynter to get here. I need a crazy distraction, like someone throwing up in the pool or having drunken sex in the guest bedroom. Everyone here is tame, speaking in polite tones, using coasters, and being careful not to make a mess or drink too much.

As I said, boring.

"Why do you look like you're about to throw up?" Callan asks, handing me a glass of something that looks and smells like my private stash of expensive as fuck bourbon.

"Now we're talking. Did you snatch this for us, or is this out on display somewhere requiring me to go and crack some skulls?" At five hundred a bottle, who could blame me?

He sighs. "This won't turn into the frat party you need it to."

I hate how well my best friends know me. And love it.

"So, this is just for us?"

"Yep. Just for you and me and possibly Aurelia, who saw me take out the bottle. But she's earned it, living with Zax so I topped her off."

"Good man. I always liked Reils, but she's got nothing on my ice queen. I might be in trouble here, brother."

He walks me over to the floor-to-ceiling windows with the view of the public gardens and Boston Common beyond, giving us a bit of privacy from everyone else. I actually bought this place from Layla's uncle, Luca Fritz, who is here making disparaging remarks about how much better it was when he lived here. The circle of famous, wealthy Bostonians is small, and we all know each other.

"I like her." Then I laugh because, first, I have no idea where the words came from. And second, I sound like I'm fifteen. "It's weird that I do, right? I mean, I met her in a bathroom over a year and a half ago, and Thursday and Friday she was nothing but antagonistic to me. Hot and sexy—the smartest woman on the planet, but antagonistic. Part of me wondered if I had been thinking about her so much because of how bad things went that night in the bathroom. Like maybe it was more pride and ego than actual desire, but after seeing her again, I'm pretty damn sure it's her." I turn to look at him, my face scrunched up. "Am I crazy?"

Callan laughs lightly and smacks my back as he takes a sip of his drink. "If she's your doctor, you can't fuck her. You know that, right?"

I smirk tauntingly. "You mean the way you weren't supposed to fuck and fall for your med student?"

He grins in return. "Yeah, exactly like that."

"Maybe I just need to fuck her again. And do it right this time. Get her out of my system, because a woman like that... she's—"

The door to the condo opens, and in she walks.

Instantly, I know I'm a dead man.

Her long, dark hair is down in silky, bouncy waves. Her makeup is minimal except for blood-red lips that make my cock jerk reflexively. She's wearing a black dress, something fitted without being too tight and a little flirty as the flared-out hem plays with the pale skin just above her knee.

My jaw hits the floor, and my tongue lags out of my mouth, rolling along the floor like it's a red carpet just for her.

"Good luck with fucking *that* out of your system," he deadpans and gives my back a shove, pushing me in her direction. "She already owns your balls; you might as well stick them in her purse and hope she plays with them later."

"If only."

"Then why are you still standing here with me? Go get her, man, before someone else does."

I falter, casting him a quick glance before turning back to her. "And when she hates me after I tell her the truth?"

"No woman has ever hated you."

"You're looking at the first." I toss back the rest of my drink, hand him my empty glass, and do as the man says; I go get her, a moth to her flame.

Before I can reach her, Fallon swoops in and steals her full attention, hugging her and laughing like two sorority sisters reunited. Only I already know—since I made Fallon tell me everything she knew about her—that they're both math and science geeks and had very limited social lives in college. Can't say I'm disappointed by that.

Wynter looks like she's in seventh heaven talking to Fallon. They're gabbing on, probably about how excited they are that Wynter is now in town and how cool it is that they're not only working in the same hospital together, but, blah, blah, blah, who cares?

"Sorry, Fall. I have to steal your date."

Because I need to tell her, yes, but I also want to be alone with her, and as Cal said, I don't want anyone else to get her before I can.

"Asher? What are you doing here?"

I grab her hand and drag her away from Fallon, who is giving me a Cheshire grin. "So, funny thing," I say over my shoulder as I lead her down the hall, debating where to take her. "This is actually my place."

"What?" She tries to yank her hand free, but that's not going to happen. I pull her into one of the powder rooms I have because bathrooms seem to be our thing. "No, Fallon invited me to a work thing. "I'm here to meet people I work with."

"You're not actually." I spin her inside the room, shut and lock the door behind us, pick her up by her hips, and drop her on the counter beside the sink.

"What the hell is going on?" she yells, her hands flying, and then jutting out to ward me off. "How do you know Fallon, and why is this your place, and what are you doing with a houseful of doctors I work with?"

"All really good questions. I love how smart you are. Keeps me on my toes." I shove her hands out of the way and stand directly in front of her. "I know all of these doctors because I'm sort of friends with them. My best friend Callan works in the emergency department of your hospital and is with Layla Fritz, whose entire family is in medicine, and half of them work at your hospital as well. Fallon works with Oliver Fritz, who is Layla's brother-in-law, and Fallon is also engaged to my best friend, Greyson Monroe. It's a lot, and I'm likely confusing you, but that's the best explanation I've got. I also attend all kinds of charity events with the Fritz family, so your doctor people are also my people. If that makes sense. To answer your other question, you're here for me because I planned this party for you, so I can talk to you. You ran out on me yesterday, and I needed to tell you something in person before Monday and work and Coach and surgery got in the way."

She stares at me like I have three heads, none of which she finds appealing. "You planned an entire party just so you could talk to me?"

I hesitate, shifting in front of her. "Yes. And when you put it that way with the tone you're using, it sounds a little crazy and desperate, but both of those accurately sum me up right now."

Her eyes hold mine. "Why would you do all that? What is it you have to say that couldn't wait? I barely know you and this seems a little... much."

"I get that. Just bear with me, okay?"

"Fine. Talk."

I cup her jaw in my hand, no longer able to hold back. "I have to tell you something important, and I didn't want to do it at the stadium or in the hospital. Especially not before you were about to take a scalpel to my shoulder."

She swallows hard. "Okay. Tell me already."

My heart starts to pound out a merciless rhythm in my chest, like a hammer striking at my ribs, making me winded. "We met before Thursday. About a year and a half ago. In a bathroom. Of a club." My hand drops to the counter beside her legs, and I hold still, standing close but still giving her space.

She blinks at me, staring harder and deeper than she ever has before. Then she gasps, loud and resonating, her hand clapping over her mouth. "I told myself I was crazy."

"You're not."

"No." She shakes her head violently. "It's not possible. It can't be. Not you. Not now. Not this."

"You remember now, don't you?"

Her eyes pinch into narrowed slits, and she nods slowly, her hand still over her mouth. "Oh my God."

"You ran out on me that night too. It was the night I won the Super Bowl. I'd had a few too many drinks and a couple too many muscle relaxants, and well, you remember what happened. Or maybe not since you didn't recognize me. It was your birthday, and I knew you had been drinking, but I didn't realize you were that drunk."

"You had longer hair. And a beard. Right?" Her face scrunches up as she looks me over again. "I didn't imagine that. But your eyes were... different."

"I grew my hair and a beard that season because a few of us on the team made a claim that we wouldn't cut it until we won the Super Bowl. I cut my hair and shaved my beard off the next day. And my eyes are the same."

"No. They were blue. I could have sworn they were blue."

"They're gray," I correct. "Kind of colorless, which means they change colors depending on the lighting. The bathroom had a slight blue tint to it."

"You're really him. The guy who fucked me without a condom, ejaculated inside me, and then ran out immediately after."

I frown. "That's not how I meant it to go down. I can promise you that."

She's shaking now. Uncontrollably. And her eyes... they're filling with tears. Tears that immediately start spilling over and onto her cheeks as she stares at me as if she's seen a ghost.

This is definitely not the reaction I thought she'd have.

"Hey. What? What is it?" I cup her face again, brushing away the tears. "I'm sorry I ran out, and I'm so sorry I didn't use the condom. That wasn't a ploy or me trying to be an asshole. I swear. I wasn't... hard as I always am in those situations, and I wasn't thinking because I was flustered, and you told me to hurry up, and so I just shoved it in. I was... freaked out. And upset. Nothing like that had ever happened to me before, and I was scared. Not only that, but I also didn't want it to be as awful for you as I knew it was. I was a mess. A little too drunk, and the muscle relaxants—"

"Asher," she cuts off my rant, her watery eyes on mine as she says, "I have something to tell you too."

## 7

### WYNTER

Oh my God. Asher. Asher Reyes is the guy from the bathroom. The father of my son. He's Mason's father, and he has no idea he has a son. I have a son with Asher Reyes. How is this happening? How could it be Asher of all people?

Everything is about to change.

My entire life will now be linked with his—if he even wants anything to do with Mason.

Tears continue to spill from my eyes as I stare at this man. This man who orchestrated a party just so he could tell me this. He's crazy. I mean, who does something like that? He could have called me up on the freaking phone and told me or asked to meet me for coffee or something. But this?

I'm sitting in a bathroom, wearing the dress I wore to my medical school graduation, an apartment full of work colleagues just beyond the door, and now I have to tell him he has a son. My heart is pounding in a way it never has before as anxiety rattles through me like a runaway train. A cold sweat breaks out on my forehead and the back of my neck, and I'm shaking so badly my teeth are chattering.

"Asher." I start only to stop. How do I say this to him?

"What is it?" he questions calmly, gently, still trying to wipe my tears. Is he a good man? Joe said he was, but Joe's not exactly someone I take my character references from.

I don't know Asher, and it's terrifying. A football player. Of course it had to be a football player. Fate and irony really have a thing for messing with me.

I open my mouth to tell him. To push the words past my lips. But a wave of nausea hits me, and I can't breathe in here. I can't think in here. It's too closed in, and I think I'm having a panic attack. "I need air. Where can I find air?"

I shove him back without waiting on his response and fly for the door. It opens, and then I'm in the hallway, and there is noise in the great room. Laughter. People talking. Holy shit, I'm in the middle of a fucking party, and this is happening.

I shake my head and start to run in the opposite direction when Asher grabs my hand and pulls me toward a large staircase that winds up and up, my heels clanging on the metal steps, all the way until he opens a door, and then we're on the roof of the building and I'm looking at... a pool? Who has a rooftop pool in their house? Well, apartment, I guess, but still.

"This is insane." Because it is. Beautiful. Super cool. But also insane. The outdoor area takes up the entire rooftop. There are loungers, seating areas, a full bar, and televisions everywhere you look. It's a sports bar that met a bachelor pad and together they made a resort.

The pool area is glassed in, showing off sweeping views of Boston everywhere you look. The pool itself is stunning and sparkling blue, lit up by underwater lights.

I realize he's still holding my hand as he walks me over in that direction. He presses a button on the wall, and the glass roof slowly retracts like a sunroof causing a gust of warm wind to hit me right in the face. I suck in a rushed breath, and then another, and collapse onto a cushioned chaise on the edge of the pool.

"How do you have this kind of money?" Then I shake my head. "Sorry, that was rude, and it's totally none of my business. My mind is too frazzled to think logically right now, and that just slipped out."

He chuckles, and the sound eases some of the knots twisting in my stomach. He sits on the lounge across from me and retakes my hand. "It's fine. I was part of the band Central Square for four years. We made more money than we ever knew what to do with, and after college and I was drafted back home to Boston, so I bought this place from one of the doctors downstairs."

"It's nice up here."

"It's why I bought it from him." He gives my hand a gentle squeeze and then shifts so he's closer to me, so our knees are touching. "What happened downstairs? Why did you panic like that after I told you what happened that night?"

My chest falls forward, my forehead resting on my knees. His hands find my hair, combing through the strands, and I don't know why I haven't stopped him from continuing to touch me like this, but I haven't, and I already know I won't. It's comforting somehow, and right now I need that. It's soothing my soul.

"Are you a good man, Asher Reyes?" I swallow and sit up, looking directly into his eyes that do in fact change color, because right now, they appear blue again as they reflect off the water.

"A good man?" He squints at me, taking both of my hands in his. "Yes," he answers easily, full of sincerity. "I'm a good man. At least I always strive to be. What is this about, Wynter?"

I look down at our linked hands, watching as mine shake in his. "Asher, that night in the bathroom..." I blow out an uneven breath and force myself to meet his gaze. "I got pregnant."

He freezes. Grows preternaturally still. He's not even blinking. Finally, he utters, "Pregnant?"

I lick my suddenly dry lips. "Yes." More tears start to spill. "I have a son. He's ten months old. He was born on October fourteenth. His name is Mason."

"Mason." With that, he explodes off the chaise and starts to pace away from me. For a moment, I think he's going to leave and head back downstairs, but he doesn't. He pauses when he reaches the bar, grips the thick, wood edge of it, and lowers his head between his outstretched arms, where he stands like that for a few minutes. Not making a sound. Just breathing heavily.

I don't dare say anything. He needs this time, and I need to let him have it because I need this time too. I don't know what I want from him. To what extent I want him in Mason's life.

Before I can come up with any answers, he shoots away from the bar and races back to me, dropping to his knees on the hardscape in front of me. I hold my breath, waiting for him to say something, but he doesn't. For the longest time, he does nothing but look up at me, his expression wrecked with turmoil, but there's something else there too.

Something I can't figure out because I don't know him, and I don't know his looks or how his mind operates.

He wipes another tear from my cheek and then whispers in a hoarse voice, "Can I see a picture of him?"

I break apart. Right here. Cracking in half and collapsing forward again. He wraps himself around me, his cheek resting against the side of my head as he whispers things in my ear. He's telling me it's okay, that it's going to be fine, that he has me, and that I don't have to cry. But I do have to cry. How can I not cry?

"I hate football players," I croak, and he laughs, which makes me laugh. I sit up and wipe my face, which is likely smeared with dripping mascara.

"But do you hate me?"

"I'm not sure." I give him a sly grin.

"I can change your mind about football players," he assures me. "I can make you love me."

A scoff climbs past my throat. "I doubt that, player."

"Don't doubt me, sweetheart. It only makes me want to prove myself more. I am the perpetual underdog in a family of football royalty."

"And what if I hate you?"

He smirks, giving me a long once-over. "You don't. You only wish you did."

"Are you sure about that?"

"One hundred percent. But if that's the game you want to play, I'll have to pull out all the stops to win you over. Not all football players are bad," he promises. "One day you'll have to tell me about your aversion to my kind."

"Maybe, but not today. I'm sorry this fell on you this way."

He shakes his head, dismissing that. "*I'm* sorry. I'm the one who didn't put on the condom. But... can I see him? Because, and I know this is going to sound really fucking weird because we don't know each other and I don't know him yet, but I'm not sure how sorry I actually am."

I blow out a breath. "You mean that?"

He bites into his lip and gives me a jerky nod. "That's weird, right? Like, how can I feel that way when I haven't met him yet?"

Holy hell. My chest clenches like someone is squeezing it in a vise.

I reach into my purse and pull out my phone. My hands fumble with it and finally, I manage to unlock it with my face. I pull up my photos app and start to scroll through. Asher is still on the ground, but now he's the one shaking.

"He has your hair," I murmur, my voice cracking, and then I pull up a video I took of him yesterday evening and hand him my phone. Asher collapses, his back against the chaise and his knees up as he holds my phone in his hand, his gaze glued to the screen.

"Fuck. Jesus fuck." He pants out a breath, his eyes immediately glassing over as he watches his son play in the bath and chew on his favorite giraffe teething toy. Once that video is done, he starts to scroll through picture after picture, video after video. "He's really beautiful, Wynter," he says as he hands me back my phone after he's gone through nearly every picture and video I have. "My mind is spinning, and I can't think all that clearly, but he's seriously fucking beautiful."

"Thank you."

He gives me a wry smirk. "Worst sex of your life, and we made that. I feel like I should ask you to marry me or something."

A laugh hits the air. "Um. No."

"That's what my dad did with my mom."

I raise an eyebrow. "How'd that turn out for them?"

He rubs at his smirking bottom lip. "They're happily divorced. I grew up in Cambridge with my mom, who now lives in Sarasota."

I shoot him with my finger. "Point proven. Thank you."

"Fine. I won't marry you until you beg me to."

I roll my eyes at him. "Don't hold your breath."

"But you'll give me mouth-to-mouth if I do. There's incentive enough."

I sigh. "Such a player."

His expression turns genuine. "I'm honestly not. Not in the way you mean it, at least. I wanted that night to be great. I was going to take you back to my hotel and then ask for your number with plans of using it. Five minutes after meeting you, and that's what I was already thinking about."

I look away, hating how that makes me feel. "That didn't happen, so what now?" It's the question I was dreading asking but has to be faced all the same.

He shifts off the ground and scooches in on the chaise beside me. "I don't know. This is my first time finding out I have a kid I knew nothing about. I don't know what I can ask for and what I can't."

"Did you ever... did you ever want kids?"

He gives me a look. "Fuck yeah, I want kids. Callan is now the guardian of his niece Katy, and I love hanging out with her. Kids are great. My brother has three little terrors I don't get to see nearly as often as I'd like since he lives in Dallas, and we don't play them often. He married his high school sweetheart. They're the couple everyone loves to hate because they're still sickeningly in love with each other."

The way he says that makes me smile. It's a far more normal response than I was expecting, and I don't even know why. Joe has jaded me pretty deeply.

"You know..." he trails off and leans into me, rubbing his shoulder with mine. "I've thought about you a lot since that night. I always said if I ever found you, I'd do everything I could to make up for the shitty sex I gave you."

I snort out a laugh. "Are you propositioning me for sex?"

"Not just any sex. Great sex," he counters, his eyes glimmering against the pool lights.

"I seem to remember that promise once before."

"Yeah, but I've only had one drink and no muscle relaxants. Trust me, I won't have performance issues with you again."

"I've thought of you too, but not in the most favorable way." I give him a sheepish grin.

He sobers. "I wasn't trying to do anything underhanded that night. I swear—"

I put my hand on his forearm, stopping him. "I know. I heard what you said downstairs in the bathroom, and I believe you. I never thought I'd meet Mason's father again. It's a lot to take in."

"It's a lot to take in," he agrees, his gaze flickering back and forth between mine before dipping down to my lips.

He exhales a breath and then starts to lean in like he's going to kiss me.

I pull back, and his hand cups the back of my neck, holding me still. "Don't pull away," he pleads, his sweet breath on my lips. "You have no idea how much I've wanted to kiss you. From the first second I saw you again, I've wanted nothing else. But seeing those pictures of Mason. Of you with him. Wynter, I want you so badly that I can hardly stand to be next to you and not touch you or kiss you."

My heart gives a reactive thud, and my body heats. So much of that night is still fuzzy, but I remember thinking that his kisses were magic. And the way he's looking at me, whispering words I'm not sure I've ever heard the equal of against me. I'm lonely and aching and emotional—and I know everything that went wrong the first time wouldn't happen again.

He'd give me the best sex of my life. He'd make damn sure of it.

"But then what?" I ask.

His brows crease. "What do you mean?"

"You kiss me, and maybe we have sex. Maybe it's great this time. Best sex of our lives, even. But what happens after that, Asher? I have a son who also happens to be your son, and we haven't worked out any of that complicated situation yet. It's not like I can date you or that this is the start of a relationship."

He blinks in rapid fire at me. "Why not?"

"For so, so many reasons. I don't know you very well. So there's that. More importantly, I can't get emotionally involved with you that way. That's how things become messy. That's how things turn ugly. I have to think of Mason. Of what's best for him."

He frowns and pulls back, scrubbing his face with his hands. "Can I be in his life?"

I pry his hands from his face, and he interlaces them with mine. "Is that what you want?"

His fingers squeeze mine. "I want to be in his life as much as you'll allow me to be. I'm not the sort of man who would have a kid and then not be their dad."

My heart hiccups in my chest, and I release him. This is what I was afraid of. This is what can't happen. He's saying and doing all the right things. It's enthralling and magnetizing and so very tempting. Asher is gorgeous and built and charming and quick-witted, and he wants me. Being desired, especially by a man who could likely have any woman he wanted, is an aphrodisiac.

But the reality is, I got pregnant from a one-night stand, and though it's easy and romantic to call this something other than coincidence, it's not.

We'd burn hot and crash fast, and that's not something that can happen now. So I tell him the only truth that will sustain us and make this work.

"If you want to be in Mason's life, then nothing can ever happen between us."

# 8

## ASHER

Her words reverberate through my skull, and immediately I realize two things. One, I hate that she just put those boundaries on us. And two, keeping them is not something I can promise her. Because, holy fuck, I have a kid. A kid! And I have that kid with *her*.

I watched those videos and flipped through every picture, and it was like my life was clicking into place before my eyes. It was more than just him. It was her too.

But that doesn't mean I don't understand where she's coming from either.

I don't address her demand. It's futile when I already plan to circumvent it.

Instead, I ask, "Can I meet him?" Because I'm dying to.

"How are you not freaking out?" she asks, and I laugh. Because good fucking question, right?

"I legit don't know. But I'm honestly not. This wasn't some situation where you intentionally got pregnant to score a big payday from me—because yes, that shit happens all the time in my world. You weren't trying to keep him from me or hide him. This was something of my own doing that resulted in a piece of me. I have money. I'm twenty-nine. I get to teach him all things football. I'm pumped."

"You're very much a big kid, aren't you?"

"Sweetheart, I play ball for a living. Of course I'm a big kid. But don't hold that against me because I'd really like to be part of this. I understand he has to get to know me, and you have to get to know me too, but I want that all to happen. The only regret I have with any of this is the last year and a half without being part of it."

I would have given anything to have seen her pregnant and then watch my son be born.

She blows out a heavy breath and stands. "I need to go home. I have a lot of thinking to do. You might be pumped and totally fine, but I'm very overwhelmed."

"I get that. Can I drive you?"

She shakes her head. "No. I drove."

I stand too. "Can I call you? Text you?"

"I was planning to take Mason to the park tomorrow. The one in the Common."

I give her a look. "You mean the one directly across the street from this building?"

She smiles gently. "Yes. That one. I forgot where you lived. You can meet us there. Does one work? That's usually a good time for him. In between naps and after lunch."

I laugh. "Any time works for me. I'll be there."

"Okay." She hesitates, unsure how to leave this. "Bye?" Yes, it comes out as a question.

"Good night, Dr. Hathaway. I'll see you tomorrow." I hug her. It's strained. I can't tell if it's because she doesn't want to touch me at all or if she wants to touch me so much she's not allowing herself to. Or if her head is simply too full with finding the father of her child.

"Good night, Asher."

Asher. Not player. I don't know if that's progress or not.

She turns and walks away. Heading toward the stairs, I let her go, thinking and feeling completely lost.

Sliding out my phone from my pocket, I open up the text message thread I have with the guys.

> Me: I need you to kick everyone out of my place and then meet me up on the rooftop.

My phone starts buzzing immediately, but I don't bother responding as I set it down. I lie back on the chaise and stare up at the night sky, all the stars above me muted by the street pollution of the city.

I have a son.

With the woman I've been low-key obsessed with since the second I met her.

A few minutes later, the door opens and out walks all four of my friends. One by one they file around me and take their seats on the lounges.

I don't move. Not yet. I continue to stare up at the sky and think about Wynter and Mason.

"Any issues getting everyone out?"

"No. Layla took care of that in a hot minute," Callan tells me. "She, Fallon, and Aurelia are cleaning up."

I scowl. "They don't have to do that. I'll do that later."

"They weren't sure if they should stay or go since we weren't sure what this was," Zax supplies.

"I don't want them going home alone in separate cars. I'll make this quick."

"I take it that it did not go well with your ice queen," Grey states.

A strange sort of smile hits my lips, and I rub it with my fingers. My chest twinges as I say, "It went a little differently than expected."

"How so?" Lenox asks.

I lift my phone and pull up the text I had sent myself from her phone, and then hand it to him.

"Who is that?"

"That's my son."

They all fall eerily quiet, and I notice Lenox passing my phone to each of them.

"That's your son?" Zax presses. "That's all you're gonna say?"

I clear my throat. "I didn't use a condom that night in the club. I was panicked because I wasn't hard, and I didn't. She got pregnant. We didn't know who the other was. No names. No identities. She ran out before I could get anything from her."

"Jesus," Grey grumbles, handing me back my phone. "Ash. Man. How did this go down? Did she know it was you?"

I shake my head and sigh. "She didn't know it was me until I told her, and then she had a panic attack. I brought her up here for some fresh air, and that's when she told me about him."

"At least she told you and didn't try to hide it."

I shake my head at Grey. "I don't think that's who Wynter is." I put my hands behind my head, my elbows butterflied out. "Is it possible to be in love with somebody after only knowing them a few days?"

Zax chokes out a laugh. "Love? Is that what this is?"

"I don't know," I admit. "Probably not. I'm being dramatic, and I know it's just emotional overload. I had sex with her in a bathroom and then couldn't stop thinking about her for a year and a half. The moment I saw her again, it was like a lightning strike, plowing through me and scorching me from the inside out. She has my kid. I watched those videos of her with him. Every picture, every smile. I think they already own me, and instead of being afraid of that, I'm... I don't know. Just not that. What do I do?"

"What do you mean?" Callan pushes out, his voice strained. Likely because I've never talked this way about a woman or even about my life.

"She's not interested in anything with me. She told me it could never happen. That it's too risky to get involved with me because she has Mason to think about, and if things don't work out between us, it could get ugly. Mason. That's my little dude's name. I get her thinking on it, but at the same time, I wouldn't mind trying either."

Everyone is quiet for a moment, and I can practically feel them exchanging glances with each other.

"But she's going to let you meet him, right?" Zax asserts, his voice growing hard.

A smile lights up my face, and I sit up, excited all over again. "I get to meet him tomorrow. She was honestly great about everything. She didn't rush me when I took my time looking at every picture and seemed pleased when I told her I wanted to be in his life as much as she'll let me. She offered to have me come meet them at the park across the street tomorrow afternoon."

"Dude." Grey smacks my shoulder. "You have a freaking son."

"I know." I laugh. Shake my head. Stare incredulously at my friends. "I have a son. It's seriously wild. Nothing in my life will be the same again."

I'm like a kid on his first day of school. I woke up early. Did an extra strenuous workout in my gym. Ate a ginormous breakfast. Popped over to the children's hospital for an hour so I could sign some stuff and hang out with the kids. Then I came home, and for the last hour, I've been trying to calm myself down, but nothing is working.

It's twelve-thirty, and I can't stand being in this apartment for another second. Throwing on my ball cap and shades, I head for the door and then shoot down the elevator. I blow past the concierge who is talking with another resident, and then out into the boiling hot sun. Cars zip past me on Beacon, and I look toward oncoming traffic before I jog across the street, heading into Boston Common.

The frog pond is filled with kids splashing in the water and stuffing their faces with ice cream and snacks from the concession stand right next to it. The small merry-go-round is at capacity, the line long and snaking around, and I meander my way along the path toward the playground.

I don't bother searching for Wynter yet. I'm still about twenty minutes early, but it doesn't take long before I'm recognized by a kid. "Are you Asher Reyes?"

I grin. "That depends on whether or not you're a Boston Rebels fan."

A smile takes over his face, his white teeth contrasting with his dark skin. "I'm your biggest fan."

"Cool. What's your name?"

"Alexander."

"Can I sign your shirt, Alexander?"

His eyes grow comically wide. "For real?"

"Sure." I motion for him to turn around, and I pull the Sharpie I always carry on me out of my pocket and sign his shirt. "All set."

"Thanks, Asher." The kid runs off, and then another is there and before I know how it happened, I have a line like the merry-go-round. Even the mothers are getting in on it—many of them are Central Square fans.

Being part of this city, signing autographs, and having fans want to talk to me—it never gets old. I love it because it gives them a story and makes them happy, and all I have to do is smile and sign my name. Just as I sign my name on a woman's shoulder, I feel a prickling in the back of my neck and turn around to find Wynter walking my way, pushing a stroller with a little boy in it.

I stare, unable to avert my gaze from him, taking him in feature by feature with my heart in my throat, which suddenly feels tight and itchy while the backs of my eyelids burn. I wasn't expecting this. This rush of pure, unrestricted affection.

No, not just affection... *love.*

His hair is short and reddish brown, and his smile... his smile is mine too. His arms and legs are flailing about, probably because he sees the playground. He's easily the most beautiful thing I've ever seen.

"Asher?" Someone else demands my attention, forcing me away from the only people I want to see. "What do you think? Will the team win the Super Bowl this year?"

"I hope so," I tell the person before I mumble out, "Excuse me."

I turn away from them and walk with determined strides toward Wynter, who has stalled on the edge of the playground without entering it. She's wearing her hair up in a high ponytail, a simple white T-shirt, jean shorts that show off the smooth, pale skin of her legs, and a frown.

"What is it?" I ask as I draw closer.

"Everyone is taking pictures and videos of you. This wasn't the best idea." She turns and starts to walk away.

Panic surges within me. "Wynter?"

"Lose the audience and come find me down by the bench under the huge oak tree." With that, she quickens her stride, and shit, I didn't think about that. About being recognized and what that would mean for her and for me meeting Mason.

I turn back to the playground and give anyone who is still watching me a wave, and then I leave, walking on the opposite path from the one she took before I double back, cutting along the grass and taking off into a sprint, desperate to find them.

I spot them tucked beneath the tree, and a pulse of relief thrums through my veins. Wynter is sitting with her back against the thick base of the tree, shaded by the large branches and heavy mantle of leaves. Her long legs are outstretched as Mason climbs all over her. Urgency moves me in their direction, and a moment later she notices me coming and glances up. Our eyes meet, and I have the biggest urge to kiss her.

The way I wanted to last night.

She doesn't feel new. She feels like months and months of yearning, of fantasizing, of not being able to get her out of my mind.

Then there's Mason.

My feet move, and then my knees give out, weakened by the sight before me. I'm crouching beside them, staring into his green eyes that match hers. "Hi."

He blinks at me, turns to Wynter as if he's checking to make sure it's okay, and then treats me to a wet smile complete with a smattering of tiny teeth. Without warning, he crawls off her lap and straight onto my thighs. My hands latch around his ribs, and then I shift so that I'm sitting with my legs folded. Only he's not content with sitting. He uses me as leverage to help him stand, bouncing his little butt and making a contented noise when I finally do.

"I take it that means he's happy?"

Wynter is quiet, but I catch her nod out of the corner of my eye.

"I'm sorry about the crowd. I didn't think it through."

"We'll have to figure it out as we go. I'd like to keep this a secret for as long as possible if you're okay with that."

I cock an eyebrow. "Ashamed I'm your baby daddy?"

She rolls her eyes at me even as she fights her smile. "I'm not calling you daddy."

"Not even when I spank you?"

She pulls a few blades of grass out of the ground and tosses them at me.

"Fine, I'll settle for you just saying my name when that happens."

"Asher!"

I grin. "Yes. Just like that. Maybe with a little moan to it."

"Oh, my God. Stop!" More grass flies my way, but her smile is something else. *She's* something else. So beautiful and yet so serious now. I wonder if becoming a mother did this to her or if that night in the bathroom was an anomaly. She said it was. That the riskiest thing she'd ever done was sneak up to the VIP floor.

But oh, how I want to peel back her petals and coax her into blooming just for me.

Mason jumps on my thighs, calling me back to the situation at hand, and I grow serious too. "I get it about the public. I don't want him in the spotlight either, and me having a kid out of nowhere will do just that. There will be a lot of questions for both of us that I don't think either of us is ready to answer. I'll do everything I can to keep this quiet for as long as I can, but eventually, it'll get out."

"I know that," she says, watching as Mason crawls all over me, standing on my thighs, pulling on my hair, and yanking on my T-shirt.

I lift him up in the air, holding him over my head. "Wow. You're a bruiser, big man."

"He's in the ninety-ninth percentile for weight and height."

I give her an arrogant smirk. "Like his daddy." Something about saying that makes me laugh. Daddy. So weird. How on earth did this happen? Yesterday at this time, I was playing ball and trying to impress her while finding a way to tell her who I am. Now, I'm a daddy. "Can I play with him?"

"Of course. That's why we're here."

I lean in and kiss her cheek. It takes us both by surprise, but I'm filled with so much love and gratitude that I can't help it. I tell myself to pull away. Knowing that my lips shouldn't linger on her skin and that I shouldn't be taking a deep inhale, trying to catch some of her fragrance.

My nose glides up her face, toward her ear, and when I feel her stiffen against me, I whisper, "Thank you." Pulling back, I give her a wink and then stand up. I carry Mason until we've cleared the tree, and then I toss him up in the air, letting him fly, and catch him as he shoots back down.

"What are you doing?!" she shrieks, on her feet in a motherly panic as I do it again. Mason belts out a squeal of laughter, loving every second of it as he flies in the air, his arms and legs outstretched, his hair catching the breeze. "Careful! You're going to drop him."

I throw her a quick side-eye after I catch him again. "Sweetheart, I'd die before I'd ever drop him. I'm a quarterback. This is what I do."

"But your shoulder!" Her wild eyes are all over me.

"Aw, how cute. You're worried about me. Is that as my doctor or my baby mama?"

"Can we please stop with the icky titles?"

"I don't think they're icky. I'm actually having a ton of fun with them. My hot doctor is my baby mama. What could be better than that?" I'm honestly not joking. I think it's the greatest thing in the world. "There should be a Hallmark card that says sorry, not sorry I came inside you."

Mason squirms in my arms, wanting another round of acrobatics, and I have that goofy grin fathers get when they have that moment when they realize their kid is awesome and fun and theirs too. How can you love someone so much after just meeting them a few minutes ago? Scratch that. How can you love someone *before* you've even met them? This kid could ask me for my spleen right now, and I'd cut the fucker out of my body and hand it right to him.

"Asher. Please."

I turn back to my beautiful ice queen. "You gotta lighten up, sweetheart. Enjoy the moment a bit more. My shoulder is totally fine right now. And he likes it. Watch." I toss him again, higher this time, and he flails through the air, landing soundly back in my hands because I'll always catch him. I bring him into me, smelling his hair and kissing his face. "I'm glad he's not older. I'm glad he's still a baby and doesn't know that I haven't been in his life all this time."

"He likes you," she says softly, running her hands through his hair, staring at the side of his face in a way that makes me wonder if it's easier to look at him than me.

"Of course he does. Everyone likes me."

"Not me," she quips, rolling up onto the balls of her feet and kissing the back of his head.

Christ, I like her. "That's a lie. If it weren't for Mason, I'd have had you pinned to that chaise last night as you begged for me to do dirty, dirty things to you."

A flush rises up her face, but she passes it off with a perturbed twist of her lips and yet another eye roll at my expense. "Yes, egotistical meatheads only after sex truly turn me on."

"Good to know, but I never said I was only after sex." I hand Mason off to her. "Why don't you both come up to my place? I think we should talk."

# 9

# Wynter

I SNAP Mason back into his stroller and then walk about ten feet behind Asher as he saunters through the park as if he owns every piece of earth he steps on. People stop him—his glasses and hat do nothing to hide who he is. He doesn't rush anyone as he signs autographs and takes selfies and smiles and laughs. He never draws attention to himself, but he never turns anyone away either.

And he never, ever, acknowledges us.

I left his place last night and lost my flipping mind. I woke my mother up and made her sit with me while I lost it with her too. In so many ways, I've wanted Mason to have a father in his life. A man who would love him and care for him and support him the way Gary Hathaway has done with me.

But fuck all if I ever wanted it to be a football player.

A football player like Asher.

A man who screams sex and oozes desire and has women staring at him like they'd use every hall pass or excuse just to have a chance with him. That was exactly who my father was. Charming. Funny when he wanted to be. I remember hearing my mother scream at him about her best friend, and he didn't even apologize for it.

He simply said there's only so much of one woman a man can take before he grows bored.

So for Mason's sake—and my own—I can never allow anything to happen with Asher. Because Asher wants Mason, and that's more important to me than anything else.

We cross the street and then shuffle into the elevator of his building. "My code is 5435," he tells me, "and I'll have the doorman put you on the list of people who don't have to ring up."

The rest of the ride is silent, and by the time we reach his penthouse, Mason is out, fast asleep in his stroller. "He didn't have much of a nap this morning. He's transitioning from needing two naps to one. I think all the excitement in the park wore him out."

"Good, because I wanted to talk to you about something specific."

My heart jolts in my chest. "What's that?"

We enter his place, and he directs us toward the kitchen. "Would you like something to drink?"

"I'd love some ice water. It's hot out there."

He moves about his top-of-the-line kitchen with ease as he pours each of us a glass of ice water. "How long will he be out for?"

I turn over my shoulder and look at Mason, fast asleep, and then turn back to Asher. "Could be ten minutes. Could be an hour."

"Will it wake him if we talk in here?"

"Only if you give me something to yell at you about."

There's discomfort in his voice and wariness in his eyes as he says, "I make no promises."

I chew on my lip and set my glass down on the counter before I've even taken a sip. "You're making me nervous, Asher. Just say it already."

He lets out a breath, his gray eyes piercing into mine. "I'd like you both to move in here with me."

I blink. Then I laugh. "Uh. No."

"Will you allow me to explain my reasoning before you immediately shut it down?"

My eyebrows bounce. "Do I have to?"

"Yes," he demands, setting his own glass down. "Wynter, I want my son to live with me."

Fuck. This is partially what I was worried about.

"Asher." I fall silent after I say his name. He's entitled to have his son in his life as much as I am. But it's hard to transition from being the only parent in his life when that's all I've been for ten months.

"Listen," he jumps in. "I'm not trying to take over, and I'm not trying to do anything that's not okay with you. I just want to see him every day, or at least as much as I can, and I'm not sure how that's possible unless you both live here. Between our schedules and the press, it'd be a nightmare. I'm a fifteen-minute walk to the hospital, and I have extra bedrooms for both of you."

"Your place isn't childproofed."

He gives me an unamused look, and I admit, that was a weak argument. "I will hire a child specialist to come in and baby-proof my place from head to toe. The stairs will have a gate, and the door to the rooftop and pool will have an extra bolt at the top. Hell, if you need me to move, I'll move."

My eyes narrow, my tone incredulous. "Just like that?"

He steps forward, the intensity in his gaze unable to be ignored. "Just like that. Is that what you want?"

"I never agreed to live with you, so I don't need your offers or promises."

This pisses him off. "But I'm offering them all the same, *ice queen*."

I raise an eyebrow at the way ice queen slithers sardonically from his tongue. "Don't get shitty with me because I didn't jump at your offer. I'm not one of those women who had you sign their stomachs or cleavage while they flirted and made bedroom eyes at you. Think of what you're saying. Living with someone is no small thing. Even with separate bedrooms and odd schedules, you're talking about co-parenting in the same space."

He growls, running his hands through his hair. "Fine. I get that I just threw that on you and expected you to jump all over it. But please, don't discount it either. If we're trying to keep this quiet, then that will make scheduled visits difficult. If he's here, if *you're* here, then it all works. I'm not asking you to share my bed. Just my home."

"And yet last night, that's exactly what you were trying to do."

He runs his finger along his bottom lip, his eyes growing darker, hooded. "Was I trying to get you into my bed last night?" His voice dips. "Yes. One hundred percent, I was. The thought of finally making you come and getting to see it, getting to *feel* it, made me wild with need for you." He takes a step in my direction, a predator stalking exactly what he wants and refusing to settle for anything less. "I've already told you I think you're the most beautiful woman I've ever seen. But you're more than that to me now. You're the mother of my son and that changes everything." More steps, and I start to back up until my butt hits the wall.

"Asher—" My voice dies as he continues to advance. My body heats at the image he painted, making my nipples tighten and blood thrum through my ears. I stand here, flat and stuck while he prowls, his eyes all over me. I shake my head, but that does nothing to stop him.

"You're smart. Fierce. I can't imagine a scenario where I don't want you. Where every inch of me doesn't burn with how much I want you."

I gulp down air, my voice sticking high in my throat. "Asher, this is what I was talking about. This can't happen."

"I know you believe that, sweetheart." He stops right in front of me, the heat from his body radiating through mine, his smoldering, intense gaze devouring. One hand plants into the wall beside my head, and he dips down until our faces are inches apart. "But if you need me to say it, I'll say it. The way I want you, hell, the way I've wanted you for the last year and a half hasn't changed. It won't change. That said, I will do whatever it takes to get both of you in my home, including keeping my hands to myself." He lets that hang before he adds, "If that's what you want."

*If that's what I want?* What a joke. "A hot look and a few choice words won't have me falling into your bed."

He smirks, his face inching in until his nose runs along mine. "I always liked a challenge."

I press my hands into his chest, ignoring the strong, blazing skin and muscles beneath my palms, and give him a shove. "That's not what I'm trying to be. I'm trying to protect myself. I'm trying to protect my son. You're telling me you'll keep your hands to yourself, and yet you're all over me."

With a growl and a grunt, he rights himself. "Move in with me, Wynter."

My body tightens. "No." Because I know exactly where that will lead.

He stares at me, long and hard. "No?"

I shake my head.

He thinks about this for a moment. "Fine. Move one floor beneath me."

"What?" Chokes out.

He thrusts himself away from the wall, away from me, and finally, I can take a breath. A breath that doesn't taste like him. That doesn't smell like him.

"The woman who lives beneath me is getting ready to sell her place. If I buy it, will you and Mason move in there?"

I hesitate.

"Say yes to that."

I don't utter a sound.

"Say yes, Wynter," he presses. "Tell me you'll move one floor beneath me so I can see my son. That's all I'm asking for."

Which considering he could haul me into court and legally demand more, is saying a lot. It's not his apartment. It's far from his bed.

"I'd want to buy it."

"It's twelve million."

I practically throw up on his floors.

"No. No way. I can't afford that, and I can't allow you to pay for that. It's too much." Christ, that's worse than living here with him. Twelve million? I shudder to think what this place cost him.

He growls in agitation, his hands interlocking and clasping behind his head as his elbows butterfly out. "Then tell me what other options I have here. I'd buy it with no strings attached. I just want to be his dad."

My heart stutters and then stops dead in my chest. *I just want to be his dad.*

How many times in my life have I wished that my own father would make such a claim over me? It's everything I want for Mason. It's certainly not something I can say no to. He just offered to drop twelve million to see his son every day.

Could I do it? Could I move in here with him?

I know how those stories go. I know what happens to those women. They give in. They fall in love. They get destroyed.

No strings, he claims. But I would still be living in a place he bought for us—that's all strings. If I were living here with him and it didn't work out, it'd be easier to leave.

"Please," he says with such desperation that I quake. "This could be a win-win for all of us."

Only it feels as though I'm already losing. Already handing over pieces of myself I don't want to relinquish.

My hands hit my knees, my head spinning. "This is all happening so fast."

"Hey," he says, his voice softening. "Here." He hands me my water and then immediately retreats, giving me space. "I'm sorry. I know it's a lot. Take time to think it through. Tomorrow you're back on the field with me for my pre-op."

His pre-op. Hell. I right myself, already frowning. "I can't be your surgeon anymore."

That pulls him up short. "Why not?"

"Because you're the father of my son." I wave a hand toward Mason's sleeping form. "It's a conflict of interest. It's unethical."

He shakes his head. "No. That's what makes you perfect for it.

More so than you were before. You have more of a vested interest in the outcome."

"Asher, I can't."

"You can," he assures me. "We're not a couple, and you're not even living with me. Yet," he tacks on. "I want you as my surgeon, Dr. Hathaway. And if you move in here with me or even downstairs, I'll have your help with my recovery. It's perfect."

"Nothing about this is perfect."

"You might be to me."

I roll my eyes. "Sweet-talking me won't get me to say yes. To any of this."

"Then what will?"

I laugh, shaking my head. "I seriously hate football players."

"Does that mean I should worry about you bringing home hockey players?"

My eyebrows bounce. "Now you're talking."

"Shit," he snarls, snatching my glass from me and marching over to put it in the sink. "I won't survive that."

"Making you rethink this living arrangement, huh?" I quip.

He emits a shaky laugh and turns, his back against the white farm sink. "I'm an excellent cockblocker."

"Nothing scares pussy away like living with your kid and baby mama."

He grins at how I say that and gives me a lazy shrug. "I don't bring *pussy* back here, Doctor. Occasionally I bring a *woman* home, but not all that often, and usually not during the season."

I bark out a slightly bitter laugh. "Good for you. I haven't had sex since that bathroom."

His eyes burst wide, and in a flash, he's before me once more. His hand grabs my shoulder, giving me a small shake. "Tell me you're kidding."

"What?" I ask, startled by his reaction. "No. I got pregnant. I had a kid and finished up my residency. When on earth was I supposed to find a man, let alone time for sex?"

He blinks sixty thousand times at me. "For real? That night was the last time, and I didn't even make you..." He grunts. "Please, please, please let me make you come right now. Please."

I gasp. "Asher—"

He gets right up in my face, his other hand hitting my waist where he grips me. Before I can make sense of what's happening, he's pulling me out of the kitchen and into the neighboring dining room, where he thrusts me up against the wall.

"What are you doing?"

He's all over me once more, eliminating the space between us. "I'll make you come, and that will be it. I swear. It'll just be now. This moment. Then you'll leave with Mason and think about my offer, and tomorrow we'll fall back into our regular roles—player and doctor. But please, Wynter, I have to make you come. The knowledge that I was the last man to touch you and it was awful is *killing* me. I can't take it."

I don't know what to say. How to react. He's beyond worked up over this. Red splotches stain his cheeks, and his eyes are wild—a little manic—filled with lust and determination.

At my silence, his face plants in my neck, and his lips begin trickling kisses. "Please," he whispers against my skin, making me shudder and my eyes roll back in my head. I need to say no, but now the hand on my shoulder is sliding across my body until it's captured my ribcage. His thumb brushes the side of my breast, and tingles of heat shoot straight to my core. "Please."

Oh God. His please in that sultry, sexy, gruff voice...

I open my mouth. I go to tell him no. But his tongue snakes out and licks over my racing pulse just as his thumb roves over my hard nipple, and a moan comes out instead.

"Please," he rasps, nipping at me, his hand covering my breast as the one on my hip slowly slides down and toward the top of my mound, where it pauses. "Let me touch you. Let me make you come. It's only this. Only now." He presses me into the wall. "You're so beautiful." He pulls away from my neck, and his smoldering gunmetal eyes meet mine before they dip to my lips. "So fucking beautiful. Please."

Only he doesn't wait. His head tilts, and then his mouth comes down over mine just as his hand slides into my shorts, beneath my thong, and cups my bare pussy.

He growls into my mouth, low and feral. "You're wet, my pretty ice queen. And there is nothing cold about what I'm feeling right now."

"Asher. This is a mistake. We can't do this." Only I grip his shoulders and rock into his touch, my head back against the wall, and my eyes closing.

"It's only now," he repeats. "You can do this with me right now."

I shake my head but continue to seek more of his touch.

"That's it, sweetheart," he urges in a dark, dirty voice. "Rub yourself on me. This is how it was supposed to be. I'm going to make you feel so good."

His lips attack mine once more, his tongue sliding inside my mouth just as two of his fingers slide inside of me. His other hand shoots up my shirt, pulling the cup of my bra away so he can squeeze my breast without any barrier between us.

"Fuck, how I've wanted to touch these. How I've missed your mouth."

It's so much. It's sensory overload. The mass and heat and scent of his body pressed against mine. His mouth and tongue ravaging my own. His hand pinching and rolling my nipple, and his fingers plunging in and out of me. Angling so they can hit that perfect spot inside me each and every time.

Restless, uncontained hips grind against my side, making his hard cock rub up and down my thigh. The feel of it—of him hard like this for me where he can't stop himself from fucking my thigh—has my core clenching around his fingers. He moans when he feels it and picks up his pace, his thumb starting to work my aching clit, rubbing it, pressing in on it. All I can do is hold on. All I can do is whimper and moan and *feel*.

"Your pussy feels so good," he praises against my lips. "Give it to me. Gush all over my hand." He's pumping into me harder, grinding deeper, working me faster. "You hear that? You hear how wet you are for me? You're going to come so hard and I'm going to watch your pretty face as you do. And then tonight, I'm going to jerk my cock until I come all over my hand—the same hand that's fucking your sweet pussy—while I picture you exactly like this. You're so fucking sexy. You make me so hard, Wynter."

His filthy words wrench a loud moan from me, my hips arching up, needing more of him. Sharp teeth graze my lower lip, and then he breaks the kiss, both of us panting for air. I don't open my eyes, but I know he's watching me. Staring at me as I unravel against his touch.

He meant what he just said. I know those words weren't simple dirty talk to get me off. Tonight, he will jerk himself off. To me. Because this is exactly what he wanted that night.

It's what I wanted, too.

I wanted his promise. I wanted him to make me come hard.

I want him to do that now.

I tell him that and he loses it. Roughly, he bites into my neck as his fingers bang in and out of me, his thumb working me harder, faster, rubbing my clit over and over until glitters of light dance behind my eyes. Calloused fingers grip my breast, squeezing it nearly to the point of pain, and I detonate. I come on a cry and a shattered moan as I ride his hand, rolling and pressing deeper against him as wave after wave of pleasure pounds through me.

His hand slows, and his grip on my breast slackens as bit by bit I start to come down. My body sags, and my eyes lazily open to find him right here in front of me. He pulls his fingers from me, and I wince slightly at that loss. Untamed, heavy-lidded eyes hold mine as he paints his bottom lip with my cum. His tongue juts out, tasting it before sucking his fingers into his mouth and licking them clean.

Jesus, if that isn't hot. I whimper, biting my lip.

"I can't believe we just did that." The words come out broken, a little panicked, slightly frazzled.

He doesn't get a chance to respond as Mason makes a noise in the other room, and I quickly adjust myself and fly out of the dining room, away from Asher, and back into the kitchen. Mason is awake in his stroller, looking around, but thankfully not upset enough to cry.

"Hey," I say in my mommy soothing voice, pinching my eyes shut

as I kiss his forehead. I just let Asher do that to me with my sleeping
son in the next room. I half stand and force a smile. "You ready to go
home? Back to Grandma and Grandpa's?"

I'm shaking. I know I am.

Asher is beside me, his hand sliding along my back until he's
crouching down in front of Mason. "I'll see you soon, big guy. Okay?"
He leans in and kisses his forehead, the tip of his nose, each cheek,
and I close my eyes, willing my heart to slow. He stands back up and
takes my hand, jerking it until I look at him. "Please think about my
offer with serious consideration."

Everything he just did to me in the dining room is gone from his
face. It's as if it never happened, and I blow out a relieved breath. It
really was only that.

"I will."

I push Mason's stroller and head for the door, needing to get out
of here. I just let Asher Reyes make me come, and now he wants me
and our son to move in with him. I'm in a lot of trouble.

## 10

### ASHER

The moment she and Mason left, I threw on running clothes and ran my ass over to Callan's. I hung out with him, Katy, and Layla for a few hours, and then I ran back home, but only after I circled the park three times. With each pass, I did my best to get the image of Wynter coming on my fingers out of my head.

By the time I dragged my exhausted ass through my door, I was sweaty and horny and had to jerk off twice in the shower because I could run to the moon and back and I'd never be able to get that visual out of my head.

Her face. Those sounds. The way she tastes.

I should have never promised her it would end there in that dining room, but anything else would result in her turning down my offer for them to live with me, and that's not an option. One afternoon, a few silly tosses in the air, and that little boy owns my heart. I want to be his dad. I want that to be how my son knows me.

And I want his mother as mine.

It's complicated. It's downright messy. It's irresistibly risky. But isn't life always?

Monday morning, I walk into the locker room an hour before

anyone else typically gets here. This is my favorite time of day here. It's quiet. No one bothers me. It sets my mental game straight as I run for thirty minutes while watching game footage, and then I do weights, extra mindful of my bad shoulder. Even in the preseason, I do this. Watch the games we lost last season so I can see what I did wrong and how I should fix it.

Only this morning, by the time I finish my pre-practice workout, I'm no longer alone. "Morning, Rookie. This is the first time I've seen you here this early."

I saunter past him, chugging down the last of my sports drink and tossing the empty bottle into the recycle bin. Pulling off my sweat-soaked shirt, I wipe my body down with my towel before going for a clean shirt and my red jersey, setting them down on the bench. I want to get a few reps in before my pre-op thing with Wynter.

"I figured since I'm going to be QB1 by the end of the week, I should try getting in earlier. Coach said I should follow your schedule. He said I had a lot to learn from you, only I don't see it."

I roll my eyes at that and swallow down my scoff of derision. "Looks like all you're doing with that extra time is standing around watching me."

Leo folds his arms over his chest as he leans against a locker two down from mine. He's dressed like an asshole. I'm not sure I have any other way to describe it. It's about ninety degrees and humid as fuck outside right now, and he's wearing a white fedora with a long feather in it, a bright blue checkered suit jacket that matches the feather, a white shirt, and neon orange pants. Oh, and enough gold and diamonds to sink a battleship.

My guess is he's here all pissed off because I embarrassed him in front of Wynter and the team on Friday when I hit him straight in the gut with the ball. The other players were teasing him about it all afternoon, from what I heard. I can also tell he *really* doesn't enjoy the fact that Coach told him to follow my routine and learn from me when he already thinks he's God's gift to the sport. He thinks he knows it all and is about to set me straight. Only, he's too chicken shit to attempt it with an audience, which is why he's doing it now, here, with only the two of us.

Except I don't care about his bullshit or his ego.

"How about you change, and we go get some reps in?" I offer, putting on my practice pads, while ignoring his juvenile attempt at a stand-off.

"I don't need the extra practice," he affirms, his tone pure arrogance. "I step on that field, and I'm lights out. Every time."

"Wow. So you've got it all figured out then," I deadpan. "Know that playbook inside and out. Know how to read every defense that you'll face. Congrats, man. I mean, I haven't seen you put in that sort of time or effort to master all that, but maybe I'm missing something."

"Your reign is over here, old man."

"Old man?" I throw him an amused side-eye. "I'm twenty-nine, Rookie. Minus the shoulder, that puts me straight in my prime."

His features harden, even as he tries to maintain his "I'm too cool for school" attitude. "Not here it won't. Fans have a very short memory, and they lose their loyalty fast. Once I start winning, they'll forget you."

That might be true in some markets, but not in Boston. Boston sports fans have memories like elephants and are amongst the most loyal out there. Just ask the Red Sox when they hadn't won a World Series in eighty-six years. I digress.

"If you're as lights out as you say you are, then I look forward to the challenge of taking you on when I return next season."

"No challenge." His words are ice-cold and full of venom. "That's what I came here to tell you." He steps toward me and pokes my bad shoulder. *Punk.* "By next season, you'll be gone. They'll trade your ass. I'm about to own your town and your team, and there's nothing you can do about it."

That hits me in every sore, soft, miserable, vulnerable part of me. He has no idea what this city means to me. Just how deep my heart goes and how red my blood runs for it.

"That useless chip on your shoulder is about as big as the plastic-looking pendant you're wearing and likely as heavy." I slam my locker shut and turn to face him, staring down at him because I'm six-seven and he's not even six-five. I give him a big once-over. "Let me guess, you blew your entire sign-on bonus on all that shit you're wearing now. You're young. What? Twenty-two, twenty-three. Did decently well in college both on and off the field, and now you think because you were drafted in the top twenty of the first round—which you shouldn't have been by all scouting reports—that you're going to be a god on that field. Your hubris will be your demise and it won't help this team."

Fire lights his cheeks and brightens his dark eyes. "Right. Like you're the person to take advice from. An ex-boy-bander has-been. You won one Super Bowl on the back of your team and former QB1. You caught a lucky break. Hell, I bet if your slutty manager didn't eat shower tile, you'd still be singing for your rent money."

In a flash, I grab him by the lapels of his stupid jacket and slam him as hard as I can into the lockers with a loud, resonating *bang*. My shoulder twinges, but I hardly feel it as I get right up in his face. My action momentarily startles him—he never thought I'd lose my cool because I never ever do. Unless you fuck with my people.

"Do you have a sister?" I bark in his face, knowing he has at least one.

He swallows hard right before he does his best to reform his smug mask that looks shaky at best.

"Do. You. Have. A. Sister?" I bite out. "A girl in your life as important to you as the blood in your veins?"

He clears his throat and shifts, trying for control when he has none since I have him good and pinned.

"Yes," he finally grits out through clenched teeth. "I have three younger sisters."

I press him harder into the locker, digging my elbows into his ribs until he grunts in discomfort. "Then you should know better than to open your idiotic mouth about Suzie. That girl was twenty-two. She was your age when she had a stroke and died in the shower. Imagine that for a moment. Imagine that's your sister—someone you love like family—that you're seeing cold and blue and dead on the bathroom floor while your brothers pump her chest and try to save her life."

He blinks at me, his expression stricken as my words resonate.

"I don't know what brought you in here this morning looking for a fight, but your pride needs to be checked at the door." I lift him up until he's forced onto his tiptoes. He might be seven years younger, but I've easily got twenty pounds of muscle on him. "I could list two-dozen quarterbacks who were drafted higher than you and burned out or couldn't cut it in the pros and were gone within their first few years. Greatness isn't born. It's taught. It's earned through hard work and dedication. You know the smartest thing you could do here, Rookie? Learn. Learn the game. Learn how to be a leader. And most of all, learn when to keep your mouth shut."

I shove him, making sure he rattles the locker, and then I turn my back on him, going for my stuff that's sitting on the bench. If he's stupid enough to retaliate, he'll be gone from this team. I pick up my stuff and walk toward the exit.

"I expect you dressed and on that field in the next ten minutes, ready to practice. You want my spot after this season? You're gonna have to take it from me."

With that, I head for the field, not looking over my shoulder once to see if the kid is coming. Instead, I get to work, running my drills and making sure my routes are solid. Eight minutes later, the rookie comes out, dressed and quiet. For once. I call the plays and make him tell me what they are, and then throw the route to Carlos, the assistant quarterback coach.

We don't talk about what happened in the locker room.

We just continue to play ball until the field starts to fill up and Coach Cardone blows his whistle. Sunday is our first preseason game, and I won't be in it. It's not uncommon for starters not to play or to play very limited amounts during those games, but still, since the moment I was drafted to this team, I have never missed a game whether I was starting or not.

My insides roll over on themselves, and though I have forced myself not to think about all the kid said this morning, I know there is merit in his words. If he does a good job, when I return from this surgery—if I'm able to make a full recovery—there is a very solid chance I might not be the starter next year. And if that happens, I will likely either be traded or ask for a trade because I won't ride the bench for the rest of my career.

And with that comes a whole new set of discord.

One, I am a Boston man, born and raised. This is my town. This is my team.

Second, I now have a son and a woman I want to make part of my life, and now their lives are here.

*All that means is you'll have to fight harder to come out on top.*

Right. Except I'm sure we all know it's never that easy. Just ask Rocky after he lost to Apollo Creed. The good guy doesn't always get what he deserves.

"Damn. Will you check out the tits and legs on that one," Ace, a wide receiver sitting two guys down from me says, and all at once our heads collectively turn. Instantly, I grit my teeth when I lock on Wynter, standing across the field talking with Dr. Horowitz, the team neurologist.

"Shut your fucking mouth before I shut it for you," I snap, losing my patience for the second time today. "That's my... doctor." Because I can't call her anything else. Not in public at least. I stand, ready to drive my point home, only Coach Cardone beats me to it. He grabs Ace by the back of the jersey and hauls him up until he's standing.

"You are to run every damn step in this stadium twice, and if I ever hear you disrespect Dr. Hathaway again, you will be fined and benched for two games. Am I understood?"

"Yes, Coach." Ace looks as shocked as Leo did this morning when I slammed him into the locker. "I meant no disrespect."

"Better not have. Now go!"

Ace throws all of us a quick parting glance and then takes off. I sit back down, and Ryder, my center, leans over and whispers in my ear, "What in the hell do you think is going on there?"

I shake my head. "No clue." But it's definitely something.

"If you hadn't spoken up, I was gonna lob him upside the head for being a misogynistic ass, but Coach reacting that way?"

"I know." Because it wasn't about him being a misogynistic ass and how that's unacceptable to *any* woman. It was about Wynter specifically.

"Do you think Coach and that new doctor are a thing?"

"What?" My head jerks his way, my expression hiding none of my revulsion. "No way. He's old enough to be her father." I'm about to say she hates him and does nothing to hide it when I get stuck on that last statement.

"Wouldn't be the first time, man. That's all I'm saying." Ryder throws a hand up and then turns back to Coach, who is still talking. Only I can't focus on anything he's saying. When I looked her up, I glossed over her family history, but I do remember reading that she had a mom, and her stepfather was Gary Hathaway.

No mention of a biological father.

I'll admit I know nothing of Coach's personal life. It's none of my business, and as a player, it's inconsequential to me doing my job.

But... the way he defended her just now and their dynamic every time I've seen them together, I knew there was something between them. I just didn't assume...

I look back over at him, studying his face for the first time. His hair is lighter than hers, and I don't catch any physical resemblance to Wynter except... his eyes. Coach has green eyes. Just like Wynter's. Just like Mason's.

Holy shit.

If it's true, that would make Coach the biological grandfather of my child. Does he even know about him?

Somehow, I'm on my feet, and Coach's head swivels in my direction, raising a "what the hell do you think you're doing" eyebrow at me.

"Dr. Hathaway is here for my pre-op evaluation," I mumble. His lips form into a thin line, clearly unhappy I interrupted whatever it is he's yelling at everyone about, but he gives me a firm nod, and I walk away, moving across the field with quick strides.

Wynter is oblivious to everything as she laughs and chats with Dr. Horowitz, who is staring at her like she's cream and he's a cat. My teeth set on edge when he touches her shoulder, and if he doesn't remove it from her body now, he's about to lose a digit.

Funny, I never considered myself a jealous man, but I nearly had a heart attack yesterday when she was talking about bringing a hockey player home, and then Ace made that comment, and now this doctor is about to die because he's pulling out his phone to get my woman's digits.

This unbearable green-eyed monster seems to have taken up permanent residence within me where she's concerned. She's messing with my head and my life in every possible way, and instead of running for the hills, I only want more.

"Sorry, Dr. Flirts Too Much, you'll have to get her digits when she's available, which will likely be sometime around the next coming of Christ."

I grab Wynter by the arm and spin her around, marching us toward the locker room without slowing my steps.

"Hey!" she barks, trying to extricate herself from me. "What the hell do you think you're doing? That was totally inappropriate. He works at the hospital with me."

I grunt. "Yet another reason why he can't have your digits." I throw her a side-eye. "I warned you. I'm the ultimate cockblocker."

"More like the ultimate caveman, only I'm not yours to club over the head and drag away to your cave."

*Wrong.* The word blares through my head but thankfully stays put and doesn't get me into even more trouble. "You're here for me, Dr. Hathaway. No one else."

"That's not how this works."

"That's where you're wrong, sweetheart. You're my surgeon. My hot baby mama. If you think I'm going to let anyone else near you, you're crazy."

The lights in the trainers' room flip on when we enter, and then

I'm pulling off my shirt and hopping up on the table. Ready. Anxious for her to put her hands back on me. Only she's standing by the door with her arms folded, eviscerating me with her eyes. Even as they smolder ever so slightly at me shirtless.

It's a good look on her, I'll admit. It certainly makes my dick hard, but then again, so does everything she does.

"This can't happen."

There she goes with that bullshit again. "Uh-huh. I know. You've already told me." I just haven't told you yet that I don't care.

I've wanted her from the second I saw her in that bathroom, and I've wanted her ever since. I wanted her before I knew about Mason. When you meet the woman you consider to be the most beautiful you've ever seen and she just so happens to not take any of your shit, marrying her is your only option. But considering I've technically only known her less than a week, I'll play by her rules while removing any man who tries to take what I already consider to be mine.

"Are we doing this or what?"

She cocks an eyebrow and then pushes away from the door. Grabbing the vitals cart, she wheels it over and slaps a blood pressure cuff on my arm, pressing the button on the screen for it to start inflating.

"Have you thought any more about my offer?" I ask, since she's not talking to me now.

"Yes."

I smirk. "And?" I press when she doesn't follow that up.

"And I haven't decided yet."

Fine. I'll let it ride for now. The monitor lights up with my blood pressure and heart rate, and then she sticks a probe on my finger while setting the earpiece of her stethoscope in her ears. The cold diaphragm hits my chest, and I make a noise.

"Shhh," she admonishes, standing against the table next to me, her body so close I can smell her shampoo. Her skin. "I'm trying to listen to your heart."

"Is it beating out your name?"

She rolls her eyes, but I catch her lips twitching. She slides the thing all around my chest and then moves it to my back. "Deep breaths."

I start sucking in deep breaths as she listens to my lungs, and when she's done with my back, she's in front of me again, putting the stethoscope right below my collarbone. After she's done with that, I snatch the diaphragm up and bring it to my lips.

"Move in with me," I whisper into it, so I don't blow out her ears. She pauses, staring into my eyes, and I see Coach in hers even more now when we're this close. "How's my son this morning?"

She smiles, despite herself. "Good. He ate two scrambled eggs and some strawberries and then watched a signing video with me before I had to leave."

I frown. "Signing? Is he hearing impaired?"

She removes the stethoscope from her ears and drapes it around her neck. "Yes. It's a minor deficit, something they're watching closely, but they told me it could get worse, or that he could require hearing aids when he's older, or that his speech might be delayed or altered. Considering he said 'mama' on Friday, I'm not so sure about all that. Anyway, signing helps him communicate things he can't yet say, like milk or cereal or more or all done. It helps to alleviate some frustrations and tantrums children might have from not being able to express what they want, and since he does have this impairment, I figured it was good for him all around."

I have so many things to learn about him. So many things I don't yet know. "I've already missed so much, and he's only ten months old. What's the sign for Daddy?"

With her eyes on me, she spreads the fingers on her hand wide and then brings her thumb to her forehead and bounces it twice.

I mimic the motion. "Can I do that with him? Please?" I tack on.

She audibly gulps, biting into her lip, but nods.

I capture some of her hair and tuck it behind her ears. "You have very green eyes, Wynter Hathaway. They're beautiful on you, but also familiar. Like I've seen very similar ones before."

She freezes, her eyes rounding and her lips parting as she sucks in a breath. Her gaze flickers between my eyes, trying to read what she suspects I'm intimating.

"Did he tell you?" she finally asks when she's weeded out the answer.

"No. He defended you rather aggressively when a player made an inappropriate comment about how hot you are. My center asked what that was all about, and in doing so, asked if you were with him. My first reaction was to kill my coach, but then I made what I thought was an off-hand comment about how he's old enough to be your father. And it hit me."

She looks away, her arms crossing over her body. "Gary Hathaway is my father."

"But not biologically. Right?"

"I don't want to talk about Joe."

I cup her jaw and turn it back until she's looking at me. "Does he know about Mason?"

She licks her lips and shakes her head in my hand. "No. At least I don't think so."

"I'm getting the impression that's how you'd like to keep it?" I check.

"Yes."

"And you don't want to tell me why?"

"No. Not right now."

"Did he hurt you, Wynter?" My tone comes out harder, more demanding than I intend, but the idea of him being abusive, whether physically, verbally, or emotionally, makes me want to do everything I can to protect both her and my son from him—by any means necessary.

"Not in the way you think," she says quickly, clearly reading me. "All you need to know is that I don't consider him my father, and I don't want anything to do with him."

"You hate football players." It's all coming together now.

"I hate football players," she parrots.

I absorb that for a moment, knowing she doesn't fully trust me yet with herself, but also knowing we'll get there, and then nod. "Okay. When do I have surgery?"

"Tomorrow."

"Tomorrow?!" I yell.

She's smiling at me now. "You said you wanted it done as soon as possible. Tomorrow by six in the morning, you'll be on my table."

Oh, hell.

# 11

---

## WYNTER

"Good morning, Mr. Reyes," I greet him, taking a sip of my much-needed coffee and ignoring how he's staring at me in my scrubs. "How are you feeling today?"

He gives me a slow drag, a smile lighting up his face when he reaches my scrub cap. "Better now."

I make an unimpressed noise. "Mr. Reyes, this is Dr. Jones. He's going to be assisting me."

"Nice to meet you, Mr. Reyes." Asher sits up and shakes Jequai's hand, and I think Jequai is about to pass out in a puddle of fan-boy mush right here on the floor. "Do you mind if I draw on your shoulder?"

Asher blinks at him. "Like an autograph?"

I hold in my laugh. "Something like that. Only it makes sure we know which shoulder we're cutting into."

Asher wipes at his jaw. "Is that a problem around here?"

"Not for me, but it's what we do to prevent any errors."

Asher waves his hand at Jequai. "Go for it, man."

"Did the nurses go over what you can expect before, during, and after your surgery?"

"Yes."

"And has anesthesiology met with you?"

"Not yet."

His short answers and stiff posture tell me he's unbelievably nervous. I turn to Jequai. "Dr. Jones, would you go and make sure everything is prepped and ready in the OR?"

"Of course."

He leaves us, and I close the curtain, coming over and sitting on the edge of Asher's bed while making sure to leave plenty of space between us. "You doing okay?"

"Uh." He laughs, running his hand back through his short hair. "Not really. I mean, yes, I'm fine. I'm not about to freak out or anything. But I'm nervous about what you'll find when you open me up."

I scoot a little closer. "Lean your head back." He does instantly. "Now close your eyes," I tell him. I take a quick moment to observe him without his eyes on me, making my insides dance the way he always does, and wow, Asher Reyes really is a beautiful man. "Now take a deep breath in through your nose and then release it slowly through your mouth."

He does, his body already starting to relax.

"Good. Stay like that for a moment while I talk. I have performed this surgery well over a hundred times, and I have never had a negative outcome. I am not promising you anything other than I will give your shoulder every ounce of my focus and skill. Okay?"

"Okay," he breathes out.

I open my mouth to say more and then hesitate. I've been thinking a lot about his offer. Weighing the pros and cons of it. I don't particularly want to live with him, but that's my own hang-up. All I know is it won't be forever. Neither of us wants this to come out during his season, so in order to protect my son and that secret, concessions and sacrifices must be made.

But once that's over and it's all out in the open, there is no reason I have to stay with him. Yet another reason not to allow him to buy me the apartment. I can get my own place with Mason, live close by to Asher, and then figure out a co-parenting situation that works for both of us if that's what he wants.

For now... I lean in and whisper by his ear, "Mason and I will move in with you."

His eyes flash open, and the biggest, brightest smile I've ever seen on him overtakes his every feature. "You will? You mean that?"

My heart thumps in my chest, and I bite into my lip, trying to squash the feeling. "Yes. We'll move in with you for a while. Once your season is over and we don't have to keep it as quiet as we do now, we'll readdress it."

He gives me that cocky, sure-fire smirk he's famous for. "You'll be in love with me by then, Doctor. No chance you'll readdress anything."

"That's really not the type of woman I am." I'm not sure if it's a lie either. Before Mason, there was a reason I never dated much, and anyone I ever did date didn't last very long.

He chuckles lightly. Contentedly. "Thank you. When will you move in?" His smile slips into a deep frown. "I won't be able to help much now, will I?"

Before I can answer, the curtain is yanked open and I immediately draw back. Dr. Callan Barrows comes flying in before stopping dead in his tracks when he takes us both in.

"Hi," he says, his voice filled with a mixture of surprise and amusement. His eyes are on Asher for a moment, as if something is passing between them, and then he turns his full focus on me. "Dr. Callan Barrows." He extends his hand. "We haven't officially met yet, though I haven't stopped hearing about you."

Heat rushes to my cheeks, and I laugh it off as I stand, shaking his hand. "Dr. Wynter Hathaway. I recognized you."

His eyebrows bounce. "Oh, is that so? Don't tell Asher that. You'll break his heart since you didn't recognize him."

"The hell?!" Asher growls. "For real? You recognized *him* and not *me*?"

I twist back to Asher with a grin. "What? I like drummers."

Callan barks out a laugh, taking the chair beside Asher's bed.

Asher leans back, covering his face with his hands. "You're killing me with that, Doctor."

I shrug unrepentantly. He doesn't need to know that I looked him up after I found out who he was.

"Will you be taking Mr. Reyes home after his surgery?" I ask Callan.

"That's what I'm here for."

"Did you want to observe it?"

Both Callan and Asher sit up straight, exchanging looks. "Can I?" Callan finally asks.

"If you'd like. But only from the gallery."

"You cool with that, man?"

Asher scoffs. "Of course I'm cool with it. At least if you're watching, then I know she won't stab me with a scalpel or cut off my balls or something."

"I can promise you, Mr. Reyes, I won't ever be touching your balls."

He tilts his head and grins in a way that makes his chin dimple pop. "Don't make promises like that, Doctor. It'll only make you a liar later."

I shake my head. A player is going to play. I just refuse to be his game. "I'll see you in there."

I leave the two of them and head to the OR. My heart starts to pound out a heavy, steady rhythm as I begin the process of scrubbing in, and then once that's done, I enter the room. There are only two places in this world I feel in control. Here and on the ice. They're the places I am most at ease, most confident.

I see all those moms whose hair and makeup are always flawless, and they never have a splatter of anything unwanted on their pristine, trendy clothes. They're living their best lives while juggling their babies on their hips, as they dominate the world on their phone while sipping their organic caffeine-infused herbal whatever, and have everything planned out and organized down to the second.

I am not that mother. I am the textbook definition of an over-achieving hot mess who can't stand the wild chaos of her hot mess life.

Except in here.

"Good morning, everyone," I greet. "How are we today? All set?"

"We are," Chandra, the scrub nurse tells me. "Just waiting on our celebrity patient."

"Good stuff." I thank her as she gowns and gloves me up. I head over to the table, going through everything with the staff and Jequai and making sure we have everything we need. A minute later, Asher is rolled in, wearing a mesh cap over his head and a petrified expression.

"Mr. Reyes, are you ready to get started?"

"Sure. Looking forward to it. I'm already a bit high from whatever this guy put in my IV." He bobs his head toward the anesthesiologist as he scoots over onto the surgical table, and the anesthesiologist adjusts him until he's where he should be.

"That was Ativan," the anesthesiologist supplies.

"Right. It's good stuff. I've never done drugs before. Not even when I was touring the world with the band. I'm starting to see the appeal."

"Lie down, rock star." Asher lies back on the table, staring up at me with the world glowing in his eyes. "Don't worry. I've got you."

"I prefer it when you call me player."

"I'm sure you do," I quip. "I think I like you on drugs better than when you're sober."

"If I forget to tell you later," he murmurs just before the propofol is pushed into his IV. "You're unbelievably sexy right now—even with your mask and hair thing on—as you tell everyone what to do and run the whole show. I might have a very serious thing for you, Doctor."

Everyone laughs, including me, and then the bright white liquid is pushed through his line, and a few seconds later, he's out.

"Well, he's a charmer," Chandra exclaims.

"You have no idea," I tell her. We run through our Time Out, making sure we have the right patient, the right surgery, and the right part of his body that we're operating on, but before I make the first incision, I call out, "Alexa, play Central Square."

"You are not!" Jequai gasps.

I wink at him. "Oh, I am."

My gaze shoots up to the gallery where Callan is watching, and I see him shake his head at me with a wry grin on his lips. I return the gesture with an unrepentant shrug and then ask for an eleven-blade as the pop-rock beat led by Greyson Monroe's croony voice fills the room.

"Let's fix the player up so I can be done with football." I open Asher's shoulder up and start inspecting my field. "Can you abduct and externally rotate the arm for me, please?" The circulating nurse springs into action, and once that's done and I get a clearer look... I squint. And recheck what I'm seeing. Then, no joke, I make sure I'm in the correct shoulder, because I should not be looking at what I'm looking at.

"Oh, aren't you a lucky man," I muse, pleasantly delighted.

"What?"

"Dr. Jones, take a look and tell me exactly what you see."

Jequai stares at the field. "Um. I'm not sure."

"Oh, it's there. Our MRI painted a completely different picture than what we're seeing here."

"Wait!" He stops me. "No labral tear! No AC joint separation either."

"Nope." I grin beneath my mask. "And do you see this?" I swipe my tool along the coarse, fibrotic tissue. "Way fewer adhesions than we thought, and they're in a good place to be removed without disrupting surrounding tissue." I blow out a breath. "Hey, Dr. Barrows?" I call out and then hear Callan's crackly voice come through since he's pressing the intercom button.

"Yes?"

"Would you like a look at this?"

"I would likely have no clue what I'm looking at. I did one ortho rotation in med school and then settled on emergency medicine right after."

I laugh. "Well, your friend is about to love me. I just cut his recovery time in half, at least. There's a very real chance he could return this season. There are no repairs to make. No tears. Just some minor cleaning up to do."

"I'm pretty sure he loved you before this, but if that's the case, you're in some trouble now."

*Don't I know it.*

"All right, Dr. Jones." I snort, and then quickly swivel toward Jequai. "Wow, that makes you totally sound like Indiana Jones. How did I never put that together until now?"

"You have no idea how many times I got that through medical school." He laughs. "I would tell them I'm a Black Indiana Jones. Patients loved it."

"I have no doubt they did. Help me clean up these adhesions. It seems Boston might have their favorite quarterback playing sooner than they're expecting."

"Is he awake yet?" I ask Alea, the PACU nurse. The PACU is empty, but it's still very early in the morning, as Limbick agreed to bump all surgeries back a couple of hours, so it would just be Asher in here.

"Not when I last checked. I was about to go back in and get another set of vitals."

"I'll go with you," I tell her.

"Going to give him the good news?" she asks me with a conspiratorial smile. "My husband will be thrilled. He's a huge Rebels fan, but also a huge Asher Reyes fan."

"That seems to be how this town runs," I note as we pull back the curtain and enter his room. He's still out, on his back, his gown covering him from the middle of the chest down, a white hospital blanket covering his lower half. "Did Dr. Barrows leave?"

"He went to make some calls," she informs me. "He said he'd be back soon to take him home."

Alea starts to check his vitals, and when the blood pressure cuff begins to inflate, that seems to stir him awake. His gray eyes—almost colorless against the harsh fluorescent lights—slowly blink open. He shifts and then winces slightly as he blinks some more, becoming more alert, and stares down at his shoulder with an obvious frown.

"Vitals look good," Alea says in a low voice. "Welcome back, Mr. Reyes. I'm Alea, your nurse. I'm going to get you some ice water. Are you nauseous?"

"No," he rasps in a groggy voice.

"What's your pain level?"

"I don't want drugs."

I roll my eyes. "Of course you don't." At the sound of my voice, he turns his head, and our eyes meet, his filled with a million questions. "You need to be honest about your pain level. On a scale of one to ten, what is it?"

"A four."

"How about some IV acetaminophen? We'll hold off on anything stronger for now."

"I'll go grab it," Alea says. "I saw the order in his chart."

She walks off, leaving us here, and I move in closer. His good hand comes up, his fingers trickling along my arm until they catch my fingers. "Tell me."

"Do you want the good news or the bad news first?"

His frown deepens, and I might be a bit evil for playing this game with him. "Bad news."

"The bad news is that the MRI was wrong. It didn't paint anywhere close to an accurate picture of what we found when we went in."

His eyes close, and he blows out a breath. I can't stop myself from running my hand through his hair, and then my mouth dips by his ear. "There was no labrum tear. No AC separation. Just some minor adhesions that we cleaned up and removed. There was nothing structurally impacted. No screws. No joint repair. No reconstruction. It was simple and clean, and because of that, with the right rehab, you could be back on the field in a couple of months."

His eyes flash open, and then he squeezes my fingers. "You're serious?"

"Yes. It was the best-case scenario. I have no idea what happened with the MRI, but your shoulder was fairly healthy. Just those minor adhesions, as I mentioned."

"Fuck," he pants like he's taking in the first breath of dawn after a moonless night. "Wynter, I could kiss you."

"If you do, I'll take you back under the knife."

He plows right past that. "I don't know what to say. You're magic. Thank you."

"Say you won't rush your rehab. Say you'll follow the regimen, including the use of pain medication if needed."

He shakes his head. "No pain meds. I know what can happen with those, and they're a slippery slope."

"Not in the first forty-eight hours after surgery."

He considers this. "I'll only take them if you come over tonight with Mason. I want both of you to sleep at my place."

I slip my fingers out of his grasp, and his hand falls to the bed. "Asher, this isn't grade school. I'm not having a sleepover at your place."

"You're moving in with me, and it's my first night after surgery. Come on. Please, Dr. Hathaway," he pleads like a lost puppy dog. "I need you."

"You don't have anything set up there."

"Please. I want to see him, and I want you there with me tonight."

The way this man says please and its resulting effect on me is nothing short of diabolical.

"Fine," I relent, hating how quickly I did that. "We'll come over this evening around five. I'll need to give him dinner and a bath."

"Great." A smile curls up his lips. "Bring as much stuff as you can because I might not let you go after tonight."

"I don't plan on making the choice yours." I step back from his bed as the nurse comes in to give him his medicine. "I'll see you later, Mr. Reyes. Get some rest."

I don't wait for him to say anything else. I leave, and I leave quickly. He talked about a slippery slope. I have a bad feeling I'm about to learn exactly what that means.

# 12

A<sup>sher</sup>

"Do you think it's too much?" I ask Lenox as we both take in one of the guest rooms.

He grunts and I turn to him. He's only in town for a few hours—my guess is he's visiting Suzie's grave—but since he loves me, he came over to check on me. And bring me barbeque, because again, he loves me.

"Really? I think it's nice. I think she'll like it."

A shrug this time. "Callan said she's a spitfire."

When I woke from my nap, I found Callan and Lenox talking about Wynter. Cal told me she played Central Square during my entire surgery and that she was fucking brilliant to watch. If he weren't in love with Layla, I'd be worried.

"You think it's too subdued for her?"

Another shrug.

"You're no help," I admonish, suddenly nervous he could be right. "What do you know about women?"

This time I get a challenging raised eyebrow, and yeah, he has a point.

"Fine. I guess I don't know much either. I've never lived with anyone except you assholes on that tour bus. The last girlfriend I had was…" I pause. Think. Glance back over at him as if he'll send me a lifeline and jog my memory.

"Meredith."

"No." My good hand meets my hip, and then my face scrunches up. "For real?"

He nods.

"That was like…"

"Three years ago. And you only dated her for a few months."

"Damn." My eyebrows hit my hairline in surprise, and I turn back to the room. "Well, shit. Do you think I should have let her decorate it herself? I was worried she never would because she's planning to jump ship after the season is over, and I hated the idea of her sleeping in an all-white room, which is what it was before." I make a displeased noise in the back of my throat. "Then again, I hate the idea of her sleeping in here and not in my bed, but I guess sacrifices must be made for the greater good."

"She'll like it."

"Right?" I exclaim. "I totally agree. What's not to like? It's feminine without being over-the-top. At least that's what Freddy said when he went nuts with my credit card." My assistant loves to give it a workout, but I have zero complaints about everything he did. My place has been transformed in a matter of hours.

Callan brought me home after the surgery, and I napped for a solid two hours while my house was filled with people and Freddy was running the show. I woke up starving like a beast, and then Lenox showed up. Bastard made me take one of those pain pills Wynter prescribed, which I might be feeling a little—or maybe even a lot. I think I'm a lightweight when it comes to any sort of medication. Just look at what happened to me in the bathroom at the club the night I met Wynter.

But at least I'm not feeling any pain, so that's something.

"I should go."

I frown. "No. Stay. You can meet my kid. He'll be here any minute."

"Kids are afraid of me."

I roll my eyes in a very Wynter way. "They are not. They just feel your strong, silent vibe."

He raises an amused eyebrow at me.

"I think next time I should go with half a pill."

He chuckles softly, his blue eyes full of mirth at my expense. "Lightweight."

"I won't even argue that because it's the truth." The buzzer for my door sounds, and a smile immediately springs to my lips, along with a jolt of nerves in my chest. "Fuck. They're here. How do I look? Hot, sexy, dependable?"

"Like a man who had surgery this morning."

"Thanks, big guy." I smack his shoulder and then wince because the motion jarred me a bit. "Always setting me straight when I need it the least. Come on. Say hi to my non-woman and kid, and then you can go do... whatever it is you're doing tonight."

"Hacking a large—"

"La, la, la, la," I start singing over him. "Plausible deniability. If you don't tell me, then I don't know what you actually do for a living other than inking people's skin." Even though I do. Tattoo artist by day. Genius hacker by night. You'd wonder when he sleeps, but after touring with him for four years, I know he doesn't. At least not often and not much.

I open the door, and there is a happy Mason chewing on something that looks like a giraffe, and Wynter looking perfectly adorable in her yoga pants, oversized shirt, and hair up in a ponytail.

"Well, hey there. Welcome home."

She rolls her eyes but pushes past me, wheeling him in. She has a huge bag on one shoulder and a long, heavy-looking rectangular thing encased in green cloth on the other. "Don't make me already reconsider this." Her words stop there as she sees Lenox standing over to the side. "Hi. Lenox Moore, right?"

"For real?!" I growl, looking between the two of them. "You recognized Callan first and now Lenox, but had no clue who I was?"

"Nice to meet you," Lenox says. "I like you already."

Wynter grins, throwing me a smug smile that only makes me want to kiss her, so she's not winning this the way she thinks she is.

Lenox kneels down and looks at Mason. "Hi."

Mason squeezes the giraffe thing, and it makes a horrendous squeaking noise like a dog's chew toy.

"Sorry," she says contritely. "It's his favorite toy, and anytime I try to make it disappear, he cries until I magically make it reappear. I'm assuming he'll outgrow it at some point and won't go to college with it, but that sound haunts my dreams."

"I can understand why. See you, little man." Lenox ruffles his hair, and Mason reaches out, grabbing his finger and tugging it back toward him.

"See. Told you kids love you."

Lenox allows Mason to hold his finger for a minute, and then he stands and gives me a fist pound. "Behave."

"Yes, Thor. I'll behave."

I get the look he always gives me when I call him that—he never liked being called Thor, though the resemblance is uncanny—and then proceeds to ignore me in favor of Wynter. "Bye, Wynter. Best of luck to you with him."

"Thank you. I have a feeling I'll need it."

"Nah. It'll be great," I promise. It's only when Lenox leaves and it's just the three of us that my heart really starts to pound. "Hi."

"Hi. How are you feeling?"

"Great!"

She tilts her head and stares straight into my eyes. "You took the pain meds."

"You told me to."

She places a hand on my face, her fingers cool as they run along my cheek up to my forehead. Even in my somewhat numb state, her touch electrifies me from within. That can't be a coincidence. Reacting to the way someone touches you—even in the most innocuous ways—has to mean something.

The fact that she's here, with my son, has to mean something.

"You need to rest, Asher." Her voice is laced with worry, but is it the worry of a doctor caring for her patient or a woman caring for a man she's catching feelings for? "You had surgery this morning. Let's go sit somewhere, and I'll take him out of this. You can hang out with him while I get his dinner ready." Then she pauses. "Crap. No high-chair." She rubs her forehead in dismay. "I didn't think this through carefully at all. Maybe we should just—"

"I have a highchair."

She pauses and peeks up at me through her lashes like I just told her aliens landed in the Public Gardens. "You do?"

"I do." I beam a smile at her because she's here and he's here, and how cool is that? "I have a lot of things. Can I show you? I want to show you. Put those heavy things down. We can deal with them later."

By some miracle, she listens and sets them on the floor. Even as she narrows her eyes. "How many of those pills did you take?"

"Only one, but this is why I never did drugs."

She grimaces. "Sorry. You're a big guy. I wrote you for a full dose. Take half next time."

"I plan to, but for real, I want to show you and Mason what I did in anticipation of you moving in." And hopefully staying. Wariness creases her features, but she follows me as I walk—albeit like an old man with limited strength—in the direction of the guest wing of my apartment. "Cal was impressed, and he's an emergency room doctor, so I think that counts for a lot. You'll notice all the outlets are covered in those plastic protective things, and there is a gate at the bottom and the top of the stairs, and there is a brand-new deadbolt completely out of a child's reach on the rooftop door."

"Asher—"

"Not yet, okay?" I glance over my shoulder at her. "Just please, not yet."

Her lips mash together, and she continues to follow me as we move down the long hallway, stopping first at the new playroom.

"My assistant had a lot of fun with this room," I tell her as I open the door, and Mason immediately starts kicking and thrashing in his stroller, anxious to get out and play, which I take to mean he loves it.

"Asher!" My name again, only this time with a lot of inflection. "When did you do all of this?"

I lean against the door for support and watch her face. She's covered her mouth with her hands, and her eyes are wide. "I texted Freddy this morning after you told me you'd move in with me."

Her head swivels in my direction. "Freddy?"

"My assistant."

"You have an assistant?"

I smirk at her surprise. "Of course I have an assistant. I have an assistant, a publicist, an agent, a lawyer, and security when needed. I'm a professional football player, sweetheart and before that, I was a rock star. I have interests and a brand to protect."

She grins. "I'm impressed. And this room..." she trails off, because yeah, this room is something. The hardwood floors are covered in brightly colored interlocking foam puzzle pieces with the alphabet and numbers one through twenty on them. There is a small playscape—really just a few steps and a slide—a jumpy thing, a house that he can crawl through that also sings to him, a television for when he watches his signing videos, and more toys than he'll likely ever use.

"There's more."

I lead us back into the hallway and point down the hall at the room at the end. "That's your room, and yes, it's decorated. I didn't know if you had furniture or anything, but Freddy loves Restoration Hardware and bought a lot of pretty stuff for you. You also have your own bathroom."

She's silent, her eyes on the door, and I can tell she's got a lot going on in that pretty head of hers. But I'm not done yet, and I know this will likely trip her up the most. I walk across the hall from the playroom and open the door.

"This is for Mason. I didn't have time for them to paint it, but we can do that later."

She steps into the room and gasps. "Asher!"

Again with my name, which I'll never grow tired of hearing her say, but I'm hoping that sound is a good one. This room has a crib with a cool mobile of exotic animals overhead, a plush rocking chair, a dresser with a changing table on it, and a bookshelf filled with kids' books. There are also pictures on the wall, and though I had asked Freddy to do football, he overrode me and went with a safari theme.

I move in behind her, my chest to her back. She's shaking, and I can't stop myself from wrapping my good arm around her waist and holding her against me. My nose hits the top of her head, right above her ponytail, and I breathe her in. "Whether you're living here or not, I wanted him to have all this. This will be his room. That will be his playroom. You will always have a room to stay here, too. I want this to be his home too, even if you do leave when the season is over."

She nods and I hear her clearing her throat.

"Are you still with me?"

Another nod, and when she reaches up to her face, I know she's not speaking because she's crying.

"I can't do much to help you right now with him, but I want to watch how you do everything, so when I'm all healed up, I can."

"Stop," she croaks. "Please, stop."

I don't know the story yet, but I can tell Joe Cardone did a real number on her. "I overwhelmed you. I know I did. So let's go give him dinner, okay? You don't have to talk to me."

She nods and presses her head into my good side and then wipes her face once more, under each eye, and then she's unsnapping Mason from his stroller and lifting him into her arms. Without hesitation, I lean in and plant a kiss on his cheek, wrapping my good arm back around her waist as I lean into them.

"Hey, big guy. Are you hungry for...?" I raise a questioning brow at Wynter.

"Mashed peas with turkey, and pears with apricots."

"I just threw up in my mouth, but I'm sure he'll love it."

She emits a wet laugh, bouncing him lightly. "It's his favorite dinner. It's why I packed it for tonight. He's always liked baby food."

"Maybe that's because it's all he's ever known." Gently, I rock the three of us from side to side. "What if you mix it up a bit? Try new things? Explore new options?"

She squints at me. "Are we talking about Mason's diet or something else?"

I keep my voice light as I say, "I'm simply suggesting that if you take the risk and try something new—something you've always believed you dislike—you might discover it's actually your favorite thing."

"Doubtful. I still dislike football players, and I don't see that changing anytime soon."

I smile as I press my lips to her cheek and murmur by her ear. "I'll change your mind. You won't even see it coming."

# 13

---

## WYNTER

I feel like this is the time when I'm supposed to level up my offense. Or is it defense? Is that even the correct word in this situation? Whatever. From the moment I walked in this door and saw him with his bum arm and then all the work he had done to his apartment today for Mason and for me, I'm having an impossible time reminding myself why I shouldn't strip naked and climb on top of his dick to see if it finally understands the assignment.

Only... he legit had surgery this morning.

A surgery I performed on him.

And now I'm sleeping in his house. In a room as far away from his as physically possible. With my son in his own nursery somewhere in between that.

It hasn't been a full week, and yet my entire world lives, breathes, and speaks the name Asher Reyes.

Asher watches me feed Mason, sits in the corner while I give him a bath, and then kisses him goodnight when I go to put him down. There are cameras in the corners of both the playroom and his bedroom. Cameras I didn't notice until this very minute.

"Do you have cameras like this in my bedroom?" It's meant to be a tease. A joke. But the idea of him having a camera in my bedroom and watching me in there—other than being sick and horrifically invasive—suddenly makes my skin hot.

He's winding down on his meds, dark purple circles ring his orbs, and with that, he gives me a withering stare as if I were serious. "Of course not. I meant to give you the username and password earlier, but I forgot."

I turn back to Mason and make sure he's comfortable in his new crib, with his new nightlight casting multicolored zoo creatures on the pale gray walls. I kiss him goodnight, but Asher can't even drag himself away from the wall to do it. He's in pain and feeling the after-effects of the anesthesia, and seriously needs some sleep.

I walk over to him and take his good hand. "Come with me."

"I know how to put myself to bed, Doctor."

Oh, he's a grump, isn't he?

"Please?" I ask, throwing his favorite word back at him.

He immediately hunches his shoulders like a bear and allows me to lead him across the apartment—which is ridiculously enormous—over to his side where his bedroom is located. I take him into his room, knowing full well I should retreat now, but also knowing I won't. He had surgery this morning. Is down a limb. And is in visible pain.

We bypass his bedroom and go into his bathroom. "Face me." He does instantly, and I work his shirt over his head and down his shoulder as gently as I can. His shoulder looks okay. Not amazing. But okay. Beneath the Dermabond are dissolvable sutures, and right now, I don't see any issues that require immediate attention.

"Do you need help brushing your teeth?"

He scowls at me. "No, Mommy. I can handle it."

"I already told you, I'm never going to call you Daddy."

Finally a grin, but it doesn't last, nor does it meet his eyes.

"Pain scale?"

"Five." Which is likely an eight for a normal human.

"Medication?"

"Unwanted."

"Not even for me?"

"You don't strike me as the pill-popping type."

I raise an eyebrow.

He curses, his chin pointing toward the ceiling. "Fine," he snarls. "A half."

"Brush up, and I'll be right back."

I pad out into his kitchen, find the prescription bottle, and break one of the tablets in half. I glance down at myself and quickly peel off my bra. I'm going to share a bed with Asher Reyes tonight because something inside me doesn't feel comfortable leaving him alone. I drape the bra over the back of the barstool, and then after I fill a glass with ice water, I bring it back to him.

His eyes scour me, rough like unpolished gems, but when they land on my pert nipples, realizing I'm no longer wearing a bra, his entire disposition alters.

"Take this for me," I ask, holding out the tablet and glass of water for him.

He hesitates, almost glaring at me now. "You know how badly I want you, and you're using that to your advantage."

I continue to stare up into his eyes. Eyes that manage to make my insides squirm, even when he's hurting and angry. "Possibly. But right now, I don't care."

He snatches the half tablet from my hand, pops it in his mouth, and then takes the glass of water and swallows down the pill with a giant sip.

"Done."

"Good." I grin. "You're a grumpy patient."

He sighs. "I don't... I don't feel well."

I cup his face and drag his forehead to my lips. "No fever. But I'm a little worried. Maybe you simply did more today than you should have, or maybe something else is going on. I'm not sure yet, but I'm going to stay with you tonight, and tomorrow if you're still looking like this in the morning, I'm going to write you a prescription for an antibiotic."

"I'll risk an infection if it gets your lips on me again."

"Don't tease, Asher. This isn't a joke."

His gray eyes hold mine. "Who said I was kidding." A silent exhale. His shirtless body practically against mine. His fingers run along my cheek and through my hair, making me shudder ever so slightly. "Are you sleeping with me tonight, Doctor?"

Doesn't he know I'm risking it all right now? How questions like that only make this worse for me?

"Yes, but sleeping is all we're doing."

"Even so, I'll be dreaming about you in bed beside me. And it won't be PG-13."

"Keep it to yourself, player."

I snatch his toothbrush and brush my teeth because mine is on the other side of his condo, and right now, I don't feel good about leaving him.

"Can you pull up Mason on the app? It's his first night in a new place."

He unlocks his phone and taps the camera app. The feed of Mason comes through, and he's out. He's a good sleeper, and I know he won't wake again until around seven. After that, we climb into his bed, in the dark, but I can feel it. His quiet grunt. The tense way his body shifts under the covers.

"You wake me if you need me. Promise?"

"Promise."

Those are the last groggy words he utters before he passes out.

I CHECKED on Asher twice overnight. He felt warm to my lips somewhere around 1:00 a.m., and I got up and called in a prescription to his pharmacy that I plan to pick it up for him once they open. Thankfully, he was sleeping soundly, though his body was tense. I think the player overdid it yesterday and it caught up to him, but I also think he's brewing a minor infection I want to get rid of before it turns into something more.

An infection is not only serious, but it could also hinder his recovery.

My lips gently press against his forehead. He's still asleep and feels relatively cool. In addition to getting his antibiotic today, I'll also get him a damn thermometer. As I slink out of his bed and silently pad from his room, I glance around his condo, peeking into rooms as I pass them. A theater room. A gym that's twice the size of the apartment I had in Miami. An office. A library. I shake my head. This place is a lot.

He's a lot.

A celebrity. A quarterback. And now I not only live here with him, but he's my son's father.

There is so much to figure out with that, but no matter what he says or how he looks at me, I need to create an emotional divide between us. He's already pushing me. Hell, a few simple pleases and that molten gaze on me, and I let him bring me to orgasm in his dining room.

He makes it easy to fall into him. He makes it easy to forget the dangers he poses.

But what happens when he grows bored of the chase? Of playing the game? What happens when he breaks my heart? It's a risk I can't take.

I shoot out a quick text to Limbick, letting him know I'm monitoring our VIP patient today because I'm concerned there might be a minor infection brewing. That's another thing. My job. Right now, it's all about Asher and his football team. The sooner I can get him healthy and back where he belongs, the sooner I'll be done with that assignment—with freaking Joe Cardone—and I can get back to my life. My job. I can move out of here, and we'll fall into a normal routine.

I just have to get there. Hold on and be patient a little longer.

I find my bra still slung over the back of the barstool in the kitchen where I left it last night, and I snatch it quickly, swinging it from my fingers as I head toward my room. A room I haven't even checked out yet. A room I'm a little terrified to see if it's anything like what he did for the playroom and Mason's room.

I need a shower before Mason wakes up. I also need to get that app Asher has on my phone. Just as I pass the entrance, the front door swings open, and I freeze as Callan and Greyson walk into the condo and then shut off the alarm that starts to buzz. They freeze as well, the three of us staring at each other until, in unison, both of their glances snag on the bra dangling from my fingers.

I turn seven thousand shades of red. I haven't even met Greyson Monroe yet and only met Callan yesterday. Plus, I work with Callan at the hospital, so there goes any professionalism I had going.

"It's not what it looks like," I squeak out, balling the lace up in my hand to hide it.

Considering I'm wearing leggings and a rumpled shirt, and my hair is very obviously sleep—or something else—tussled, I doubt I'm selling it.

"Uh." Greyson clears his throat, amusement dancing in his dark eyes. "We wanted to check on the patient."

Callan is fighting his smile. "Yes. Before I have to head into the hospital."

"He's still sleeping." And if I thought I was red a second ago, I'm a freaking fire engine now because I'm holding my bra and just admitted to having knowledge of Asher in his bed.

Greyson wipes at the smile on his lips. "We'll, um, we'll wait then."

"If that's okay with you," Callan tacks on.

"That's fine. I'm worried he has an infection. I just checked on him." I shift. "That's how I know he's still sleeping. Not that anything else happened."

Did I actually just say that? I mentally smack my forehead.

Could this be any more awkward?

"There you are, Doctor. You left me in bed to wake up all alone." Asher's voice rings out through the condo, and I close my eyes, beyond mortified. I can't bear to handle the looks on Callan's and

Greyson's faces. As it is, I hear their muffled snickers as Asher's steps grow louder. "Oh, hey guys. What's up? You come to check on me?"

I creak open my lids as Asher moves in beside me. He's exactly how I left him. Wearing no shirt and low-slung pajama pants. His reddish-brown hair is sticking up every which way. Then there's me with my bra in my hand. Awesome.

Callan clears his throat. "Yeah. Just wanted to see how you're feeling."

"Not bad since my beautiful doctor is taking such excellent care of me." He drops his arm over my shoulder, and that's my cue.

"I'm going to go shower before Mason wakes up. I called you in some antibiotics, and I'll run and pick them up when the pharmacy opens. Nice seeing you both." I rush off, throwing a wave over my shoulder when Greyson calls out that it was nice meeting me too, and Callan says that it was good to see me again.

Shoot. Me. Now.

I fly down the hallway, snatch my overnight bag off the floor, and head straight into the room Asher had pointed out as mine. The second I shut the door behind me, I want to cry. The room is so pretty. Cream fabric headboard with a bunch of throw pillows on the bed, and even a pretty crystal chandelier. The color scheme is simple and clean—all pale grays and creams.

I know he said his assistant did everything, so I shouldn't think too much about this, but the fact that he created a space just for me...

I shake it off and pull out my clothes and toiletries before heading for the bathroom. The walk-in shower is loaded with expensive shampoos and conditioners, and the huge soaking tub has bath bombs, candles, and bubble bath on the shelf beside it.

*His assistant did all this. I doubt Asher is even aware this stuff is in here.*

What I really want—what I really *need*—is to go hit the ice for a while. Burn off some of these excess thoughts in my skates. Unfortunately, it'll have to wait. I strip down and take a quick shower, sampling some of everything the player has in here for me. I get dressed and brush out my hair, about to put on a bit of makeup, when I hear a knock on the door.

"Come in!"

"Ice queen, are you decent?"

I smirk at the playful way he says that. "More so than I was fifteen minutes ago."

He laughs. "If it helps, both of those guys are madly in love with their women and didn't notice your braless tits the way I did. If they had, trust me, I would have gouged out their eyes Oedipus style, best friends or not."

I groan, my face falling to my hands. "They think we slept together."

"Slept, yes. Fucked, no."

He enters the bathroom, coming in behind me, and my hands slip to my sides, my face meeting his in the reflection of the steamy mirror. It's déjà vu from the night we first met. He smirks, clearly having the same thought.

"You were so adorable that night."

"Was I?" My brows scrunch. I don't remember much. "Adorable isn't a word used with me very often."

"You were chatty and nervous and so innocent, I nearly felt as though I was stealing your virtue."

I sigh. He practically did. I lost my virginity in my third year of college—hello, trust issues—and it was with a guy I had been dating for three months. He broke up with me a week later, and I learned not long after that he'd had a bet with some of his friends that he could win my V-card from me. The guy after him came over a year later—hello, more trust issues than before—and we dated for four months. He was nice. Dependable. Boring as fuck, but I also knew he'd never burn me or break my heart. We fizzled out when I left for medical school. In medical school, there were two men, and I had zero feelings for either. I think by that point my heart had all but been frozen over—ice queen for the win—and I was okay with that until my eyes locked on a gorgeous guy in the wrong bathroom, who made me laugh and feel comfortable, but then gave me the worst sex in the history of the world, and once again renewed my lack of faith in men.

Until now. Until once again, this man made my head spin and my heart buzz.

"I remember you being so charming," I tell him, smiling despite the ugly memory of it. "I remember you making me laugh, when laughing wasn't something I did all that often." I remember thinking how I knew I'd never see him again, so what did it matter if I let loose and stopped thinking for once?

"And now?"

I swallow past the lump in my throat. "Now I might laugh even less." The admission hurts. I don't want to be this mother. I don't want to be this woman. But I'm not sure how to be any other way. I was carefree that night for the first time in my life, and though I wouldn't change it because it brought me Mason, being carefree no longer feels like an option.

I'm a single mother, and I know Asher says he's in this with me, but I can't rely on that. I had a father once, and then I didn't. I know everyone is different. I appreciate that Asher isn't Joe. But that doesn't make it easy to unwind the decades of distrust from my head.

I'm trying to take everything one *are you fucking kidding me* at a time, but some moments prove harder to do that than others. Like right now.

"I make you laugh."

"You do," I concede. "Like I said, you're very charming."

"Maybe," he whispers. Another step, and his chest is against my back. His hand snakes around my waist, his fingers splaying out on my abdomen. "But with you it's real. It's not an act." His gaze burns into mine, intense and unrelenting, forcing me to believe him. Thankfully he allows the topic to die there. "How was the shower?"

"Great." I force a smile.

"And your room? Do you like it?" His voice is a soft purr. A seductive whisper in the humid bathroom. What is it about this man that catches me and then reels me in?

"It's beautiful. I love it." And I love all the things he did for Mason.

It took everything in me not to turn into an ugly-crying mess last night. He's wrecking every part of me, finding every soft spot I wish was calloused over.

I don't want him to. I don't want to get attached.

"I came in here to tell you Mason is awake. He's hanging out with Cal and Grey in the playroom."

"Okay. I'll come get him. He needs a diaper change and some breakfast."

"Are you staying home with me today?"

I swallow. The way he's staring at me is making my heart race. "Yes. We both will. How's your shoulder? How are you feeling?"

"My shoulder is more sore today, and no, before you ask, I won't take more painkillers. I don't react well to them. It's Ibuprofen for me only."

"Fine. I won't push it, as long as you promise to take the antibiotics I'm going to go and pick up at the pharmacy for you and take it easy today."

His mouth dips to the side of my neck. "Promise. Did you see the bath bombs? They smell really good." He takes a deep inhale, and I do everything I can not to tremble, but it's hopeless, and when he feels it, he smiles against my skin. "You smell really good too. You used the stuff in the shower I had Freddy buy for you. But the bath stuff... I didn't know if you were a bath person or not."

Damn him. "I saw them. They look nice. I haven't taken a bath in a long time, but maybe I will." I roll my shoulder, pushing his mouth away from my neck. "You're playing with that line again, player."

"I might be, but it's a line I love to play with." He pulls away and spins me around to face him, tilting my chin until our eyes meet without the buffer of glass. "You seem tense, my queen. What's up?"

*My queen?* That's new. And I freaking love it way more than I should.

"This past week has felt like Mr. Toad's Wild Ride. I'm having trouble adjusting to it."

"I will do my best not to comment on the trouble adjusting to a wild ride thing, because my mind just went all kinds of dirty. But what can I do to help?"

Stop being perfect. Stop acting like you want this thing between us to be real. To last forever.

"Nothing," I tell him, swallowing it all down the way I always have. "I'll work it out. I always do." Only this time I'm not so sure I believe it.

# 14

## ASHER

In theory, I'm supposed to hate everything about my situation. I am in pain—better today than yesterday, but still in pain. I have a low-grade infection and am now taking antibiotics. I'm not on the field, and I'm not throwing a ball, and I'm not leaving with my team for Houston tomorrow.

So yes, I'm supposed to hate everything right now.

Only Wynter is in the pool wearing a small black bikini and making tiny splashes and ridiculous faces at my son, who is tucked into a baby ducky floaty thing, giggling his head off at his mother.

I'm trying not to stare at her tits and hard nipples encased in the thin, wet triangles. I promise you, I am. But let's be real, she looks *damn* fine in that bikini. Delicious curves and sexy pale skin I can't get enough of. Wynter hasn't slept in my bed again. In fact, since our conversation in the bathroom yesterday morning, she's pulled back from me. Again.

And while that's not what I want, her distance mixed with intermittent moments of forgetting why she's determined to hate me is certainly what I've come to count on.

She's the challenge I never expected, the desire I never wanted, and the woman I was never looking for.

"Asher?"

My head snaps up. "Yes?"

A raised eyebrow. "What do you think?"

*What do I think? I think I have no idea what you asked me.* "Uh-huh. Sure."

"You agree I should take off my top, so I don't get tan lines from all the sun filtering in through the open glass?"

I hesitate. Am I dreaming, or is this a trap? "Ummm... Yes?"

"Will you help me untie the strings then? With your good hand, of course."

My gaze bounces back down to her tits, which are so pretty and perky, overflowing the confines of the meager black fabric containing them. "I'm dreaming, right?"

"No." She snaps her fingers in front of my face. "You weren't listening, so I'm putting things on your level until you figure out how to focus on something other than my tits."

I legit might be in love. I know I was posturing or being flippant about it when I first spoke to my guys, but now, I'm hopelessly lost in her. She can't stand me, but that's only another turn-on.

"Impossible. Your beauty is spellbinding."

She rolls her eyes as she twirls Mason's floaty in a circle. His arms fly up, and he lets out a squeal every time she does it. The kid is so damn easy to please. Like me. He didn't even whine or fuss when she lathered him with enough sunscreen to not just protect him from the sun but to refract it.

"Fine. Fake apologies. What can I do for you, my ice queen?"

"Move your arm in twelve circles, six forward, six backward."

She's trying to rehab me, which is adorable. Her boss point-blank told her she had to spend the rest of the week looking after me and that she wasn't allowed in the hospital. You can imagine how well she liked that. Especially when Coach jumped on the bandwagon and made it clear I'm her number one priority.

She *hates* it.

She hates being sidelined to care for me, especially when I don't exactly require a lot of care. She does, however, love being home with

our big guy, so there were no complaints about spending an afternoon in a rooftop pool when I suggested it.

"Yes, Doctor. I'm on it."

I do the movements she forces me to do about ten times a day,
and I feel the tightness—and a decent amount of discomfort—but
push through it. I'm a football player. Sore muscles and tight joints
and pain come with the gig. She told me immobility would be my
worst enemy, and I believe her, so I do what she tells me.

"Good boy. Should I give you a treat?"

I give her a crooked smile, scissoring my legs back and forth in
the cool water as I sit on the edge of the pool. "You think degrading
me like I'm a dog will throw me off your scent, but sweetheart, the
only treat I want from you right now is to kiss your pretty lips. Either
set."

She splashes water in my direction that falls way short of getting
me wet, but I've had a margarita today—for medicinal purposes only
—and I think we've already established I'm a lightweight, so for me,
that was game on. I hop off the ledge and trudge through the waist-
deep water in her direction. She shrieks, her hands flying outward as
if that will stop me.

"No! You can't get your shoulder wet. Out of the pool, player."

Just before I reach her, I dip down, careful not to get my
shoulder wet, and swoosh in, faking her out, left, right, left, and land
a kiss on the side of her neck. "I bet you wish I had gone for your
lips."

"Jerk!" She pinches the nipple on my good side as hard as she can,
as if that simple act of impulsivity is a deterrent against my main
motivation—her. She doesn't know that shit turns me on, but she's
about to. Only I can't swoop her up over my shoulder fireman style,
and I can't drag her up into my chest like a bride. I'm a man with limi-
tations for the first time in his life.

It sucks.

My good arm bands around her body, and I toss Mason a wink as
I haul his mother against my chest. "If I loosen just one knot, the
whole thing comes undone."

"You try it and I'll pinch your earlobe, and trust me when I tell you, you won't like that nearly as much as the nipple tweak."

"You like me." I lick her neck again, just to prove the point that she's mine. "Admit it. It's okay. Everyone does."

"Gross! Stop it with that! I don't like you," she protests. "You're aggravating and arrogant and rarely serious."

"That's..." I pause, thinking that through. "Fair. I am all those things. But you're stuck with me, so you might as well learn to love me."

"I already love your offspring. That's enough Asher Reyes for me."

My phone rings from the side of the pool, interrupting my witty retort. With a groan and a hell of a lot of reluctance, I release my feisty doctor and wade back through the water, only to groan again when I see it's my PR manager.

"Crap. I have to take this."

Wynter waves me on, and I pick up the phone, slide my finger across the screen, and head for the steps at the far end of the pool since I can't hoist myself out of it.

"Jean," I answer as I trudge up the steps and go for a towel. "What's up?" I tuck the phone against my good shoulder and then wrap the towel around my waist.

"The news on your shoulder broke about ten minutes ago. It hit Boston Sports Network first but quickly spread like wildfire over the internet."

"Shit," I hiss, and Wynter's head snaps in my direction with a concerned frown. I shake my head and turn partially away. "There goes my perfectly planned press conference for Monday."

"Yes. We need to get damage control on this now."

"Great. Okay. Give me five minutes, and I'll call you back. I'm just getting out of the pool."

"Sounds good. I'll call Freddy and your agent now."

Jean hates my agent, Hunter, and never refers to him by his first name. Ever. My theory is they had a thing once that didn't end too well.

We disconnect the call, and I turn back to Wynter, who is pulling

Mason out of his floaty and walking him toward the stairs. "Everything okay?"

"The news on my shoulder broke before we could release it ourselves."

Her head tilts as she tucks Mason against her, but hell, even with this news, Wynter walking toward me wet and in that bikini is all kinds of distracting.

"Do you know who broke it?"

"I'm not sure. That was Jean, my PR person. I told her I'd call her back."

"Then you should go do that."

"I can help you with him first." I hand her a towel that she wraps around both her and Mason.

"We're fine, Asher. Go. You've got business to deal with. He's ready for a nap now anyway."

"Thanks." I drop a kiss on each of his cheeks. "See you in a bit, big guy. Sweet dreams. Dada loves you." I make the sign for father as I say dada—since dada is easier to say than daddy—and then drop a kiss on Wynter's cheek, and quickly step back with my hand in the air when she looks like she's ready to cut off my balls. "That was for luck. For me. I might need it."

I toss her a wink and then open the door for them, following closely behind as they head down the stairs, Wynter and Mason going in one direction, me in the other. I speed across the apartment into my master, where I strip out of my wet trunks and step into a pair of sweatpants, and forgo the shirt because it's too hard to do one-handed right now.

Then I head into my office and tap on my keyboard, illuminating both monitors I have on the desk. I go to the Boston Sports Network page, and there it is in big bold font. "Asher Reyes has shoulder surgery. Questions on the season and his future with the Rebels uncertain."

Dickheads.

I dial up Jean, setting my phone on the desk and pressing the speakerphone button so I can talk hands-free. As it rings, I do a quick

Google search, and hundreds of articles already pop up. I rub my hand across my forehead and back through my hair. My contract is up in two years. I never considered the team wouldn't resign me, but then they brought in Leo and Joe Cardone, and now with my injury, I have no idea what's headed my way.

There's a chance I could be playing for another team by this time next year.

"Hey," she answers on the third ring. "I'm going to patch you in with Freddy and your agent."

"K. Sounds good." My voice sounds empty, even to my own ears.

A second later, the three of them are on the phone, all talking at once and over the others.

"One at a time," I bark, clicking on link after link, all saying a variation of the same thing. "I hate it when you all do this shit. Just tell me what the deal is, who leaked it, and what I have to do now."

"We don't know who leaked it," Jean starts. "The story is very vague other than to say you had potentially season-ending surgery earlier this week. The story claimed a reliable source close to you leaked it. That could mean a player, someone on the coaching staff, a hospital employee, your doctor—"

"It's not my doctor," I clip out. "Dr. Hathaway would never do that."

"Okay," Jean says, backpedaling. "Then not her. But the point is, we don't know who leaked it."

"It had to be someone who benefits from the press knowing," Hunter growls—since he always growls—into the speaker. "Who could that be?"

"Leo comes to mind" I answer easily because that's true.

"Maybe," he agrees. "I'll look into it."

And I'll have Lenox look into it as well because he has ways of getting information no one else does. Because if I learn it's Leo—

"Great," Freddy chimes in, cutting off my thoughts. "Moving on. When is the press conference? I'm assuming we now need to do one before Monday, which means I need to go shopping ASAP for the perfect outfit."

"I think it needs to be tomorrow morning," Jean states emphatically.

"I agree," Hunter declares. "News is buzzing, and the speculation is rampant. We need to get a grip on this before it spins even more out of control. We'll call a press conference for tomorrow at the stadium."

"Wow, you agreeing with me is a first," Jean smarts.

"A first, and likely a last."

I roll my eyes Wynter style. "Let's not start with this. I agree we should do a press conference tomorrow. Freddy, that means I'm wearing what I already own. The team leaves tomorrow for Houston, so it'll be quiet there. They won't be able to get any immediate sound-bites from anyone."

"Right. Good." Hunter clears his throat. "Then you need to be seen out tomorrow night."

I lean back in my chair, the leather creaking beneath my weight. "What do you mean by out? I'm supposed to be recovering from surgery."

"I'm not suggesting you go clubbing or anything, but fans need to see you're out and doing well. A quiet dinner somewhere. We need to believe you will, in fact, be back this season. Hiding away suggests the opposite."

"I hate to agree with your agent because I won't be starting that trend, but yes, you need to be seen out and looking healthy."

"Fine. I'll get the guys and we'll—"

"No," Hunter cuts me off. "With a woman. Go out with a woman. You haven't been photographed with one in a while, and we can move the talk from your shoulder to a female."

"Um. No." I glance toward my open doorway, thinking of Wynter. I'd love to take her out to a quiet dinner. Hell, I'd love to take her out to a rowdy dinner with Mason, but not only would she never agree to the date, but the reasons I can't date her in public are also numerous. And now that my face is front-page news, it's even riskier to be seen with her. I'm glad they moved in. Hell knows how else I'd be able to make seeing my son work.

"Yes." Hunter is adamant. "Go out with a woman. Have dinner

with her. Fuck her or not, but let the press see that you're feeling good enough to be with someone, and let that someone churn the gossip mill into off-the-field talk."

"I don't even know who I'd ask, and I'd rather not use a woman I've had a thing with in the past. I'd need someone new, and I don't have anyone new." Because I haven't dated anyone in a while, and the only woman who *is* new in my life is the one woman I can't have on my arm. Even if she's the only one I want there.

"I have someone," Freddy states, but I can hear the discomfort in his voice. He knows about Wynter. He knows I moved her in here, but I haven't told my agent or my PR person yet because I've heard of things like that getting leaked as well, and though I trust them, I don't trust them enough to risk my son or Wynter. Especially if they're looking for something to take the heat off my shoulder, and my future on the team.

"Who is someone?" I question, tapping my fingers impatiently on my desk.

"A model slash influencer. Beautiful with a big following on Instagram and TikTok. She'd be perfect. She'd take a selfie and post it and it would likely go viral, and then boom, your shoulder is no longer front-page news. You can deny any relationship and simply blow it off, but as much as I hate to agree, I think a date could help."

"Hell, get yourself laid." Hunter chuckles into the phone, and I groan. The last thing I plan to do is fuck some influencer-model chic.

"Okay," I grumble reluctantly. "Set it up."

I have a bad feeling I'm going to regret this.

# 15

## WYNTER

I shouldn't be angry. I shouldn't be surprised or annoyed or ready to flip off the world and scream, *I told you so*. Asher is exactly who I thought he was. A man who would say *anything* to get what he wants while planning dates with beautiful models at the same time. Now I'm living in his house. *His* house. I moved my stuff in yesterday.

*What if he brings her home? What if they hit it off and start dating?*

Ugh.

I can't stand the uncertainty he breeds within me. He's like cancer, infiltrating my body, taking over my cells one by one.

I never should have agreed to this. He made me feel seen and beautiful and special, and even though the larger part of me knew better, the smaller, softer part of me began believing that he wanted me beyond Mason.

This is what I didn't want. This is why feelings are so dangerous in this situation.

I'm jealous, and I have no right or desire to be.

He's a single man who can date whomever he wants. He can fuck whomever he wants. I shouldn't factor into that. That's how this works. That's what is best for Mason.

I had walked down to his office to tell him that I was going to bring Mason to my mom's. He didn't want to go down for his nap, and she called in the middle of my trying and offered to take him for a bit so I could get some ice time. I stopped outside his office when I heard voices, and then I listened as they planned the date. I heard the mention of the beautiful model. I heard someone suggest he get laid, and then I heard Asher say, "Okay, set it up."

I couldn't face him after that. I ended up texting him right before I pulled out of the garage, and he hasn't texted me back to acknowledge it.

Whatever. At least I know the truth now, and thank God nothing else has happened between us. I'll set firmer ground rules. I'll start apartment hunting. It'll be fine.

I inhale a deep breath as icy air fills my lungs, the glow of smooth, white ice a landscape before me. A smile catches on my lips. Gary had the Zamboni do this since I know his players cleared the ice only about twenty minutes ago. I finish lacing up my skates with a bit more gusto than likely needed, but then I push onto the ice, my arms floating on either side of me, my head back, and my eyes closed.

Taylor Swift's "Enchanted" courses through my ears and into my blood for no other reason than to torture myself. I twist into a spin and then skate backward along the edge of the boards, picking up speed and heading into my first jump. My free leg extends out behind me as I bend my other knee, then I step forward and jump into the air and rotate one and a half times, landing blindly, but no less soundly.

My skates pick up excitement, and I hit center ice where I do all kinds of spins and jumps, going faster and faster until I land a double loop—I used to be able to do triples. It's solid, and I swirl around until I shift into a sit spin, my hand holding the foot of my blade as I twirl.

I come out of it, my spin slowing as the song ends, and then I shriek at the top of my lungs.

"Shit!" The guy holds his hands out toward me. "I'm sorry. Gary told me you were here, and I wanted to watch you skate. I remember seeing you when you were in the Olympics."

I press a hand over my racing heart. "It's fine. I just usually skate without an audience now."

He grins and steps on the ice toward me. He's cute. Tall and built with sandy-brown hair and darker eyes. "I get it. I prefer to knock the puck around solo now. I busted up my knee during the Stanley Cup finals my third year in the pros. Never made it back."

"You had a shitty surgeon then," I comment, only to grimace. "Sorry!" That feels wrong to say, but he laughs it off.

"Probably. I was a kid and didn't know better."

"And now?"

"Now I'm an assistant hockey coach for a D1 team, so I'm still in the game. My name is Heath."

"Are you going to stay out here and watch me, Heath?"

He smiles. "Actually, I was hoping I could ask you out for dinner tomorrow night instead."

"Oh." It comes out in a shocked whisper.

"I've seen you on the ice before. I've wanted to come and speak to you, but the timing didn't work out until now."

My eyebrows hit my hairline, and he nervously runs a hand through his hair.

"So, would you like to go out with me tomorrow night? I know you don't know me, but I thought it would be fun. Gary mentioned you're single."

"Uh." Well... "I'm also a single mother."

"He mentioned that too."

Okay then. I would usually say no. Inherently, I would. He works with Gary and is a man, and I hate men—especially in this moment —but it's also because of this moment that tempts me to say, "Okay. Dinner tomorrow sounds nice."

A bright smile blooms on his face. "Great! Can I pick you up?"

That would be a definite no. "I can meet you somewhere," I offer instead.

He slips across the ice on his sneakers and then removes the phone from the side of my leggings, unlocks it with my face, and types something in. "This is where I want to take you."

He sends a text.

"This is also my number. Meet me there at eight?"

I gulp. Something in his chocolate brown eyes hits me strangely, but I push it away. "See you then."

He hands me my phone and then walks off the ice, leaving me to myself once more. Only now I have a date tomorrow night.

Me: How did your press conference go this morning?

Player: It went pretty well. I answered a lot of questions. Made you the star of the show.

Me: *eye roll emoji* Great! That's my favorite thing to be. I'm glad it went well though.

Player: Me too. It's a relief to have it done. Where are you? You're not home.

Me: Nope. I'm not. I'm at my parents'. Mason is spending the night here and I had to drop him off.

Player: Oh. Okay. I guess that's better actually because I have plans tonight.

Me: Good for you. I do too. That's why he's staying there.

Player: What kind of plans?

Me: You tell me yours first.

Player: I'd rather not.

Me: Same.

Player: I don't like this.

Me: Get used to it. I gotta go. It's getting late.
Glad your press conference went well.

Player: Queen, what kind of plans do you
have?

Player: Will I see you later tonight?

Player: You are sleeping at the condo, right?

Player: Why aren't you answering me?

Player: Wynter! Answer me. Tell me you're
sleeping at the condo tonight. Or at your
parents' place.

I STUFF myself into a dress I haven't worn in years and twist my hair
around a curling iron until it's in soft, tight waves. I draw the cat eye
sharp enough to kill a man and paint a smoky dusting of shadow over
it. Then I curve red around my lips because red makes me feel like a
warrior.

I gave Mason dinner and a bath, and then my mom shooed me
out the door with a knowing smile. I nearly canceled this date a
dozen times today. My heart isn't in it. I had turned off my phone after
I told Asher I had to go. I don't want to text him, but now as I sit in the
back of the Uber heading to the restaurant, I turn my phone back on
just in case my mom needs to reach me.

And when it powers on and all of Asher's texts come through, I
sigh, reading through his frantic texts. With a shake of my head, I put
it back in my purse. I don't know where I'm sleeping tonight—the
condo or my parents'—but I don't feel inclined to answer him.

*"Hell, get yourself laid."*

*"Okay, set it up."*

I'm trying to focus on tonight. On the date I'm forcing myself to go
on. But the truth is, I'm hurt. And annoyed. And wanting to kill
Asher, so that's not helping anything. Did he not think I'd hear about
it or see it somewhere on the internet if he's dating a freaking model?!

I blow out a breath and run my hands down my dress. It doesn't
matter. I'm here for me. Not for Asher. And I plan to give this man a

real chance. He was cute and uncomplicated and normal. He has no ties to Joe, and he's not a celebrity, and he's not Mason's father.

All reasons why I should be happy about Asher's date.

The valet opens the door for me and helps me out. I walk into the lavish restaurant, the space large and sprawling with high ceilings and hypnotic music playing in the background. The bar is at least two layers deep, and the crowd around the hostess stand is intense. I manage to slip through, but I don't get far before a warm hand hits my lower back.

"Hey," Heath breathes by my ear. "You made it."

I spin around against the warmth of his palm and face him. He's wearing a black button-down and jeans. His hair is brushed back, and his dark eyes are all over me.

"You look beautiful."

"Thank you."

He leans in and kisses my cheek, and considering I barely know his first name, that feels forward. Then again, maybe I'm the outdated one. Maybe this is how it's all done, and I just don't know better. I can't remember the last time I went on an actual date with someone.

With his hand on my lower back, he guides me to our table somewhere in the center of the enormous space. He helps me into my chair and then takes his own, menus on the table as if he's already been here a while when I was exactly on time.

"I've wanted to eat here since it opened," he tells me, staring down at his menu. "I finally have an excuse." A smile brightens his eyes. "I'm glad you agreed to meet me."

"Me too," I tell him, not fully sure if I mean it yet. Gary told me he was new to the team and doesn't know him all that well yet. I never would have given him a chance if it weren't for Asher's date. Perusing the menu, I settle on an entrée—no appetizer or dessert—and then set it down over the empty place setting.

"I wasn't sure you would," he admits, his features softening. "I know I was a bit forward yesterday, but I didn't want to let the chance go. I knew the first time I saw you skating that I had to ask you out."

"Oh." That surprises me.

He blushes slightly "Anyway, I heard everything here is good, so let's have some fun."

I relax at that. Smiling and laughing along and not protesting when he orders some appetizers and a bottle of wine for us to share.

The wine comes along with our appetizers and I settle in, forgetting everything else until he asks, "Did you always want to be a doctor?" He's sipping from his wine glass, carefree and totally interested, without knowing the blackbox that is my past. That's a hard question for me to answer without getting into the details of my fifth birthday. Usually, I answer that by talking about my knee injury and decide that's the course I'd rather take.

"No. I was at a competition, getting ready to head into my second Olympics the following year, when a skater came too close to me during practice. I was mid-jump and I saw them out of the corner of my eye, and when I came down, I landed funny to avoid hitting them. But in the process, I tore three ligaments in my right knee."

He frowns, dropping his elbow onto the table. "That must have been awful. I'm sorry."

"It was... pretty rough," I admit, shifting some of the tomato and burrata around on my plate. "It was going to be my last Olympics anyway. I wanted to go to college and had gotten early acceptance to Yale that I had deferred."

His eyes widen. "How? You were... what?"

"I was seventeen, but I had done high school entirely with tutors since I was competing and training so much. I technically graduated at sixteen."

He looks impressed. "You never got to compete in the Olympics."

"No. Definitely not." I shrug. "I retired."

"So you know what I went through then."

I laugh lightly at his playful tone. "I guess I do." I take a sip of my wine as our appetizers are cleared and our entrees are set before us. "Wow. This looks amazing."

"It does. Do you want to try mine?"

"Um. Sure." He cuts into his steak and then offers me the bite from his fork. It's intimate as hell, and I falter. *Just do it.* Pushing myself up, I extend toward him and take the bite, chewing as I sit back in my seat. "It's delicious. Do you want some of mine?"

"I'd love to try it."

I do the same thing he did to me, and he eats from my fork.

"That's great." He sets to cutting more into his steak, eating his own meal now, and I do the same, forcing myself not to overthink anything. "You didn't finish your story," he prompts.

"Oh. Right. Well, it's difficult coming back from an injury like that. Knees especially take a long time to heal. But I loved the idea of being able to repair injuries like that, and sports medicine is where I ended up."

"I think it's great—"

My phone chimes in my purse, cutting him off. "Sorry," I say, pulling my purse onto my lap and digging for my phone. "It could be my mother about my son."

He waves me away. "Not a problem. I get it."

Unlocking the screen, I read the message. It's not from my mother. It's from Asher. And at first, it has my eyebrows knitting together in confusion.

Player: Look to your left.

What in the hell? Reflexively, I turn my head, scanning through the sea of diners until, about ten tables over, my gaze collides with a set of furious silver eyes, intensely trained on me.

# 16

## ASHER

The girl is barely a minute over twenty-one, has the IQ of a flagpole, and the most annoying high-pitched, squeaky voice I've ever heard in my life. There's also not an inch of her face that hasn't been injected or surgically altered, which, at her age, feels sad. But the real bonus of this is that she hasn't stopped talking about herself once since I picked her up half an hour ago.

I hate that I'm here. I hate that I agreed to this.

I hate that Wynter never replied to me, and I have an awful feeling she's out on a date. I keep checking my phone, but I know she won't respond, and I continue to resist the overwhelming urge to blow up her texts until she does.

"Mr. Reyes?"

My head snaps up, away from my phone. "Yes?"

"Your table, sir."

I nod, gripping my phone in my hand like a psycho, as the host leads us to our table. People are whispering as we walk by. They're taking covert pictures that aren't the least bit covert. I grit my teeth and push out a grin, then take my seat across from... Fuck. I forgot her name.

She drops forward on the table, her fake tits using the tablecloth like a shelf, pushing them up and causing them to spill even further out of her tiny dress. I don't take the bait. I'm not even tempted to, and generally, I have zero problems with fake tits.

"We should get a bottle of champagne to celebrate."

I hold in my snicker. "What precisely are we celebrating?" I ask, giving the menu a quick perusal. Freddy said the food here is very good. I wonder if I could fake an emergency and get something packaged to go.

"Us, silly." She laughs. It's like nails on a chalkboard.

"Us?" I raise an unimpressed eyebrow.

"Yeah. You know. Like us hooking up and stuff."

My dick has never been less interested. "We're not hooking up."

She rolls her eyes, and it's not nearly as adorable as when Wynter does it. "Obviously not now since we're in a restaurant. But later, I'll fuck you. We can video it if you want. I know someone who will leak it for us."

I blink, stunned and completely at a loss for anything to say to that.

Thankfully, the waiter comes over and interrupts us. The mouse orders a bottle of freaking Cristal like I'm a rapper at a club. A few minutes later, he returns with the bottle, and I decline a glass because, not only is champagne seriously not my drink of choice, I am not toasting or celebrating *us* with her.

I pull out my phone and check it again. Still nothing. Dammit, Wynter. You're killing me.

I text Freddy instead.

> Me: How do you know this girl, and what's her name again?

> Freddy: I met Saline at a party a few months back. She's a friend of a friend of a friend. She seemed nice. A bit fake, but who isn't these days?

> Me: Saline as in saltwater?

Freddy: No. Saline as in Celine. I don't think
she knew how to spell it when she picked it
as her name.

I wipe my hand across my lips to hold in my smile.

Me: I might need to fake an emergency. I
can't do this. It's awful and we're only at
champagne.

Freddy: Champagne?

Me: Don't ask.

Freddy: Give it thirty minutes and if you still
need me, I'm here to help.

Me: Fine. Thirty. Thank you.

I set my phone face down on the table as the waiter starts going over the specials.

"Um. I'm on keto and paleo. Is there anything I can eat here?"

I tune her out as the waiter goes over a few items and then gives us a minute to decide. She starts spouting off about how she wants to be a model and eventually move to New York, and blah, blah, blah—I'm not listening. Instead, I survey the restaurant, seeing just how closely we're being watched, when my eyes snag on a woman across the room.

My heart instantly takes off into a crazy rhythm as I stare at her talking and laughing and eating and drinking and looking so fucking stunning that my chest hurts all with someone who isn't me. My jaw clenches so tight, I'm shocked I'm not cracking teeth.

"Ashy, are you listening?"

"No. And my name isn't Ashy."

She shrugs and keeps talking, and I keep staring at my woman on a date with another man. I pick up my phone and text her, watching as she goes to check it, her face scrunching up as if she doesn't understand my message. I watch as she looks and looks, and then bingo.

Her eyes widen, and her lips part.

For a few moments, we continue to stare at each other. The douche she's with says something to her, and I watch her lips move, but I can't tell what she's saying. I sign *nice friend* to her since I've learned a few things from watching those sign language videos with Mason.

She smirks and quirks an eyebrow as if to say *you too.*

I'm ready to fly across the restaurant and pull her away from him, take her home, and officially make her mine. Instead, I hold myself steady and sign *bathroom.*

She shakes her head at me, and then the waiter steps in front of me, cutting off my view of her. Saltwater orders something, and I tell the waiter to pick whatever his favorite dish is, and I'll go with that. He starts to leave, and my head ducks and weaves around him, anxious to see Wynter again. To demand she go to the bathroom and meet me.

Only now she's not looking at me. In fact—I chuckle lightly—she just covertly flipped me off by wiping her middle finger along the side of her face in my direction. God, that woman drives me crazy. And makes me hard. And makes me want to curl up under the covers with her and Mason and never come up for air.

The more time I spend with her, the stronger my feelings for her get.

She continues to eat and be on her date, and I continue to watch her like some deranged stalker because as much as I'd like to, I can't go over there and make a scene. I have no right. She's technically not mine, and she's told me that more times than I can count at this point.

That doesn't mean I don't want to break her date's nose so I can watch him bleed.

I can't stand this. She's with someone else. Giving him her full attention. He gets to stare into her eyes from across the table. He gets to listen to her laugh and know what it feels like when she smiles just for him.

Jealousy churns like poison ivy in my stomach, growing tentacles that make my skin itchy. She's on a date, and technically so am I, but this is not how it's supposed to be. It's supposed to be her. It's supposed to be us. Goddammit, doesn't she know that? Haven't I told her and shown her a hundred different ways?

Our food arrives, and Saline is still talking because she's not eating much of her... I don't even know what she got. Mechanically, I cut into whatever my dish is and take a bite while Wynter and her dead date have dessert, and he pays the bill. He stands and offers her his hand, and she accepts it, letting him drop his fucking hand to her motherfucking lower back.

My body tenses, and I angle around, watching them walk toward the exit. *Look at me, Wynter. Look at me!* She doesn't, and I'm going out of my mind. Just as she reaches the exit, she drops something black, and I watch as it cascades to the floor. In a heartbeat I'm on my feet.

"Asher?"

My head snaps back over to the rabbit. "I'm sorry. An emergency just came up. I have to go."

She glances around, noting the people watching us. "So, no sex tonight?"

"No. Definitely not." I reach for my wallet and tug out a bunch of bills, dropping them on the table. "For dinner and your Uber home. I'm sorry. This isn't going to happen between us. It never was."

"Really?" she snaps, growing angry. "What do you mean this isn't going to happen between us and it never was? No one rejects me. Everyone wants to fuck me. Look at me." She waves a hand over herself. "I'm beautiful and famous. I have over two hundred thousand followers."

"I'm thrilled for you. Bye now."

I spin and race for the exit, snatching Wynter's sweater thing just as the host goes to pick it up. "I've got it. I know who it belongs to. Can you have them bring my car around immediately?"

"Certainly, Mr. Reyes."

"Thank you." I hand him my valet ticket and then run outside, but Wynter and her date are already gone. My good hand rakes through my hair as I pace in an impatient circle. A few people come up to me, asking for selfies and about my shoulder. I smile and give them the standard answer they're looking for, and then finally my car arrives, and I hop in, racing home.

Praying she's there.

I need to make sure she's not with him, but I also need to explain about my date. I was foolish in not telling her, but I didn't know what to say or how to put it. Her trust in men is already about as limited as it gets, and then I went and proved her right.

I am such a fool.

I might have potentially risked everything I've been trying to build with her. And for what? To pull the heat off my shoulder? Who gives a fuck? Why did I give into that? Why did I listen when, in my gut, I knew better?

Parking in my spot, I fly to the elevator and then up to my place, storming through the condo. She's here. The light in the foyer is on, and I'm nearly positive I flipped it off before I left tonight. I jog toward her bedroom, and then I'm pounding on her door.

"Ice queen? Are you in there?"

No answer. Dammit, I know she is. The hall is dark, but there's a light glowing from under the crack of her door.

"I'm sorry." I pound again, only to collapse against the wood, my forehead pressing into it. "It's not what you think. I swear it's not."

"I don't care, and it doesn't matter."

"It does! It all matters. I need to see you. I need to talk to you."

"Go away, Asher."

My eyes cinch tight. "I can't do that."

"You're free to date, and so am I. There's nothing to say beyond that."

"Like hell, there's not," I growl and then temper my voice. "Please. I have the sweater you dropped on your way out."

Nothing.

"*Please*, talk to me." I scramble for a way to reach her. To get my stubborn woman to comply. "This isn't healthy for Mason. We have to be able to communicate with each other."

My face pinches up in nervous anticipation as I wait for her to either give in or verbally eviscerate me for that one. But to my surprise, the door shifts and then opens. Only before she fully opens it, I start to lose my shit, thrusting it all the way open and getting right up in her face with my hands all over her.

"What happened?"

Her eyes are puffy and red-rimmed, but the bright swollen patch on her right cheek, along with the scrape slicing right through it, has me seeing red.

"It's not how it looks," she starts, and that alone makes me postal.

Fury shoots a blazing path through my veins. "Wynter, tell me where he is and what he did to you because he is a fucking dead man. No one touches you. No one."

"It was an accident."

"You see," I start, walking her into the bedroom and then straight into her bathroom, her feet stumbling behind her as I push her along, "to me, that's bullshit. Because in my twenty-nine years, I've never accidentally hurt anyone, let alone a woman."

"Asher—"

I scoop my good arm around her waist and pick her up, dropping her ass on the counter. Then I get right up in her face again. "Do not Asher me. Tell me the truth right now before I have Lenox look the motherfucker up and we destroy his life."

She can tell that nothing I'm saying is in jest. I'm one hundred percent serious right now.

Her hand goes to my chest, over my blood-thirsty heart. "We left the restaurant," she starts, her voice calm. "He offered to drive me home since I Ubered there. I agreed. I had two glasses of wine with dinner, and maybe that's why, but he seemed nice, and it was just a ride home."

I clench my jaw and look away. I never should have gone on that date. Never.

Her hand cups my face, and she drags my gaze back to hers. "He asked if he could come up. I told him no. He asked if he could come up for just a little while without anything happening, and again, I said no. He didn't like that, I don't think. By that point, I was a little standoffish. Your eyes on me the whole night threw me off, and I was angry and upset. Then he moved on me, going in for a kiss, and I didn't want him to. He really didn't like that. I went for a hug instead, and he was still going in for the kiss, and somehow his fist hit my cheek, along with the pinkie ring he had on."

"Pinkie ring?" My eyebrows hit my hairline. "Who is he, the godfather? Who wears pinkie rings anymore?"

"Maybe not on his pinkie. I don't know. It was a big ring. Maybe a championship ring from when his team won the Stanley Cup the year he was injured. I didn't pay much attention to it, but it scratched my face when it made contact."

"He's a hockey player? Christ, woman. That's the devil you taunted me with me?" I drag a hand roughly across my face, trying to calm my breathing when it feels like knives are shredding my lungs. I open my eyes and give it to her straight. "I'm sorry, but him going in to kiss you and you going in for a hug does not translate to what you have on your cheek or the tears in your eyes."

"He didn't mean to, Asher. I could see it all over his face. He freaked out and apologized profusely. He'd had a few glasses of wine too, and that's another reason I shouldn't have gotten in the car with him." Her face tilts down. "I didn't expect it. It hurt, and I reacted. I shoved him away and fled the car. It's done. I'll never see him again."

"Jesus." My hand is all over my face and through my hair. With a vicious shake of my head, I snatch one of the white hand towels from the towel bar and turn on the faucet as cold as it'll go, running the cotton through it and then ringing it out as best as I can, since my other hand is far from at full strength. I press the cold, wet cloth to her face.

"You don't need to do this. I can take care of the cut myself. I'm the doctor here."

I run my fingers along her forehead and down the slope of her other cheek. "Stop being brave when you don't have to be. I want to do this. I want to take care of you and make sure you know that not all men are like that. Some men will take care of you with no ulterior motive."

A noise clears the back of her throat, but she won't meet my eyes. "What are you doing here anyway? Shouldn't you be out with the blonde still?"

"No. Definitely not." I force her gaze. "It was a setup date. Not one I wanted to be on. My PR team felt I needed something to distract the public from my shoulder, and they felt some influencer with a decent-sized following would be the ticket. I was done with that date long before I knew you were there."

"Hmmm."

"No hmmm, sweetheart. It wasn't going anywhere beyond that restaurant. Trust me." I step in between the V of her legs, pressing my chest to hers as I continue to hold the cloth to her face. "She couldn't hold a candle to you. It was you who I couldn't take my eyes off. You who I wanted there as my date. Not her. I never wanted her. In fact, I couldn't wait to get rid of her."

"Asher—"

"I know," I interject. "I know what you're going to say and I'm not pushing anything." *Tonight*, I add. "But promise me you won't go out with him again."

"I promise."

"Good girl. Okay. Now, let's see this."

I pull the cloth away and swallow down curses. I might still kill the man and have Lenox cover it up. He'd be good at that. Him or Zax for that matter.

I lean in and press my lips to the spot right above it. "Does it hurt?"

"Not much."

I frown. "Come with me."

"Where?"

"To bed. Obviously."

"I'm not sharing my bed with you."

"You will for a bit," I tell her, my voice firm. "But I won't stay, and I swear, I won't try anything. I just want to hold you for a while, and I think you could use that too."

She starts to shake, and I hate this. Her trust was already so fractured. It was paper thin, and then this happened. I need to know more. I need the details. But now isn't the time. And frankly, maybe it doesn't matter.

I'm not him, and that's what's important.

Me proving that to her.

"I don't know," she hesitates, still so goddamn uncertain and rattled.

"I do. Don't fight it. Let me take care of you the way you take care of everyone else."

I exit the bathroom so she can get ready for bed, and while she does that, I text Freddy, Hunter, and Jean to inform them I will never take their date suggestions again. They're already over it. According to them, us at dinner is all over the internet, so mission accomplished.

Whatever. Who cares.

I hear Wynter entering the bedroom, and I turn around to find her wearing a T-shirt and possibly nothing else. I look—I can't help it with her—but I don't linger. Instead, I switch out the light, bathing us both in darkness. Wordlessly she climbs into bed, and I follow her, using my good arm to hold her.

She settles against my chest, but I can tell the damage has been done, and I'm still not her favorite person. But if she didn't care, she wouldn't have cared that I was on a date. And if she hated me, she wouldn't allow me to hold her now.

That's something to build on.

Until then, I plant my lips in her hair, and I hold her body against mine until she falls asleep. And with her body limp against mine, I make a decision. No more fucking around. Wynter Hathaway is mine.

## 17

### WYNTER

"No. I won't do it." My words are sharp, refusing to be challenged. Yet the asshole does it anyway.

"Yes, you will," Joe states calmly from behind his desk, his hands neatly folded on top of the wood. Hell, I hate this man. "It's part of your job requirement here. You have to travel with the team for games. Last week you didn't because of Asher's surgery. This week you have no excuse."

Except for a son I don't want him to know about. A son I have with his injured quarterback.

"You have an orthopedist on staff, and I am only licensed in Florida and Massachusetts. If I travel with the team, it's not like I'm about to do any sort of surgery until the team returns home. Anything emergent would have to be done by a local physician."

"I don't care. Team doctors travel with the team."

I grit my teeth. "I do not work for the team. I work for the hospital."

His green eyes hold mine. Green eyes that match my own. That match my son's. "You are the team orthopedic surgeon for the season, Wynter. You will travel with us to Cincinnati on Saturday for the game Sunday."

"No." My insides fester. How do I get out of this without telling him I have a son I won't leave? I may work long hours, but traveling for work isn't part of my gig. No matter what, I see my son every day. He is always my first priority. That was the promise I made to him when I held him in my arms for the first time. I refuse to be away for a minimum of seven weekends over the next four months.

"Yes."

I plant my hands on the other side of his desk, beyond furious. "Find another surgeon, Joe. I don't want to be here. I did Asher's surgery, and it's done. You didn't need me to travel last week with the team, and now suddenly you do? I'm calling bullshit. Why the fuck do I still have to be here?"

"Because I want you here."

I hate how calm he is. Always so cool. So apathetic.

"Why? I've already told you I don't want you in my life. Stop trying to steal a piece of it now. It's too late."

"It's never too late."

His words freeze me in place, stealing the air from my lungs. My first thought is that moving here was a mistake. Only it's difficult to think that after the last two weeks with Asher. Mason is in love with him. Totally. Completely. In. Love. He laughs at everything Asher says and does. Crawls over to him for hugs and snuggles every chance he gets. Prefers Asher to feed him dinner because—let's face it—Asher is a lot more fun than I am.

It's been cruelly beautiful watching my son bond with his father. And watching Asher fall just as much in love with him.

But now it's Tuesday, Asher's surgery was a week ago, and I'm forced to deal with yet another emotional blow. This one is from the man who started them all. At least the scratch on my cheek and any redness that had been there are already gone.

I straighten my spine. "I'm not traveling with the team, and that's final. Feel free to fire me."

A knock on the door interrupts us. "Come in!" Joe barks.

The door swings open, and in walks Asher. He's not surprised to find me here, and it shows as he quickly studies me, scowls ever so slightly, and then turns his full focus on Joe. "You wanted to see me, Coach."

He doesn't apologize for interrupting. He doesn't offer to come back another time. Instead, he moves deeper into the room and shuts the door behind himself.

Joe leans back in his chair, wiping a hand across his sun-weathered forehead. "Yes. How's the shoulder feeling?"

"The pain is mostly gone, but I haven't tested it much. Dr. Hathaway gave me very strict post-op instructions that I've been following. I'm here to meet with the rehab team this morning."

"Do you feel you can travel with the team this Saturday even though you won't be playing and you're on injured reserve?"

"Absolutely."

"Good. I think the kid will need you there." Joe stands, shuffling useless bullshit on his desk so he can seem important. "Why don't the three of us go down and meet with the training staff?" He moves past us, having to lead the pack because, again, he's just *so* important.

"After you, Dr. Hathaway."

"Oh, a gentleman," I quip acerbically. "How rare your breed is to find in this sport."

Joe makes a noise, and I grin as I move in behind him, walking toward the main hallway that will lead us back down to the locker rooms and training area. Asher slides in beside me, his hand reaching out and brushing mine before he snatches two of my fingers.

My head snaps in his direction, but he's facing forward, his expression stoic, giving nothing away. His fingers squeeze mine and then he releases them, shifting to place distance between us.

He doesn't know anything more than what I initially told him about Joe, and he hasn't asked. I need boundaries after what happened Saturday night. I fell asleep in his arms, and other than checking my cheek daily, he hasn't said anything else about it. But he was there for me when I needed him, and I believed him about the date with the model.

His eyes weren't on her that night. They were all over me.

My mind is tripping on that, and I can't seem to find my balance with him.

The moment we enter the gym and then move through to the training room, loud music blasts through the speakers, and all the players who are scattered around various pieces of gym equipment stop to sing along, pointing their fingers at Asher and using their fists as fake microphones. Asher groans, but there is no hiding the amusement on his face.

"Is this a Central Square song?"

It has to be. I don't know for sure because I've never heard it before, and I'm not all that familiar with their music, but it has to be.

"Our first hit," he grumbles. "Baby, This Is Where You Belong."

"Excuse me?" My eyebrows shoot up to my hairline.

He rolls his eyes at me. "That's the name of the song, Doctor. They play it after every win."

"Only the team didn't win Sunday's game," Joe barks sharply. "So there's no business playing that nonsense."

"No," I snap in response. "But their quarterback had a successful surgery and could return this season. I'd count that as a win for the team, wouldn't you, Joe?"

Joe ignores me as he keeps going, storming down the hall and into the training room with a slam of the door behind him.

Asher stares bewilderedly at me. "You just stood up for me to Coach."

"Don't let it go your head, player. I simply dislike you less than I hate him."

He gives me that cocky grin. "All I got from that was that you like me more."

"Come on, Reyes," one of the players yells. "Let's see those sweet dance moves."

The guys start to whistle, whipping their sweat towels around in the air. *Gross.*

"Only if Dr. Hathaway will dance with me," he calls back, his gaze still on me, that arrogant grin growing as now everyone is into it, hollering and whooping and stomping their feet.

"I can't believe you just did that!" I scream as the music in the room intensifies.

Asher is not the least bit remorseful as he goes into full-on taunt mode. "What's the matter, ice queen? You don't know how to dance?"

I fold my arms. "Ha! That's a good one. I was a figure skater, player. I took more dance lessons than you have brain cells."

"Prove it," he challenges, taking my hand and spinning me around in front of the entire team.

"You're going to hurt yourself!" I cry as he shoots me out and then reels me back in until I practically slam into his chest.

He loops me under his good shoulder and then twists me around until I'm back in front of him, and then his bad hand goes to my hip because he can keep it low and tight to his body. He moves our hips in a swivel that is pure sex, much to the appreciation of everyone in the room.

"I happen to know this amazing doctor with the sweetest lips and sharpest tongue who can fix me up."

"I didn't know it was like that between you and Callan."

He cracks up, his smile showcasing all his pearly white teeth. "A lot can happen between five boys on the road." He winks at me. "Are you ready for the big finale?"

"Absolutely not."

"Sure, you are." He releases me and then breaks out into some sort of choreographed dance that the other players get in on, all seemingly knowing every move. He turns to face me and then starts singing the words, his good hand his microphone, only to end it on his knees in front of me, serenading me.

I'm laughing. Hard. I wish I had this on video because it'd go viral in a second and I'd make millions off it.

The song ends and the room erupts in applause. Asher jumps to his feet, spins around, and does a bow I'm positive he's done hundreds of times over in front of screaming fans.

The music cuts out, and Asher calls out, "Back to work now, boys. Those muscles won't get bigger on their own, and we certainly won't kick Cincinnati's ass unless we put in the effort."

The team does some sort of man chant, and then Asher is pushing me along toward the trainers' room.

"Is there anyone who doesn't worship at your feet and does exactly as you ask of them?" I question, staring around the room at the men who look like they'd do anything for their fearless leader.

"Only you, but that's part of what makes pushing your buttons so much fun."

ICY WIND WHIPS across my face as I skate backward, my head over my shoulder, my arms poised, out on either side of me. The music in my AirPods picks up, and I skate faster, getting ready to attempt a double loop. I bend my knees, get on an outside edge and explode up into the air in a tight twist—one, two rotations—and then I land on one skate, my other leg out behind me.

Heath wasn't here today when I came in. I made sure of it. He sent me a text on Sunday apologizing profusely yet again for the blunder of punching me in the face, and I never bothered to respond.

That's that as far as I'm concerned.

I move through a series of twizzles across the ice before I swivel in a rapid circle to a stop when my phone chimes with an incoming message. Sucking in breath after breath, I tug my phone from the restrictive side pocket on my leggings and take a look.

> Mom: Your Asher had me bring Mason back home early.

*My* Asher? What in the hell is that nonsense? My eyes flare as another text comes in.

Mom: We spent an hour chatting and giving Mason a snack while I told him story after story about you. All at his request. Then he asked for any pictures I could get from my phone that you haven't shown him on yours. If I didn't love Gary and Asher were into older women, I'd be all over that.

I roll my eyes. You and every other woman—and man, for that matter—on the planet.

Me: Where is Mason now?

Mom: Home with Asher. He insisted he could handle it.

Me: Mom! Are you kidding me? He has a bad shoulder. He can't lift Mason. He can't even change his diaper.

Mom: He showed me he could. He wanted daddy time with his son. He's the real deal, Wyn. Joe never behaved that way around you. Not even when you were a baby.

I growl. And curse. I'm the only one on the ice so I can swear up a storm and no one other than myself will be the wiser.

Me: Stop. I know what you're doing.

Mom: He also couldn't stop talking about you. He asked me about your favorite color and flower and food and if I had a video of your face when you found out you won the Olympics. He wanted a video of your face, Wynter. For God's sake, why haven't you married him already? He's a postcard of a man. A total dream.

Me: You just proved my point exactly.
Postcards and dreams show the best
versions of themselves and are far from
reality. No thanks.

Mom: Did it ever occur to you that he's a
Gary and not a Joe?

I grumble a whole new version of a swear, making up new ones as I spew them. Because yes, it obviously occurred to me. I'm not blind, and I'm not totally ignorant of Asher. I just don't want to believe he's one way and then be proven wrong because then Mason suffers. I've been duped more than once, and that is not okay with me when it comes to my son. I want Asher to love him, and I want Mason to be his number one.

And I don't want Asher to feel obligated to me because I'm the mother of his child. Asher is a golden retriever. He falls in love easily, and he falls in love quickly, but that doesn't mean he wouldn't love any new owner who came along and petted him just right.

He's an attention whore, and men like that don't stay loyal.

Thirty minutes later, I'm back at Asher's place and find it eerily silent. I check the app, and they're not in the playroom or Mason's bedroom. "Asher?"

No answer, and my heart rate spikes to unfounded decibels.

I start racing from room to room, coming up empty each time, until I hear a thick snore.

*What in the world?*

I follow the sound as Asher lets out yet another noise and find him passed out on his great room sofa with Mason fast asleep on his chest, pressed against his good shoulder, wearing only a diaper. Asher has his arm fastened around him like a seatbelt—like a football he'd never dare fumble.

My heart twinges, and my eyes immediately water.

It's the sweetest image I've ever seen in my life.

I pull out my phone and snap a picture of my son fast asleep on his daddy's chest, curled tightly into him.

I step closer and run my fingers first through Mason's hair and then Asher's, which is the same exact color. "Are you the real deal, or the man who will scar me and leave both me and our child in ruin?"

Asher stirs, his eyes blinking open, and when he sees me standing over them, he smiles.

"Hey," he murmurs, his voice thick and crackly with sleep. Locking his arm tighter around Mason, he shifts, taking me in. "Wow."

"What?"

I glance down at myself. I'm wearing leggings and a fitted long-sleeved sports shirt.

"Nothing. You just look..." He laughs, and my gaze flashes back up to his.

"What?"

He hitches up his shoulder, his smile turning impish. "Hot. Like seriously hot. The whole just after a workout thing is... yeah. It's my favorite look on a woman, but the way you wear it..." He laughs again in a slightly self-deprecating way. "Let's just say it's a good thing our son is asleep on my chest, or his mother would be in serious trouble."

"You're flirting again," I accuse, but there is no hiding the butter-flies his words elicit.

"Oh, no, sweetheart. This isn't flirting. This is stating a straight-up fact. I've seen you in a dozen different ways, and each one I can't get enough of, but you like this is the sexiest thing I've ever seen."

I roll my eyes in disdain, even though I doubt I'm selling it. "Keep it in your pants, player."

My tone was sarcastic, but his is anything but as he says, "For now, I have to. But tonight, when I'm in bed alone and my cock is painfully hard and wanting you, I'm going to picture you like this. Then I'm going to picture pulling off those tight-as-sin leggings and having you sit on my face."

"Asher!" Holy hell. I flush and then flush some more, my pussy aching and empty feeling. My nipples harden, and I know he can see that through my sports bra and thin shirt.

"Have you ever done that?" he persists, his voice dipping. "Sat on a man's face while he ate you out like he was starving for you?"

"Knock it off." I slide my hands under Mason, picking him up and bringing him into my arms because I need the distraction, and nothing is more distracting and less sexy than having your baby in your arms.

Asher sits up. "Answer me," he demands, his gray eyes consuming the hunger in mine and returning it tenfold. "Have you?"

Mason wiggles against my chest as he starts to wake up from his nap. "I'm going to go change his diaper."

Because again, there's nothing sexy about that.

"Wynter." Asher is on his feet. "Just tell me."

"No, okay? No. I've never done that before." My voice climbs along with my ire as I hotfoot it toward Mason's bedroom. "I haven't done a lot of things. I've had boring, vanilla sex with boring, vanilla men. Missionary at its worst. I've never had an orgasm during sex. Half the time I hardly had one during foreplay, if there was foreplay at all. The freaking orgasm you gave me in record time in your dining room was the first time anything like that had ever happened to me. No one has ever touched me just to touch me without expecting sex. Happy now?"

I set Mason down on his changing table and get to work on removing his diaper. The diaper is dry, and I curse because, for the first time in my life, I was hoping for something beyond gross to be waiting for me in there.

I make a noise of frustration and then pick him up again, walking him across the hall to his playroom. Asher is still with us, but after I dropped my lovely sex truth bomb on him, he's thankfully quiet.

That is until Mason starts climbing up the small playscape and sliding down. I didn't even put him in clothes. That's how flustered Asher had me. Then he comes in behind me, his mouth on my neck, and I realize that's his favorite spot to kiss. Every time he's kissed me, he's kissed me there.

"I'm not vanilla. I'm far from boring. The orgasm I gave you in the dining room was just a taste of what I can do to your body. The idea of making you come over and over makes me painfully hard." He pushes into my back, proving his point with every hard inch of himself. "I know you don't trust me yet. I know there's a lot about yourself you're holding in, and I haven't pushed it because I need to earn your trust before you'll do that. But Wynter, I am telling you this now so there is no confusion in your head, and then you can sit with it and think it all over. I am crazy about you. It's more than sex. It's more than a do-over. It's more than Mason. It's you. I want *you*. No one else. I want to show you how good this can all be because I have no doubt it could be incredible."

Another kiss, and I hate how his words hit every vulnerable spot inside me. I want to be more than a second chance at getting one night right. I want to matter. I want to be just as important to him as Mason is. I don't trust him, but I feel things for him, and I can lie and deny that all I want, but there is only so much lying a person can do to themselves, especially when they already know the truth.

Because I'm not sure I've ever mattered to anyone beyond my mother and Gary, and then later Mason. I believe I am strong and will never need a man, and that is unchanged. But that doesn't mean I don't want someone to stare into my eyes and view me as their world. It doesn't mean I don't want a man to make me feel special and loved—truly desired for the first time in my life.

"Think about it. I'm not going anywhere."

# 18

## ASHER

Rain comes down in torrents, in heavy sheets of fat water. It's the kind of rain that seeps into your bones and makes you shiver even when the temperature is sweltering enough to make you sweat on top of the rain. It's oppressive and miserable, but thankfully I'm wearing rain gear since I'm not playing.

"Settle down, Rookie," I speak into my mouthpiece that goes directly into his helmet speaker. "Balls are going to drop like panties on prom night in this weather. Focus on the defense. If you're slow, so is the defense coming at you. Fade right and hand off left. They won't expect it. We're six minutes away from tying this game, and I don't know about you, but I don't want to stand out here for fucking overtime. Let's win this shit now."

The rookie grunts, but he calls out the play I just suggested in the huddle. There isn't much of a crowd here tonight. Preseason, mixed with monsoon-like conditions, keeps fans watching from the dry comfort of their sofas. Right now, it feels like a scrimmage or a shitty high school game, but we lost our first preseason game, and as much as it chides my ass to help this kid take over my role, I also want my team to win.

I won't have a shot to win back my spot for another two months, at the earliest, and when—*if*—I return to the team as the starting quarterback, I want us to be in a position to make the playoffs and win it all.

The center snaps the ball to the kid, and he drops back into the pocket, tucking the wet ball against his chest. He does the fake to the right only to spin around and hand it off left. The spin was some unnecessary fancy bullshit, and he's lucky it didn't cost him because the fake worked. Our running back secures the ball with two hands and shoots straight up the field with hurried, determined strides, his singular focus, the end zone.

One. Two. Three defenders all come chasing, but our running back is fast and books it toward that patch of green turf that will deliver six points our way. No one catches him. No one stands a chance. He stiff-arms the last defender and jumps over a guy sprawling out as he attempts to catch his legs, and there he is in the end zone.

Touchdown Rebels.

I shoot straight in the air, jumping high off the ground—smart enough to remember to not shoot my arms up with my body—and hollering out in a way you'd think we just won the Super Bowl. I might not be playing tonight, but the high still gets me every time. Our kicker nails the extra point, and with just over four minutes left on the clock, I'm feeling good. The game is far from over, but our defense has held Cinci pretty well all night. Not to mention, no one wants to get hurt during the preseason.

Trust me, it sucks balls.

The kid comes racing off the field, a smile on his face that easily matches my own. "Nice move, Rookie."

"Nice call, old man."

I roll my eyes, but he sobers quickly. "Hey, listen. I didn't mean what I said about that girl."

I stare stunned and then wave him off. "We're cool, man."

"No." He grips my arm. "I'd burn down your world if the roles had been reversed and you were talking about one of my sisters that way. I mean it. I'm sorry. Thank you for your help tonight. I needed it."

Color me shocked.

I hold out my fist and he gives me a solid pound. The kid's finally learning. Maybe we have a shot this season after all, though it's *far* too soon for that kind of talk.

Time ticks off the clock, and Cincy doesn't pull much in terms of an offense, and we win our first preseason game. Coach goes into the locker room barking at everyone, and I'm starting to like him less and less.

He's Wynter's father, but she calls him Joe, and Gary Hathaway, Dad. She hates him, and I'm starting to need to know why more and more. Hiding my situation with Wynter, as well as Mason, is risky for me. It could mean the end of my career here if he found out.

Boston, this team—they're everything to me.

But so are Wynter and Mason.

I push that off and congratulate my teammates—because that's my job now that he's done berating them.

After showering and changing—thank God for hot water and dry clothes—we climb onto the team plane and end up sitting on the tarmac due to thunderstorms back in Boston.

I've avoided it all night. All day. I haven't pulled up the video apps once, but now that we're sitting and it's dark and stormy outside and I have nothing better to occupy my thoughts than my big guy and my ice queen back home, I no longer resist. The video feed immediately comes in, and there he is on his back in his crib, arms splayed out on either side of his head.

A hard swallow sticks in my throat.

*Good night, big guy. Sweet dreams. I love you. I'll see you when you wake up.*

I continue to watch the feed, still mesmerized by my son and knowing that will never change. I've missed so much. Ten months of his life. Ten months of growing and changing. I hated leaving him, even for a couple of nights.

I tap my screen and pull up my text message thread with Wynter, debating if I should write anything. I put all my cards on the table with her the other day, and since that time, I've given her space. It hasn't been easy.

I'm a bull. I charge in and dominate any situation with horns and a lot of snuffing, using my weight and size when necessary.

But that's not what she needs. She needs to know she can rely on me. That my words are genuine. I need her trust the way I need oxygen. Hell, I simply *need* her. Body, soul, mind, and spirit. I want to do this. I want to see where it can go. I've never met anyone like her, and I can't stop thinking about her.

It's constant and pervasive, and I love it as much as I hate it.

I tap the screen some more and then start writing, only to immediately delete it. It's after ten now, and if she's asleep, I don't want to wake her. Joe wasn't happy about her not accompanying the team to Cincy, but she held firm on her stance about not going, and he relented. I don't even know if she knows I'm coming home tonight. I told her I'd see her Monday because we don't land until late. She's living with me, and I know she sets limits on us for reasons I understand, but I don't care.

I think she's it. The real deal.

Now I just have to prove it to her.

The plane finally kicks off the runway, and I settle in for the short flight, my eyes closing only to snap back open when we have a bumpy landing. Rain is coming down hard in Boston too, along with rumbles of thunder and streaks of lightning. I drive home, pull into my spot in the underground garage, and park next to Wynter's car.

Her car is old. And not my first choice for her and my son. I know she must make good money as a surgeon, but I also know how Wynter's mind works, and I know she'd view a car as a frivolous purchase. She's pragmatic, whereas I'm adventurous.

We are opposites in so many ways.

Still, I wonder if she'd agree to allow me to buy them one if I said it was in the name of safety and not bestowing gifts. Gifts I'm dying to shower her in.

With a yawn, I get in the elevator and shoot up to my place at the top, ready to crawl into bed and then spend tomorrow with my guy since I have a day off. Only as I reach the edge of my room, I stop dead in my tracks.

Squinting against the thick darkness I take in the form under rumpled blankets and the dark hair spread across my white pillow.

Wynter is fast asleep in my bed.

My groin tightens, making my slacks uncomfortable, so I take them off along with my shirt. Unmasked desire rages through me, and I climb on the bed, the mattress dipping beneath my weight as I move in toward her.

Her body stirs as I climb beneath the covers, and then I roll her until she's on top of me. She's not wearing a lot. I can't see much of anything, but I can feel, and my hands rove her curves of their own volition. A thong and a T-shirt—my T-shirt, if the size and smell of it are anything to go by. She's so sexy, I can hardly stand not thrusting straight into her.

Her in my clothes, sleeping in my bed like a sneak. Like a thief. It makes me impossibly hard, and I know she feels it since I'm doing nothing to hide it from her.

"Look at this sweet surprise I found waiting for me in my bed."

She pushes up, planting her hands on the bed on either side of me, her eyes wide in shock. "I didn't know you were coming home tonight."

I grin. "That doesn't explain how you got here."

She licks her lips, the outline of her features barely visible against the streetlamps that filter through my blinds. "I had a nightmare. A bad one and I woke up, and then it was storming."

I run my fingers across her face and back through her hair, my other hand on her hip beneath the shirt.

"And?"

Her face twists in annoyance. "And I'm leaving."

In a flash, I roll us until she's pinned beneath me. "Try again."

"Get off me, Asher."

"Why did you come to sleep in my bed and put on my T-shirt?" I want her to answer because there are only so many explanations for it.

"Screw you."

"It'll be the other way around. But first I'd like your answer." My hand pinches her ass, and she yelps.

"Move!"

"Tell me first, and then I'll move."

"Argh." She smacks my good shoulder—ever the conscientious doctor—in frustration. "You're such an ass. Fine. I was scared. I was alone in this big, dark apartment that's not mine and... I needed... I don't know."

"The smell of me to comfort you?"

Her head turns away, her expression pinched. "Yes. Happy now? Move!"

With a wicked grin she's missing, I slide down her body, heading beneath the blanket. Straight for her pussy.

"What are you doing?!" She gasps, lifting the covers up so she can see me.

"I told you I'd move. I never said which direction I'd go though." I lick my lips, spread her thighs, and then press my nose straight into her thong-covered cunt.

"Jesus!" she cries out, her hand ripping at my hair, her back arching. "Asher. No."

"Yes. Please let me do this. Please." I pull her panties aside and blow cool air on her. She squeals this time, ripping harder at my hair, but now she's not telling me to stop, and she's not pushing me away. She won't now that I said please. It's her kryptonite. A spell I cast that lures her in and weaves her under my control.

But more than that, she wants this. She just doesn't know how to ask for it or accept it.

She's wet. So very wet. And smells like fucking heaven. I haven't gotten a good look at her pussy yet, and now in the dark, I'm not getting the best view either, even as I toss the blankets off my back. That'll have to wait for another time.

She told me no one has ever had her sit on their face before, but I have to wonder... "Has anyone ever licked your pussy before, sweetheart?"

"Asher, I—"

I gently smack her clit, and she whimpers. My rough, stubble-lined cheek grazes the soft flesh of her inner thigh. "Answer me, Wynter. Has anyone ever eaten out your pussy before?"

Her eyes cinch tight. "No."

Fucking hell.

"I'm about to change that right now, unless you tell me no again."

No sound. She's hardly even breathing, but I smile like the wicked devil she makes me.

"I'm going to give you so many firsts, my queen, you won't be able to keep up."

Balling the thin material of her thong up in my fist, I tear it off and then shove my tongue straight inside her. She cries out, startled almost, her hand held firm in my hair as if she's unsure what to do now that we're in this position.

I solve the dilemma for her. I show her exactly what we're going to do as I start to fuck her pussy with my tongue. Wild. Unhinged. Positively feral. This woman is mine and with every lick, every touch, and every kiss, I will make her even more so. She will be branded to me, body and soul.

At that thought, a blazing flame crackles and scorches my skin.

Because I realize I am branded to her too. Possibly forever. And instead of terrifying me, it awakens me, transforming my purpose. I'm hers. Her man. Her lover. Her protector. The father of her child.

My breathing loses rhythm as I circle her opening with my tongue before flattening it and sliding up to her clit. My hunger is a raw, palpable beast. My fingers dig into her thighs, holding her open for me as wide as she can go. I flick her clit with my tongue, swirl around it, and then suck it between my lips.

She moans, rocking into me, her hips uncoordinated as she moves against my face, fucking me as I fuck her. Two fingers slide inside her, pumping in and out as my lips and tongue continue to play with her swollen nub. A hoarse growl slips past my lungs, vibrating into her.

"You taste so good."

I pull my fingers from her pussy and slide them into my mouth before thrusting them back inside her. Her hips jerk as my tongue joins them, pushing in as they drag out, and I repeat that motion over and over. Swirling my tongue only to pump straight in as deep as they'll go. My hands are big, and my fingers are thick, and she feels every inch of me, only it's not compared to what I plan to give her after I make her come on my face.

I slide my fingers out and use my thumb to play with her clit, shifting her body so I can bury my face in deeper. With my tongue inside her as far as it will go, I flick it against her walls and her hips shoot up. She grips my hair tighter, angling up, wanting me to go even deeper. It's wet. And fun. And I can't get enough as I eat at her like I might never get the chance again.

"Holy fuck, Asher."

I pull away, angling up to catch her eyes, even as hers are closed. I use my finger to ring her entrance, playing with her. "That's it, sweetheart. You're such a good girl letting me eat your pussy like this. Now, I'm going to reward you. Are you ready for it? Are you ready for how messy I'm going to make both of us?"

She likes my praise. I know she does. I saw it the first time in the dining room when I had my fingers in her. How no man has ever worshipped her before is beyond me, but it thrills me that I get to be the one to do it now. It has my possessiveness over her lashing out and fueling me on.

"Your pussy is mine, Wynter. I own the way you come. I give you pleasure. Me. No one else." Fucking ever.

Her answer is immediate, her sounds unlike any I've heard from her before. They make my cock ache and drip, my hips canting into the bed, needing to rub and rut and feel friction. Needing to fuck— and to do it hard. She was tired of boring. Tired of vanilla.

I'm about to be her fairy godfucker and grant her every wish and desire.

My mouth covers her pussy as I suck and lick and devour her.

Her legs wrap around my head, holding me against her, her head back, denying me a view of her face. She claws at my headboard, grinding against my movements, taking me in deeper, demanding I give it to her harder. Her clit rubs against my face, her sounds growing louder and more urgent, and I decide I want to feel her clit pulse as she comes on my fingers. My lips wrap around it, and I suck it hard into my mouth, gently using my teeth to scrape her, and she explodes.

Bucking and moaning and whimpering and swiveling her hips tighter against my lips. Her pussy flutters around my fingers as I send her soaring. I continue to lick her through her orgasm, my fingers still pumping in and out of her even as my pace slows. I want to do this again. I want to eat her out to another orgasm, but I can tell she's already sensitive as she squirms.

Her body sags, her grip on my neck slackens, and I raise my head, staring at the magnificent sight before me. Wynter's eyes are closed, but there is the most breathtaking smile on her face. Her shirt is rucked up, revealing her smooth abdomen and the underside of one breast.

Breasts—much like her cunt—I haven't seen yet.

"Give me your eyes, Wynter."

She blinks her eyes open halfway, staring up at me as if she's not quite sure what to do next. Stay or go. Fuck or flee. I solve her mental quandary for her. Once again, her serpent, her Hades.

"In my nightstand drawer, you'll find a condom. Roll it on my cock and then ride me until you come at least two more times. And if I hear an ounce of protest from you, I'll spank you. Am I understood?"

# 19

WYNTER

Asher's silver eyes blaze into me, a white-hot intensity I feel covering every inch of my body. I woke up from my nightmare earlier, nervous and jittery, my heart pumping adrenaline that wouldn't quit. Then thunder shook the penthouse, and I hated that Asher wasn't here for me to curl up against. He would have taken me in his arms. He would have held me all night if I had asked him to.

That realization hit me hard.

It's what found me wandering down the hall into his empty room. It's what made me strip out of my own nightshirt and then climb into one of his discarded ones that was hanging over the back of a chair. It's what had me crawling into his bed, burying my face in his pillow, and drifting off into dreamless bliss.

There is so much about this man that overpowers me. It terrifies me as much as it appeals to me. I let my guard down with him, and his words and actions infiltrated, and now I'm pushing him away, forcing him onto his back. His lips part in surprise, and I inwardly laugh.

I haven't kissed him yet.

Not once.

And while part of me wants the dirty edge of his promises, the other part, the part that's still unsure and distrustful, needs more. I falter, staring down at him, and he sees it. His head tilts, those smoldering eyes observing me as he uses his good hand to push himself up until he's sitting.

"Oh, my beautiful ice queen." He makes a tsking noise in the back of his throat as he shakes his head in a self-deprecating way. "I got so wrapped up in the fun and the filthy, I forgot to give you the sweet first." And then he's smiling. His chin dimple deepens, slicing his sharp jaw in two, and then he's quirking two fingers at me. "Come 'ere."

He takes my hand, lacing our fingers together and helping me straddle his hips until I'm seated on his lap, my naked pussy over his hard cock, with only the thin cotton of his boxer briefs separating us. But as he gazes at me, brushing back a few wayward strands of hair from my face, he doesn't seem to notice.

"My queen." His fingers trace the lines of my face, his eyes following the movement. "Do you have any idea how in over my head I am with you? I've done nothing but think of you and Mason and football for the last two days." Then he laughs. "For the last few weeks, more like." His eyes pin mine as his hand cups my cheek. "And yet, for the first time in my life, I found myself wanting to be here with the two of you rather than out on that field tonight." His gaze flickers back and forth between my eyes. "You're owning my heart, Wynter Hathaway. I know you're afraid I'm going to ruin yours, but I think for me, you've already ruined mine."

I believe him. It's a shuddering realization.

My heart trembles, making it hard to breathe.

With a restless fear low in my belly and on a shaky breath, my hand flattens against his chest, over his racing heart, and then I lean in and press my lips to his. I relinquish control. I hand him the reins. His focus is single-minded and entirely on me. This man turns my insides into a quivering mess of needy uncertainty, but at this point, what choice do I have but to throw caution to the wind and chance the irresistibly risky temptation he comes with?

My tongue dances with his, tasting and exploring, but all too quickly our kisses become urgent, fueled by lust. I rip my lips from his and throw his shirt up and over my head. It's still dark in here, but by this point our eyes have adjusted enough that he can see me completely nude and straddling his cock.

He makes a noise in the back of his throat that is all male, rugged, and slightly deranged, and then his lips slam back down on mine as his hand comes up and cups my breast. His mouth ravages and consumes, his breaths hot and urgent against my own.

"Condom, now. I need to be inside you." His control slips as his hand moves to my hair, and he tugs it in a way that ensures my full attention. Ensures I'll comply, which I do. I scoot to my knees, my blood thrashing through my chest and ears, a heavy bass I'm positive he can hear.

He lifts up for me, and I remove his boxer briefs, allowing his long, thick cock to spring free. I'm like a virgin in a cheap porn film, about to ask if that thing will fit inside me. Then I remember he wasn't hard that night in the bathroom, and panic ensues.

"No. Never mind."

"What?" he chokes out a laugh.

I point at the massive, *angry*-looking beast. "You're a football player. Really tall and seriously built, and I see now that comes with a certain caliber of equipment, but no thanks, I'm all set."

He blinks. Then a smile takes over his entire face, and he starts cracking up. "You don't think you can handle me?"

I shake my head. "It's not I think. It's I know. I might be tall myself and have some decent curves, but your son had to be removed from my body by a C-section because he was too big to fit down my... canal." I take his fingers and run them over my C-section scar.

"Your canal?"

He's mocking me now.

"Shut up, Asher. Your dick is too big to fit."

He's laughing. Hard.

"Stop laughing at me."

I move to climb off his body, but his hands grip my hips, and he holds me firmly seated against him. "Sweetheart, my dick was made for your pussy. Is it going to be a tight fit? Sure. One I look forward to actually. But it will fit."

"It'll hurt."

His features soften. "I promise if it hurts at first, you'll adjust and then I'll make it feel so good. I'll go slow. I'll get you nice and wet before I enter you, and if you want, I even have some lube we can use. Besides, the ice queen I know never backs down from a challenge or an occasion to prove me wrong. Prove me wrong, my queen. Prove to me that my big cock won't fit in your tight little pussy. Prove to me that I'm too big to make you come over and over again."

"I hate you."

He nips my bottom lip. "First comes hate. Then comes love. Then comes marriage and the baby in the—oh wait, we did that last part already."

I pinch his nipple, making him jerk and smack my hand away. "Ow. Those are sensitive. Okay. I can't pin you to the bed because my shoulder couldn't handle the weight, so I need you to ride me, sweetheart. Can you do that? Can you try?" He reaches between us and starts playing with my clit, rubbing it in soft circles that make my breath hitch and my nipples automatically tighten. He grins. "There it is. There's my girl. That flush in your cheeks is the sweetest and sexiest thing. Start riding my cock like this. Move your pussy up and down against my shaft. Make it feel so good. Get yourself so wet."

He begins to thrust up, and my breathing grows shallow. It does feel good. *So* good. And I want it inside of me. But to say I've never experienced a man his size is putting it mildly, and I'm not even trying to feed his ego here.

Between his fingers still rubbing my clit, his lips stealing kisses in between staring down at where our bodies are connected, and his dick rimming the edge of my opening, I'm starting to lose my cadence.

His lips layer with mine, and his crooked, arrogant-boy smirk only seems to make me hotter for him. "Are you on the pill?"

"No," I admit. "I don't do well with the hormones. Hence why you knocked me up in the bathroom."

"Condom then."

"Yes, and this time *I'll* make sure it goes where it's supposed to." I dismount my new favorite toy and go for his nightstand. And "wow." Because I wasn't prepared for that.

"What?" His head snaps in my direction.

"Just... all this." I gesture to the open drawer.

"Do you know why I have so many condoms in there?"

"Because you fuck a lot of women?"

He rolls his eyes at my droll tone. "Because I *haven't* fucked a lot of women. At least not in a while. Pick a condom, ladies' choice. Grab some lube if you're really worried, and hop on my cock."

"So romantic."

"Sorry. It's just that I'm so painfully turned on and I'm..." Consternation strikes a path across his face.

Oh. He doesn't want a redo of the first time where he came too quickly, and I didn't come at all.

I grab a condom and then return to him, opening it up and rolling it down over his length. Then with my hand on his good shoulder for balance, I start to lower myself on him. He breathes my name as I slowly sink down, spots of red highlighting his cheeks and his eyes growing bright like twin flames.

"Fuck," he hisses, blowing out a heavy breath. "Hell. I'm going to die, but at least I'll die really fucking happy. You okay?" He wheezes when I reach the halfway point and freeze as a slice of pain skates up my spine. He's shaking. I know it's killing him to sit here and let me do this. To not thrust up and start pounding into me.

I nod shakily, blowing out an uneven breath, forcing myself to relax. Rising, I then sink back down, going farther and farther each time I do it. "You're not even in my ass, and it's this tight of a fit."

His head falls back and his eyes pinch tight as a pained groan rips from his lungs. "Wynter." Sweat coats his brow. "A thread. That's all

I'm hanging on by, and then you go and mention me fucking your ass?"

I lean in and whisper by his ear, "Come on. Man up. I told you I've never had an orgasm during sex. What did you say about me riding your cock until I came twice? Or..." I bite my lip, giddy and a little nervous. "You'd spank me."

His eyes flare open, and my primal alpha beast has returned with purpose in his gaze. "Just wait till I'm fully healed. Then I'll really unleash myself on you. Until then, use me. Fuck me. Learn what feels good and how you like it. If you like it dirty and naughty, awesome. If you like it sweet and playful, that's great too. Slow, fast, rough, gentle. However you want it, is how I want to give it to you."

Christ, if that's not the world's biggest turn-on, I don't know what is.

With his eyes on mine, I push myself all the way down until I'm fully seated on him. This man fills me up and then some. I hold still, my muscles testing, squeezing, ripping another groan from him.

He pants. "I can tell you unequivocally, this is the best thing I've ever felt in my life."

I smile and press my lips to his. "Really? I think we can do better."

He smacks my ass. Hard. The sound and sting shocking me. "Prove it."

I slide up and then back down, taking in every inch of him. I do it again, and then on the third time, I slam myself down, shredding both our lungs with moans. How does this already feel better than any sex I've ever had? His hand grips my hip, and he drags me back and forth, making my clit rub against his lower abdomen.

My head flies back, and my hand squeezes his shoulder. "Asher."

"Yes, baby."

I smile at that. The man is all pet names for me. "Can you use your bad arm?"

"Depends. What do you want me to do with it?"

"Play with my tits."

"That I can definitely do."

His hand starts squeezing me, lifting the weight in his hand, and pinching my nipple until it borders on pain. I gasp and then move my hips. Forward and backward, up and down. Using him the way he told me to. My mouth seeks his, our breaths sharp pants against each other's lips.

"Are you ready?"

"Ready for what?" I whimper breathlessly.

"More."

I shake my head, but then he starts moving his hips, thrusting up just as I thrust down, and holy *fuck,* that's deep. So deep that I swear, I feel him in my uterus. We moan together, and then he does it again, setting a pace. Moving faster. Forcing me to do the same in order to keep up. I'm bouncing on him as he pistons his powerful hips and cock into me until I'm utterly lost to everything other than what he's doing to me.

Our tongues rub and tangle and fight, lost in the rhythmic, mind-bending pleasure. His hand abandons my breast, and his thumb starts rubbing my clit in earnest. Sweet, tight circles with a delicious amount of pressure that has me scraping my nails down his arms. That has me grinding harder against his cock and fingers, wrapping myself around him as I lose my ability to move on my own.

"I'm... Asher, I'm..."

I can't finish that, as I'm sideswiped by my orgasm. It raids through me like a thief, stealing the air from my lungs and muscle control from my limbs. All I can do is hold on and press deeper.

Asher watches me come on him as he growls and groans and grunts, but I don't think he's coming with me. A point he proves as suddenly arms move, legs shift, and then he has me on all fours with him kneeling behind me. He spanks my ass and then slides right back inside my swollen, wet heat.

"Goddamn, Wynter. How fucking tight is your pussy? Do you feel that? The way you're still clamping down on me?"

"Yes," I cry because I feel everything. I just came, but I already feel like I could again.

"Fuck, you feel incredible." He drives into me, surging with all the power in his strong thighs. "Ahhh. God, yes. Fucking perfect."

His hands roam along my back and my sides, swooping around to cup my breasts and pinch my nipples. All the while he fucks me, his sweaty chest against my back, his mouth by my ear, whispering words I can hardly make out. His body smacks into mine, the sound filling the room along with his unrestrained grunts.

Every time he slides out, I whimper, needing him to fill me up again. And he does. He doesn't stop or slow his pace. I twist my head over my shoulder and catch him staring down at where he's fucking me. It's unbelievably hot. The concentration lining his forehead and the unbridled lust burning his eyes and cheeks.

He notices me looking and smirks, his grip on my hip tightening as he plunges in as deep as he can go and then swivels his hips in a circle. My eyes instantly roll back in my head, and I cry out, rocking against him.

"Again?"

"Please. That…"

He does it again, and I feel my orgasm building, picking up speed and heat like a blowtorch. I lower myself to my forearms, my head dipping between my shoulders, and dare him to take me deeper. He does without hesitation, his body trembling behind me as he gets closer and closer to his release.

"I want to feel you come inside me," I tell him, and he smacks my ass again.

"You want my cum, my filthy queen? If I could fuck you without this condom, I'd have you dripping my cum for days. I'd rub it all over your clit, using it as lube until you came with it. I'd ring it around your asshole and then shove it deep inside there too. You'd be so full of me and then I'd fuck you again and give you more."

My eyes pinch tight and I feel my pussy clenches around him at the image he's painting for me.

"For now, I'll give it to you like this, but only after you come for me again. Rub your clit, Wynter. Rub yourself while I fuck you." He picks up his pace, making sure his huge cock hits that spot inside me, and I reach between my spread thighs and find my clit. I start rubbing myself with abandon, and between that and his cock hitting my G-spot, I quickly tumble over the edge a second time.

I scream into the comforter, my fist balling up the fabric as wave upon wave shocks through.

"Fuck! Wynter!" he bellows, his hand on my hip bruising as he grips me. His hips jerk, his cock throbs, and he stiffens as he comes inside me with my name on his lips, shooting everything he has until we're both spent.

He pulls out of me, quickly discardes the condom, and then he's back, bringing us both under the covers and dragging me into his chest on his good side. His fingers stroke reverently through my hair, gently uncoiling any tangles he snags on.

"I'm really glad you had a nightmare tonight."

I laugh, my body shaking against his. "I bet you are. You finally got your do-over. But don't think this means it'll be a regular thing. The sex wasn't *that* good."

He cups my jaw in his hand and drags my eyes up to his. "Nice try. But the sex *was* that good, and this *will* be a regular thing."

"Was it... was it okay for you?" I hate how I sound insecure or vulnerable. I don't mean to, and that's not what this is. It's more of a curiosity because it's hard to be into sex when the sex is boring and not all that great. But part of me always wondered if sex was that way because I wasn't all that great at it.

His eyebrows bounce. "Okay for me? No. It wasn't *okay* for me. That was life-changing, never-going-back, best-sex-of-my-life sex." His fingers trace my jaw. "Try this with me, Wynter. I know it's risky. I know there's too much at stake. But life's too short not to take that risk and see where it can lead you. Do that with me. Please."

This man and that word. Still, it's not like I stood a chance anyway. I was his the moment I walked into his room and put on his shirt. Or maybe it was the night he cleaned up the cut on my face and then held me till I fell asleep.

I knew it was only a matter of time.

So, I say, "I'll try. But this doesn't affect Mason if it doesn't work out."

"Never," he promises me. "He'll always be our number one priority. But this *will* work out."

With that determination, he kisses me again. And enters me again. And by the time we fall asleep, snaked around each other, I can only hope this irresistibly risky move doesn't lead us both to ruin.

# 20

## ASHER

I'm singing The Cure's "Friday I'm in Love" even though it's not Friday. Thankfully, it's in my head, but I woke up before dawn —after very little sleep—and suddenly it's like I'm Robert Smith minus the makeup and wild hair. Wynter is still asleep in my arms, and I'm terrified to move so much as a twitch of a muscle and wake her because what if that pops this magical bubble? I get it now.

The fairy tales.

I'm even man enough to admit it.

But I suppose my very male question is, what happens in those stories after the prince gives his woman the very prim and proper and frankly boring kiss? Does he whisk her off to his castle and fuck her like mad? Does he steal her away behind her awful stepparent's estate and fuck her against the wall? How could he resist?

She's finally his.

The prince or beast or thief, or whatever he is, had to have been thinking about her pussy nonstop. So it only makes sense that he'd slip down her sweet, naked body and move her hips so she's fully supine, and then spread her thighs wide open. Right?

I mean, we are talking about the pussy of his dreams here.

"Asher?" My name is a question on the tail end of a moan when she feels what I'm doing.

"Were you expecting Prince Charming to be between your thighs?"

"I've always been partial to Flynn Ryder."

I grin against her wet skin. "At your service. My niece Katy loves all things Disney, and we went on a princess-watching binge."

Her hand slides beneath the covers, and she grips my hair in her fist. "But can a prince fuck me dirty like a villain can?"

Holy fuck. I'm legit in love. Like, no going back, this is it, she's my forever, I'm eternally obsessed, in love. It doesn't even hit me sideways or linger like a smile or a joke. It's like, yeah, bro, we've known this shit since you first laid eyes on her, so it's time you catch up.

"Oh, sweetheart. I've got the tongue and mind of a villain and the appearance and smile of a prince. I'm a freak in the sheets and a hot guy on the streets."

She laughs, but I quickly cut that off when I shove my tongue straight into her wet cunt. Her back arches and her grip tightens, but I love doing this. I'm the first man, and I already know I will be the last to do this to her. To make her come with my lips, tongue, and teeth. Those fools. What kinds of men was she with before now? How could anyone look at her, touch her, kiss her, and not want to make her scream out their name over and over again?

"Fuck my face, baby. Show me exactly what your pussy needs."

"You're very good at this," she hums in appreciation, wiggling her hips, seeking more contact.

I rip the blanket back so I can breathe better and so I can see her pretty face and tits. Her tits, man... they're fucking sensational. I slip my fingers inside her and give her a few good pumps, my eyes glued to hers. "I'm good at everything I love doing. But fucking you all the ways I can until you come is my new favorite. It's the challenge I can't help but want to keep winning."

"Always so competitive," she moans as I flick her clit with my tongue while my fingers pump in and out of her. Only having one good hand sucks. Because I *really* want to reach up and squeeze her tits right now. Unfortunately, that'll have to wait, but I'm not happy about it. Her head falls back, her eyes closing, as I increase my pace until her head snaps up and she pulls my hair to make me stop. "Wait. What time is it?"

I laugh, ringing her entrance with my finger. "You on the clock?"

"Yes. I have patients this morning starting at eight. And Mason."

I suck her clit into my mouth before releasing it with a wet kiss. "It's early. A little before six. When Mason wakes up, both of our phones will ping with a notification from the camera app's motion detector. Now shut up and enjoy the perks of being my woman."

I dive back into her pussy, making out with her clit as my fingers thrust back in.

Her thighs squeeze my head, and I know she's being extra cautious with my shoulder, but she's still pressing down on it, and fuck, it does *not* feel good.

"Roll over and put your ass in the air. I want to eat you from behind."

Worry strikes her features as her legs immediately remove themselves from me. "I'm sorry—"

I shake my head, cutting her off as I sit up and lean in to give her a dirty kiss, making her taste herself on my tongue. "I'm fine. On your hands and knees."

Her hands cup my face, deepening the kiss, and then she's moving, flipping over, her perfect fucking ass in the air, and I can't stop myself from admiring it with my mouth and my hands.

"Asher, I want you inside me. Now." Her head swivels over her shoulder, and that look in her eyes is my total undoing. But I don't want to fuck her on the bed, and I don't want to fuck her on all fours. We've done that. And we'll do it again a thousand more times at least, but right now I want to keep exploring. I want to try something new with her.

Climbing off the bed, I snatch a condom out of my nightstand drawer and then take her hand. She gives me a curious look but doesn't question me as I guide her to the sliding door that leads to the balcony off my bedroom. I unlock the door and then slide it open.

"What the hell?!" She tries to jerk her hand free of mine, only I grip it tighter and turn back to face her.

"Trust me?"

"I thought I did."

I grin. "No one will see you. The walls are thick and high, and the building next to mine has no balconies. I want to fuck you as the sun rises over Boston."

"You're sure no one will see me?"

I cup her face in my hand and layer my lips with hers. "I'd never let that happen. I'd never risk your safety or comfort for anything."

With a nervous nod, she lets me lead her out into the cool morning air. Whispering kisses of light trickle along her pale skin, making her glow like a radiant angel. Like an ethereal being, and I wrap my arms around her, tucking her chest against mine and then lowering us onto the chaise. We're surrounded by stone, tucked into an alcove of privacy, but we can both hear the sounds of the awakening city, ready to start its Monday.

I'd love to stand her up and fuck her as she stares down at the street, but maybe that's a game to play at night.

I roll the condom on, and then she lowers herself onto me. But instead of having her sit up and ride me, I bring her back down against my chest, her legs pressed together between mine as she settles perfectly over my cock.

"It'll be tight," I warn, and then groan just thinking about it. My good hand slings around her chest, fondling one full breast. And then I sink inside of her. Thrusting up, I angle my hips skyward, shoving myself in deeper. It steals her breath and makes her nails dig into my thigh. "You okay?"

"Yes. Don't stop. I love the feeling of being full of you."

My eyes pinch shut, and I blow out an uneven breath before I shoot my load this second. Wynter Hathaway is nothing if not candid and unapologetically honest, and I don't even think she realizes half the time just what a weapon that is, but fuck. It absolutely rips me apart time and time again.

"Then you better hold on because I'm going to fill you up so good, you'll feel what my cock did to you every time you move today."

My cock slides in, hitting her front wall with every fierce pound, rough as it meets resistance with our positions and keeps going. Her whole body is hot against mine, and her nipples are hard, and her pussy is like fucking magic with how it chokes my cock. My nose runs along her jaw, inhaling her sweet scent until I'm by her ear.

I press her deeper against my chest, my hips pistoning into her with all the strength I have in my thighs and ass. Her breathing is ragged, her hands gripping my thighs, and then I take the hand on her breast and slide it up and up until I'm wrapping my fingers around her neck.

"Tell me if this is too much."

Her grip on my thighs is crushing, and I know I'm pushing her past her point of comfort. I know I've taken control from her—something she thrives on—and am playing not just with that but with her ability to breathe. It's a lot. I'm fucking her outdoors, and I'm fucking her hard, and it's tight, and now I have my hand on her neck.

One of her hands flees my thighs and goes for the one I have wrapped around her neck. I expect her to pull my fingers away. I expect her to shake her head and tell me it's too much and that she's not the type of girl who would be into that.

What I don't expect is for her to cover my hand and squeeze, indicating that's what she wants me to do. With a feral growl, I sink my teeth into the soft flesh just below her ear, and then I squeeze her throat as I continue to pound into her.

She makes a noise and then swallows. The feel of her throat constricting and her muscles working beneath my palm drives me mad. I've never done this before with a woman, and I tell her that. I tell her this is another first for us and that makes her moan and clench.

Sweat covers me from head to toe, my body buzzing with endorphins and adrenaline and whatever the hell else it can throw at me. I never thought it was sexy to restrict breathing, and I'm not even sure why I'm doing it now with her other than it makes me feel like I'm collaring her. Like it's my ultimate form of possession and that if we can do this—trust each other with this—then we can do anything.

I'm her prince and her villain.

Her hero and her captor.

It turns my already hard cock into steel, and I pant in her ear as I fuck her like a man possessed while I restrict her breathing to the point where her moans become raspy, whispered cries. I cross my ankles over her shins, restricting her ability to move even more, having her at my total mercy.

I control how I fuck her. I control what she takes. I control how she breathes.

It's a total head trip and a mind fuck and something so new and forbidden and wild for me that I start to tremble with how my body reacts to it. With how good she feels.

"You belong to me," I grunt. "My beautiful queen."

And then I do something reckless. I release her neck, listening as she rakes in a sharp gust of air. I pull out of her and flip her over onto the chaise until she's lying on her stomach, her face resting on its side. Keeping her legs pressed firmly together, I climb back over her and rip the condom off.

Her eyes burst open wide, and she starts to move, but I press her back down with my hand in the center of her back. And then I start fucking her bare. Shoving myself into her, watching as my wet, glistening cock slides past her ass cheeks and into her tight, sweet heaven.

"Asher!"

"I know," I manage. "I'll pull out."

I know she's not on the pill. I know if I come inside her, I could get her pregnant again.

That thought makes me want to give her every ounce of cum I have, but I won't do that. Her eyes widen further but then roll back in her head as I start to screw her like a man possessed, my hand back on her throat, using it for leverage and breath play. I pound into her, angling forward and driving my fucks in deep and hard, penetrating her while targeting her front wall.

"You feel so good like this. So fucking good, and you're so goddamn tight and warm. I'm giving it to you rough, Wynter. That's the game we're playing now, but tonight, when you crawl into my bed, I'm going to fuck you so sweet, baby. So sweet your head will spin, and you'll come just as hard for me then as you're going to now."

Her lips are parted, and she's moaning, but it's quiet and low, and I have to bend closer to hear it. Her pussy starts quivering around me, clenching and unclenching, driving me to the point where I almost can't take it another second. I give her neck a solid squeeze, and then she's coming and coming, her body thrashing beneath me, her eyes closed and locked tight.

The moment she starts to come down, I remove my hand from her neck and pull out of her, using that hand to jerk myself until I'm coming all over her back with a savage roar. Stars burst behind my eyes, and then I collapse onto my good side, sighing and panting for air.

"I think that might be the hardest I've ever come in my life."

"Mmmm," is the only sound she makes.

Blinking open my eyes, I stare over at her, moving her to her side on the narrow chaise and running my fingers along her neck, shifting her head as I look for marks.

"Will I need makeup?" she asks softly, a little shaky, and I slide beside her as worry and guilt slam into me. I pull her body against mine and rest on my side so I can put my bad hand on her back. My cum is beneath my fingers, cold and wet, but I don't care.

I kiss her neck where my fingers held her and then pop up to meet her eyes. "No. It's just a little red, but it doesn't look like it'll bruise or anything. Are you okay? Was it too much? Did I go too far?"

"It was... unexpected." She giggles lightly, her lips spreading into a smile. "It's certainly not something I ever thought I'd try."

"Me neither, truth be told. You bring out a very possessive, feral beast in me. I'm sorry."

She shakes her head as she stares directly into my eyes. "Don't be. You didn't go too far. I never felt unsafe. And well"—she blushes—"I liked it."

I gaze down at her in wonder. "Yeah?"

"Yeah. It's not something I want to do all the time, but it was hot." She lets out another giggle. "You didn't wear a condom. Again."

I smirk, nuzzling against her. "I pulled out. Your back is covered in my cum. Now *that's* hot. Like seriously hot." I swirl it around with my fingers, painting her skin with it.

"You're a real caveman. But seriously, we're going to have to figure this out. I can't go on the pill, and it seems you have a problem with condoms."

"Only with you." No joke. I lose my mind and common sense with her. "But I agree. We need to figure something out, and I know you can't go on the pill. You told me last night it messes with your hormones, and I'd never want that for you. You're already cruel and bitchy to me."

She pokes my side and I laugh. "Only when you have it coming."

I kiss the tip of her nose. "You know I'm totally falling for you, right?"

She smiles and rolls her eyes dismissively. "I think that's all the dopamine your body is releasing talking."

It's not, but I don't argue it because she's the tortoise and I'm the hare. I'm always racing ahead, trying to outrun everyone, determined to win. Slowing down is not in my DNA, but if I don't wise up, I'll come on too strong, too fast and I'll lose her, which is not an option.

"Come on." I slowly maneuver myself up and off the chaise and then extend my good hand to her. "Let's get you cleaned up and ready for your day, Doctor."

She takes my hand, and we walk like that back inside. I close and relock the door, and then I walk us into the shower after checking the app and making sure Mason is still asleep. We shower together, talking about the day we both have ahead—me with calls to a few local sports talk radio shows and then in-home PT, and her with patients in the office. She told her boss she's not needed at the field now that she's fixed my shoulder, but I have a feeling that won't fly for long.

There's a reason Joe wanted her as the team doctor. I don't know him well, but from what I can tell, he's a methodical man. A planner. A deep thinker. He doesn't do anything on the fly. Which has me growing quiet as we exit the shower and head back into my room. She's about to leave. All of her stuff is in her room because this all happened last night, and I don't even know if I can ask her to move into my room or not.

What a fucking mess this all is.

But before that, I have to know this. I have to know what I'm up against with my coach. I'm lying to him by omission, and while my private life is my own, this part of my private life is potentially bleeding into my career.

"Wynter, what happened with your father?"

She stops midsentence—because she was talking about something I wasn't listening to—and then turns to face me.

She takes a step away from me and opens her mouth when two things happen at once. Our phones start blowing up with pings from the camera app, and the sound of Mason crying reaches us all the way across the apartment. We both run down the hall and straight into his room. He's fine, just fussy and wanting out of his crib.

Wynter goes to him, tucking her towel in tighter against her chest, and then picking him up. She kisses his forehead and then starts speaking softly. "He's starting daycare at the hospital today."

I blink, my head on a swivel as I take her in. "He is? I didn't know that was even a thing."

She gives me a sheepish look without meeting my eyes. "Yes. Sorry. I registered him for it when I started at the hospital, but there was a waitlist. I got the text yesterday that he's able to start there today."

"Oh." I'm not even sure what to say. Her tone is off, and so is her body language.

"It'll be better that way. Makes it a lot easier for me not having to take him back and forth to my parents' house."

"Right. Makes sense." Only I was hoping I'd get to spend time with him today. That he'd be hanging around with Wynter's mom watching him here.

"Yeah, so we need to get going. I'm going to get him dressed and then bring him into my room with me while I get myself ready."

I frown. "You don't have to do that. I can watch him. My call isn't until later this morning, and my game film can wait."

She waves me away with a smile that doesn't reach her eyes. "It's fine. I'm used to it. I know you have a busy day too. I'll make us all eggs before we leave though. He loves it when you feed him."

She carries him over to his changing table and starts to get him out of his pajamas, and I have no idea what I'm supposed to say or do now. She told me she'd try with me, and we spent an incredible night and morning together, but since I mentioned her father, it's like I shut out her light. A switch has been flipped in her head, and I have no idea how to fix that.

All day, I haven't been able to stop thinking about it. My reaction. Asher asked me a simple question. One he's entitled to ask and to know about, and I mentally shut down. On him. On myself. On everything. It needs to stop, but I don't know how to make it.

I drop off Mason at his new daycare—he does better with the drop-off than I do—and then, with thirty minutes to spare before my first patient, I call my mom.

"How'd it go with dropping Mason off?" she asks. I shut the door to my office and then collapse into my chair.

"Good. He did great. It's not his first time in daycare, so it was like he never left."

"Wonderful. But why do you sound anything but?"

I blow out a breath, running my finger along the edge of my desk. "I'm with Asher now." The words come out sounding hollow, and they feel that way in my chest. It's strange to say that aloud. I'm not sure I've ever truly considered myself *with* someone before and this isn't a small thing. I'm not casually dating him. There is no casually dating the father of your child, and if this doesn't work out...

"When did that happen?"

"Last night, but I saw it coming for a while. At least he hasn't been shy about letting me know that's what he wants."

"Yes," she agrees. "I knew that too. He wasn't shy about telling me that either. Are you not feeling good about that decision? Did you make it for the wrong reasons?"

A wry grin hits my lips but quickly fades. "I am feeling good about it. Asher is..." I fade off as I think about this, leaning back in my chair. "Impossible not to like. He's funny and charming and sweet, and in my heart, I believe him to be a good man. I mean, he didn't even hesitate when I told him about Mason. Not even for a second. It was like, okay, I'm in."

"Then what's going on?"

I stare down at my hands. "He asked me about Joe this morning, and I froze. Suddenly I was hit with every reason why I hate football and football players and why I don't trust men. I'm thirty-one years old, Mom. I was five when Joe left. Why am I still like this?"

"Because you were five when Joe left, and it was traumatizing." She sighs. "I didn't do the best job with it either. I was heartbroken myself, and I tried to comfort you and make you believe it wasn't your fault, but you blamed yourself for catching him with Loretta, and you blamed yourself for him leaving because he told you both were your fault. They weren't, but you didn't believe that. Then you grew bitter and angry and resentful when he cut you out. I don't know. I should have put you in therapy, but then you started skating, and Gary came along, and you seemed better. I didn't know how deep all of this went with you until much, much later."

"I don't want to be this mother to Mason. I love Gary, and I trust Gary. He's my dad. But I am inherently distrustful of every other man. With Asher, it's as if I'm waiting for the other shoe to drop, and it has me on edge. I don't want him to prove me right, and so far, he's given me no reason to think he will. But that doesn't mean I trust him yet."

"How about this, then? I'll take Mason tonight, and you and Asher have an evening for just the two of you. Talk to him. See what he has to say. Give him a chance. Remember, Wyn, if I had never reopened my heart after Joe, I wouldn't have met Gary. Try to imagine that Asher is your Gary and not your Joe."

I swallow past the lump in my throat and nod even though she can't see me.

"Okay. I'll talk to Asher tonight."

I disconnect the call and then go and see patients, already feeling lighter after speaking to my mother. But more than that, I'm back in the hospital. I'm doing injections and scheduling surgeries. I'm the doctor I've always dreamed of being. Mason is downstairs in the daycare, and I feel like I'm finding that groove. The one I've been searching for since I found out I was pregnant with him.

There's only one thing that can derail that.

"Joe Cardone says he needs you back on the field tomorrow," Dr. Limp—er Limbick says to me just as I leave a patient room. I sag. Dammit. Limbick gives me a displeased look. "You told me that he didn't require you there. What's going on, Wynter? We don't typically blow off our high-profile clients and patients here."

"He's my father," I admit, moving over to an empty patient room so our conversation is private. "Joe Cardone is my biological father, and we do not have the best history with each other."

Limbick shuts the door behind himself and then leans against it. "I figured it had to be something like that since he was so adamant it be you and no one else. You had just started with us and are a new attending. It didn't make a lot of sense." He folds his arms. "Still, it's the Boston Rebels." Meaning over his dead body will he give up the prestige and income that comes with them. I don't blame him for that. "Joe says it can only be you. I don't want to put you in a position where you're uncomfortable, but I don't know what else to do."

My hands go to my hips. I asked Joe why me when I first started there. I asked him what he was trying to do by forcing me to be there. And he gave me no straight answers. But unless I want to quit—which isn't an option—I'm stuck.

"I'll be fine. I can handle it. I'll report back to the field tomorrow."

ALL THE LEVITY I felt after my call with my mom vanished the moment I was done talking to Limbick. Not even five minutes later, a text from Joe came in.

Joe: See you back here tomorrow morning.

I didn't reply. Anything I would have responded with would have been impudently childish, and that is not the woman or doctor I want to be. Then the last patient of the day was a total asshole. A retired football player—I swear I can't make this shit up—who demanded I give him a cortisone injection even though his last films are over three years old, and he's had two this year already. He needs knee replacement but wasn't happy hearing that from a woman, so he called me a lying bitch and stormed out. The only reason he was on my schedule was because his last—male—doctor told him the same thing, and he didn't like it then either.

Whatever.

I drop Mason at my mom's, and then on my drive home, I try calling Asher. He doesn't pick up, so I text him letting him know the plan for the night. Twenty minutes later, I park in my spot in the garage and fly up the elevator. But the moment I enter the apartment, my skin prickles with awareness, and my feet turn to lead, begging me not to move. Not to explore. Not to seek out the source of what I'm hearing.

Asher grunting and groaning. A female moaning. A repetitive smacking sound.

My heart gallops in my chest, and the backs of my eyes burn in shame and humiliation. I'm so sick I'm shaking with it. The reaction comes on so swiftly it actually shocks me, zapping any logical thought from my mind.

"Yes, Ash. More. Give me more."

He groans louder. "Fuck, Sara. Jesus."

I creep along, getting closer to his bedroom, where the sound appears to be coming from. Only a flash of something in his gym stops me, and I pause, finding the reflection in the mirror. Asher is shirtless sitting on a workout bench, and a blonde woman in a sports bra is straddling him. Bouncing on him. I forgot he has physical therapy today, and I know he has a female therapist in his crew, though I haven't met her, and I'm positive that's what that is, but...

Why is she in a sports bra? And why is she straddling and bouncing on him? He wouldn't be the first athlete to fuck his therapist.

"Yes." Her voice is ragged and breathless. "There. That's it. More, more, more. Don't stop," she begs.

"Fuck! Yes!" Asher cries out, his face pinched up in concentration, flushed and sweaty. He sounds exactly as he did this morning on his balcony when he was inside me. Out of nowhere, my father's words to my mother all those years ago venomously snake through me. *There's only so much of one woman a man can take before he grows bored.*

My hand slams over my mouth to stifle my sob, and then before I know what I'm doing, I'm running for the door, needing to flee. Hot tears stream down my face the moment the elevator doors close and I fall back against the metal wall, barely able to catch my breath.

What do I do?

I make it to my car on autopilot, and then I'm peeling out, driving away from the building. Deep, shaking breaths burn my lungs, and I do my best to clear my thoughts. I try to think this through logically. But I can't do it. All I can see is her on his lap. All I can hear are the sounds they were making.

Music blasts through the speakers of my ancient car as I drive out to the skating rink. I need to be alone. I need to skate and lose myself for a bit before I'm forced to deal with this. The rink is magnificently empty, dark, and cool as I set my bag down on the ground and pull out my skates. The tears keep coming, but they begin to stall along with my thoughts.

I keep coming back to one question: Would Asher really do that to me?

I know what I heard, and I know what I saw. But my brain and my heart are having trouble reconciling that with the man I've come to know over the last few weeks. No. I don't think Asher would do that. And I'm furious with myself for running and not seeing the entire picture for myself.

I want to trust him.

I don't want to be the scarred, damaged girl anymore. The one who sets up roadblocks and is afraid of any man who speaks to her. I've avoided getting my heart broken for so long, and I believe it's served me well. But maybe it's time I run toward someone instead of away from them.

Maybe the risk will be worth the fall.

Then again, when I was five, I never would have imagined my father would ruthlessly cheat on my mother right under her nose and then not only blame me for it because I caught him in the act but then abandon me.

Only... that's not Asher. He's never been that man.

Still working through my thoughts, I lace up my skates and push myself onto the ice, skating around as I slip my AirPods into my ears and then unlock my phone. I have three missed calls from Asher as well as about a half dozen texts that I didn't notice. The blaring music in my car must have drowned out the sound.

I come to a stop, pulling up the first message, when movement out of the corner of my eye startles me so badly that I drop my phone onto the ice.

Absently I know it broke. I could hear the crack.

But I can't remove my gaze from the man walking my way.

# 22

### ASHER

"Come on, Ash. That's weak as hell. You can do better."

I growl out a slew of curses as I pull on the resistance band, working on rebuilding the strength in my arm and shoulder. "I hate you," I snarl.

"You'll love me in November."

"Fuck November. Tell me October."

"If you want October, I need to see more sweat."

More sweat? The woman wants more of my sweat? Any more and I'm going to pass out from dehydration. Sara is one of the two sadists I've hired to help me rehab, but considering this is my first major injury, I had no clue what I was in for.

"I can't do it."

I release the band and fall back on the bench when my shoulder feels like it's about to give out. My good arm falls over my eyes, and I die just a little. I'm in pain. Like serious fucking pain. It's also the good kind of pain that you feel when something is healing and you're working it hard, but still.

"Come on, pussy. My wife lifts more than you do."

Sara drops herself on my lap and smacks my abs, making me flinch and wince. "I hate you."

"So you keep saying. Come on, Ash. Sit up. Give me five more reps, and then you can call it quits. Until tomorrow, of course."

With a toddler-quality pout and moan, I sit up and take the band from her hands.

"I get a drink after this."

She nods. "Sure. A sports or protein one."

"Have I mentioned I hate you?"

"Only fifteen times today, which I consider an improvement from last week. Five more. Let's do it."

Five more. I can do five more. And then I'm going to fill a bathtub with ice and drop myself into it. And then, after that, I'm going to take the longest shower of my life. And then after that, I'm going to be too tired to do anything other than eat and snuggle with my girl and my baby.

Shit. I hope Wynter isn't looking for sex tonight because I'm not sure I'll have any stamina left in me. I told her I'd give it to her sweet after giving it to her so rough this morning, but I'm not sure I can move.

"You're ruining my sex life," I tell her.

Sara rolls her eyes. "You're supposed to be a professional athlete. Man up and give your woman the orgasms I'm positive she deserves for putting up with you. We grow bored if you don't, though, for the life of me, I can't imagine why my fairer sex turns to your lesser breed for anything, including sex."

"I'm not sure how to comment on that."

She gives me an annoyed look because she knows I'm stalling. "Then don't. Go!"

"Argh! Okay." I start to stretch the band outward across my chest, moving my shoulders back and my elbows out to my sides. And FUCK! It hurts worse than it did five minutes ago.

"Yes, Ash. More. Give me more."

A groan tears from my throat. "Fuck, Sara. Jesus."

I'm dying. I am. The band retracts, and then I do it two more times. Each time pushing myself a little farther than the last.

"Yes." Sara's voice climbs with excitement as she bounces on my lower thighs. "There. That's it. More, more, more. Don't stop," she encourages.

"Fuck! Yes!" After the fifth one, the band snaps from my hand, and I fall back once again.

"You did it!"

"I did it. Someone lead me to the ice."

A strange noise jolts me upright and has Sara's head turning over her shoulder as she stands. "What was that? It sounded like—"

"A cry."

Her brows furrow. "Yeah. I was thinking that, but it didn't make sense—"

Her words are sharply cut off a second time by the slamming of my front door. Automatically, I'm on my feet. "Fuck. What time is it?"

I look down at my Apple Watch. It's already after five. How did that happen? That must have been Wynter, but why did it sound like she was crying, and why did she come home only to immediately leave?

Something must have happened.

"I'll see you tomorrow, Sara." I fly out of my gym and into the hallway, but I'm too late to catch the elevator, even as I slam my fist into the button. I race back inside, searching for a T-shirt and sneakers. I dial up Wynter's phone, but it rings and rings only to go to voicemail. Same thing when I call the second and third time.

Then I start with the texts that also go unanswered.

By the time I make it to my car and pull out onto the street, I'm worried out of my mind about Mason and call her mother.

"He's fine. I have him for the night," her mother tells me.

"For the night?"

"Yes," she says, her voice catching a bit on the end in surprise by my tone. This is all news to me. "Didn't she tell you?"

"No," I start to say, only to pause when I reach the traffic light and scroll through my texts from her. "Yes. She did, only I didn't see her text until now. She said she wanted to talk, but then she ran out, and I don't know why."

"If she's anywhere, she's on the ice. You'll be able to find her there. And Asher, what she wanted to talk to you about?"

"Yeah?"

"It's about your coach."

"Her father."

"Her father," she echoes. "He did a real number on her. Be gentle."

My fists clench the steering wheel so hard the leather creaks. "I will."

She disconnects the call, and a moment later, a text pings in with the address of the rink. But her mother's words reverberate through my skull. *He did a real number on her.* And I had Sara on my lap. Not that it was the least bit sexual, but if Wynter walked in and saw Sara like that... it would be easy to misinterpret.

Is that what happened? Is that what caused her to run?

Is her trust truly that thin?

I know the answer. I've known it for weeks. Now I have to figure out a way to change that.

I arrive at the rink and discover that her car is the only one there. That instantly drives me crazy. Does she have any clue how vulnerable that makes her? This is where she had to go?

But it's more than that, and it's more than her being alone in this building.

It's Joe. I need to learn once and for all just what he did to her before I seek him out and ruin his life for ruining hers.

I enter the dark building, past the spectator area, and over to the glowing ice, illuminated by a few soft bulbs overhead. Wynter is aimlessly gliding around the ice, staring down at her phone. I watch her for a moment, her face splotchy and her eyes red-rimmed. Has it not reached her giant brain yet that I fucking love her and would never, *could* never hurt her?

I step onto the ice, walking carefully in her direction when she catches sight of me and drops her phone. The phone cracks immediately, the glass splintering. But her eyes never leave mine.

"What are you doing here?"

I don't stop until my good hand dives into her hair and my bad one does its best to wrap around her waist, and then I'm pulling her into my body and slamming my lips down on hers. I kiss her deeply, her head angled, her back arched, her body knitted against mine. My tongue sweeps against hers, claiming, possessing, telling her with unequivocal certainty that I am hers and no one else's.

She kisses me back, which feels like a miracle, and then after a few minutes, I pull back and hold her face in the palm of my hand. "You ran. So I did what I always do with you. I chased."

Her head tilts up toward the rafter-exposed ceiling, her eyes glassing over. "You weren't having sex with that woman."

Somehow it doesn't come out as a question, though I answer her all the same. "No."

She gulps and nods. "I knew it. I mean, I didn't know it. It took me longer than it should have to realize that. I saw her on your lap. Both of you half-naked. She was bouncing. I heard you. I heard her. And my brain short-circuited."

"Sara is one of my trainers. It was groans of pain and over-worked muscles. Trust me, it was awful and not the least bit pleasurable."

Another nod. "I overreacted, and I ran, but... part of me knew that whatever I was seeing wasn't what was actually happening. It just took me a bit to grasp that because it didn't look good. And I think I'm..."

"You think you're what?"

She shakes her head, refusing to answer.

"Sara's married to a woman, and they have three boys together—which I secretly love because they torture and abuse her the way she tortures and abuses me."

A shaky laugh. "I'm sorry I ran."

"Look at me, Wynter." I force her stormy green gaze to mine. "Don't apologize for running and don't apologize for caring enough about me to be hurt and upset. I'll continue chasing because you're worth catching."

I want to tell her. I want to look into her eyes and tell her that I think I'm in love with her. That I think I've been in love with her since she walked into the bathroom of a club and smiled at me.

Except I can't force the words out.

I've never said them to a woman before, and once I do, once I set them free and they become hers, there is no more trying. There is no more attempting to see where this goes. I'll need her more than I already do, and that will scare her. It's too much too soon, and too far too fast.

So instead, I seal my lips and I leave it at that.

Her body leans into mine, her hand climbing up my back and into my hair. I press my forehead to hers, and she emits a soft sigh that turns into a gentle hum.

"What I was going to say before is, I think I'm pretty messed up. I have a serious fear of abandonment along with some massive, preconceived notions that I'll be cheated on. I don't think all men are evil, but I don't trust them either."

"Will you explain why to me?"

"Here?" She laughs the word and then pulls back, looking around at the abandoned ice rink surrounding us.

"Yes. I can't tell you how sore I am, and the cold air feels amazing. I'm honestly contemplating lying down on the ice and watching you skate. You ran out before I could take an ice bath or even a shower after. I'm positive I don't smell very good right now."

She smiles up at me. "You actually smell pretty good. Even your sweat is sweet." She kisses my neck. "You lie down on the ice, and I'll skate and talk."

She laughs at how quickly I release her and do just that, my body thanking me even though the ice is obviously freezing and isn't the most pleasant or accommodating.

"Too bad you don't have your skates. I could show you some moves."

I squint up at her, using my good hand to block the overhead lights from shining straight into my eyes. "Even if my shoulder or body were up to it, I wouldn't risk it. I haven't skated since I was fifteen and Suzie made me go on a double date with her and Zax."

"Oh? Who was the girl?"

I think about it for a moment. "I don't remember her name. Only that she let me get to second base behind the concession stand."

She rolls her eyes at me, but she can't fight her smile. I'll admit, when I initially chased after her, I thought I was going to have a lot of explaining and groveling to do. I'm beyond floored by her trust and faith in me.

"Show me how pretty you skate. I want to see all the moves."

She twists around and starts skating backward, her eyes still on me as I lie here like a gimpy starfish. She flips around and skates away from me as she starts to talk. "On my fifth birthday, I fell out of the tree in our front yard, breaking my arm. My mom was out, grabbing some last-minute items for the party I was having later that day. My dad and her best friend were inside, supposedly setting up, but when I screamed for help, no one came." She goes into a spin, her head tilted back, and her hands arched behind her back, holding the blade of her skate and her leg up to her head, as she twirls around and around. When she's done with her spin she continues with her story. "When I went inside, I'm sure you can imagine what I walked in on."

I grimace. The thought of a five-year-old child walking in on her parent having sex with another person is repugnant.

"I didn't know what they were doing," she admits, coming to a stop and then pushing off again, just skating around, twisting and spinning and moving across the ice. "My father yelled at me for being stupid enough to climb the tree and then fall out of it as he shoved himself back into his clothes, and my mother's friend sat there with a stunned look on her face since my bone was protruding through my skin. I made him call my mother, and at first, he wouldn't let me talk to her, but I was screaming and crying and in so much pain, and I could hear her yelling at him to call an ambulance. He told her it would make the news if he did. Like somehow the potential disgrace of his child being injured was more important to him than getting me medical attention. Anyway, he drove me to the hospital, and my mother met him there, and I told her exactly what happened when she asked."

She increases her speed and launches herself into a jump, twisting around at least twice before landing on one skate. I clap my hands, and she gives me a curtsy before skating back over to me, stopping a few feet away.

"They fought in the room beside mine, and I heard everything he said. He told her that a man grows bored with only one woman after a while and then he blamed me for everything. He said having a kid wasn't what he wanted and that it was holding his career back. He said if I hadn't fallen out of the tree, I wouldn't have seen anything, and then my mother could have continued to be pleasantly blind to his affairs. Those are the words he said. Pleasantly blind to his affairs."

She puffs out a breath and then takes a seat on the ice beside me, her hands in her lap and her legs stretched outward, crossed at the ankles.

I reach over with my good hand and take one of hers, resting it on her lap.

"He left after that. He didn't even stick around for when I had surgery. He told me he was leaving and that he might not see me for a long time. By the time I got out of the hospital, he had moved, somehow got himself traded to a new team, and that was that. I'd call him from my mom's phone and leave him voice messages. I'd apologize and beg him to come home. I'd promise to be good and never cause trouble. He never called me back. He never reached out. That morning I ran into you in the bathroom at the stadium was the first time I saw him in twenty-six years."

Jesus. What a motherfucker. What kind of man does that, not only to their wife but to their child? Who puts that sort of bullshit blame on a five-year-old when the fault lies at his feet and no one else's and then abandons them completely?

She can see I'm burning with rage and runs the fingers of her other hand across my face, trying to smooth out my scowl and furrow, but to no avail. I see red. A haze so thick and deep and consuming, I can practically taste it.

It's bloodlust.

I want to kill the man with my bare hands.

"He's not a man." The words cleave past my lips with a razor-sharp edge. Maybe I shouldn't have said that, but it's true. I force myself to rein in my temper. "That's why you hate football players."

Her fingers comb through my sweat-damp hair. "I did. Now I just hate him."

"I'm not him."

She nods. "I know."

"I won't ever be him."

She smiles and leans down, kissing my lips. "I know," she whispers against me before sitting back up. "I have a lot of old wounds I never worked at trying to heal. You asked me to try with you, and I can't think of a more perfect way to put it. I want to try and heal this. With you."

"If I could move, I'd kiss you."

She laughs, the sound loud as it hits the hard surfaces and echoes back to us. "Good thing I'm flexible and can kiss you." She bends in half and kisses me again, only this time I slip her some tongue.

"Your mom told me we have a kid-free night."

She nips my bottom lip. "You called my mother?"

"How else do you think I knew where to find you?"

"I like that you're determined."

"Determined is my middle name. Along with hot cock."

She chokes out a noise. "Asher Determined Hot Cock Reyes?"

"At your service, Doctor."

She giggles, and I'm not sure I've ever heard her laugh this much.

"I don't suppose I can talk you into having dinner out with me?"

She sits back up, and I force myself to do the same, even though every muscle in my body is screaming at me.

"Nope. Not gonna happen. Considering the paparazzi have been living outside your building hoping to catch you with a woman or get a soundbite about your shoulder, I'm all set."

"That's been a bit of a bitch. Okay. Quiet dinner at home. With candles. And no clothes. Maybe a naked movie too."

"A naked candle-lit dinner and a movie?" She raises an eyebrow.

"What?" I feign innocence. "Isn't that how you do them?"

"I suppose it is tonight."

"Damn straight."

"After you shower."

"After I shower," I agree. "Help me up?" I bat my eyelashes at her, and she rolls her pretty green eyes at me but does it anyway, and when we're both upright, I take her into my arms and kiss her because I have to kiss her until we're both breathless. I have to kiss her so she knows it's real, but also so I do too.

I have my first real girlfriend since... I don't know. Maybe ever. None of those other girls count when I think about them versus her. The stakes are high. The risk is extreme. I might end up indicted for murder after I kill my coach, but the jury will let me off once they know the story and I smile at them a few times.

I don't dwell on the negative. I focus on what I have control over and let fate drive the rest. But since my shoulder injury and my position on the team became uncertain and Wynter walked back into my life with a child I knew nothing about, I feel as though things are spinning too fast on a trajectory I can't direct. I have too many balls up in the air, and at any moment, one could be intercepted, and this will all fall apart on me.

As I drive home, keeping Wynter in front of me because I hate her driving that goddamn car, I can't stop thinking... just let me hold onto this for as long as I can.

# 23

## WYNTER

Somehow, I beat Asher back to the condo, but after I enter the apartment, I get a text from him.

Asher: Meet me on the roof.

A surge of jitters shoots through me as I immediately get in the shower. Only five minutes later, when I'm putting a razor to my leg, the glass door opens, and in walks a naked Asher.

"I said to meet me on the roof."

"And I had to shave my legs," I sharply retort.

"That's not nearly as fun as naked swimming."

I glance over my shoulder at him, raising an eyebrow and catching him staring at my ass. Considering I have one foot propped up on the bench, I'm giving him an unholy view he's taking full advantage of. "What's it with you and naked events?"

He grins devilishly when he realizes I caught him. His hands go to my hips, his thumbs dragging along my wet skin. "You're the Olympian. I'm merely following in your predecessor's footsteps."

"Are you sending out a tribute to Zeus or me?" I quip.

"Both." He wraps his arm around me, pulling me upright. "Come up on the roof with me. I ordered food, and we can pull up a movie on one of the televisions, and then swim under the stars."

My head falls to his chest. "You're good at this."

"I've never done it before, so I'm happy to hear that. Incidentally, do you think you can wear the gold medal and nothing else?"

I smirk. "Football will never be an Olympic sport."

I can feel his returning smirk against my neck. "Now you're just crushing my dreams."

"If you leave, I might let you try it on later."

"Fine. Finish shaving, but I'm not leaving. Pass the shampoo." I roll my eyes but hand him the bottle. "Do you think you want to move into my room?" he asks, and I freeze mid-swipe of my razor. "You don't have to, and I'm not trying to pressure you before you're ready for that," he continues when I don't reply, stepping beneath the spray to wash out the shampoo from his hair. "I figured it would make more sense since we both know you already like sleeping in my bed and clothes and there is always the risk of thunderstorms and nightmares that you'll need me to rescue you from."

I shake my head, biting into my bottom lip as I resume my shaving. "Are you always going to be this clingy?"

"Clingy?" he chokes, stealing my body wash and using it on himself.

I roll my head over my shoulder and meet his perplexed gaze. "You're a bit obsessed with me," I note.

He gives me that sexy, self-assured, cocky grin. "You have no idea how much."

"I'll think about moving into your room."

"Just remember, I may be clingy, but I make up for it with orgasms." He gives me a wink and then steps out of the shower. "Rooftop, Doctor. I'll be waiting."

He steps out of the shower, wraps a white towel around his waist, and then leaves. Lord, I am in a lot of trouble with that man. I finish shaving and showering, and then I get myself dried off and ready. Despite what he says, I am not going up to the rooftop naked. I brush out my hair and put on a bit of makeup, and then after deliberating for too long, I decide on a tank top with a shelf bra and cotton shorts.

By the time I wind my way up the stairs, my stomach is rumbling. Asher is sitting at a table between the bar and the pool, staring at his phone, but when he catches me approaching, his face lights up, and my heart skips a beat accordingly.

"You're not naked," he accuses.

"Neither are you." He's wearing a blue shirt that makes his eyes appear nearly the same color, and joggers.

He stands, and then pulls out the chair beside his for me, taking my hand and helping me into it. "I knew you wouldn't come up here naked. It's fine. I'll enjoy stripping you down later."

He takes his seat and then opens up the bags of food. My stomach rumbles again, much louder this time, and I giggle.

He cocks an eyebrow. "Hungry?"

"Shut up. It's late."

"It is." He yawns.

"Tired?"

"Shut up. I worked hard today."

He opens the bag of food and takes out a bunch of sushi. "I didn't think this place delivered," I tell him, lifting one of the cartons.

"They don't. It's Callan's restaurant. Well, he's a secret owner of it, but they deliver for me. Dig in."

These guys, with their fame and money, are something else.

We both start munching down, too hungry to even talk. The roof is open, sending in a late summer breeze that feels nothing short of heavenly. The only lighting is two hurricane lanterns with fake candles in them and multiple strings of Edison bulbs that line the glass wall on the other side of the pool. It gives it a very romantic feel.

Dining on the roof of a building under the stars like this is nothing short of fantasy-like, and I know that's what he was going for. He's trying to win my heart and make falling in love with him irresistible. It's easy to let him continue to sweep me off my feet, but I'd be a fool not to force myself to stay grounded too.

We finish eating, both of us contently full until he gets a mischievous glimmer in his eyes.

"What is it?"

"Want to go on an adventure with me?"

I laugh. "What kind of adventure?"

"I don't have dessert here." He sits up. "I don't eat junk during the season."

"I'm not following," I admit.

"I want to get you something sweet and I know a cookie place not too far from here. They make these peanut butter protein bomb things that have no sugar or carbs."

I scrunch up my nose. "Sounds delicious."

He chuckles. "They're an acquired taste, but their regular cookies are amazing."

"I thought you said you were tired."

"I've gotten my second wind. Come on. It'll be fun."

He grabs my hand and pulls me up to my feet. "What are you doing? We can't go out together."

"Sure, we can. We're under the cloak of darkness. We'll sneak out the back way and slink around the city."

He grabs the to-go bag filled with the remains of our dinner, and then we're flying down the stairs, back into the apartment. The bag gets thrown into the trash, and then he's tossing the flip-flops I have by the front door at me. I slip them on as he's stuffing his giant feet into his sneakers and throwing on a Red Sox ball cap.

"Let's do this shit."

"Wait! I don't have my purse or my phone!" I cry out as he flings the door open and pushes me through.

"I have money and my phone. If your mom needs us, she'll call me."

The elevator chimes, and then we step on, quickly descending to the first floor of the building. He steps out first, glancing left toward the front entrance. The doorman is helping a woman with two large suitcases into the building, and Asher gives my hand a squeeze, nodding to the right.

"What?"

He gives me a look. "You're the worst on covert missions. Go!" Without waiting for my reply, he races off in the direction of the back of the building, his body ducked down as he weaves us toward the back exit. Paparazzi have been populating the front of the building like cockroaches in a New York City basement. It's been aggravating the hell out of everyone in the building, but especially Asher.

We reach the back exit unobserved, and then he flings the door open, putting us on a side street in Beacon Hill. "Where to next, Mission Impossible?"

"This way."

We start down the street, holding hands and chatting about Mason's first day of daycare and how I have to report back to the field tomorrow.

"You do know it will be damn impossible for me not to want to kick his ass, right?" Asher states as we turn left toward Beacon Street, making a loop around the neighborhood simply to avoid the front of the building.

"You can't. Not if you want to keep your position on the team. Separation of church and state," I tell him.

"You're my church, and football is my state? Is that how we're playing this?"

"The roles are up to you. All I'm saying is, I don't need you to fight my battles for me. Especially not with your coach. We agreed to keep us separate from the world, and that includes football."

"My queen, that was when you were only my baby mama. Now you're my woman and my baby mama. The game has changed."

"But the stakes haven't. If anything, they're higher now." I glance up at him as we walk. His face is trained ahead, but I can tell he's not happy about this. I appreciate that he's protective of me, but facing off with Joe won't benefit either of us.

Thankfully, he lets it drop, and when we turn the corner on Beacon, heading away from his building he hisses out a curse. "Freaking rats. You'd think they'd have moved on by now. They've never been all over me like this before. That's always been one of the beauties of Boston. It's not New York or LA. The press usually gives us breathing room."

"Not anymore it seems."

He grunts in dismay and quickens our pace, keeping his head tilted down, the brim of his hat shadowing his face. The dude is six-seven and built, well, like a football player. He stands out no matter what. After another block, we stop in front of a shop with neon blue signage.

"That's The Way...?" I read questioningly.

"The cookie crumbles," he finishes for me. "It's a play on words, even though they never finished the sentence."

"Got it. Very cute."

He opens the door and leads me in, but I pause, jerking my hand from his. He turns his head to find me, and I shake my head, staring around the shop that has about a half-dozen patrons plus the staff inside.

"I come in here enough that the staff all know me, and I tip them like I'm a Kennedy for their quiet loyalty. It'll be fine."

"What about them?" I bounce my head in the direction of the occupied tables.

He shrugs. "Maybe they won't notice."

I give him a *you cannot be serious* look.

"It'll be a test."

He retakes my hand and drags my reluctant body inside and up to the counter.

"Ash! Hey, man!" one of the kids behind the counter crows, reaching out his fist. Asher releases my hand and gives him a fist pump.

"Hey, Kev. How's it going? How's school?"

"Good!" the kid exclaims. "Senior year is coming this fall. It'll be epic. What can I get you"—his gaze swishes over to me—"and your lady friend tonight?" That's the moment we hear the click of a camera phone behind us.

I stomp on Asher's foot, and he winces. "This is actually the amazing doctor who saved my shoulder. I wanted to thank her by buying her the best cookies in the city." He turns around and addresses the café full of people who are all staring at us. "And if you all delete any pictures or videos you just took and promise not to post anything about my lovely doctor who is very camera shy, I will buy you all cookies, sign anything you want me to sign, and have my assistant send you each a ticket to a game this year."

That quickly wins everyone over, and Asher ends up dropping hundreds on cookies and taking selfies—which he's fine with—and signing everything anyone hands him with the marker he keeps in his pocket at all times. He also texts Freddy to inform him of the offer he just made and gets a returning thumbs-up.

By the time we leave the cookie shop, I've eaten my weight in salted caramel and chocolate chip cookies, and Asher has a very contended smile on his lips.

"You love that," I remark. "Don't you?"

He gives a half-shrug as we stroll. "What's not to love? It's a trip that's never gotten old. I like signing autographs and taking selfies and dropping money to make someone's day better. I love being able to pay it forward. It's why I love going to the hospital. All I do is throw a ball around a field, but it's magic to those people and those kids, and I think that's the coolest part of this gig. Sure, it's annoying when I can't leave my apartment or take my girlfriend and son out to the park without being mobbed or photographed. But I've been dealing with the celebrity side of life since I was sixteen, so it's not new, and for the most part, I've learned how to manage it."

"I don't know how you do it," I admit. "I never had anything like that when I was skating. Not even with endorsements or winning gold."

"You'll get used to it."

That thought hits me, and hits me hard. Regardless of this thing between the two of us, Mason being Asher's son, will be in the spotlight. I didn't get knocked up by a regular guy; I got knocked up by a football god. A man who stems from a family of football legends. My instinct is to shelter and protect Mason from all of that, but the clock is already ticking on that particular time bomb.

The world will discover what we've been hiding sooner or later.

And when they do, they'll want a piece of it for themselves.

We reach the back door of the building and slip back inside, both of us quiet and a bit stoic. It's late, and we're both exhausted. Wordlessly, he guides me down the hall to his room, even though I never told him I'd move in here with him. We brush our teeth, and then he exits the bathroom to give me privacy.

I wash my face, fighting the jolt of butterflies that comes over me. Last night, this all sparked into action, but tonight we're actually doing this. It's real now. I'm his girlfriend. That's what he called me, and I told myself I was done with second-guessing when Asher walked out on the ice after chasing after me.

Something catches my eye and brings a smirk to my lips. He has a T-shirt in here, slung over the side of his bathtub. It's a team shirt with his number and name on it. I strip out of my clothes and slip it on, the soft cotton falling around the middle of my thighs. The butterflies only intensify as I switch off the light and step into the dark bedroom.

My feet pad softly toward the edge of the bed, and then a laugh tickles the back of my throat. Asher is shirtless, on his back, his reddish-brown hair already rumpled because he's fast asleep. His breaths are deep and slow, his full lips softly parted.

"So much for the end to our hot date," I whisper, running my hand through his soft hair, reveling at how I can do that now. At how this larger-than-life man is now mine. I'm going to fall in love with him. I'm positive of it. And it scares the absolute crap out of me.

# 24

---

## ASHER

After falling asleep before sealing the deal on my first real date with Wynter, I woke up to the best surprise in the world. Even thinking about it now, I'm hard. Wynter's mouth wrapped around my dick while she was wearing my jersey with my name and team number plastered across the back.

Hottest. Fucking. Thing. Ever.

My girl sucked me off like she was trying to win the gold medal for blowjobs, and then I swooped her up into my arms, plastered her sweet pussy over my face, and ate her out. I've never had that happen to me before. I've never woken up with a woman's mouth on my morning wood. I've never had her sit on my face until I made her come, and then spent the remaining few minutes we had before the alarm went off just kissing and snuggling and holding her.

In the early morning light, she looked so beautiful. So peaceful and content, and it hit me like a marching band that it's a look on her face I don't see very often. It's a look I swore then and there to work my ass off to replicate morning after morning, day after day.

She might not fully grasp this yet, but she's not alone anymore. She has me, and I'm her guy, and I'm not going anywhere. It's what

I've been trying to prove to her for the last week since we became official. A week of being together and living a secret life.

But last week, after hearing what Coach did to her when she was a child, it's been hell on wheels not confronting the man or simply grasping him by his neck and squeezing until all the available oxygen in his body is snuffed out.

Like right now as I walk past the owner's office and hear the two of them speaking. Randolph never closes his door, and with that, I can hear everything.

"He's green, Joe. If the reports on Reyes' shoulder are accurate, then he'll be back on the field in a couple of months at most. I still don't know how we got so lucky with that."

"*He* got lucky with that Super Bowl, Randolph. The team carried him on their back, and last year was flat at best. It's why you brought me in. Leo's stats in college showed growth from year to year. That's what we need. I'm just not sure how much more growth Asher has in him."

I frown as grief slams into me, the force of it knocking me against the wall.

"I agree we need more growth. Especially after a mostly unproductive year last year. But Reyes is this team. He's this city. You'll face one hell of a fight if you try to replace him."

"Maybe. But winning is why we're here and I think Leo can be a winner. He's looked good on the field so far."

"Perhaps. Winning *is* why I brought you here. Show me you can, and we'll talk again."

I move away from the door, unsure if their conversation is done but already knowing I don't want to be there when Joe leaves. Coach doesn't like me. That much is clear. I still don't understand why Randolph drafted Leo so high in the first round. He was good in college but far from lights out.

And I really don't understand what he has against me.

I've been helping the kid because it helps my team, but ultimately my loyalty to that will hurt me in the end.

On numb legs, I make my way through the tunnels, into the

locker room, and then into the weight room. Naturally, the rookie is here, and naturally, he's chatting with my woman, making her smile and laugh.

"Morning, has-been," he greets me, and though this has become our routine, ribbing each other because that's what ball players do, it grates especially rough this morning. Leo is actually a good kid, and I've grown to like him a lot more than I ever thought I would. I want him to succeed, and I want him to lead a team at the highest level.

I just don't want him to do that with *my* team.

"Morning, will-never-be." I toss him a wave and then go over to the leg press, needing some serious heat on my muscles to burn off all this extra emotion I can't seem to shake.

I set myself into the machine and then push the metal plate and weights with a heavy grunt and a thrust. My thighs already burn, the weight on the machine set to thirty pounds more than my usual lift.

"Good morning, Mr. Reyes. How's the shoulder treating you?"

"Good morning, Dr. Hathaway. It's still attached, so I guess that's something."

I can't see her face from this angle, but I know her well enough to know she does not like that response. "Are you in pain?" she asks softly after a quiet half-beat.

"Nope. But ask me that again after PT later this morning."

I grunt and continue to push myself, ignoring the woman, who is impossible to ignore, standing somewhere beside me.

After my tenth rep, I hear her move, and for a moment, I think she's leaving me without another word, but then she hands me a white towel since I'm already sweating like a sinner in church. "Thank you."

"Last I checked, you're Asher Reyes. Remember that and never let anyone change it. You've got this, player. I know you do."

Her hand brushes my hair briefly, a passing swipe no one else can see, and then she's walking off, heading for the trainers' room. The metal weights click back into place as I reset the machine, panting out a harsh breath as I do.

Wynter's words sit heavy on my chest, while somehow managing to lighten me. People enter your life when you least expect them. I never saw her coming. I wasn't even looking for her. But I'll forever be grateful to the universe, which brought her to me not just once but twice.

"DA-DA," I say, enunciating the syllables in the word. I lift Mason in the air, his full weight centered in his chest that's held by my palm. This is his favorite thing for me to do with him, I think. He crawls or scoots himself over to me and tugs on my hand, placing it on his chest for me to lift him. If he already likes the feel of being weightless, the kid is going to be a daredevil and give his mother and me hives when he's a teenager.

Still, he's easily the coolest kid on the planet, and I'm not just saying that because he's mine.

"Come on. You can do it. Say, dada." I do another press into the air as I sign "Father" with my other hand. My muscles are screaming at me from all the pressure I put on them today—well, all the pressure I've been putting them under since the surgery—but I'd do just about anything to hear his giggle and see his smile, so my muscles will just have to deal.

"Mama," he chirps in delight, and I groan.

"Big guy, you're killing me. We've been at this since you moved in here. That's more than three weeks of this. If I didn't know better, I'd suggest you were intentionally not saying dada just to mess with me."

"Cookie."

I groan. "Are you kidding me? Cookie over dada?" Those are his two words now. Cookie and mama. Incidentally, he learned cookie after spending the night at Wynter's parents' house last week. Not a stretch to figure out how he learned that word. I guess that's grandparents for you.

I do another rep with him, down and then back up into the air where he giggles in delight.

"Dada. Please. Just one time? For me?"

He stares curiously at me as if the word isn't computing when I've only said it to him about a million times.

"I hate it when you do that," Wynter remarks from the doorway.

"Sweetheart, he doesn't weigh more than twenty-five pounds. I could do this with you and still be fine."

She enters the room, sitting on the large yellow yoga ball near us. I give Mason another push into the air. "Dada."

Little booger looks directly at Wynter, extends his arms, and says, "Mama."

She laughs, giving me a *what can you do* shrug. "Don't look so glum," she tells me. "He'll get it. He's just paying homage to the fact that I spent thirty hours in labor with him."

My eyes bulge. "*Thirty hours?* Jesus, remind *me* to pay homage to your pus—er—vagina later. When I spoke to my mother last night, she told me both me and my brother were planned C-sections because we were so big."

She snickers. "This boy wasn't small. He came out at almost nine pounds, and that was two weeks early. It's why I eventually ended up having a C-section too, only I endured hours of labor first."

"I hate that I wasn't there."

Mason reaches for her again, and this time she snatches him away, bringing him into her chest to give him a kiss on both cheeks before setting him down so he can crawl over to his toys. I sit up, inch over to her, and drop my head on her lap. Her fingers start combing through the strands of my hair, and my eyes close as a contented hum passes my lips.

I've never had this before. Where I could just hang out and be myself and snuggle as much as I want—evidently, I'm a snugger. Who knew? I've always had to be Asher Reyes, whether that was the rock star or the professional football player. Money, and fame, that's what drew women to me.

Wynter doesn't give a rat's ass about either. It's just us like this, and it's quite possibly the most freeing and relaxing thing I've ever experienced.

Her fingers trickle along my healing scar. Oddly, it feels good. Sensitive. "Do you ever wear a shirt?"

"Not since it became a total mother-effer to put one on or take one off. Plus, I happen to live with this incredibly hot woman who thinks I'm insanely sexy when I'm shirtless."

"True. That *is* why I'm here. The visual man candy is where it's at. The fact that you're decent in bed and are the biological father of my child is all a bonus."

I roll my head and quirk an eyebrow up at her. "*Decent* in bed?"

"Just calling it as I see it."

I bury my face in the V between her thighs and blow a raspberry, making her screech and wiggle on the ball as she tries to push me away from her pussy.

"Stop!" she cries, laughing as I nip at her inner thigh and then blow more vibrations into her center. I plant a series of kisses and then rest my head on her thighs again, my good arm around her back, holding her upright on the ball and closer to me.

"Can I buy you something special?"

She coughs out a laugh. "What? Why? I don't need anything."

My head pops up and I gaze into her eyes. I've had it for over a week now, and I've been too nervous to give it to her. I ordered it after I followed her home from the ice skating rink last week. This thing between us is still so new, and I wasn't sure how she would take to me doing something like this without consulting her first.

"Maybe I shouldn't have asked if I could, but you don't seem like the type of woman who does surprises well."

She stares warily at me. "Not typically, no."

"I got you something."

Her head tilts. "So, you went from asking if you *could* buy me something to telling me you already *did*?"

I slide my phone out of my pocket, unlock it with my face, pull up the picture of the car, and then flip my phone around so she can see it.

She studies the image for a moment and then trains her surprised gaze back to mine. "What's this?"

"Safety."

"Asher—"

"I have so much money," I quickly interject before she can mount her argument. "Too much money. If you'd let me, I'd buy you and Mason the world. You have no idea how badly I want to spoil you both. But I can't handle either of you in your car for another second. This one received top safety ratings, it's all-wheel drive, which you will need in Boston when winter comes, and it's pretty and luxurious, which are both things my woman deserves."

"You already bought this," she states. "That is in the garage downstairs."

"Yep."

She bobs her head absently, her eyes trained on the picture again as the seconds tick by like an eternity.

"It's silver."

Nervousness starts to swell in me. "Is that a problem? Did you want a different color?"

"I won gold."

I chuckle at her aghast expression. "That wasn't an option."

"That's criminal," she asserts in feigned outrage.

My lips twitch. "Perhaps."

I get a shake of her head, and then she's staring at the picture once more. "Hmmm. I guess I could live with silver if it can't be gold."

"Yeah?" Hope surges through me like a geyser.

Her fingers trickle along my jaw. "Yeah." Her lips glide against mine, and a soft smile plays on her lips. "Thank you." Another kiss. "It's more than generous, and extremely sweet and thoughtful. My instinct is to argue this, but I won't. Your heart, Asher Reyes, is quite possibly the most impressive and beautiful thing about you, and I adore you for it.

Adore me? That's like a hop, skip, and a jump from love. This makes my heart go thump, thump, thump.

"I adore you. All of you. Just as you are." I drag her lips back to mine and kiss her, and all the worry from today, everything I over-heard Joe say about me, starts to dissolve. At least for a little while.

# 25

---

## WYNTER

Asher has been on edge all week leading up to today. It's Sunday. One p.m. First game of the season for the Boston Rebels, and he's not playing in it. Much like me, he's forced to the sideline, wearing a Rebels T-shirt and track pants and an anxious look. It's killing him. I know it is.

This is his team. His heart.

And while I don't care about football necessarily, I do care about him. And my guy is visibly hurting. I want to hug him. I want to hold his hand. But I am forced back into that realm of indifferent acquaintance. No one here knows our truth.

No one knows that this Asher Reyes, the football god, is actually mine.

That he wakes me up at all hours with his mouth between my thighs and his fingers inside of me. That he stares deep into my eyes every time he enters me for the first time. That he is so unlike the man he works for, I can only hope our son is more like his father and nothing like his biological grandfather.

In the two weeks since the ice skating rink, things between us have found their rhythm. I've talked Asher away from confronting Joe —it won't help me and it will only hurt him—and I've sort of moved into his bedroom. I'm fully aware that I'm irrevocably lost to this man because he's hot and sweet and loves our boy with his entire heart and is on a boundless mission to find all the ways to make me come.

I'm trying to take it day by day. I'm trying not to get in too deep too quickly. But Asher makes it so effortless to love him.

So it breaks my heart that he's here on the sideline, mic'd into the kid on the field who is starting the game instead of Asher. It's been nearly a month since his surgery, but he's got another month, at least, of rehab before he can even think about taking the field.

The opposing team just deferred the ball and kicked off to us. Asher paces the sidelines as the rookie hits the field. He passes me on one of his paces, and I grasp his hand on the back side of it, giving it a squeeze and then immediately releasing him. His eyes train back to mine, and I can see the ache in his.

"You've got this, player."

A wan half-smile. "I'm glad you're here." *Because this sucks.* He didn't have to say it; his expression screams it for him.

"Soon enough you'll be back out there."

But the grim crease of his face tells me that he's not sure if he'll ever start again for this team, and I don't know what to say. Joe spoke about seeing what the kid could do when he and I met that first time. He talked about possibly trading Asher. And then what? This is where my dream job is. Where my family is.

What happens to all of this if Asher gets traded?

Yet another reason why I'm trying to force myself not to get too emotionally involved, but that feels like a joke.

I haven't mentioned any of this to Asher. I'm not sure what good it would do anyone, especially him. Instinctively, I'm positive he already knows the score and that being traded is a very real possibility for him.

"Maybe."

It's all he says, and then he's game-on. Nothing else registers but the plays.

I'll admit it, it's sort of fun to watch. Even if I don't understand much of it. It's not hockey, and it's far from basketball, but I get it. The gridiron roughness of it. The putting your body on the line for each play.

I slink to the back of the sideline, away from the players and the action. Joe is standing on the edge of the sideline, barking and growling as he stares at a laminated sheet with plays on it. He shouts something at Asher, who simply nods his head in acknowledgment, though the clench of his jaw does nothing to hide his resentment.

Asher wears his heart on his sleeve, and that won't help him with this. Joe, for better or worse, is his coach. And if he wants to continue to play for the Rebels, then he has to learn how to manage that. I love that he's protective over me, but I can take care of myself. Ignoring Joe has become an art and science that I've mastered.

I don't have to speak to him. He has very little to do with what I do here.

Letting go of the past means removing his importance in it, and I will no longer give him any power to affect anything in me.

"You look tense," Dean, the team neurologist says, coming over to stand beside me. He's a nice guy. In the weeks I've been here, we've become friendly. He also works at the same hospital I do. Not that I ever see him there since I'm no longer working there, except for occasional Mondays.

"It's my first football game."

His eyebrows bounce in surprise. "What do you think of it so far?"

I hitch up a shoulder. "I'd rather be home with my son."

He laughs. "How did you get this gig again?"

"I drew the short straw."

"Interesting considering I practically had to offer up my firstborn child to get it."

I throw him a side-eye. "How do they feel about that?"

"No kids yet, so I'll let you know when I have one."

"Well, I have no plans to give up mine, so I'd gladly pass this off to someone else."

He steps in closer to me, nudging me with his elbow. "From what I heard about what you did for Reyes' shoulder, I doubt they're letting you go anytime soon."

"His shoulder wasn't that bad," I admit. "I'm not sure what was up with the MRI. It was a completely different field when I got in there." It's still something I don't understand. I reviewed the MRI after the surgery to make sure I hadn't been imagining things, and the MRI showed a torn labrum, an AC joint separation, and a ton of scarring that wasn't present inside his shoulder.

The truth is, anyone could have done Asher's surgery. He might have even been able to get away with some physical therapy for it instead of surgery, which would have gotten him through the season. I'm still not sure what to make of it.

"Even so, you're the team hero if Reyes can manage to get back on the field this season. The rookie is talented but very green." He juts his chin toward the field just as the quarterback takes a sack. "See what I mean. He never should have taken that hit, and he should have thrown the ball away before he did. He not only cost the team a bad third down, he cost them field position for the resulting punt."

I glance over at Asher, who is swearing, but when the kid comes running off the field looking forlorn, Asher grabs him, smacks the back of his helmet, and then puts his arm around him, saying something to him that no one else can hear.

"Do you think they'll keep Asher?" I ask, since Dean has been with the team a lot longer than I have, and from the way he's speaking, it sounds as if he has insider information I don't.

"No clue," he admits. "Everyone was surprised when they drafted the rookie as high as they did in the first round. Rumor has it, it was all Coach Cardone's doing, but he kept Asher as his primary QB until Asher's shoulder became a problem after that big hit."

Huh. My eyes track over to the back of Joe's head as he yells at some offensive lineman. "I thought Cardone wasn't hired on until this summer."

"He didn't move here until shortly before training camp, but he had signed a secret agreement with the team before the draft back in April. That's privileged information though. I'm not supposed to know about any of this."

I turn back to Dean, my brows furrowed. "I don't understand."

"They didn't fire the old coach until two months after the draft."

I shake my head. "Why wait if they made a deal with Cardone?"

He throws his hands up. "No clue. No one knows, and it's all been kept very quiet. I only know about the deal because I overheard the owner talking on the phone with Joe before the draft. I was standing outside his office and heard everything. When Randolph realized I knew, he told me I couldn't mention anything about Joe coming on or that Joe wanted the rookie in the draft as part of the deal."

"Wow." That's all I've got. Admittedly, I don't know much about football or how it all works for contracts and owners and coaches. Still, something feels very off about that.

About all of this.

The game continues, and I end up in the locker room with a wide receiver who I suspect tore his ACL in his right knee. Poor kid is devastated when I tell him I want to see him tomorrow at the hospital for an MRI. By the time I finish up with him, the game is over, and the locker room is filling up with players and staff.

I head for the exit only to have Asher grab my hand before I can leave, pulling me over to the side where no one can see us. He leans in and whispers in my ear, "Are you good if my friends come over this afternoon to swim, eat, and watch the later games?"

"Of course. My mom and dad will be there though, remember?"

"That's fine. Grey loves hockey. He'll pester your dad all afternoon."

I grin. "He'll love that." I glance over my shoulder, and when I find we're still alone, I plant a kiss on his cheek. "Congrats on a team win."

"Thanks. It hurts but it also feels good, you know? A win is a win."

"A win is a win," I parrot. "See you at home, player."

He leans in and presses his lips to mine, then releases me, heading into the locker room for the post-game stuff they do.

A couple hours later, we're all up on the roof deck. I'm in the water with Mason, who is clinging to me like a monkey while I talk with Fallon, Layla, and Aurelia. In the weeks Asher and I have been together, I've learned this group is tight and they spend a lot of time together. I already knew Fallon from med school, but I've started growing close with her and the other women, which has been nice. It's an added bonus of being in Asher's life.

My mom is resting on a lounger with sunglasses over her eyes and a margarita in her hand. She loves being a grandma, but I don't think she's minding the break right now. All the men are over by the bar, watching the games, sipping on beers, and picking at the spread of food Asher brought in for everyone.

"How'd Asher do today?" Aurelia questions. I've noticed they're pretty close. They have an easy banter with each other. Asher told me he used to flirt with her to get a rise out of Zax—one of his favorite hobbies—but that seems to have stopped now that he and I are together.

"He did okay, I think. I know it was hard for him."

"I can't imagine how it wouldn't be," she says. "That team is his life. I have no doubt it was good for him that you were on the field too."

I shrug, swirling Mason around in the water. "I didn't see him or talk to him much. He was doing his football thing, and I was doing my doctor thing. Though…" I pause, wondering if I should say anything. If what Dean told me means anything at all. "I don't know. He's been working his ass off, and I have no doubt he'll make it back on the field this season."

I just hope it's with the Rebels.

"Zax has been trying to get him to come to New York at the end of the month for fashion week. He thinks it'll help clear his head, but I don't think Asher will walk the runway."

I snicker. "I still can't believe he models for Monroe Fashions."

She laughs. "Are you kidding? He sells our clothes every time he's photographed in them. Especially lately. He's so hot right now."

Layla starts to crack up as she sips her lemon-drop martini. "You sound like that dude from *Zoolander*."

Aurelia throws her hands up, splashing pool water about as she does. "I know! But it's so true. He is!"

"I don't think he's going to New York anytime soon. At least not to model. The press is especially hot for him right now—as you said—and I know it's driving him crazy."

Fallon gives me a look. "It only drives him crazy because he can't take you out anywhere without it becoming front-page news."

Aurelia gets a sparkle to her eye. "True, and that sucks, but I love seeing him like this."

My brows furrow as I adjust Mason on my hip, making sure his toes dangle in the water. "What do you mean?"

"He's in love," she says, almost flippantly, like the answer is obvious to everyone. "Because of you, he's grown up a bit. For once, he's serious about something other than football."

I shake my head. "You mean he's in love with Mason," I counter.

Aurelia, Fallon, and Layla share a smirk between themselves. "Take a look over your shoulder and see for yourself." Fallon's head bobs in the direction of the bar, and reflexively I turn to find Asher watching us in the pool, an absent, almost dopey grin on his face. His eyes meet mine, and that grin turns into a smile that makes my heart jolt in my chest and butterflies take flight in my belly.

"See what we mean?" Aurelia murmurs. "That's the smile of a man head over heels in love."

"I mean, I don't know Asher all that well," Layla chimes in, "but yeah, dude's obsessed. Anytime he's with Callan, he can't stop talking about you or Mason."

I turn back to them, all those butterflies suddenly becoming flesh-eating as they gnaw at the lining of my stomach. "I'm worried we won't have a real future with each other."

If what Dean said is true about Joe demanding Leo in the draft as part of the deal for him to come to the Rebels, that means he doesn't want Asher for the long term. If that happens, a decision might have to be made in the coming months, and I'm not sure how that will go. If he's traded, will he want us to move with him? And if he does, is that something I'm willing to do? I'm here for the Boston sports teams. For the job and the market, but also because my mom and dad are here. I want Mason to be in their lives as much as possible, but... Asher is his father.

We have no legal documents. No court dictating anything.

Other than not wanting anything to become public yet, we haven't needed it. Mason and I live here with him, and after what I went through with Joe, I'd never keep Mason from a father who wants to be in his son's life.

But if this falls apart on us, what will that look like?

"I think it's pretty clear that Asher would move heaven and earth to make a real future with you," Fallon declares. "It's all a matter of what you want that future to look like with him."

Mason starts squirming in my arms, interrupting my thoughts and our conversation. His arms and legs start flailing out, and he's making a high-pitched squeal.

"What's all this?" I laugh, looking down at him, only his gaze is trained over my shoulder. I turn to find Asher making goofy faces at him. "What's Daddy doing? Is he being silly?"

Mason is going nuts in my arms, anxious to get to Asher so I walk through the pool, headed for Asher, who now has his arms out for him when Mason says, "Dada."

Clear as freaking day, he says, "Dada."

I freeze midstep in the water, staring down at Mason, who is still reaching for Asher, completely unaware of the enormity of what he just did.

"Did he say my name? Did he say, dada? And sign it?" Asher is on his feet, looking like someone just sucker-punched him in the best of ways.

My throat closes, and I have to swallow past the lump of emotion hindering my ability to speak. "He did. Oh my God! Asher, he said dada." He also did sign it at the same time, which is just freaking awesome.

Asher's eyes glass over, and awe fills his expression. In his next breath, he walks down the steps, straight into the pool, still in his track pants, and buries his head in Mason's neck. "Say it again, big man. Say dada." Mason is silent, so Asher pulls back and makes the sign for Father while saying, "Dada."

"Dada," Mason repeats.

"Yeah! That's my boy!"

I laugh, even as a tear hits my cheek. My mom is sitting up. and my dad walks over to her, taking her hand because I know my mom is crying too. They told us when he was three weeks old, failed the hearing test in one ear, and then did further testing after, that they didn't know what his auditory future would be. In fact, they painted the grimmest possible picture for us.

But he's using words and signing, and for him to say dada is just so fucking sweet.

Asher pellets Mason's face with kisses and then scoops him out of my arms and tucks him into his good side. I know it's killing him that he can't toss him up in the air or do half the things he'd like because of his shoulder.

Asher's forehead drops to mine, using his free hand to wipe away my tears, and then he kisses me. Right here in front of all his friends. In front of my parents. In front of our son.

"Thank you," he whispers against my lips. "Thank you for him. Thank you for you. Thank you for completing my life in ways I never knew it was lacking."

His gray eyes, nearly colorless against the sunlight filtering in from above and the blue glow of the water, swim with love and gratitude. He's standing waist-deep, soaking wet, holding our son, staring at me like this, and all I can think is, *I feel the exact same way.*

# 26

## ASHER

I've changed out of my wet clothes, and I've got my big guy sitting on my lap. He's picking at some puffed rice, carrot and cheese ring things that he seems to love but that taste like stale pieces of air to me. Who cares. My son called me dada. Actually, he signed and said it, which makes him a fucking genius.

Something he likely gets from his mother.

And while I've been working with him on saying it, I wasn't expecting how it would make me *feel* when he finally did it. It's becoming harder and harder to pretend that this isn't everything I want. That they don't own my heart and soul.

Today was impossible for me, but Wynter was there, touching my hand and reassuring me, and visually checking in with me at random points in the game. Then Mason said dada, and I wasn't sure my heart could handle how quickly it swelled in my chest.

"Do you think if I bought her a ring, she'd say yes?" Callan—not me—asks, though I won't lie and say I haven't been having similar thoughts.

"I think she'll say no," Grey says with a grimace. "Layla has told you from the start that she is not looking for that, and she's only...

what? Twenty-three? She's entering her second year of medical school. I think you need to wait."

Callan does not like hearing that. "What the hell does age matter? Aurelia is the same age as Layla, and she's wearing Zax's ring."

"Different," Zax states in that gruff way of his. "Aurelia has been on her own since she was sixteen. She was an adult before Layla was out of braces."

Callan pouts a bit and then tosses back his drink. "Fine. You are all right. I'll wait. But would it be such a bad thing if she needed me half as much as I need her?"

We all fall silent, each of us secretly feeling the exact same way about our women. Well, all except Lenox, since he's now the only single holdout of all of us.

He makes a noise. "Pussy-whipped."

We all turn in his direction. "That's no joke, brother," I tell him. "It's a defining moment when you meet the woman destined to own your balls and your heart. One day, it will happen to you. Though for the life of me, I have no clue who could tolerate your surly, silent ass."

He grins pompously at me. But it'll happen. One day, it will. I hope.

Some big plays go down on the television, and it calls us back to the screens. My boys are all around me, sipping on beers and bourbon while I drink snobby electrolyte-infused water. The end of the 4:00 p.m. games is playing on RedZone on the television above me, but that's not what concerns me right now.

It's the man on my right who holds my undivided attention.

"I wanted to ask Wynter's mom to marry me after a week of dating. But after all she went through, I knew I had to wait for the right time. Especially considering she had Wynter. When I met Wynter, it took her months and months to consider me as a man who wouldn't run out on her."

I freeze at Gary's words. We all do.

"She would be kind and smile, but I had to work so damn hard to prove to her that I wouldn't abandon her or her mother. I married her mother when Wynter was ten, but it took the Olympics for everything between us to change. She turned fifteen a week before those games and by that point, I'd done everything I could think of to prove myself, including marrying her mother."

I swallow audibly, and I catch the way my guys are watching me.

"What happened there?"

"We were teammates—on Team USA, that is—and though I had been introducing her as my daughter for five years, something about doing it there, something about being there for her, is what finally won her over. Joe was at the games too."

My breath snags in my chest.

Wynter and the women are on the other side of the pool area, so we're trying to make this look like light, friendly bro banter, and to them, it probably does. Even when it's anything but.

"Does Wynter know he was there?" I ask, even though I'm pretty sure I already know the answer.

"No," Gary replies, swirling a chip around in the pile of salsa on his plate. "I never told her. And not because Joe asked me not to— which he did—but because I felt it would only break her heart more, and those Olympic games meant the world to her. She truly came back to life in those two weeks, and there was no way I was going to let him take anything else from her. Or from me, truth be told. I wanted to be her dad, and he didn't deserve her the way I did."

I smile softly to myself. Gary is a good man. A good father. Joe is clearly not.

"But he was there?" Grey questions, still unable to wrap his head around it.

"He was," Gary confirms, popping the chip in his mouth and chewing while I make some noise about the game. He swallows, takes a sip of his beer, and then continues. "I was sitting in the stands with a teammate of mine. Wynter and her mom were backstage, or what-ever it's called, waiting for her turn to skate. I looked to my left, and up in the very top row, hidden in the shadows, was Joe. I got up and sat beside him, and for the longest time, I didn't say anything. I just sat there and waited him out. I wanted to threaten him. I wanted to tell him what a piece of shit I thought he was. But I held my tongue, knowing he was up to something."

"What did he do?" Callan asks as he polishes off his beer.

"He told me he wanted to see her skate in person, but that he didn't want her to know he was there."

"But why?" Zax questions. "I don't understand it. Why bother flying all that way if you're not going to make your presence known?"

"He didn't do it for her. He did it for himself. She was his offspring, and he was a competitor. A champion. He was also at her medical school graduation, where she gave a speech to the class since she graduated on top. Same deal."

I wipe a hand across my forehead and absently point at the television, just in case we have any curious eyes on us. "What you're saying is he basically stalks her for his own ego, which I can totally buy. I mean, he knew she moved up to Boston. He knew what practice she was working for. Do we not think he knows about Mason?"

"No reason to think that right now," he says. "To the best of my knowledge, he's followed her career but hasn't tracked her as a person until she moved up here."

"Does her mom know?" Lenox asks, which, as always with him, is another good question.

Gary shakes his head. "It would have upset her too, and I didn't want to ruin those special days for them. Plus, Wynter and Sonya are very close. She never would have been able to keep that from Wynter."

"But you're telling Asher this for a reason," Zax surmises, glancing over his shoulder at the women and then back to us.

"All those times he showed up, he made sure it stayed a secret," Gary maintains. "He didn't want to be in her life. He just liked how her accomplishments made him feel. So why after all these years has he suddenly changed his mind and made himself part of her situation?"

I scrub a hand over my face and shrug. "I don't know. I don't think Wynter does either, and he's been evasive when she's asked."

"You work with him," Gary asserts. "Your career is almost based on him. Joe is methodical. He doesn't do anything without a reason. I don't know what his reason for bringing Wynter back into his life is, but I know he has one. Now you're as wrapped up in it as she is." He shifts in his chair, pinning me with this dark gaze. "It might be nothing. It might just be he's finally learned the error of his ways after all these years and regrets the choices he made with her. Or it could be about something else. Just keep an eye out. That's all I'm suggesting."

My friends and I exchange looks. We're not strangers to this sort of thing. We grew up as famous rock stars, our every move tracked by the paparazzi and fans. Now—with the exception of Lenox, who lives off the grid, and Callan, who is a doctor—we're all still famous. Grey and I most of all.

But this is different.

This *feels* different.

I don't get the sense that Gary would say anything if he wasn't suspecting that Joe was up to something, and he's right. Why now?

～

> Me: Where are you?

> Me: Wynter? Where are you? Why can I not find you when I know you're in the apartment?

WITH A GROWL OF FRUSTRATION, I wander from room to room. I had been hoping to coax my pretty lady back up to the roof for a naked swim, but I can't find her, and she's not returning my texts. Mason is asleep. Big man passed out early tonight—I think it was all the swimming and being passed around like a joint at a concert from person to person all afternoon.

But that means it's adult time, and it's barely eight, and where the fuck is Wynter?

The door to her old room is closed and I tap gently on the wood and then plant my ear against it. I don't hear anything, but I give it a try anyway, turning the knob and entering. The light is on, and I hear noise coming from the bathroom.

"Ice queen?"

She doesn't answer, but I notice the sound of water sloshing. There's a white robe on the bed, and I touch the soft cotton, debating if I should go in the bathroom. She's obviously taking a bath, but why not do it in my bathtub unless she wants privacy?

Something on the floor catches my eye, and I bend down, finding a chain for a necklace I've seen her wear, but it's missing the jade stone that's usually dangling from it. I search the floor and even under the bed but come up empty. When I stand back up, I notice the nightstand drawer is open a tiny crack, and I wonder if maybe it fell in there.

I slide the drawer further open, and a shit-eating grin splits my lips. No jade stone, but there is a very pretty pink vibrator in here.

Oh, ice queen. You naughty, sexy woman. Lifting the smooth silicone device, I run my hand over it. It's not very big, a few inches at most, and shaped like a bullet. My head swivels toward the bathroom and the enticing sound of Wynter naked in the bath.

With a wicked grin on my lips, I walk toward the bathroom and slide the door open. "My queen?"

She doesn't reply, but that's because she can't hear me. She's in the bath, head back on the rim of the tub, eyes closed, with her AirPods in her ears. The room is dark, with the lights dimmed and candles flickering. The air is thick with humidity and the scent of the bath bombs I had Freddy buy her. It's a sensual, romantic wonderland.

I don't want to startle her, so I march with heavy steps, hoping the vibrations will alert her to my presence. Especially if she has the noise canceling on.

"Wynter?" I call, louder this time.

Her head snaps up, her eyes bolt open, and she emits a tiny, startled scream. One of her AirPods goes flying out of her ear, and by the grace of all that is holy, she manages to catch it before it plummets into the water. She pulls the other one out and sets them down on the shelf beside the tub.

"The hell, Asher?!"

"Sorry. I couldn't find you."

"I told you I was going to take a bath."

I kneel down next to the tub, dropping my forearm on the edge of the white porcelain and then my chin on my arm. "No, you didn't."

She rolls her eyes, not pleased at all. "Um. Yes, I did. You were checking your phone, and I told you I was going to take a bath. I asked if you heard me, and you said yes."

I give her a sheepish smile. "I have zero recollection of that."

"Shocker of all shockers. Now out. I'm relaxing."

"That's not nearly as fun as naked swimming." I stare down at her perky breasts and firm nipples peeking, up through the thin layer of bubbles floating on top of the water.

"We already did that. Remember?" She flicks my ear, making me jolt, and my gaze snaps back up to hers. A full-blown smile erupts across my face. I like that she just caught me staring. Especially considering it made her nipples harden. "Out. You're interrupting the sanctity of alone bath time."

Instead of doing what she asks, I pull off my T-shirt and then strip out of my track shorts and boxer briefs.

"What are you doing? I didn't invite you in here with me."

The way her green eyes grow dark and hungry isn't exactly selling that.

"I had wanted to swim naked with you under the stars, but when I came into your room to find you, I found something in your nightstand drawer instead," I tell her, bypassing her half-assed rejection completely.

I step into the opposite side of the tub and then sink down into the warm, girly-scented water and fluffy bubbles. Our eyes fight a silent war, and then she harrumphs in feigned defeat. She's the worst at playing hard to get, but I love the game and the chase, and she knows it. Shifting to make room for me, my large frame quickly crowds her, but to make up for it, I grab one foot and then the other and place them over my legs, taking turns using my good hand to rub them.

Her head falls back, and her eyes close. She loves the hell out of this.

"What did you find?" she murmurs distantly.

"Do you not know?" I click the button on the end of the toy that's enclosed in my other fist, and it starts to vibrate in the water.

Her eyes spark open. "Oh." She laughs. "I forgot about him."

"He's not very impressive."

She quirks a taunting eyebrow. "He more than gets the job done."

"Let's see how well."

I give her foot a firm tug, pulling her toward me until her ass slides through the water and over my shins and knees. Water sloshes everywhere as she straddles me, her tits practically in my face, her skin wet and warm and flushed. So fucking delicious.

"I think I can do better," I tell her, leaning back against the tub and getting comfortable.

"I doubt that. Hemi is a magic bullet. It's his official title."

"Hemi?" I choke out, my eyebrows at my hairline.

She smiles victoriously. "Like Chris Hemsworth and the truck engine all in one."

"This tiny thing is a total insult to Thor." And frankly, I always think of Lenox as Thor. Large, muscular, blonde, saves the world like a goddamn superhero... it's who he is.

She shrugs indifferently. "Not to me, it isn't. He's fantasy material."

I frown disparagingly. "I look nothing like him."

"A tragedy I cry myself to sleep over every night."

I bark out a laugh. Christ, this woman and her fucking mouth. I bring the vibrator up to her nipple and press it in, pinching the other with my good hand. A punishment the little minx loves far too much.

"What other secret toys do you have in your arsenal?" I ask as I swirl the toy around her nipple in a circle.

She hums in pleasure, her hips grinding on my thighs ever so slightly, almost as if she's not even aware she's doing it. "He's the only one."

"No Avengers set of pleasure dicks? We'll have to change that. And of course, name them all Asher. But for now…"

I let that hang in the air between us as I glide the pink bullet down the underside of her breast, down the sloped dip of her stomach, and into the water. Her eyes spark with fire, and her full lips part to accommodate her heavy breaths as the toy reaches the top of her mound.

"You're so beautiful, my queen." My other hand runs along her tits, up her throat, across her jaw, and into her wet hair that's knotted on top of her head. I grip it by the roots and then drag her forehead to mine. "One day, when I've finally managed to convince you that you can't live without me, I'm going to marry you."

She starts to roll her eyes, but they end up rolling in the back of her head when I press the vibrator on her clit. "Not a chance."

"Oh, sweetheart, that's where you're wrong. You may not be there yet, but I already know you're the one for me. When you're ready, I'm going to tell you just how in love with you I am."

Her eyes shoot open, her face a delightfully twisted display of intense pleasure and shocked consternation. I smile, no longer caring if she's the tortoise and I'm the hare. Today our son called me dada, and I'm done taking it slow.

"I love you," I tell her, pulling the toy back so she hears me. "I know it's ridiculously too soon. I know you're not even halfway there with me. I know I'm the last guy you want. But I'm telling you, I love you. And it's not because of Mason. I love you *more* because of him. I looked into your eyes that night in the club, and there was something about you that immediately stole a piece of me, and since you came back into my life, that's all you seem to do."

She blinks at me, her eyes rounding as a different sort of blush takes over her features. "You really love me?" Her voice is a shaky whisper.

"I really love you."

She lets that sit, her mind working overtime to try and absorb that. Or maybe argue it, but she's staring into my eyes, and she can see that I meant every word as I hold nothing of myself back.

"Poor bastard," she finally murmurs, a quirked half-smile pulling up the edge of her lips. Her hand comes up, running along my smooth jaw and through my hair, where she cups the back of my head, holding me tighter against her. Our mouths layer as her nose runs back and forth against mine.

I lick the seam of her lips and then nip at her jaw. "Maybe. But remember this, my ice queen, I play to win, and I never lose. You're mine now."

"Is that so?" She gasps when I press the toy directly back on her swollen clit.

"Sweetheart, you're about to learn all the dirty ways I play this game."

## 27

### WYNTER

Asher loves me. While the cynical, scarred side of me wants to dismiss that, the rest of me refuses. Asher loves me and I believe him. I see it in his eyes and feel it in his every action. I knew it today when we were in the pool and Mason called him dada. I could continue to push back. I could continue to hold my ground and maintain my distance.

But why would I do that?

Why would I fight back when I have a man like Asher Reyes fighting for me?

I don't want the scars of my past to mar my future any longer.

Asher is holding the back of my head, and I'm holding the back of his. Our foreheads are one, as are our lips. He still has my fun little toy pressed to my clit, and maybe this isn't the time to say it with him doing that to me, but he deserves to know the truth—and he deserves to know it now.

With my eyes holding his, I swallow down my nerves and say, "I love you."

He freezes, his entire body growing still. I don't even think he's breathing. Finally, he utters, "You mean that?"

"I wouldn't say it if I didn't."

He tilts his head, and then stares down into the water between us. "Wait. Are you saying this to Asher Jr. or to me?"

I smile so big, I'm positive all my teeth are showing. "Asher Jr.?"

"The toy formerly known as Hemi."

I can't stop my giggle. "We'll discuss his name later, but I'm saying it to you, you goof."

"Oh good. I just wanted to make sure. But you interrupted all my plans for dirty play with your boring proclamations of love."

I twist his nipple until he yelps, but then he grows serious, his gaze earnest.

"I love you." He uses the hand in my hair to guide my mouth fully onto his. "I love you," he repeats. Then he's kissing me with everything he's got. His tongue sweeps into my open mouth, and then he's pressing the toy against my clit, moving it in circles, filling me with the most incredible vibrations that have my toes curling.

He shifts me, moving me around, then he's pushing me down on his hard cock all the way to the hilt.

"Jesus," I cry out, my head flinging back, my hand slapping down on the side of the tub. "Asher!"

This vibrator may be small, but he's fucking mighty, and with that pulsing into my clit, and his cock filling every inch of me, it's so much that I'm not sure how long I can hold off coming or if I'll be quiet when I do. As it is, I can hardly catch my breath.

"I'm coming inside of you tonight, sweetheart," he growls, his mouth by my ear, his breathing harsh and ragged. "You're going to be dripping me all night, and then I'm going to fuck you again just to push it back inside of you where it belongs."

God. Why is that so hot? I love it when he gets like this. Like he has to own me, and claim me. It's barbaric, but I crave it all the same. I can't even argue it. I got my IUD on Friday, and we haven't tested it out yet. All I can manage is a nod because I'm overcome with sensation. With the heat building from my core. With the tingles racing up through me and electrifying my skin. I'm rocking and bouncing and shifting and shaking.

"Asher... I'm..."

That's all I've got before my orgasm slams into me with the power of a thousand suns. I lose coordination, my body unable to do anything other than lean against his and ride it out, but he's not satisfied with that. No, he starts slamming up into me, pushing the toy in deeper, and intensifying what is already the most intense orgasm of my life.

I'm coming and coming and *coming*.

The vibrator clicks off, and my body sags, still trembling. Only that doesn't last long. In my next breath he's pulling me off him, and then somehow he's standing, making me do the same on unsteady legs.

"What are you doing—" My words cut off with a screech when he picks me up and drops me over his good shoulder. "Stop! You're going to hurt yourself."

"Not a chance." He's out of the tub and carrying me across the bathroom before he sets me down on the counter. It's slippery, and we're both soaking wet, but before I can get my bearings, he's on his knees with my thighs around his head.

"Asher, I can't!"

"You can," he tells me, giving me a dirty lick from my ass up to my clit, where he then swirls his tongue around and around making me writhe and squirm. It's so much. It's too much. I'm sensitive from the warm water and the vibrator, and he knows it. In fact, I'm positive that's why he's doing it.

One hand catches his hair, the other on the counter so I don't fall. I don't know how much more of this I can take. That first orgasm nearly did me in, and now he's doing this.

"Please," I beg. "I need you. I need you. It's too much."

His tongue punches inside me swirling around, and my grip on his hair tightens.

He slips it out and then gives my pussy a long, wet French kiss before standing. With his gunmetal eyes locked on mine, he steps forward, wraps my legs around his waist, and grasps the back of my neck. Using that as leverage, he sits me up just as he slides himself back inside of me.

My lungs empty with a moan. It's beyond deep like this. So close, so intimate, there's no distance between us. No more games. No more pretending. All our cards are out on the table now. It's just us, naked and raw and exposed in front of the other, and the look in his eyes tells me he knows it too. For a moment he holds himself steady, letting me adjust to his size, and then he starts to slide out only to pump back in just as slowly.

He sets a grueling, mind-numbing pace, exquisite with how it feels. Time stretches between us, the heat of his body fighting the cool bathroom air on my wet skin. He latches our foreheads together and stares down at the space between us where our bodies are connected. All the while maintaining this slower, leisurely pace.

A pace that's spinning me up and driving me to the brink of madness.

I can hardly take it.

His cock glistens, coated in my arousal and cum, and with every thrust in, he arches up, driving deeper for that spot he knows makes me his. His other hand comes up, playing with my tits, pinching and rolling my nipples, all the while he fucks me like we're not in any hurry, and he has all the time in the world. Like we have a lifetime to do this, and he refuses to be rushed as he watches his wet cock being swallowed up by my pussy.

"I think this is the hottest thing I've ever seen," he rasps, his voice like gravel. The way he burns for me sets my skin on fire. "Look at the way you suck me in. That's how hungry your body is for mine." His head falls back, and he curses when I shift, angling myself to try and take more of him in. He doesn't make it long before his molten gaze returns, unwilling to miss a second of this. "Do you want more? Can you take more?"

I give him a shaky nod, and then he starts to move his hips faster, angling up to drive himself all the way to the hilt causing a burst of pleasure to spike through me. My hips roll forward like a wave, chasing this high, seeking every inch of him. His face pinches up, and he bites into his bottom lip, his head falling back on a heavy, deep growl.

"Fuck. Do that again."

I do, and the sound he makes causes my pussy to convulse and a moan to tear from my lungs. It's intoxicating to watch him like this. To watch him lose control, knowing it's me who's owning him just the way he owns me.

"So fucking good. Your cunt is so fucking sweet and perfect. Hold on, sweetheart. I'm going to take us both on a ride."

He doesn't stop, and he doesn't slow. He's tempered and even, but deep and grinding and powerful. He starts to build and build, getting us closer. Sweat replaces the water on his brow, and then he switches back on the vibrator and swirls it across my clit. Grasping my ankle, he moves my foot up onto the counter, widening my position and opening me up fully to him.

His gaze turns liquid, fascinated and mesmerized by the movement of the toy on my clit, and his cock inside of me. The intensity has me crying out. The way the toy pulses into me as his large cock fills me from within is a new form of torture and heaven.

"I feel that too. Jesus Christ, Wynter. It's like nothing else. It's both of us vibrating together."

Something about that unhinges him, and he uses all his force to pump into me, his skin slapping mine now, his thrusts harder and harder. I rip at his hair, my body on the verge of falling to pieces that I'm not sure I can be rebuilt from. I'm trembling, shaking, panting, gasping, and moaning. So loud I can hardly stand it all the while he's pounding into me, thrusting in deeper and harder, rubbing the toy faster with every swipe.

My pussy squeezes his cock, and it drives him wild. "Come for me, my queen. I can't hold off any longer. It's too much. It's all too much, and you feel too good."

He doesn't even have to tell me. My body is already one step ahead of him, coiled tight like a spring, until I snap and explode. I scream, falling forward, my cries muffled in his shoulder as he bellows out a sound I've never heard come from his lips. My vision frays at the edges as a delicious, never-ending euphoria barrels through me.

"Fuck, yes. Fuck!" And then he's shooting himself inside me, coming in me for the first time since the night we made Mason in the club bathroom. I feel his cock throbbing with every jerk of his seizing body. His teeth sink into my shoulder, clamping down, biting me, but his tongue is there to lick away the sting.

The toy shuts off, and I feel like I can finally catch my breath.

Little by little, his movements slow and then stop. He pulls his cock out of me, dragging a wince from both of us. His cum immediately starts to leak out of me, and he reaches down, playing with it, rubbing it over my pussy, and then shoving some of it back in.

"You weren't kidding," I remark.

"You're the only woman I've ever come inside of. Watching it leak out of you is gratifying in a very male way, but it also feels criminal. Come 'ere." He sweeps his arm around my back, drawing me to his chest, and then he takes us both to the floor on the plush, white bathmat.

"There's a bed in the other room, you know."

"But doesn't that feel like ten miles away right now?"

"It sort of does," I agree.

Gathering me onto his chest, he holds me close, my body wrapped around his like a vine.

"That was like nothing I've ever experienced before. How does that happen?" His voice is bewildered. "How can each time with you be so different and yet better than the last?"

"You're asking me? You're the one with all the experience here."

His fingers trace a pattern on my hip. "I've never had that type of experience before, Wynter. It's never been like this with anyone. Everything with you is a first. Everything is new. And it's all remarkable because it's with you." A soft breath exhales from his lungs, though the sound is deep and resonating and maybe a bit regretful. "You know what this means now that we're together, right? I said I love you, and you said it back. That means this isn't temporary." He angles his head down, making sure to catch my eyes. Making sure I'm listening to his words and gathering their meaning. "It means it isn't just for now. It's us, and it's forever."

"Asher, we can't make that sort of promise with each other right now. We have no idea what the future will grant us. We have no idea what's headed our way. There's a real possibility this might not go the way we want it to go. We knew the risks when we started this. Those haven't changed. If anything, they've grown now that we're here."

His expression turns fierce. Unrelenting. Determined.

"Do you think I'm gonna allow something to come between us? Do you think I'm gonna let anything—or anyone—keep me from the woman and son I love? Impossible."

"What happens if you get traded? What happens if you have to move?"

"Then we figure it out, Wynter. In case you missed it, I'm a foot-ball player. We don't quit, and we never give up, and we play for the win or nothing at all. You're my win. Without you and Mason, there's nothing to play for. It's just emptiness. You're both my endgame. Trust me that I'll figure this all out for both of us."

Trust. That's never exactly been something I'm good at, but there's no sense in arguing about it now either. That will come later, I'm sure of it. But for now, I lie here in his arms, feeling safe, protected, loved, and it's enough to make me never want to let go.

# 28

---

## WYNTER

"Jerome Rice needs surgery," I tell Joe Tuesday morning after being summoned to his office and trudging down here with as much enthusiasm as a troublemaker being called to the principal's office. "It's possibly season-ending," I continue when the man does little more than stare at me stoically from behind his desk. "When he lacerated his hand on the other player's cleats, he tore a ligament."

Joe curses. It's the third player—including Asher—to have surgery this season, and they're only heading into their fourth game on Monday night.

"When do you plan to operate?"

"I don't. I've referred him to a hand specialist. I do mostly knees and shoulders. Hands are delicate."

"Fine. You're traveling with the team this weekend."

I roll my eyes at him, loving how it makes his jaw tick. "No, I'm not. We've had this discussion already, Joe, and I told you then that I will not be traveling with the team. If you don't like it, find someone else."

The first game of the season was an away game, and he didn't mention anything about traveling with the team that week. The last two weeks have been home games, so it wasn't necessary. Now he's back at this crap again apparently.

"And I already told you it's part of your job requirement. What if a player is hurt when we're on the road?"

"I feel as though we're going around in circles. If a player is hurt while you're traveling, he can be attended to by the team's general physician, the training staff, or a local surgeon if need be. But I'm not traveling with the team," I say firmly. "Fire me if you don't like it."

He sits forward, placing his folded hands on his desk. "I have no plans to fire you, Wynter, much to your dismay. How about you tell me *why* you won't travel with us?"

Something in his tone gives me pause. "Hatred of football. Hatred of you. No desire to spend more of my time with a pack of meat-heads." I throw them out, ticking each one off on my fingers.

I'm stalling.

I can see it in his eyes. He knows about Mason. I don't know how he knows, but he does.

"And what about your son? Does he enter into that decision at all?"

My breath hitches high in my chest, and I take an instinctive step forward, the mother in me needing to protect my son. And if he knows about Mason, does he also know that Asher is the father? It's been more than six weeks since Mason and I moved in with him, and in all that time, we've been careful not to be seen together in public.

"How do you know about my son?" I grip the back of the empty chair facing him, half ready to strangle Joe yet again. He has a way of bringing out the worst side of me and reducing my patience and cool to nothing.

He doesn't even blink or register any emotion. God, I hate this man.

"Limbick told me about him."

Fucking Limpdick and his big mouth.

"What right did he have to tell you anything personal about me?"

"He assumed I already knew. Since *he* already knew I'm your father."

"That's simply DNA, Joe. You're not my father. Gary is my father."

His nostrils flaring is his only reaction.

"In any event," he continues smoothly, "I told him I required you to travel with the team, and he told me he wouldn't push that on you since you're a single mother, and he can't ask you to travel like that when you have an infant son to look after."

Wow. Color me shocked that Limbick—now I feel a bit guilty for calling him Limpdick—stood up to Joe on my behalf.

"So I'm asking if that's your reason for not wanting to travel with the team?" He finishes without missing a beat.

I grit my teeth. "Yes. My son is the reason I won't travel with the team."

"Were you ever going to tell me about him?"

"No," I answer honestly, and that does something to him. I'm not even sure what, but in a flash, he's on his feet and pacing to the window behind him. His hands meet his hips, and then he's staring out at the field, and I can't see his expression. For reasons beyond my comprehension, I feel a twinge of guilt and regret, but I quickly push that away in favor of needing answers. "Why am I here, Joe? Why did you bring me on? I've asked you before and you wouldn't tell me."

He releases an audible breath, keeping his back to me as he speaks. "Similar to how you weren't going to tell me about my grandson, I won't explain my reasons for having you here beyond what I've already told you."

I shake my head. It hurts to hear him call Mason his grandson. He has no right to make such a personal claim to him.

"Who's the father?"

I laugh caustically. "None of your business."

"Do you even know?"

"Fuck you, Joseph," I snap. "You're the last man to ever lecture about fathers or their presence in their children's lives."

"Perhaps, but that doesn't mean I want that for you."

There is an ornate cylindrical glass paperweight sitting heavy on his desk. I bet it would shatter the window by his head if I chucked it. "You don't give a shit about me!" I yell, at my wits' end, hating that he got me here with a few choice words. "You never did! I was five when you left, and you didn't give two shits about doing that to me or my mother. She became a single mom thanks to you, or did you forget that?"

He spins around in a flurry just as the door to his office bursts open and Asher is there. No knock, no, *you wanted to see me*. There is fire and protective resolve in his eyes. "I heard shouting. Is everything okay?"

His attention is on me. Not on Joe.

Asher needs to go. He needs to be careful. He needs to not insert himself into anything that happens between me and Joe. He needs to be Switzerland in order to protect himself and his career, but that's not how Asher Reyes works.

Especially when it comes to me.

"Everything is fine. Just a disagreement between me and your coach. It's over now." I look back at Joe. "I'll update you after the surgery on Mr. Rice. The matter of me traveling with the team is now closed."

It's not a question, but he gives me a firm nod all the same. Good.

I spin around and storm out—not waiting on Asher because I obviously can't—heading for the freaking field because that's where I'm supposed to be for the next five flipping hours that they hold their practice.

"Hey, everything good?" Dean exits the locker room and catches me in the middle of my march, my face no doubt a mask of anarchy and rage.

"Sure. Awesome."

"Looks that way," he deadpans.

I don't respond, and he follows me out onto the field, where some of the players and assistant coaches are gathering. The cool bite of early autumn in New England hits my face, simmering some of my heat.

"Now's a bad time to ask you out, right?"

I come to an abrupt halt and turn to look at Dean, who does the same only to have someone slam into his back. Hard. "Oh, sorry, Doctor. Didn't mean to bump you like that."

The look in Asher's eyes tells me that's exactly what he meant to do.

"No problem," Dean remarks, not sparing Asher so much as a glance. He's waiting me out, only Asher isn't leaving.

"Good stuff. Dr. Hathaway, do you have a minute? I had a question about my shoulder."

I blink up at Asher and then nod before turning back to Dean. "I'll see you out there."

"Great. We can talk more then."

Dean saunters off, and then Asher is grabbing my arm and pulling me to the edge of the field on the opposite side from where the players and staff are congregating.

"What are you doing?" I hiss, looking around and then taking a step back away from him to create some distance.

"That's my question to you."

"What's that supposed to mean?" I cut back, not liking his accusatory tone.

He runs a hand through his hair and blows out a heavy sigh. "Sorry. I just... I hate this. I hate that men ask you out because they don't know you're mine. I hate that I can't protect you from Joe. I hate having to pretend and keep us a secret. I'm not good at it. It's not the way I'm built."

"He knows about Mason," I tell him instead of addressing that because there is no answer or immediate solution to any of that.

Asher's back stiffens, and he glances over his shoulder at where Joe is now starting practice. Asher should be over there. He should not be standing here with me, and we should not be talking like this.

He turns back to me. "How?"

"My boss mentioned it without knowing he shouldn't. Joe doesn't know about you. He thinks I'm a completely single mother with no father in the picture."

"Wynter, I don't like this."

"What's he going to do, Asher? Kidnap him? He may be a selfish, self-serving asshole, but he's not a psycho, and he's not dangerous."

He huffs out a breath, his hands on his lean hips, and he nods. "You better say no to Dr. Horowitz."

"You think?"

His eyes narrow. "I know."

I smirk. "But he's a neurologist."

Asher growls, but he can't fight his grin either. "You're dangerous for my heart, Doctor. You make it beat in all kinds of new, unfamiliar ways."

"Right back atcha, player. Now go get out there before this becomes obvious."

"I love you," he mouths, and then jogs away, heading straight onto the field with the other players. A queasiness flutters over me as I walk in Dean's direction, already dreading this conversation.

"Reyes certainly requires a lot of your time and attention," he drawls casually when I fall in beside him. Only I know the male species enough after living with Asher to understand nothing is casual when they're asking about another man.

"Football players seem to be needier than hockey and basketball players are after they're injured."

He chuckles at my brush-off, liking that answer.

"What do you think though? About dinner?"

"It's a nice offer, and if I weren't seeing someone right now, I'd consider it."

He taps his fingers on his khaki-clad thigh, but I can hear the surprise in his voice since I've never mentioned anyone in all the times we've chatted. "You're seeing someone? Is that new?"

"It's new but serious."

He bobs his head. "I get it. No worries. I just thought I'd try."

I offer him a wan smile, and we both let it go. Practice drags and drags, but we fall back into friendly chit-chat, which is a relief. We tell stories about med school and residency until my phone rings in my pocket. I give him a sheepish look and then slip it out, walking away in a hurry for privacy when I see it's the daycare.

"Hello?"

"Dr. Hathaway?"

"Speaking."

"I'm so sorry to bother you, but Mason doesn't seem to be feeling well. He's been fussy for most of the morning, and he just threw up. When we checked his temperature, it shows he has a fever."

"Oh my gosh." My hand covers my mouth and I spin around, facing the field. "How high is his temperature?"

"It's 103.8."

My heart picks up a few extra beats. That's not a crazy high fever for a child. I know this. But still, it's the first time he's ever been sick or had a fever, and it being high like that makes me nervous. The medical part of my brain implodes when it comes to my son.

"I'm on my way to get him now."

"Thank you. We'll see you soon."

She disconnects the call, and I shove my phone back in my pocket and race over to Dean. "I have to go. My son is sick. Can you let them know?" I don't even know why I'm asking or who I want him to let know. Certainly not Joe, and it's not like he can go over and tell Asher.

"Of course. Is everything okay?"

"Yeah. Just a fever, and he threw up." I give him a goodbye wave, and then start to run off the field, all the while I throw quick, darting glances at Asher, hoping to catch his eye. On my third try, right before I reach the tunnel, he glances at me with worry creasing his brow. I don't know what to do, so I pull out my phone and wave it back and forth by my hip so he can see it. Then I shoot him a text telling him about Mason and leave.

I doubt he can do anything right now. His phone is in the locker room, and he's stuck on the field with the team.

What a morning this has been.

On my way over to the hospital, I call Fallon, who's his pediatrician. She's seeing patients but tells me she'll pop over to Asher's place after her shift to take a look at Mason. Gotta love doctor friends who will make house calls.

I reach the hospital, park in my spot, and then fly through the building up to the daycare. My poor baby is tucked into his teacher's chest, his cheeks bright and rosy. "Mason," I call gently as I approach, running my hand over his hair. He lets out a whiny cry when I pick him up. I kiss his forehead. "Yikes. He's burning up."

"Yes, he is," his teacher agrees. "We can't give him anything here to bring it down."

"That's okay. I'll bring him home and give him something there." I pull him into my arms and hug him tightly against me. "Let's get you home, baby boy."

# 29

## ASHER

The *thump, thump, thump* of my heart only intensifies as the afternoon progresses. I don't have access to my phone, so I don't know what the hell is going on. Wynter left the field in a rush and while I want to race after her, I not only can't for myself, but I know she'd be angry if I did. So I'm stuck. And it sucks.

The second we're done on the field, I run to my locker, pull out my phone, and read her text.

> Ice queen: I received a call from Mason's daycare. He has a fever and threw up. I'm on my way to get him. He's fine and I'm on it. Call me when you're on your way home. Love you.

Dammit. That was three hours ago.

I don't even bother changing or de-sweating. Who cares? I wasn't doing much on the field anyway. Instead, I tell my quarterback coach that I have a family emergency and leave. After the shouting I heard between Joe and Wynter earlier today, I'm not even sure what to do or think anymore. My team demands my allegiance, but so does my family, and I'm stuck somewhere in between that.

I dial up Wynter in my car the moment I put it in drive. She picks up on the third ring and I can hear Mason crying in the background.

"Hey," I say. "What's going on? Is he okay?"

"Yes. Fallon is here and looked him over. She thinks it's a virus. Likely something he picked up in daycare, which of course fills me with guilt."

"Stop it. You work, and so do I. Though maybe when we're out in the open, we'll discuss getting a nanny for him."

"Maybe," she says and then comforts Mason. "Shh. It's okay."

"I'm on my way home. Do you need me to pick anything up?"

"Actually, if you could stop at the pharmacy and get some acetaminophen, that would be great. Dye-free if they have it. I have ibuprofen here, but Fallon suggested alternating that with acetaminophen for his fever."

"I'm not quite sure what all that means, but I'm on it. Anything else?"

"I can't think of anything."

"Well, if you do, text me. I love you both."

I can hear the smile in her voice when she says, "We love you too."

She disconnects the call, and I drive home, restless and edgy. It's been a strange day. I took some reps on the field. Light throwing. Nothing too much, and definitely no contact. But I could feel it. The way my arm responded. How well I threw the ball. How accurate I was. I could feel it all coming back, and the buzz of playing hit me hard.

Leo has been doing well despite a few rookie hiccups, and I have no illusions he's Coach's favorite son at the moment. The team has won two of our first three games, which is great for the team but bad for me. I will be ready to hit the field again in the next few weeks, and I'm not sure how that will shake out. Coach hasn't said a word about it.

I park in my spot in the garage and then walk up through the building to the front. There's a pharmacy three blocks down, but when I exit my building, there are a few paparazzi lingering around, which I don't understand at this point.

If I didn't know better, I'd think someone was feeding them something to keep them interested in me all this time.

"Asher!" they yell in unison, immediately running over to me and getting right up in my face. "Have you heard from Saline since you walked out on her at the restaurant? Rumor has it she's now dating Derek Sandibal of the Yankees. Any comments on that?"

I give the customary smile and wave and start off, keeping my head tucked down as I hot-foot it down the sidewalk.

"How do you feel about Leo Dodd leading the team?" one continues, persistent as hell. "Do you think there's room for both of you on the Rebels? Care to comment on LA's interest in you?"

*LA?* That's news to me.

Then again, these guys throw shit around hoping something will stick and make me react.

They give up the chase after half a block, and by the time I make it to the pharmacy, I'm positive I'm alone. Only I'm in a pharmacy looking for children's medicine with zero disguise on. I'm not even wearing a hat. And it gets worse from there when I reach the children's cold medicine aisle and find about ten thousand different options.

Brand name, off-brand name, store brand, grape, cherry, bubble gum.

I stare at the shelves of boxes and start to panic myself into a sweat. So I do what any brilliant man in my position would do. I phone a friend.

"What's going on, brother?"

"Callan, I need my second favorite doctor to help me out."

"You call me your second favorite and expect my help after that?"

"My lady love fixed my shoulder, dude. Sorry, but you've been demoted. For real though, Mason has a fever, and I guess Fallon told Wynter that he needs acetaminophen in addition to ibuprofen?"

"Is it just a fever or something else?"

I shake my head in frustration. Like I have real answers to these questions. Doesn't he know I'm on the clock here? "I don't know, man. She told me Fallon told her it's likely a virus. He threw up before, but I don't know about now. What do I do about the meds?"

"If his fever is high, then you might need to alternate the meds, so he gets better fever coverage."

"Right. Whatever." I roll my eyes at his doctor language. "But I'm in the pharmacy and there are about ten thousand options, and I don't want to bother Wynter when she's with Mason, and if I call Fallon, I look like a man who can't handle the assignment."

"True. Smart to call me. Never let them know all the ways we struggle. He'll be a year old next week, so you want infant acetaminophen, not children's."

My eyes widen, and I take a step to the left where it looks like the infant stuff is. "I totally would have fucked that up. Next."

"There really is no difference between brand and off-brand, but who are we kidding here? You're obviously buying name brand, so go with that."

"Truth. She mentioned dye-free. How can I tell if it is?"

"It'll say it on the box. Dye-free means it won't have artificial dyes in it. It'll be a milky, semi-translucent whiteish color instead." He starts cracking up. "Actually, it sort of looks like cum."

My face scrunches up in disgust. "That's the grossest thing I've ever heard."

He's laughing his ass off now. "I know, but it does. I will never look at that the same way again."

"Me either. What do I do about flavor?"

"Kids usually do well with grape or berry flavor."

I pick up a box of each, read over the packaging to make sure it says dye-free and infant formulation, and then tuck them under my arm. "Got 'em. Thanks, brother. I owe you one. Or maybe not for the cum comment. You do know I'm about to give this to my son, right?"

"Yeah. My bad. I shouldn't have gone there. Text me later to tell me how he's doing."

"Will do. Later."

I disconnect the call and slide my phone back into the pocket of my track pants. Tugging the two boxes out from beneath my arm, I turn toward the register when I stop short. Joe Cardone is standing at the end of the aisle, staring at me as if I'm a convicted felon. He takes a few steps in my direction, and part of me is reveling in this.

A showdown with him away from the field.

"Coach," I greet him.

"I suspected there was something between you and my daughter when you blew into my office today and looked like you were ready to tear me apart for upsetting her. Then when I saw you two talking on the field and later running off claiming a family emergency, I knew my hunch was right. What I didn't know when I followed you home is that you're the father of my grandson." His gaze pointedly drops to the two boxes in my hands, and he clearly overheard me on the phone with Callan. I called Mason my son not even a minute ago.

"Since we're showing our hands, you should know that I know about you too. Everything."

He squints at me, wondering what I'm getting at, suggesting that there is more beyond him simply being Wynter's father, which he just admitted to when he referred to Mason as his grandson. I was posturing, riding on my own hunch after my conversation with Gary that day by the pool.

But his expression tells me I'm dead on with that.

"What exactly is it that you think you know about me?"

All I offer him in return is a smirk.

"Tell me how you got to be the father because as far as I know, Wynter never stepped foot in Boston before she moved up here."

"Honestly Joe, it's none of your business, nor is my relationship with Wynter. You haven't earned any details from her, so you sure as hell haven't earned any from me."

"She's living with you?"

I shrug and watch as his nostrils flare and his jaw tics. It's his tell. I may always lose at poker to Aurelia, but I've played football long enough to know how to read an opponent.

"She's too good for you," he barks.

I laugh because that's about the least insulting thing this man could say to me. "I know."

"She's with you because of the kid. Not because she cares about you. Wynter hates football players."

"The way I see it, Coach, she only hates one."

He takes a step forward, trying to get into my personal space. He's a big guy. Tall and broad and, at one time, a hell of a quarterback. Only I've got two inches and about thirty pounds of muscle on him. I might be fucking up my career in all kinds of ways, but he needs to know he doesn't intimidate me.

"What happens when I trade you at the end of the season?" he asks coolly. "No matter the outcome of the surgery, I was getting rid of you anyway. You're worth a lot for a trade and Leo can easily be the future of this team. Not you. What happens then? You think she'll move with you?" He makes a tsking noise as he shakes his head. "Her career is far more important to her than you will ever be. I know your kind, Reyes. I *was* you. And while I might not have done right by my daughter in the past, I won't allow her to make the same mistakes her mother did."

He just confirmed what I had already suspected. I'll never play for the Boston Rebels again. The pain that comes with that discovery is nothing short of a slice through the heart. My team, my town, my family. They're all here.

"By mistake you mean marrying a lying, cheating, child-abandoning asshole?" I take a step this time, getting right up in his face and using my height and size to my advantage. "You think you know me? Why? Because I was a rock star for a while and now, I play professional football? Because I fucked around a bit before I met Wynter?" I glare down at him. "You're a fool. You know nothing about me, and nothing about Wynter. You think intentionally trying to tear her family apart will help you win her favor? It won't. I know exactly what you're attempting to do with her and let me save you the time. She's not interested in having anything to do with you. Wynter, unlike you, is loyal. She is loving. She wants what's best for *our* son. She is my fucking north star, and I will always find my way home to her and our son. *Always*."

I shoulder past him, making sure I bump him as I go. At this point, it doesn't matter. I'm gone from the team in his eyes, and he's the coach with the power to make it happen. I'm simply the ball player. One with limited options if I want to continue to play.

"Nice to know you're so worried about my son that you didn't even ask if he's okay or why I'm purchasing fever medicine for him. Asshole."

I walk up to the register, pay for the medicine, and then walk home to my family, fuming and burning with a rage so deep I'm positive there is no end to it. I'm not an angry man. It's not who I am. Until you fuck with me. Until you fuck with my people.

Then I'm ruthless.

Joe Cardone might mistake my easy smiles and quick laughs for being stupid. For being a pushover. For not being all that serious. But he's got another think coming his way.

I pull up Lenox's number the second the elevator doors close behind me because there is no way I'd dare text him this. He picks up on the second ring with a grunt.

"I need intel on Cardone. Get me everything you can."

I can practically hear him smiling when he says, "I was wondering when you'd ask. You sure you want to go down this road, and how deep are we talking?"

I start to pace around the small metal box as it climbs floors. "As deep as you can go. He's fighting dirty, and I plan to fight even dirtier."

"I'm on it."

"Good. Thanks, man, I owe you."

"Give your big man a fist-pound for me and we're even." He disconnects the call, but I can't even muster a grin at that. Lenox will get me any skeletons Joe is trying to keep hidden in his closet. Something tells me I'm going to need them.

Whatever they are.

But as I'm riding up, I'm hit with what Joe said. Truly hit by it. I can't idly sit around and allow Joe to control my life. My career. My future. With a heaviness in my chest that resembles something like grief, I text Hunter. I'm under contract through next season, which is why Joe has the power to trade me anytime he likes. But being a player, I have some options if I'm proactive. I can position myself in a way that's advantageous to where I'm willing to end up—even if it's not in Boston.

I'm not sure I have any other choice but to put out feelers and see what catches.

A few minutes later, I enter the apartment and go searching for Wynter and Mason, only to find them in his room in the rocking chair. The lights are off, and his nightlight is on. Mason's head is against her chest, his little butt on her lap. She holds him as she gently rocks him in the chair.

I raise the brown bag up like a triumphant warrior returning from battle, and she gives me a soft, approving smile. "Thank you. Is he asleep? I'm afraid to move to check."

"Looks to be that way." I walk in and crouch down beside them, running my hand along the back of his soft head. "How's he doing? He feels cool."

"Poor baby threw up all over himself, and I had to give him a quick bath. That broke his fever along with the ibuprofen, though I wonder how much of the ibuprofen he vomited. Every time I try to put him down, he cries though."

"Let me try?"

She worries her lip with her teeth but then gives me a nod. I slip my hands around his little body and then carefully shift him to my good shoulder. He comes easily, hardly stirring, even as I stand and walk him over to his crib. I plant a gentle kiss on the top of his head and then set him down.

Wynter stands, both of us holding our breath, waiting for him to wake up, and when he doesn't, we creep out of the room, shutting the door behind us as quietly as we can.

"I think I might sleep in my old room tonight so I'm close to him," she whispers, looking tired already even though it's not even eight.

I take her hand and walk her toward the kitchen, where I direct her onto a bar stool, and then go about fixing us up a couple of chicken burritos because I have the stuff for them in the fridge.

"That's fine. Can I sleep in there with you?" I ask.

She laughs as if my question is ridiculous. "I already assumed you would since I know you'd never want to sleep across the apartment from us."

Something in the way she says that, in the way she *knows* how I feel about her and how I feel about Mason, has me rounding the island and taking her face in my hands. I kiss her. Urgently. Desperately. Like a man who feels as though he's only holding onto things by a thin thread.

Her hand cups my jaw, running along my smooth cheek before she pushes her finger into my chin dimple playfully. "What was that for?"

I need to tell her that Joe knows I'm Mason's father, and I will. But if I tell her I'm being traded and there is no plan in place for it, she'll freak out. I know she will. I have to figure that part out so I can better reassure her that everything can still work with us.

But right now, I need her. I need to touch her and hear her moan my name. I need to know that this thing between us is real and lasting. No matter what.

So instead of answering her, I lift her out of her seat and drop her on the stone counter. She eyes me curiously, likely because I'm not smiling or flirting the way I always do. I'm dead-ass serious right now, truly afraid for the first time in my life because for the first time in my life, I have something I'm unwilling to lose.

I tear her shirt off, throwing it somewhere behind me, and then my mouth dives in, kissing my favorite spot on her neck and inhaling her sweet fragrance. Her hands get lost in my hair, her body swaying backward on the counter, and I grab her thigh, dragging her closer to me until my body is cradled in the V of her thighs.

She's not going anywhere.

"Asher?" She moans, but there's a question on the back end of it. I shake my head, silently telling her not now, as I suck on her neck and begin to trail open-mouthed kisses down to her chest. My hand comes up, cupping and lifting one breast until the soft swell meets my lips. In a flash, I rip down the cup, and then capture her nipple in my mouth, sucking roughly on it.

Wynter lets out a low whimper as I eagerly devour her nipple, swirling my tongue around the stiff peak, and then immediately sucking it back into my mouth. Reaching around her back, I unclasp her bra, and toss it in the same direction her shirt went. And with her completely bare to me from the waist up, I take full advantage, my mouth shifting over to her other full tit. My teeth scrape along her pert nipple while my fingers pinch and twist her other.

My hand returns to her thigh, dragging up her leggings until I reach her warm, wet center. She rocks into my touch as I start to rub her there, needing more contact than I can give her with the barrier of cotton between us. Abandoning her nipple, I use both hands to grasp the seam of her leggings at the crotch, and then in one swift motion, tear it apart, shredding the fabric and making her gasp in surprise.

I continue to feast on her tits while I pull her thong to the side and start rubbing her clit. She hums in pleasure, her nails scraping down the fabric of my shirt before she balls it up in her fists and rips it up and over my head.

"Asher, I need you."

I smile against her skin as I trail up to her mouth. "How much?" I ask, staring into her dark, green eyes just as I shove two fingers inside her.

"Ah!" she cries, her eyelids flickering, fighting the urge to close. I slide my fingers in and out of her dripping wet pussy while my thumb plays with her clit.

"So much," she pants, her nails digging into my good shoulder. She's a volcano, already so close to erupting, always so fucking responsive to everything I do. I'll never tire of her. I'll always want —*need*—more of her. And with that, I need her so irrevocably lost in me that nothing else matters but us and this.

My free hand cups her jaw, forcing her to see the storm in my eyes, how wound tight I am, the way I'm trembling for her. "I love you."

And then I kiss her, my tongue swirling with hers, my mouth stealing every available breath from her I can. My fingers pick up their pace, matching the speed and motion of my tongue in her mouth.

"My tongue or my fingers?" I ask, sucking her plump bottom lip into my mouth and then releasing it with a slow drag of my teeth. I want to fuck her sweaty and fast until she's gasping my name, but I also want my queen to come once before she comes again on my cock.

"That," she moans, her cheeks flushed and her eyes wild with desire. "Keep doing that. I'm already so close."

"How's this? I'm going to fuck you like this..." I pump faster and press harder on her clit until she gasps, her eyes closing and her head flying back, no longer able to fight it. "And the second you start to come, I'm going to slam inside you."

"Oh, God. Yes. Please, yes."

Shoving down the waist of my track pants, my heavy, hard cock springs free and I give it a lazy jerk. I slip my fingers from her pussy and move them up to her clit, focusing on that as I use the fat tip of my dick to rub her entrance. Her chin drops, her greedy eyes matching my own as we both stare shamelessly at the erotic display before us.

"Oh, fuck," she whimpers. "Oh, fuck."

I'm right there with her, having to bite my lip and tighten my body so I don't come this instant. "I love watching your pussy come," I manage, my voice strained, the brutal need to drive into her over-whelming, but this visual... this fucking visual is so goddamn hot, I don't want it to end either.

Only, in her next breath, she starts to come. Her back arches and her arms give out, and then her face plants against my chest as she shudders and shakes, moaning and groaning. And that's when I thrust all the way inside her as deep as my cock can go.

A scream wrenches the air and my lips slam down on hers,

kissing her through her orgasm as I begin to fuck her into another one. I push her down onto the counter of the island, my forearms on either side of her, and I use my hips as weapons to piston me in and out of her. Her legs are wrapped around my waist, and her arms are snaked around my neck as she holds me to her, chest to chest.

Sweat shivers across my back, and my heart flutters out a crazy rhythm as I stare into her eyes. Our foreheads meet, and then I take her hands, intertwining our fingers and setting our joined hands just above her head. I continue driving in deep, swirling my hips and pressing down so my pubic bone rubs her clit with every thrust.

I take her like this until fire burns in her eyes.

Until neither of us can hold off another second. Until flashes of light dance behind my eyes and she chants my name, moaning and quivering beneath me. Then I come inside of her, throbbing, and pulsing, and giving her every piece of me I have.

"I love you," I breathe against her lips.

She smiles, her eyes clear and bright even as we're both still winded. "Love you."

"Forever," I promise. Because that's the only truth that will get me through this right now.

# 30

## WYNTER

Asher was officially cleared to play by me and the training staff on Tuesday. I've never seen an athlete, or anyone for that matter, work as hard to get themselves back into game form as he has. Hours and hours of physical therapy, weights, running, and training. He's been throwing the ball for a couple of weeks now, but Tuesday he went out on the field for practice and proved he was ready.

And yet he's riding the bench.

Something the fans in the stadium are *not* happy about and are not shy about letting Joe and the entire team know.

Leo lost horrifically last week. Three interceptions and one fumble. And after Asher's press conference on Wednesday, declaring himself physically ready to play, the crowd is demanding their hero take the field to lead them to victory.

I haven't seen Asher much today. He woke up this morning, went for a very early run, and then he got a phone call, and before I knew what was happening, he told me he had to get to the field early and practically raced out the door. Since he ran out on the field with the team, he's been... I don't know... agitated, maybe.

Like lava simmering beneath the surface, ready to blow.

I'm bundled up on the sidelines, wearing more layers than I can count, topped off with a Rebels puffy coat. It's the middle of October, and it's especially miserable out today as the temperature huddles around freezing and light icy rain falls from the sky.

"I miss Miami," I grumble to Dean, who looks like he's about to go yachting in khaki pants and a navy Rebels sweater. "Aren't you freezing?"

"Are you kidding me? This is football weather."

I roll my eyes skyward, only they start to freeze as ice pellets them making me wince. There are heaters blasting on the sidelines, but those are for the players, and Asher told me I'd look like a wimp if I stand in front of them the entire game. I flipped him off and put myself in a position where I can catch the very edge of one of them.

I'm fine with being a wimp if it means I'm warm.

Asher is pacing the sideline, talking to Leo, and grumbling out curses when plays don't go well. The team is playing five hundred football, Dean explained to me, which means their record isn't winning or losing. Considering the expectations for the team this year, I think it's safe to say no one is happy.

Least of all Asher right now.

He's changed a bit over the last few weeks. He smiles less, and his manner seems... harder. Less go-with-the-flow. Less himself. I've pushed a little bit, but he won't talk about it. I know it's related to everything that's happening with his position on the team and its future.

Joe knows about me and Asher, and how Asher is Mason's father. Asher told me he followed him to the drug store and confronted him there, but then Joe had the audacity to tell me I should end it with him because he's not good enough for me.

I laughed in his face and walked away.

But I also know that Joe doesn't like Asher and that his time on this team is borrowed. What that means for me and Mason, I don't know. Only time will tell, and I force myself not to dwell on it. At least not until I have to.

"Remind me why we have to be on the field?"

Just as the words leave my mouth a defensive player comes barreling at Leo, who doesn't run or shift to deflect the onslaught. The defensive player plows through one of our offensive guys and straight into Leo, knocking him to the ground with so much force that I immediately cover my mouth with my hands to stifle my shriek of horror.

"Fuck," Dean hisses.

"Oh my God!" I grip his forearm. "Is he moving? Is he getting up? Is he okay?" I rise up on my toes to try and get a better look, but I'm shorter than all of these players by several inches.

A player waves over the training staff. "Doesn't look that way. This is why we stay on the field."

Dean grabs his medicine bag and runs out onto the field, and I find myself walking over to the sideline to where Asher is standing with his hands on his head, elbows butterflied out, and distress all over his face.

"He's unconscious," he tells me, and I feel my eyes prickling with tears. "I tried talking to him, and he hasn't responded, and I heard Ryder call that out to the staff."

"Dean is on it."

He gives me an absent nod, but that's it. Joe is on the field, standing over Leo and talking with the crew who are working on him. He wipes at his face, his expression grim, and then he points at Asher.

My heart gallops faster in my chest. "What does that mean?"

Asher blows out a breath. "It means I'm up."

"No."

The word is out of my mouth before I can stop it. Asher peers down at me, but after seeing that hit Leo just took and watching as they bring out the fucking cart and put him on a backboard with a neck collar, I can't help it.

"Asher." I follow him back to the bench where he grabs his helmet off a holder.

He turns back to me, stares around at everyone around us, and then back up at the crowd in the stands. And when he turns back to me, I see the grit and raw determination in his eyes and the locked set of his jaw.

"I'll be fine."

The crowd erupts in applause as Leo gives a small thumbs-up as they load him onto the cart and drive him out toward the tunnel. Thank God for that!

"I have to get warmed up."

"Asher!"

His hand cups my jaw, and then his mouth slams down on mine. Rough and passionate, and taking no prisoners. Right here on the field. In front of the entire world, most likely because I'm positive there are cameras trained on the returning quarterback. But at this moment, I don't care.

I'm scared.

I don't want him to go out there, and I never thought about it in those terms before, but he could get *hurt*.

"You don't have to watch," he whispers against my mouth. "But this is what I do. And I'm damn fucking good at it." He steps back and gives me an arrogant boy wink. "I love you." And then he puts his helmet on as a kid comes racing over, holding a ball, and ready to take some passes with him.

"I love you too," I murmur, but he's already gone, and now I'm stuck here like this. With my face plastered across the massive screens that line the upper portion of each endzone. Awesome.

I head back over to the returning training staff, doing my best to pretend not to notice that my face is blown up to the size of a blue whale in high definition or the players who are all staring and talking about me and their quarterback.

"Is he okay?" I ask one of the trainers.

"Yes. He got his bell rung and most definitely has a concussion. Dean is taking him back for an X-ray and possibly a CT scan, depending on what he discovers during his neuro exam."

"Good." I breathe out a sigh of relief. "I'm glad Dean is on it." Leo is a nice kid. A bit too cocky for his own good, but a nice kid.

Joe glares at me from the sideline, and I give him a cheeky grin.

He grumbles something I can't hear and then turns back to the field. What his problem with Asher is, I have no clue, but it doesn't matter. We're out there now. Asher just made us public, and any peace and quiet we had before is now gone.

I should be angry about that. It's not what we talked about at all, but I can't find my ire anywhere. My guy is on the field, and that seems to trump everything else at the moment.

"Don't worry," one of the players, whose name is Aaron I think, says to me. "They'll keep him safe, and Asher is the best in the league at evading the sack. I think he only had six all of last season."

"That's not a lot?" I ask, gnawing on my lip.

He grins at me. "There are quarterbacks who have six in a game."

"Oh." I grimace. "Okay. Got it."

"You get used to it," he tells me. "My wife never used to watch my games, but now she comes to every home game we have."

"Thank you for that," I tell him. "It helps."

My phone buzzes in my pocket, and I slip it out to see it's Fallon. "Excuse me."

I shift over toward the side—and the heater, let's be honest—for some privacy that I doubt I have any of.

Fallon: Asher kissing you is all over every sports network right now, whether they're broadcasting the game or not. You can also tell that he says I love you to you.

Me: Fabulous. What are the odds we make it home without a media storm or without people discovering that Asher is my baby daddy?

Fallon: Next to none. They'll know your name and who you are by the end of the game. I'm sorry.

Me: Thank you. It was bound to come out at some point.

That's the spin I'm going to put on it because it's the only one I've got. Asher steps onto the field, and the place erupts into thunder and lightning, vibrating the earth beneath my feet with its intensity and flashing endless light from camera phones. Asher throws his hand up in the air, thanking the fans, and then he's all business, going into the huddle and leading his team.

My heart hiccups into my throat and stays there, lodged like a lump of clay unable to be expelled. My fingers knot up and tuck under my chin like a six-year-old. I never really watch the games when I'm out here. I mean, I watch some of it. But I don't follow plays or downs or the score—or much of anything—other than the clock that I was always counting down.

But right now, I'm invested, my breath held along with every other fan here.

Ryder snaps the ball, and right off the damn bat, two guys on either side of the field go running the distance along with another guy I've heard referred to as a tight end. Asher fakes handing off the ball to the runner and then he sidesteps, dodging the advance of a defensive player, and lets the ball fly. Joe curses audibly, ripping his headset from his head and thrashing his arm out as if he's about to chuck it. The ball sails in a high, tight spiral that hits one of the players downfield midstride.

With the ball in his hands, he sprints down the field, only to be tackled on the twenty-yard line. Asher fist pumps into the air and then points at his wide receiver, but that's the only emotion he shows. Just like that, he's clapping his hands, and getting his team to run down the field, calling something out to each of them as they go.

Joe is losing his absolute mind on the sideline and then calls a timeout.

Asher is furious, yelling at Joe in a way I've never seen him do before as he comes running over to the sideline. The two of them go head-to-head, shouting words no one else can hear due to the roar of the crowd. Ryder inserts himself between the two of them and then starts walking forward, pushing Asher back onto the field.

"Follow the fucking plays I call!" I hear Joe belt out, and all Asher does is shake his head.

"I know!" He points at Joe over Ryder's shoulder. "I fucking know all about you, Joe. You're not calling shit today."

I have no idea what's going on, but I've never seen Asher like this. And what the hell did that mean? He knows about Joe? What does he know? Ryder grabs Asher by the facemask of his helmet, and then he's saying something that has Asher nodding. The timeout ends, and Asher is on the field, calling the play, going completely rogue.

Joe's headset goes flying, skidding across the grass, forcing two players to jump so it doesn't smash into them, and then it crashes against one of the heaters. He's ripping at his hair and for a man who is notoriously cool and composed, he's completely unhinged. The players shift, giving Joe a wider berth. Not even his assistant coaches will go near him.

My phone vibrates in my pocket again.

> Fallon: What the hell is going on? The announcers are going nuts, speculating about all kinds of things. Is Asher running the show and not listening to Joe? They're also saying he's been traded to LA.

My skin prickles with uneasiness.

> Me: What? No. That can't be. Asher would have told me if he was being traded.

Wouldn't he have?

> Fallon: I don't know. Layla, Aurelia, and I are watching. The guys are in another room talking about something. Did Asher say anything to you this morning? The announcers are now saying there's a deal in the works for a rare mid-season trade to LA, but now that Leo is hurt and Asher is on the field, they're stating that deal might end up on hold.

> Me: He went for a run and then left in a rush. He's been quiet and maybe a bit more inward and distant, but I assumed it was related to being benched. Then he just yelled at Joe that he knows about him. I don't know what he's talking about or what's going on.

Could she be right? Is Asher being traded to LA? And why wouldn't he have told me? He told me he wouldn't do this. I told him how I work. Where my mind tends to go. That I have freaking abandonment issues. So no. He wouldn't do this.

Right?

> Fallon: The guys know something for sure, but they're not sharing it yet. There's something going on beneath the surface. All I know is that Lenox was doing some digging into Joe. Grey let something slip before they went into the other room to talk. Maybe he found something on Joe. If I learn what it is, I'll text you.

> Me: Thank you.

I don't even know what else to say. What on earth could Lenox have found on Joe that would have Asher so furious? And what if Fallon is right? What if Asher is being traded to LA? And he didn't tell me.

## 31

---

### ASHER

Fuck Joe. He can actually just go and fuck right off if he thinks I'll ever listen to anything he has to say or follow his lead again. I received not one, but two calls this morning. It was the first one that really got my attention. Lenox had me running out the door, and after meeting up with him and learning everything he had to share, Joe is lucky that I made it through pregame warmups and the first half of the game without causing a mutiny.

My team deserves better from me, and they're the only reason I didn't lose my mind until he tried to start calling plays that would not only cause our team to lose but make me look weak and scared.

"Hand off for every down." That's what he said into my helmet. "You're not to throw the ball."

"That's exactly what the defense will expect me to do," I spat back.

"I don't give a shit, Reyes. You're on my team, and you'll do what I tell you to do."

Fat fucking chance I was going to do that.

Especially when my throwing arm is in top condition. He forgot that it wasn't my throwing arm that underwent surgery.

"You running this show?" Myers, my tight end questions when I get back into the huddle after completing that beauty of a pass.

"I am," I state resolutely, meeting the eyes of my guys one by one. "If anyone has a problem with that, now's the time to speak up."

Silence.

"All right. Denver draw left to Myers. Ready... break!"

We all clap our hands, and then my guys run into position. Ryder smacks my back, gives me a firm nod, and then I'm lined up behind him, calling out a dozen things to throw off the pace of the defense. Adrenaline pumps through my veins like a delicious drug, honing my muscles, sharpening my reflexes, and tightening my focus.

I go through my motions and then yell, "*Hike.*"

The ball snaps straight into my hands, and then I'm stepping back in the pocket, reading the defense and searching for my receivers, looking in the opposite direction of where I plan to throw the ball. I shift right, knowing my offensive line will do their jobs and keep me safe. Myers runs his fade route left. I fake right and then let the ball sail in his direction, watching as he turns his head over his shoulder at the right moment, and catches my bullet with two hands.

Right in the end zone.

"Yeah!" I jump in the air and then get slammed by my guys who lift me and carry me all the way to the sideline. The fans in the stands are going nuts, the sound a deafening roar. And because I'm a child at heart and in practice, I throw Joe—who is glaring so hard his face is redder than a fire engine—a smug grin and then turn to face the field, dismissing him.

It's funny; I almost wasn't sure what I was going to do when Lenox spilled all the tea to me. There were a lot of mixed emotions. A lot of wayward, fire-enraged, vengeful thoughts. But nothing is sweeter than stealing the team out from under him without him being able to do a damn thing about it.

This may very well be my last game as a Boston Rebel. I could be suspended or traded or even cut tomorrow. But this is my moment.

And right now, I own this.

Wynter is somewhere behind me, but I haven't dared look in her direction since I ran on the field. I know she has questions. I owe her more answers than she's even aware of. This involves her too. More so than ever before. But this isn't the moment to lose focus. Not when we're this close to victory.

She must sense that because she hasn't come over to me since I took the field.

The extra point kick is good, and then I head back to the bench where my offense has congregated. Kneeling on the cold earth, I start going through plays and strategy, when the offensive coordinator comes over to me.

"Asher, what the hell are you doing?"

I glance up at him. "My job. Leading my team to a W."

He shakes his head, his mouth twisted up. "You can't go against your coach like that, man. It's career suicide."

"When this is all over, I won't be the only one with things to answer for. Not by a long shot."

And something about that seems to do the trick because suddenly, my offensive coordinator is coaching us up, running through plays with me, and that's how we do things for the rest of the game. Joe doesn't come near us. Not once. In fact, he keeps his mouth shut and his eyes on the field.

But I know better than to think that he's declared defeat.

If anything, he's resting up, recharging his batteries in preparation for our next battle. Only he has no clue what's coming for him. None.

THE GAME COMES DOWN to a field goal in the final seconds of the game. We won, but there's a heaviness in the air as we all trudge into the locker room, Joe leading the pack to give the illusion that he still maintains control. I don't answer any of the reporters' questions, though they swarm me and Joe the second they're allowed on the field.

I started a coup, and generally, that doesn't hold so well in sports.

I search around for Wynter but don't see her anywhere, and then

I push my way toward the locker room, ignoring the questioning looks from my guys as we go. I will need to address this with them. With Wynter. With everyone.

I stop one of the trainers and ask about Leo. He tells me that Dr. Horowitz took him to the hospital, and that's all he knows right now. I can only hope he's okay.

Joe is nowhere to be found—evidently deciding to forgo his postgame speech—so I stand in the middle of the locker room and address my guys.

"I know you all have a lot of questions about today. I can't give you answers yet, but I will. I promise. You all played a hell of a game out there today, and I want us to all send up a silent, healing prayer for Leo."

The guys grunt and all circle around me, and then I head for the showers to get myself put together. The press conference is scheduled for after the game, and I know the press are already in there, waiting on me after what I pulled today.

In fact, I bet it's standing room only with reporters. Hell, ESPN is less than a two-hour drive. I'm not sure what I'm going to say. I need to speak directly to Joe, and I need Wynter and the team owner, Randolph there for that.

I shower quickly and change back into the suit I wore here since the team has a dress code for us. Slipping my phone out of my pocket, I take a look and see I have dozens of missed calls and texts. But it's the text from Wynter that has my breath stalled.

Ice Queen: Is this true?

There's a link to an ESPN news article with the headline. "Asher Reyes Rare Mid-Season Trade Deal With LA Possibly Put On Hold With Leo Dodd Injury."

Fuck. Chaos brews within me. I bolt up to my feet and head for the exit. How on earth did they hear about the trade? I can only imagine the thoughts going through Wynter's head.

Me: Where are you?

The dots start to dance on the screen, and anxious relief swarms through me. At least she's still talking to me. I should have told her. I should have talked to her this morning, but after meeting with Lenox, I ran out of time before I had to report to the field, and then I didn't see her much, and I certainly didn't have the opportunity to speak with her about anything this involved.

I couldn't do that on the field. But I had planned to talk to her tonight. I was going to tell her everything.

What I hadn't planned on was Leo's head injury or overthrowing my coach or coming out publicly about my relationship with Wynter or her finding out about the trade from a goddamn news article.

She won't understand this. I know she won't, and I already know her mind is going to some very dark places.

Ice Queen: Answer my question.

*Dammit.* I run an agitated hand through my hair, gripping it by the roots. I plow through the door and straight into a horde of waiting reporters. Fuck! I hold up my hand and press through them, pushing toward the staff-only part of the building as they rapid-fire question after question at me.

About the trade. About Joe. About Wynter—who they refer to by name.

All of this is blowing up at once, and with it, there's a very real chance I could lose my girl if I can't get to her and explain.

"Ash? Where are you going?" Arnold the press secretary for the team questions frantically. "You're expected in the press room. You have to give your post-game conference."

I shake my head as I quickly type out a reply to Wynter.

Me: Yes, but it's not what you think and it's not how it looks. I can explain. Where are you?

> Ice Queen: Not how it looks, and you can
> explain. Said by every man who was ever
> painted into a corner and guilty of their
> crimes.

Hell, if she isn't right with that.

> Me: That's not how this is. I promise. Please,
> I have a lot to tell you. A lot you need to know
> and not just about this stupid trade. Where
> are you?

*Come on, Wynter. Don't do this. I know I fucked up, but don't quit on me yet.*

> Me: I love you, and I swear on that love
> you've got the wrong idea on this. Please, my
> queen. I have so much to tell you and I was
> going to tell you everything tonight and then
> this blew up before I got my chance.

She doesn't respond, but something tells me she didn't leave the grounds either. She would have been mobbed, and I know that's not what she wants right now. Plus, I don't think she wants to run from me. I think in her heart she wants to trust me, and she wants me to tell her I didn't let her down.

> Me: Please. Tell me where you are so we can
> talk.

"Asher." Arnold grabs my arm, forcing my gaze to snap up to his. "Now, man. It's not a choice."

Fuck!

> Me: I'm being dragged into the press room.
> Don't leave. Just watch the post-game
> conference and we'll talk after. Please.

Reluctantly and with my stomach twisted into knots, I follow after

Arnold, passing by the press and then up to the podium of the press room where I'm immediately inundated with questions.

"Asher! Asher!" reporters cry out. "Is it true you're being traded to LA?"

I speak directly into the microphone, maintaining a relaxed expression and even eye contact. "I don't know any of the details on that at this point, but I can tell you that I did not request a trade, nor do I want one."

"Tell us what happened out there today with you and Coach Cardone."

"I won't go into specifics," I state, using my years of media training to guide me. "It's not to protect Coach Cardone but the other people involved. All I can say is that I'm excited to see where the rest of the season will take the Rebels and I look forward to working closely with Leo after he makes a full recovery. We're a team. Not a one-man operation. That's how we work and that's how we win. As a team."

"Except what sort of future can you have with the Rebels now that clearly you and Coach Cardone don't see eye-to-eye on how the team should be run? Especially when there's already a trade in the works."

I shrug at the reporter. "Again, I'm not going to comment on anything that has to do with Coach Cardone at this time. LA is a great team, but my heart is here in Boston."

"Asher?! What about the reports you have a son with Wynter Hathaway?"

My breath catches, but I quickly hide my reaction. Damn, that was fast.

I clear my throat, hoping Wynter is listening. Hoping she's still willing to give me a chance. "I do have a son with Dr. Hathaway. An incredible son who makes me the happiest and luckiest of fathers. But that's all I'll say on the subject, probably ever. Next question."

"You mouthed the words, I love you to Dr. Hathaway. Does this mean you're officially off the market?"

I laugh at the female reporter's suggestive eyebrow bouncing. "Yes, I'm one hundred percent off the market. With any luck and if I don't do something to screw it up, it'll stay that way for the rest of my life. Now if you're all done with your questions, I'd like to get to my family. We ask for your respect and to give us privacy. See you next weekend on the field."

I throw them a wave but proceed to ignore the rest of the questions. I have to find Wynter. I have to force her to listen to me.

So I do what I've done since I met her. I chase after her.

Running around the building in a frenzy, I'm not sure what to do or how to find her. That is, until I think a bit deeper, and then I smile, because I think I know where my girl is. Spinning on my heels and using my forearm to wipe at the fresh coat of sweat on my brow, I push through the men's room door—the bathroom where I ran into her for the second time—and sure enough, she's here.

Her hands are pressed onto the counter, her shoulders hunched forward, and her gaze is directed down as she stares at her phone with the streaming video of the press conference pulled up on it. When she hears the door, her head snaps in my direction, but before she can open her mouth and tell me to fuck off, I have her by the hips, and I'm hoisting her up and then dropping her onto the counter.

I step between her legs and cup her tear-streaked face in my hands. "I was never going to take the trade deal to LA," I start, my words rushing past my lips, desperate to get them out. "I didn't sign any contract or approve of any deal. The night Mason was sick and Joe followed me to the pharmacy, he threatened me and told me he was going to have me traded at the end of the season."

She sniffles, staring up at me through watery, furious eyes. "And you didn't feel that was something I should know? You told me about what happened between you and Joe at the pharmacy, but you left out that huge fucking part of it. How could you not tell me that you were going to be traded at the end of the season? You knew that was one of my major concerns. A very solid reason why I was so reluctant to get involved with you. You let me be blindsided by this."

"I'm sorry."

She gives me a shove, demanding distance. "I'm sorry is a crappy response. How on earth could you ever imagine I'd be okay with that?

Was that why you didn't tell me? Because you thought I'd end things?" Her face twists with anger and frustration, her features hiding none of the hurt I've caused her.

"I don't know. Maybe that was part of it," I admit truthfully. "There was a lot going on at the time and Joe had just learned about Mason and Mason was sick and I was overwhelmed and frankly, crushed by the notion that Joe was trying to get rid of me. I didn't want to tell you until I had things figured out, because I knew you'd freak out on me when you learned of Joe's plan."

"That was two weeks ago." She shakes her head incredulously. "Jesus, Asher, you should have told me you were going to be traded. I knew it was a possibility, but not a certainty."

I hold her face steady, not willing to let her slip away, even an inch. "I should have told you. You're right, and I was wrong for not doing that. At the time, I thought it would only upset you more. I didn't want you to doubt me, and I was worried you would. I thought I was handling it."

"Without me." She shoves me away for a second time. "Did it not occur to you that this involves me too?"

"I was trying to protect you."

"Fuck you!" she snaps. "You don't get to decide what I need protection from and what I don't. That's my call to make, and I can tell you unequivocally that lying and hiding things—as I've already told you—are about the worst things you can do with me. That instantly kills my trust when trust isn't something I'm ever quick to hand out."

I take a step back and spin in a circle, my hands on my head, the air in this bathroom stifling and unsettled. "I'm sorry, sweetheart. So very sorry. Please, you have to know that I'm not going anywhere you're not."

"I don't want to move."

"You don't have to."

"Oh really? That's not what it looks like right now." She blows out a flustered breath. "It's more than just this trade deal. It's that you hid things from me. Important things. And I know you're hiding more."

I nod. I am hiding more. "I have no excuse," I admit, turning back to face her and throwing my hands up in defeat. "I don't know why I did it. I thought I was doing the right thing. I thought I was protecting you because that's all I ever want to do. Joe is a sneaky motherfucker, and I needed time to formulate a plan while other things fell into place. I was worried you'd lose faith in me, but that's exactly what happened anyway, and I have no one to blame for that but myself."

I take a step in her direction, and she holds her hand out to me, stopping me.

I frantically search my brain for a way to fix this when it might already be too late for that. "Don't leave me, Wynter. I can handle losing a lot of things, but you aren't one of them. Don't end this. Let this be something we work through, not something that tears us apart."

"I don't want to end this," she declares, another tear slipping out and then dancing down her cheek. "But I don't know how to be with someone who hides things from me. That's what Joe did with my mom, and I won't be that woman. I won't live that life. You knew that when we got involved and yet, you did it anyway."

"I'll tell you everything," I plead, my hands out in front of me, desperate to touch her. "Every last detail. Right here and now."

She laughs sardonically, flicking disdainfully at the tears on her face. "Oh, I know you will. Start with this trade, Asher Reyes, and pray I take pity on your soul because right now, I'm a hot second from walking out of here and never coming back."

My stomach knots up. "You know I'd never let that happen, right? I'd always chase after you."

She slashes the air in front of us. "Shut up. I don't want you to be alpha, and I don't want you to be charming. I want you to be honest."

Fair enough.

"What happened is, the morning after my encounter with Joe, I went into Randolph's office and told him all about it. I also told him that I wanted to stay and he told me that Joe had called him right after he and I spoke in the pharmacy and demanded that I be traded as far from Boston as possible. Randolph told him he'd only consider that if he could get a good deal and I was agreeable. I told him I wasn't, but with Joe trying to get rid of me, I wasn't sure where to go from there. I did have my agent, Hunter, putting out some feelers to other East Coast teams. Places where, if I had to leave the team, at least I could fly home to you and Mason easily enough. Then this morning Randolph called me and told me that LA wanted to discuss the particulars of a mid-season trade for me. That the key players on their end had already been lined up and were agreeable."

"LA is Joe's previous team."

I tap my nose. "Exactly. LA had been informed by Joe that I wanted out, and they were anxious to make a deal. Going so far as to send over a preliminary contract for us to look over. Somehow the press got wind of the contract and then assumed it would be put on hold with Leo getting hurt. It's not going to happen. Any of it."

She squints bewilderedly. "Then why are they reporting that it is? They made it sound like it's a done deal."

"It's not. That's all I can tell you. I told Randolph this morning I wouldn't do it. LA is too far, and I won't consider any team on the West Coast. Joe took liberties he had no right to take simply to get rid of me. Randolph told me we'd discuss it all after the game. Then everything else happened."

She stares at me for a very long time as she processes what I'm telling her. "You were going to discuss a trade deal I knew nothing about."

My hands hit my hips, my insides stirring uncomfortably. "I was going to tell you about it tonight. I was going to tell you everything because there's a hell of a lot to this. More than just the trade bull-shit." My eyes cling to hers. "Wynter, I wasn't going to take the trade, so there wasn't anything to discuss with that."

That's not an answer she likes. "Explain to me how you're not out of here. Because it sounds like whether that trade happens now or later, it's going to happen."

"Before this morning, that was likely going to happen, yes. Now that's no longer the case. I promise you, I'm not going anywhere, and I will make sure of it once I speak to Randolph."

She shakes her head, her lips twisting into a frown. "I don't see how that's possible if Joe wants you gone that badly and he's the head coach."

"Trust me—"

"I don't," she interjects, her tone sharper than a blade as it cuts over me. "I'm pissed. Like seriously, supercharged pissed that I had to hear about it from Fallon and fucking ESPN."

I step back into the space between her legs. This time, she doesn't try to stop me. "Understood. It'll never happen again. From now on, you'll hear everything from me without delay. I'll never keep anything from you again."

Her face pivots to the side, and her eyes narrow in warning. "Nice try, asshole, but you're not forgiven. Not by a long shot. I could still leave you, and I'd be well within my rights to."

I plant my hands on the counter on either side of her thighs, bracketing her in. "True, but you won't," I tell her with an assurance I haven't earned.

"I wouldn't be so sure of that, Asher. I'm serious. I don't know how to trust you right now."

"I know and I deserve that."

"What you did was really shitty, and I'm hurt and angry. Now we're stuck in a media storm, and I feel like I was the last to know everything. You tell me the deal isn't happening, but ESPN sure as hell thinks it is. I don't see how this ends in a favorable way for us."

## 32

### ASHER

Wynter can say that. She might even believe it. But she's wrong. Doesn't she know that I'll never give up? That I'll never stop fighting for her? For us?

"It will," I promise. "Please, I'm sorry about how you found everything out, and I'm sorry I didn't tell you from the start. I swear, I'll never do that again. From here on out, I will always communicate with you first. Which is what I need to do now because I have more things to tell you."

Her hands fly. "Oh, *now* you want to tell me things."

"I was going to tell you everything tonight."

"Too late!" she yells. "Tell me right now, Asher, and I swear, if you ever withhold anything from me ever again, I will slice off your balls and feed them to a neighborhood dog. Don't think I won't. I have scalpels at my disposal."

I lean in and kiss her, my hand diving into her hair and cupping the back of her neck. I stare at her, hoping she can see that she is my whole world. "I love you, and I'm sorry. Please forgive me. I promise, it'll never happen again," I repeat as I press our foreheads together and drag my nose along hers. "Tonight, I'll rain orgasms on your body until you're so exhausted you can't help but love me again. But for now, I do have a lot to tell you, and none of it is easy."

"Okay." Her voice trembles. "Just tell me. I don't like the build-up."

"I had Lenox do some digging into your father."

She rolls her eyes. "I know. Fallon told me."

A wry grin hits my lips. "When did she tell you that?"

"Today," she hisses, still fiery. "Since you didn't."

I hold up a consolatory hand. "That's fair. What did she tell you?"

"She said the guys were all in another room talking, and that she knew it must be something like this. She didn't know what specifically though."

"Are you mad?"

"Not about that." She quirks a *you're an asshole* eyebrow at me. "That's a drop in the freaking bucket compared to everything else. But I'd like to know what's going on."

I thread our fingers together. "Lenox found a lot of information Joe has been trying to hide. In fact, he had quite the system built up with a lot of cyber protection on it. He didn't want anyone to discover his secrets. They're going to be upsetting. Nearly all of them will be and for different reasons and in different ways."

She swallows hard, nervously licking her lips. "Is it about me?"

"Not directly, though it does impact you greatly."

"What about Mason?"

I shake my head. "No." I cup her jaw. "Wynter, Joe is—"

"Reyes," Randolph barks as he bursts into the bathroom. "I've been searching everywhere for you." He wipes at his forehead, his round face ruddy. "What in the absolute fuck happened on that field today?"

"Sir—"

He holds up his hand, stopping me. "Not here. Not like this. Joe is in my office, and I think it's time we all hashed this out once and for all. Now move your ass."

He turns and leaves the bathroom, the door closing with a heavy bang behind him.

Wynter gives me a grim look. "I guess you'll have to explain everything to me upstairs."

The fact that Wynter is sitting here with me, listening to what I have to say, feels like a miracle. It's a gift. A second chance I wasn't sure I'd be granted after everything that happened today. And it isn't over yet. Not even close. I messed up epically with her, and it's certainly not something to play with or chance again, so everything else will have to wait.

I shake my head. "No," I say to her. "He can wait a moment. I need you to hear this, and I need you to hear it from me." I swallow and shift her to the edge of the counter, bringing her body closer to me, and then I stare into her eyes as I say, "Joe has cancer."

She sucks in a sharp breath. "What kind?"

"Prostate. He had surgery and then a round of chemo in April, which is why he didn't actually sign a contract with the team or move here until the summer. It's advanced though, and I'm not sure what he's doing about it at this point or if they're watching it. I don't have all the details on that nor am I a doctor."

Her head is twisted away from me so all I can do is squeeze her hand for comfort. She clears her throat. "There's more, I take it?"

"Yes. And this is the hardest part." I pull her into my body, cup her jaw, and force her gaze up to mine. "Leo is your half-brother."

Her eyes round, and I think her heart just stopped beating entirely. "He's what?!"

I soften my tone and my expression. "Your half-brother, sweetheart. Your father had an affair with his mother and paid her off after. I don't know what Leo knows, but I don't think it's much."

She blows out a breath, her eyes glassing over. "They're keeping him in the hospital overnight for observation. He has a severe concussion."

"I know. I couldn't get more information than that. Is he okay?"

She nods, nibbling on her lip. "Dean is with him. I texted with him a bit. Leo won't be able to play for a few weeks." A fresh tear hits her cheek, her chin trembling. "Half-brother?"

"Joe wasn't ever part of his life."

A scowl twists her face. "God, he's a son of a bitch." Then she changes course. "Joe brought him here." She pauses, her lips parting. "Joe brought me here too. Not to Boston, but to the team."

"Yes. And there's more to that."

She shakes her head. "It's already too much."

I drag my thumb across her cheek, swiping away her errant tears. "I know. I can tell you the rest upstairs because it involves Joe and the team and both of us."

"All right. I need a few minutes to process this anyway." She hops off the counter, and then I hold her hand, leading her out of the bathroom. Before we get too far, she twists and pinches my nipple with vengeance. I screech like a little girl and jump about five feet in the air, making her laugh. "That's for keeping things from me."

What can I say, I have sensitive nipples, and sometimes that's a good thing, and sometimes—like right now—that's a very bad thing because now is *not* the time to be hard. "Just don't do that to my dick."

She shrugs. "I make no promises."

"What if I buy you a diamond? Will that smooth everything over with us?"

She glares hatefully at me. "Um. No. Definitely not. And don't you dare get any ideas about that."

I grin, bumping my shoulder into hers and then rubbing them together up and down. "Too late," I whisper playfully.

"Asher!"

I laugh at her horrified expression. "I meant with the ideas, not the actual diamond shopping. Relax, ice queen. When I'm ready to pop the question, I won't tell you about it beforehand. That's a rookie move, and I am not a rookie."

She grumbles something under her breath that I don't have to hear to know isn't all that kind. She's mad, but she has a forgiving heart, and I'll earn her trust back.

"I love you madly," I tell her, stopping us before we enter Randolph's office. I turn and hold her gaze, keeping her close. My heart thrashes inside me as I look at her, and a soft, almost incredulous smile curls up my lips. "I don't know how to describe it. It's almost beyond words or comprehension. Some things are better felt than expressed, and that's you."

"What do you mean?" she whispers, clearing her throat.

"You, Wynter Hathaway. It's this incredible trick of reality, but you somehow make my soul both hungry and satisfied. There are places in my heart I never knew existed before, but you've unlocked them and made them your new home. You and Mason live inside me. There isn't a part of my day where my thoughts don't automatically drift to you both and are reluctant to leave. You've awakened my soul and taken over my dreams." I step into her and place my hand over her thrumming heart. "It's simple, Wynter. You're my passion, my obsession, my someone I can't live without. Please remember that. Even when I screw up, which I will likely do again. It's you and Mason. Forever."

She leans up on her toes and kisses my lips. "You're forgiven."

I grin. "I knew you found me irresistible."

She rolls her eyes. "Irresistibly risky. Troublesome. Arrogant. Aggravating—"

I shut her up with a kiss. That is until Randolph pops his head out and ruins it with a grizzly growl. "In here now."

I take Wynter's hand and lead her into his office. Joe is already here, standing by the window, refusing to turn and face us. He doesn't know all that's headed his way, but if he thinks I'm not here to fight him, he's a goddamn fool.

"What in the fuck happened out there today?" Randolph starts without any preamble. "Joe told me you went rogue. It's all over the goddamn news. Not even just sports networks, but regular fucking news, Asher."

"I went rogue because Joe wanted us to lose the game," I tell him bluntly, taking a seat in one of his chairs even though everyone else is standing. I'm not the one who should be sweating bullets right now. "Well, he wanted *me* to lose, that is. He wanted me to only hand off the ball and nothing else, and to me, that was unacceptable. But it comes down to one simple fact. I don't trust Joe. I don't trust any man who sets out to sabotage another man's career."

"What?" Randolph exclaims.

"Do you want to tell them about it, Joe, or should I?" I toss the words casually out to him, just to see how he'll bite, when really, my throat burns and my skin itches with all the things I want to yell at him for. Instead, Wynter surprises me by walking across the room and yanking on Joe's arm, forcing him to turn and face her.

"You have cancer?" she questions.

Joe stares down into his daughter's eyes, and then his head snaps in my direction. I toss my hands behind my head and give him a smug look that tells him I know everything. I warned him on the field. I told him straight up. He should have listened. Frankly, he should have never fucked with me to begin with.

"Don't look at him," Wynter snaps. "Look at me. You owe me a million explanations. Start with that one first."

Joe turns back to her and sighs plaintively. "Yes."

She exhales a heavy breath, her hands on her hips. "How advanced?"

A palpable pressure settles in the room. "I had surgery and chemo. I'm currently on hormone therapy."

"Did it metastasize?"

He makes an evasive noise that she's not having any part of.

"Tell me," she demands sharply.

His eyes narrow. "Yes. To my lymph nodes and bones. They tell me it's relatively under control now."

She shoves him. Not hard but enough to startle him. "And Leo?!"

Now Joe is supremely pissed. His gaze slashes dangerously over to me. "How the fuck do you know all this?"

"What about Leo? The head injury wasn't Joe's fault." Randolph is befuddled, his eyes volleying back and forth between me and Joe like he's watching a tennis match as he seeks answers.

Joe curses and turns away from Wynter for a beat, only to think better of it and race over to me. He grabs me by my suit jacket, balling it up on his firsts, and hauling me up and out of my chair until I'm right up in his face. "How the fuck do you know?!"

"Back off, Joe," Randolph orders.

I don't move, and I don't attempt to shirk him off. I get that he's pissed. I invaded his privacy. I dug into shit I had no business digging into, and I crossed a lot of lines with that. But it doesn't change the facts, and it doesn't change what he did.

If anyone crossed lines, it's him.

"Do you remember what you told me when I was crying in the hospital?" Wynter calls out, her voice calm and composed. "Before you told me that I wouldn't see you for a very long time that is."

Joe pulls me in, putting us nose to nose before he shoves me away. He blows out a strained breath and then shakes his head as his chin drops toward the floor.

"You told me that when a person makes a mistake, they need to own up to it and accept the consequences of their actions. Even if it's hard." She laughs acerbically. "Then again, you were talking about me falling out of the tree and breaking my arm. You weren't talking about yourself, which, in retrospect, makes you the biggest hypocrite of all. But for once, be a man of your word and tell me the truth."

"What the hell are you talking about? What is all this about Leo, and what do you mean Joe said that to you when you were five?" Randolph is getting more and more riled up by the second, glaring into Joe's back. "Joe!" he bellows, pounding his fist on his desk as if he's calling this courtroom to order when Joe doesn't so much as move a muscle to answer.

Joe, ever the shark, glares at me once more, ignoring everyone else. "Tell me how you knew?"

"I will never divulge my sources," I tell him flatly, only to edge toward Randolph's desk, giving Joe my back and Randolph my full attention. "I was curious if you already knew who Leo is to Joe, but given your reaction, I'm going to say no."

Randolph stares dumbfounded at me, his eyes owl wide. "What do you mean? Who is Leo to Joe?"

"Leo is Joe's son," Wynter supplies. "And I'm his daughter."

Randolph curses under his breath. "Goddammit, Joe!" He releases a harsh growl. "What other secrets are you keeping from us?"

# 33

## WYNTER

I'm thrown. Totally. Completely. Undeniably.

I'm not even sure how to come up for air after this. I might as well grow gills and learn how to breathe underwater. Leo is my half-brother. Joe has cancer. It's one thing after another, and yet, instinctively, I know we're nowhere near done with this.

"Plenty," Asher declares. "He's keeping plenty of other secrets." His unrelenting gaze nails Joe where he stands. He folds his arms and leans casually against the edge of Randolph's desk. "He's the one who leaked my shoulder injury to the press and the one who's had the paparazzi stalking my building. But that's nothing compared to the rest of it. You need to tell Wynter what you did." The hardline, suffering-no-fools steadiness in his eyes has me turning back to Joe.

Joe bristles. "I don't know—"

"You know!" Asher bellows, his hands now gripping the edge of the desk as if he's restraining himself. "Don't do that! Don't look at me and lie, but worse yet, don't look at her and lie. You have been a miserable piece of shit father your entire life, and this is not the time. Tell her how you used her! Tell her how you manipulated her! Tell her how you deceived everyone!" He takes a deliberate step in Joe's direction, his finger pointed at Joe in accusation. "Because I swear to God, if I have to do it, you will forever be sorry."

Joe picks up something from Randolph's desk and chucks it straight across the room, making it shatter on impact, and I jump. Randolph is at just as much of a loss as I am, neither of us sure what to do or how to react.

"You can't know!" Joe yells, his face red with rage.

"I know," Asher declares with so much certainty that there is no mistaking him. "I know everything. Firewalls are only as good as the man hacking it, and my man is the best."

"Fuck!" Joe growls, raking his flustered hands through his hair as he starts pacing.

"Tell me," I plead, even as my heart rate starts to spike, and my palms sweat.

Joe shakes his head and storms toward the window, where he pounds his fist against the glass.

I turn to Asher who is furious and repeat myself. "Tell me."

When Joe still refuses to talk, Asher snarls, calling him a coward and a weakling, and then he marches over to me and takes my hand, staring intently into my eyes with so much sorrow and vehemence, my knees nearly give out on me.

"He falsified my MRI results."

I blink about sixty thousand times, a wave of some malformed adrenaline shooting through my veins, making my vision hazy. "No. That's not..." Only I trail off because it makes so much sense it's almost obvious, and I'm suddenly irate that I didn't come to that conclusion before. There was nothing on the MRI that would have indicated it was from a different man. No degenerative changes in the bones. Nothing. Other than the scarring that indicated a previous injury, which Asher had claimed to have had, there was nothing. "That's why the MRI showed a completely different picture from what I found when I went in." I'm not even questioning. I'm nodding like the fool this man made me as it all comes together.

My stomach roils.

"Asher?" Randolph looks like his head is about to pop off his body.

Asher turns to Randolph. "Your coach forced your hand to get Leo higher in the draft because he's his son. In doing so, he wanted Leo—not me—to start. I got hit in the left shoulder during training camp, and it was the perfect opportunity for him to make that happen."

"I don't... I'm not sure I..." Randolph walks over to his desk and pulls out a cigarette, of all things, and lights it, the caustic smoke pluming from the flaming end of the butt as he puffs. "I haven't smoked one of these in two years." He takes a deep inhale and then exhales a stream of gray smoke into the air. I scrunch my nose and step back, so I don't have to inhale it. "Tell me it's a lie, Joe."

Joe remains silent, still over by the window as his life—and his lies—fall apart around him.

"You did that to force Asher's surgery?" Randolph exclaims, pointing the cigarette at Joe, ashes scattering to the carpet before he takes another hasty drag and then turns to Asher. I swear, the man is one inhale away from a heart attack. "And it was designed to keep you out for the entire season?"

"Yes," Asher confirms since Joe isn't saying anything. "Or at the very least, out for half the season. But it wasn't my true MRI. I don't know whose it was, and I don't know how Joe managed to get it into my medical record as mine, but somehow, he did."

I stagger a step, nauseated. Dizzy. I lean against the far wall, my hand on my forehead as I grapple with this. "I performed surgery on a patient who didn't need it." I committed an egregious medical error. Not necessarily at my own fault, but does it really matter in the grand scheme of things?

I rechecked the MRI after the surgery, but the films all appeared to be authentic. They just didn't line up with what I found when I started cutting, but I blew that off. Imaging isn't one hundred percent accurate. There is fault in it.

But... I knew better.

Instinctively and medically, I knew what I saw on the films was bogus compared to what I found when I opened Asher up, but I was so relieved at the outcome, that I didn't question it beyond that. I didn't think deeper than what it was. I just didn't.

Joe risked my license.

My reputation.

Asher's future.

All so he could get Leo on the field instead of Asher.

I turn to Joe. "Did you do that? Did you compromise my integrity as a physician? My license?"

He makes a noncommittal noise, still staring out the window as if the empty field holds promise and hope of rescue for him.

I start to lose it. His nonchalance about what he did drives me absolutely insane. "Have you no conscience? No moral code? How could you do that to me?!" I scream at him, ready to pound my fists against him. "How could you be so... remorseless? So calculating. I knew you didn't love me—you never did and made that clear—but I never fathomed you could still be *so* heartless and uncaring."

He heaves a heavy breath and keeps his back to me, and it only makes me want to shake him.

"It was my MRI," he states solemnly, his voice low as it pierces the cloud of smoke and tension in the air. "It was taken two years ago. No doctor would touch me after I injured my shoulder in my last year of playing. It's why I retired early. I had hoped the years would have healed some of the injuries I sustained, and it would finally be operable. It is, if I want a shoulder full of screws." He turns, folding his arms over his chest, attempting to look foreboding, and yet it comes across as meek and broken. His eyes meet mine. "I talked you into the surgery knowing you'd do it, and Asher's shoulder wouldn't require much surgical intervention. He'd heal, and his career wouldn't be over, but in the meantime, Leo would shine and take over the team, and I'd have a valid reason to get rid of Asher and keep the kid as the starter."

I can't even begin to describe how infuriating that is. My fists ball up, my body *shaking* with rage. What a bullshit attempt at an excuse. "You falsified medical documents. That's a felony," I tell him in no uncertain terms. "That's why you brought me in. Because I was stupid and emotional and took the bait when you pushed me just right."

Joe looks rattled. Lost. Desperate. I know the feeling.

"No," he swears. "I brought you here because you moved to this city, and I felt it was a sign. I'd been watching you your whole life, Wynter. Even when you didn't know it, I was there."

"Fuck you! You have no right to say that. You were never there. Never! I was a little girl who blamed herself for her father leaving. For her father no longer loving her. I cried myself to sleep every night for years, praying you'd come home and forgive me. How dare you say you were there. How dare you."

Asher walks over and takes me in his arms, holding me close as I tremble and fall apart and fight my tears.

"I never wanted children," Joe states, his voice cracking ever so slightly. "I never wanted to be a father, and I sure as hell never wanted to be a husband. Then I met your mother, and I fell in love. You were born ten months later, and that was that. I did love you, Wynter. Both you and your mother. But I couldn't make it work. I just didn't know how to make it stick."

I glare disdainfully at him. "You mean you were selfish."

He nods. "Yes. I was selfish. I did everything wrong that day you broke your arm. It wasn't your fault; it was mine, but I was angry, and I took it out on you because I could. I had been looking for a way out, and when you presented it to me, I suddenly didn't want it the way I thought I did, but it was too late. I knew you were better off without me in your life. So, I left. Then I did the same thing with Leo's mother. It was a fuck up. Anyway, like with you, I watched him from afar. Then I was diagnosed with cancer, and when I saw that Leo had a shot in the NFL as a quarterback like I was—that a piece of me would live on in the game—I didn't hesitate. With him or with you. I wanted to see you because even though you no longer figure skate, I knew you were a brilliant surgeon, and again, I had a part in that. Plus, well, I suppose part of me wanted to make amends for what I had done to you as a small child."

I scoff so hard I'm shocked I don't crack a rib. "Um, no. Not even close, Joe. And may I just say, your massive ego is a serious trip you need to get in check. You had zero part in my life and that includes both my figure skating and medical careers. Falsifying an MRI to force an unnecessary surgery is about as fucked-up and sadistic as it can get. I opened up a shoulder that didn't need it. You risked Asher's health, his career—my career—all for your own selfish needs and gain. Now Leo is in the hospital with a concussion. I don't care if cancer gave you some half-assed, I'm the master of the universe and want to live on through my unwanted spawn or some bullshit, I want to make amends with the daughter I knowingly destroyed when she was only five, come to Jesus moment. I don't want anything to do with you ever again."

Joe's lips flatline and he looks away. What he was expecting from this, I don't know. But using me, trying to ruin Asher, lying and cheating his way through... I can't even with any of that.

So I tack on, "Honestly, I can't tell you how grateful I am that you left when you did. Because of that, I had Gary Hathaway as my dad. A man who showed me what it is to love without condition and was always there for me, no matter what."

He makes a noise, his face stricken, but it does nothing to soften anyone.

"Joe, you're fired," Randolph barks harshly. "If you attempt to become a coach anywhere else in this league, hell, anywhere else in this world, I will make all of this public. You're finished. Done. You hear me? Carl will be the interim head coach until I can find a replacement. Wynter and Asher, you are well within your rights to press charges, and I will not stand in your way or ask you to keep it quiet if you decide to take that course of action. Both of you have been wronged by him, and his actions are reprehensible. As for the trade, I think we can all safely say that's not happening."

Joe storms out of the room, not even sparing me a backward glance, and though I try not to let it happen, the part of my heart he still occupied breaks once and for all. I imagine it will never be fully healed. He has cancer, and he's alone, but I can't be part of it. I don't want him in my life, but more than that, I don't want him in Mason's.

Mentally, I say goodbye to him. Mourning him one final time. But I'm not sure that sort of ache ever fully goes away. Even when we hate someone, they're still a part of you.

I sag into Asher, his fingers combing down the back of my hair. "Told you I wasn't going anywhere," he whispers in my ear.

"Awesome," I croak. "I still better not ever hear about you again from a third party."

He tilts my chin and presses his lips softly to mine. "Never."

"Tell me you found out all of this, this morning and that you weren't hiding that from me as well."

His eyes ensnare mine as he rocks me ever so gently. "I found it out about an hour before I had to be on the field. I was going to tell you everything the moment I could, which meant tonight before everything else happened. Are you okay?"

"Not really, no. But I will be." It'll just take time to get there.

"Asher, I'm sorry to break this up, but we have a room full of players downstairs still here waiting on you to say something."

"I have to go," he says to me with genuine regret. "It might be better if you leave while I'm in there because I don't think the press will leave until I do."

"Great," I deadpan. "This is going to be a thing, isn't it?"

"Honestly? Yes. At least for a little while, and then something else will come along and they'll move onto that."

I push up on my toes and kiss him. "Good luck. Sounds like you're going to need it."

I MANAGE to sneak out of the stadium undetected. Asher was right, the press was focused on him. My phone is full of texts from my mom and Fallon, but for a few minutes, I just need to be alone with my thoughts. Alone in my car. I need a moment to come to grips with everything, and it's not as easy as it sounds.

Putting everything Joe did aside, I've seen how the world reacts to Asher. Hell, we couldn't even go out for late-night cookies without it being a problem. What will it be like now that the world knows about me? What will it be like for Mason?

Loving Asher won't be easy. But I also know he's worth the risk.

My phone rings, and I answer it using the fancy screen on my new car that I'm still not fully used to.

"Hey," Asher says, his voice coming through my speakers. "Where are you?"

"On my way home."

"The guys on the team are in, but... it's a mess, sweetheart. The next few weeks might be a bit nuts. I'm sorry."

"We'll manage. I think."

He chuckles. "I was tired of hiding the lie. I was tired of pretending you weren't mine."

"You sound like Greyson writing song lyrics."

I can hear the amusement in his voice as he says, "Grey does a way better job at that. But I want alone time with you. Your mom has Mason overnight, right?"

My eyebrows shoot up. "Since when does my mom have Mason for the night?"

"Clearly you didn't read your texts from her."

I snicker, turning on my signal to get off Storrow Drive. "Nope. I needed a minute of quiet solitude."

"Well, now that you're hopefully more Zen, you should know our building is surrounded by press, and she felt it was safer to keep Mason, at least for a while. I told her about Joe."

I sigh. "You and my parents are growing very close."

"Yep. They love me. Just like everyone else."

I roll my eyes, even though he can't see me do it. "I'm almost home."

"I'll be there shortly." I go to disconnect the call when his voice stops me. "And my queen?"

"Yes?"

"I plan to make good on my promise."

My brows scrunch. "What promise?"

"To rain orgasms on your body. See you soon."

# 34

## WYNTER

The orgasms don't come—pun intended—the way he promised. Instead, I'm met with a houseful of people. I open the door to the apartment after having to fight my way through reporters getting into the garage, and Fallon is here, rushing across Asher's penthouse to hug me. With her arms wide and her raven hair flying, she slams into me, and that's that.

His people are here.

They're like your great-uncle whatever-his-name-is who shows up uninvited on Sunday afternoons and stays way past his welcome because you never quite know how to get him to leave. At least that's them right now, because I'm exhausted. Mentally, physically, just cooked. And I liked the idea of Asher raining orgasms on me.

Like a lot.

Now those are on hold for the foreseeable future. Still, I love that he has his people. That they rally around him in his time of need.

Only no one told Asher they'd be here because when he walks in the door, he's already stripping out of his suit, his shirt half-unbuttoned, and yelling out, "My queen, where is your pretty body? It better be naked for me to ravage."

I blush about ten thousand shades of red and then offer his

friends, who aren't even bothering to hide their smirks, a *what can you do* shrug.

Asher starts on his pants only to freeze when he enters the great room and sees all his friends sitting here, eating, drinking, and hanging out.

"Uh, what in the actual fuck are you doing here other than cock-blocking me?"

Zax gives him an unimpressed look. "You invited us, dickhead. Remember?"

Asher shakes his head. "No, I didn't—"

"Last night when we were on the phone, you told us to come over for our usual postgame stuff," Callan supplies, tossing a chip loaded with guacamole into his mouth.

"Oh." Asher grunts. "I might have done that."

"And we brought food, so the sex will have to wait," Callan continues through a mouthful. "Sorry, dude, but I'm eating, and I have no plans to stop right now."

"Same," Grey agrees as he munches down on a chicken wing. These people and their food spreads are no joke. My stomach growls accordingly because I haven't had anything to eat since this morning, and everything smells really good.

Plus, let's be honest here, I could seriously use a drink after the day I had.

Asher rakes a hand through his hair and glances at me as he openly debates kicking his friends out. That is until something catches his eye, and it's all over. "Is that spinach dip?"

"Yes," Aurelia tells him. "I made it with Greek yogurt and extra fresh garlic, the way you like it."

He groans, his head falling back. "That's my favorite dip."

She puffs out a breath. "I know. Why do you think I made it?" Her blue eyes roll, and then she dives forward, covering the dish with her hands when he makes a move for it. "Uh-uh. You get no dip until you put your shirt back on. Man boobs are not appetizing."

"Man boobs?!" he chokes and then smacks his chest like Tarzan.

"These are pecs, not *boobs*." His nose scrunches, his voice full of disdain.

I hold in my snort, as do his friends.

"Come on, doll," he pleads, going for the dip again only to be denied. "You love me shirtless."

"Um. No. Not so much." Layla jumps in from her position on the floor, her mouth twisting in disgust. She's sort of confiscated the cheese board along with Fallon. It might be a cage fight to get some of the goat cheese I'm eyeing. "In fact, it's definitely ruining my appetite, which I never would have thought possible. I'm that chick who can *always* eat."

They continue going back and forth, ribbing Asher, which is always amusing to watch. Lenox chuckles, and it draws my attention over to him. Rising up off the sofa, I walk over to him as he stands alone by the balcony door, just doing his own thing.

"Hi," I say sweetly.

He blinks at me and then grins but doesn't say anything in return.

"Thank you for digging into Joe's... stuff, I guess you'd call it. I don't know what you do, or how you do it, and frankly, I don't want to know. I'm grateful though. For me and for Asher."

He gives me a firm nod and that's about it. For how much Asher—and even Greyson—talk, Lenox is the total opposite. Asher said he's always been this way, but after he lost his sister, it's been worse. He also seems like a bit of a loner but clearly loves his people with an undeniable ferocity.

I reach up and give him a hug, which he returns—albeit a bit awkwardly—and then I go back for the cheese, ready to fight my way in if necessary while Asher digs into a plate of spinach dip with pita and veggies since he now has his shirt back on. Greyson turns on the television to put the evening games on, but even though another team is playing, Asher is all anyone is talking about.

"Oh my God!" I cry when they do a replay of me and Asher on the sidelines. "I look like a crazy woman." Layla and Aurelia giggle lightly at my outrage.

"It's not so bad," Fallon attests, lying through her teeth.

"Uh, no. That's tragic girl hair right there. My hair is legit all over the place. Why didn't you tell me?" I throw Asher a scathing glare, but all he does is shrug it off.

"I thought you looked beautiful, and honestly, I didn't notice the hair."

I cast a hand in the direction of the television that's displaying the madness in like eighty inches of high definition. "It's a ball of electrified frizz. Remind me next time it's shitty New England weather to wear it up."

"I hate to break it to you, but your face is going to be everywhere now," Aurelia tells me. "I didn't expect it when I got together with Zax, but yeah, it happened, and it wasn't all that fun."

"Reils, your face was already everywhere. You're a model. Or were."

She waves Greyson away. "That was different. It was like I was dating a Beatle or"—she snickers—"a member of Central Square."

"Same," Fallon commiserates. "It was madness for me and Grey. We had press posted outside the warehouse we live in for weeks. Then Grey proposed, and it started all over again." She points at the television. "Oh look, they're showing you standing on the podium holding up your gold medal. You look so cute."

It goes from that to my freaking medical school graduation, like some warped *this is your life* video montage. I groan and collapse on the floor, splayed out like a starfish. "I take it back, Asher. We're breaking up. Officially. You can visit Mason whenever you want, as long as I'm not there."

"Oh, come on," he drawls, sipping his water to wash down his food. "Don't be such a wimp. You had your chance to run—not that I would have let that happen—but now it's too late. In for a pint, in for a pound. Besides, it'll blow over in like a week. And Fallon is right, you did look cute."

"They're practically reporting my final score in the Olympics and my GPA in college!" I half-yell. "Next thing you know, they'll learn you knocked me up in the bathroom of a club. It's a lot. I haven't been on television since the Olympics, and this is different. *So, so* different."

"Here, sweetheart. Sit up. I'll get you some wine because I think you could use a drink, and it'll make you more willing to do the naughty stuff later. Oh, and there's goat cheese. Have some goat cheese. You'll feel better."

Asher jogs into the kitchen and returns with a glass and a bottle of wine—like I'm going to drink the whole thing—and pours me a mammoth glass. I take a sip and then a gulp as he makes me a cheese plate and even adds on the fig spread I like with a bounty of crackers beside it.

"There. Better now?" he checks.

"Marginally. Today sucked."

He agrees. So does everyone else, since they all seem to know about what Joe did. I'm going to have to tell Limbick. That's not something that can be ignored, whether it becomes public knowledge or not. I can't imagine he'll be too pleased, but he saw the MRI just the same as I did, and if it had been him instead of me, he would have opened up Asher's shoulder too.

That's what's sitting with me the hardest. The manipulation. The lies. The deceit. I have a half-brother I never knew anything about, and he just so happens to be Asher's teammate. His rival, I guess. What will that be like?

Asher smacks a kiss on my lips, and then we just settle into a groove of watching football—still not my favorite sport—and eating good food and laughing with his friends, who are starting to feel like they're my people too.

It's nice.

I'm not sure I've ever had people before, so I like the notion of a girl squad. I like the feeling of being *home*. It's not one I've had for as long as I can remember. After Joe left, that all sort of fell apart, and then I was traveling nonstop for skating, and then after that, it was college, med school, residency... it didn't stop.

But being here with Asher, our son, his people... it's home. *He's* my home.

Something I tell him after everyone has left and it's just us, snuggled up on the couch together finally *not* watching football. We had my mom and dad bring Mason home to us and we snuck him through the back way. After the day we had, I wanted him home with us and his friends set up a perfect distraction for the press out front when they left.

In a flash, Asher tugs me by the thigh until I'm supine on the couch, and then he climbs over me, staring down at me from above, straight into my eyes. "It's been an intense few months."

I snort. "That's putting it mildly."

"No," he says softly, his eyes dancing about my face as a smile curls up the corner of his lips. "What I mean is, I think we're going to hit an even patch."

I groan. "You did not just jinx us like that, did you? Next thing you know, we'll have some weird celebrity obsession thing and you'll be kidnapped, and then Mason and I will have to hire... well, I guess Lenox in this case, to find you."

He's thoroughly amused. "Celebrity kidnapping?"

I shrug up a shoulder. "You have a lot of obsessed fans."

"Funny considering the only person I want to be obsessed with me is you."

I roll my eyes. "Never gonna happen, player."

He drops his body weight down on me and then grinds up until I'm forced to feel every hard inch of him. "I bet I can change your mind, ice queen."

"You have your work cut out for you. Most women would not be so forgiving."

"True," he acknowledges, as if he's genuinely giving this some consideration.

"In fact," I tell him, doing my best to hide my grin. "I don't think I forgive you after all. I think I'm still mad."

He grinds into me again, stealing the breath from my lungs. "How mad?"

"Furious," I exclaim on a pant. "I might hate you again."

Brimstone burns in his eyes turning them to a smoldering charcoal. "Is that so?"

"Yes." I squint at him tauntingly. "Player."

He gives me that devilish crooked smirk. "Hmmm." In one swift movement, he rips my shirt up and over my head. He tosses it away and then plants his hands on either side of my head. "Let me see what I can do to change that."

Yanking down the cup of my bra, his tongue swirls around my nipple, making me arch into him. My hands grip his hair, my fingers ripping at his strands. I do forgive him, but that doesn't stop the part of me that's still miffed by his action. Besides, a little punishment never hurt anyone.

His hand dives into my pants and underwear, pressing down on the top of my mound with his palm while swirling a finger around my opening.

"Fucking soaked," he hisses and then plunges two fingers inside me. He starts to pump in and out of me. "Still hate me now?"

"More than ever." I moan, my eyes closing as the pleasure intensifies when his fingertips find that magic spot inside me.

He nips at my jaw. "That's what I thought." His fingers continue their delicious pounding, the pace so fast and delirious I can't do anything other than feel what he's doing to me. His mouth dips by my ear. "This is going to be one of many. The next one will be on my cock. How close are you?"

"So close," I manage, my body swirling higher as he rubs the base of his palm on my needy clit.

"I know, my queen. I can feel it. Your pussy is gripping my fingers the same way it'll grip my cock the second you come. So how about you be a good girl and do that for me now?"

Mother. Fuck. That should not have *any* impact on my body, but it does. It totally does. I come, just as he tells me to. And the second I start to wind down from that high, my pants are off, and he's hiking my knee up and over his good shoulder, and then he's slamming straight into me.

"Jesus! Asher!"

"Shhh. Mason is sleeping."

I smile as he starts to take me, knowing this is exactly how we're going to do it for the rest of our lives. Hot. Dirty. Playful. Experimental. Risky. And all of it filled with so much love.

Two separate entities so perfectly and thoroughly intertwined, there's no telling where he starts and I end. It's him. A football player of all people. The last man I ever intended to fall for is, without a doubt, the one I never stood a chance of resisting. And I wouldn't change a thing about it.

# EPILOGUE

W ynter
     Four months later

IT'S THE CRAZIEST THING. All of it is. After Joe was fired, no one expected the Boston Rebels to do much of anything. They had an interim head coach. Quarterback battles—or so the media played it. Not to mention, they were already going into this without much of a winning record. The playoffs seemed like a lofty goal to everyone.

Everyone except Asher.

Asher and I went to visit Leo in the hospital the day after his injury, and we both told him everything. He was shocked. His mother never spoke about who his father was, and I could see how hard it hit him to learn that he had been drafted and working with his biological father without actually knowing it.

He was also furious when he learned all that Joe had done to secure his spot on the team. After Joe was fired, he officially retired from football, knowing his demons would follow him if he ever tried to coach anywhere else. He moved back to LA, and though I don't want anything to do with him personally, I do follow his care through his oncologist.

As for the team, there was a lot to figure out. A lot to sort through, both emotionally and figuratively since sorting through what was best for the team going forward wasn't so cut and dry. Asher did what any great leader would do. Once Leo was out of the hospital and feeling a bit better, he invited the entire team, including coaches, over to the apartment, and they all talked it out. They figured out a strategy for the rest of the season. Something that went beyond one game at a time.

And it worked for them.

Because here we are at the same club I met Asher in three years ago, practically to the day.

And the Boston Rebels won the Super Bowl—again.

The first team to ever do so with an interim coach and two starting quarterbacks. Asher takes the majority of the snaps and does the majority of the playing, but they use Leo for Wild Cat formations and other plays when they want to throw off the defense.

The VIP floor of the club is pounding so loud with thumping house music and the loud chatter of the team and their significant others that you can feel it vibrating in your bones. I didn't have to sneak up here this time, which is sort of a bummer actually.

That was a total thrill that night.

Until things got all mucked up in the bathroom after that, of course.

But now I'm here as not only the team's orthopedic surgeon but also as the MVP's girlfriend. Asher led the team to a twenty-one to ten victory over Badlands and is flying higher than I've ever seen him. Thankfully, without the aid of muscle relaxants or too many shots. His boys and their women are here—because they never seem to go or do anything without each other—and we've all been dancing our collective asses off.

The song morphs into a slower, more hypnotic rhythm, and

suddenly Leo is before me, pulling me into his arms and moving us in a slow dance. In the months since I found out that he's my half-brother, we've grown impossibly close. I've met his mother and his sisters, and he loves 'uncle time' with Mason.

I may have lost my biological father—hell, I'm not sure I ever had him to begin with—but the one thing Joe did manage to do for me is give me a brother.

"I have something to tell you," he says after we hit a lull in the excited chatter of discussing the game.

"Why do you look nervous, Leo?"

He spins me out and then twirls me back into his chest. "Because I am."

My heart rate picks up a few extra beats at the serious expression on his face. "What's going on? Are you okay?"

"Vegas reached out to my agent. They want me to be their starting QB next season."

"Vegas?" I echo, my voice hollow as swirls of Rebels red and blue colored lights skate over us. "But that's so far away. And aren't you under contract with the Rebels?"

"Yes, but I don't think Randolph will be opposed to making a deal for me, and now is the time for me to strike. We just won the Super Bowl. I was part of that as a rookie. This is my chance to land a big contract and be the starter for a team."

As much as I'm reluctant to admit this, I know he's right. This is his shot. Joe got him drafted high, but no one knows how it happened. His team just won the Super Bowl with his help. He's a young kid at the start of his career, and he should take it and see how high he can go with it.

I wrap my arms around his neck and bring him in for a hug. "I'm going to miss you."

He squeezes me. "I'm going to miss you. You and Mason will come to visit because the weather in Vegas is nicer than in Boston."

I laugh. He knows how much I dislike the cold of New England.

"Buy a place with a pool," I tell him, making him chuckle in my ear.

"No doubt. You can even bring that mediocre quarterback of yours." He and Asher are very close but love ribbing each other every chance they get.

I pull back, suddenly emotional. "You'll take care of yourself out there?"

He rolls his eyes at me. A habit we clearly both have. "I'll be fine. My mama is moving out there with me."

"Oh good." I snicker. "She'll keep you in line."

I feel hands on my hips from behind me, and I turn my head over my shoulder to find Asher there, peering down at us. "Did you tell her?"

I scowl at Asher. "You knew?"

"He told me earlier when we got here."

"And you didn't say anything?"

Asher smirks at me. Jerk is lucky I can't pinch his nipple in here for it. "It wasn't for me to tell you."

"Ugh!" I turn back to Leo. "You're leaving me alone with him? That's just mean."

"You can handle him."

"That's hardly the point," I grumble, not happy about this at all but already knowing it's what's best for Leo, and I'll adapt. "Fine." I hug him again. "I'm very happy for you, and I hope the deal goes through."

"Can I steal my woman back yet?" Asher asks, tugging on my hips as if to say it's not really a question or an option. Leo releases me, and then Asher twirls me around and takes me straight into his arms. The music starts to pick up, but he doesn't increase his pace as he moves us along the dance floor. "You okay with that?"

"I'm sad," I admit. "I feel like I just got him, and now he's going to be moving away."

"I know, sweetheart. I'm sorry." Asher holds me for a moment and then tilts my face up so he can lean down and kiss me. "I know what would make you feel better."

"What?" I ask softly, my voice practically absorbed into the music surrounding us.

"Let's go into the bathroom we met for a quickie"

I snort out a laugh. "You're kidding me, right?"

He smiles against my lips, his gray eyes swirling with colors. "Nope. Not even a little. I owe you a hot bathroom makeup session. Let's do it."

I glance around the room and then return my gaze to him. "Someone could come in, and I'm not drunk the way I was last time."

"We'll lock the door," he assures me.

My eyebrows shoot to my hairline. "There's a lock?"

He tilts his head. "You, know, I don't know if there is one. Let's go test it out."

I balk, chewing on the corner of my lip.

"Come on, ice queen. Take the risk with me. I promise, this time, I'll make it worth it. Please."

I can't resist that smile. The one that makes his eyes sparkle and his chin dimple pop. I never could. Obviously. It's how we got Mason. His please isn't so bad either.

"Okay. Just don't make me regret it."

He winks at me and takes my hand, threading our fingers and then shooting us across the club floor. I'm in heels and a dress— similar to how I was the first time I was here—and since I am not a woman who is comfortable in heels, I stumble a bit. Asher is there, pulling me into his side as we bob and weave around people vying for his attention. We find our way to the back, to the quieter side of the floor, and over to the bathrooms.

"You're sure about this?" I question.

"Trust me."

Ugh. "I got pregnant the last time I did that in this place."

He laughs but doesn't comment further as he takes us into the empty women's room. The automatic light flickers on, still the same blue it was the last time we were in here.

"It's like déjà vu," I quip, skipping over to the counter. "How did we do this last time? I don't remember much."

Asher comes in behind me, his hands planting on the counter on either side of me, his eyes molten as they meet mine in the reflection of the mirror. His lips skim along my exposed shoulder.

"You're so beautiful," he whispers reverently. "I couldn't take my eyes off you that night. I'd never wanted a woman like that before. I knew instantly there was something special and different about you."

A flutter hits my belly. Deft fingers swoop my hair over to my other shoulder, and then his mouth continues its assault on my shoulder, slipping up to my neck. A soft moan trickles out from the back of my throat.

"I love you," he says, swinging one arm around my waist. "So much. We haven't been together that long, but these months with you and Mason have been the best of my life. I can't imagine being with anyone else. You're perfect for me, Wynter. I can't tell you how happy you make me, and all I want is to make you this happy in return."

I lean back into him, tilting my head to give him better access to my sensitive skin. "You do. Always."

"You mean that?" he questions, nibbling on my earlobe.

I meet his cautious eyes in the mirror. "Of course. It hasn't been easy. In fact, it's been a pretty crazy several months, but I wouldn't change it either. It brought us here. Both literally and figuratively. These months with you have been the best of my life too."

He grins. "Hands on the counter."

My heart races as I do as he instructs, my skin turning hot, humming with an electrical current. He starts digging into his pocket, pressing himself against me. "What are you doing?" I question.

"Getting a condom."

"Are you kidding?" I laugh. "We haven't used one of those in a long time."

"I told you I had to make this up to you. That means I right all my wrongs."

I roll my eyes and wiggle my ass against him, urging him on. He may put on the condom, but knowing him, there is no way it stays on.

"Shit," he hisses, and I hear it smack against the floor. "Crap. Can you help?"

"What?" A bemused laugh escapes my lungs. I spin around to find Asher down on one knee, holding a small red box up at me. "Are you kidding me?!" This time I shriek. "What are you doing?"

He flips open the box, suddenly quiet for what is very likely the first time in his life, to reveal a large solitaire emerald on a platinum band. It's absolutely stunning and simple and perfect. But...

"We're in the bathroom of a club."

He takes my hand with the one not holding the box. "I know. I thought of that. And I knew that's exactly what you'd say, so I'm here with my argument."

"Okay," I say in a shaky voice, my gaze flipping back and forth between the ring and his eyes.

"This bathroom, believe it or not, represents a special place for me. It's where I met you. It's where we made our son. It was the start of something I never anticipated to be possible. I want to rewrite this bathroom for us. I want to rewrite our beginning while I make you my future."

Oh, hell. "You're really proposing?"

"I really am. I want to marry you, Wynter. I know some people will say it's too soon or it happened too fast. But I don't believe in too soon or too fast. I believe when it's right it's right, and when it's meant to be, nothing can stop it. I want your last name to be my last name— Mason's too—and I want my ring on your finger, and I want to be there when our children grow inside of you. I want all your moments to be my moments too. It's you, my queen. It'll always be. And I will spend my life by your side, holding your hand, kissing your lips, and telling you every day how I grow more and more in love with you."

Oh, God.

I tug him up by the collar of his shirt and slam my lips to his. There is one word ringing in my head, besides yes, of course. It's beloved. This man is my beloved. That's who I'll be to him. It's how we'll live our lives together. Always.

THE END.

Thank you so much for taking the time to read Irresistibly Risky! I hope you enjoyed it.

**Want an exclusive look at Asher and Wynter's HEA? Scan the code for their bonus epilogue!**

Keep reading for chapter one of Irresistibly Broken.

# IRRESISTIBLY BROKEN

*Zaxton*

The headline was all anyone cared about. It was all that was repeated over and over and over again ad nauseam across every news network, entertainment magazine, and blog. "Suzie Ward, manager of the hugely successful pop band, Central Square, and girlfriend of Zaxton Monroe, found dead in the shower."

The headline was followed by mass speculation because even though there were some leaks and a few statements here and there, no one knew what actually happened except for us. And even then, I'm the only one who knows the truth. A secret I will take to my grave. A fucking heartbreak that has turned me into the delightful mother-fucker I am today.

*Especially today.*

Eight years ago, I lost the love of my life.

And it doesn't seem to get any easier with the passing of time. Maybe it's because I lost more than just her that day. I lost a piece of myself I haven't been able to retrieve.

My phone vibrates on the seat beside me, but I don't bother checking it. It's either one of the guys, my brother, or work. None of which I want to deal with right now. I should have stayed home today. I shouldn't have gotten out of bed this morning, but today we have a photo shoot for a few pieces in the new women's fall line, and I have to be in it, and who gives a shit?

Bed and whiskey for breakfast were a much better option.

My driver, Ashley, sits quietly and patiently up front, staring straight ahead and allowing me this moment. He knows. He's been with me long enough to know I'll get out when I'm ready and I'm just not there yet.

Will I ever get past this? Will the hurt ever dissipate?

"What happens if I call in sick?" I mumble under my breath and notice Ashley stirring up front. I'm not asking him, but I wouldn't mind if he answered me all the same. He's the closest thing I have to a fatherlike figure in my life even though I pay him to be here because my actual father is a world-class piece of shit. He's the reason I'm the CEO of Monroe Fashion instead of him.

"May I suggest, if you talked about that day, it might help to unburden your soul."

"One has to have a soul for it to be unburdened."

He breathes out a mournful sigh in a way that tells me he's not amused.

"Talking about it won't unburden me. It will only burden others." The truth shall not set me free. It shall ruin someone who is already suffering more than he should.

"You know—"

"I know. And thank you. If I ever do want to talk about it, you might hear more than you ever wanted."

He chuckles at my wry tone just as a flash of whitish-blond whisks past my window, snapping me out of my miserable thoughts. Inadvertently, I follow the trail it makes, transfixed by the unique color and wavelike flow as it bounces and plays in the summer sunshine and breeze. That is until it drops from my view in a sudden swish and swoop along with the body it's attached to. Then there's the scream.

"Shit."

Snatching my phone, I fly out of the car and race up the three cement steps to the first landing where a woman is yelling and fighting with a man trying to snatch her purse. Gripping the leather handle, he gives a solid yank, managing the upper hand with the purse while simultaneously shoving her to the ground. Hard.

Without thinking twice, I collide with him, the full force of my size and weight knocking him back. The purse slips from his hand, skidding on the steps, but before he can catch himself from falling or right his body and flee, I grab him by the shirt and haul him up. Feet dangling from the ground, I get a better look at him.

"Jesus," I hiss in dismay. "What the hell are you doing snatching purses at your age?"

The kid, who can't be any older than seventeen, sneers at me, all punk-ass bravado despite the fact that I have him dangling like a proverbial worm on a hook. "Fuck you, man. The fuck you care what I do? You don't know me."

I set him down, but I don't release my hold on his shirt. "You think stealing from women makes you tough? Makes you a man? Do you know what being tough is?" I get right up in his face. "Tough is being a man even when the odds are stacked against you. It's doing the right thing when the wrong thing is easier. Grow up. Get out of your shit and do better. Now go before I call the cops."

I shove him away but make sure he sees me staring after him. For a second, he falters, his gaze snapping down at the woman who is still on the ground, then back up at me before he runs off.

I turn, taking in the now-seated woman swearing under her breath and staring incredulously at a high heel clutched angrily in her fist. The long, narrow heel of the shoe hangs limply from the black stiletto, having snapped.

"You're not supposed to do this," she bemoans. "Not today! Your job is to carry me from point A to point B without snapping like a twig. Don't you know what this means for me? Now look." Her hands fly about her body. "I'm a bloody mess. Literally." She threateningly shakes the shoe. "I'm gonna tell Marie you did this to us, and she won't be pleased. Not at all."

Marie? I take a better look at the shoes. Marie Marcato. Exclusive and expensive. But clearly, she's speaking in jest and ire because no one knows or speaks to Marie directly. Not even me and I've been trying for longer than I care to admit. Still, I can't understand how she's more upset about her heel snapping than she is about the fact that she was almost *mugged*.

My shadow looms over her, blocking the blinding summer sun. "What were you thinking fighting with him? He could have been armed or seriously hurt you. Are you okay?" The cuts on her knees are dripping blood down her shins and onto the concrete steps, but she's more focused on her broken shoe.

Alarmingly bright cornflower-blue eyes snap up and glue themselves to my face. And the moment they register me, they grow round as dinner plates, her plump pink lips parting. "Shit," she breathes harshly.

"Now you're catching up. That's what I said when I saw you were struggling with him. Are. You. Okay?" I repeat, my annoyance dripping through into my tone now that she's staring at me like, well, like everyone else does. Starstruck, awed, and terrified. "Do you not know how to answer questions or is English along with common sense a difficulty for you?"

She scowls at my sharp, curt words. "Did you honestly just ask that? Do you have any sense of how insanely rude and condescending that is after what just happened?"

My lips bounce, attempting to curl up into a smirk, but I beat it instantly away. "Whatever gets you to speak."

She blinks away from me, staring down at her knees that are bleeding and oozing everywhere. "He shoved me, and my shoe broke," she shoots back. "Obviously, I'm not having the best of mornings."

"Obviously," I deadpan, mocking her snarky, sardonic tone. "And now you're hurt. For the third time, are you okay?"

"Um. I don't know," she admits with a shaky breath. "I'm pissed. And hurt. And annoyed. At so many, *many* things right now."

"Can I help you up?"

"You might be the last person on earth I should ever ask for or accept help from."

Okay. I'm not sure what to do with that. "Do you work here?"

"Probably not for much longer. I'm a design intern. First day." Regret immediately strikes her features, and she frowns, shaking her head violently. "I seriously wish I hadn't just told you that."

I chuckle and with the sound of my laughter at what she inaccurately assumes is at her expense, she scathingly glares back up at me with those arresting eyes. Then there is her hair and those sexy lips and those entrancing pinpoint freckles on the bridge of an adorably petite nose and across the upslope of her perfect high cheekbones and shit.

I can't stop looking at her.

Though I know I've seen her face before, I'm struggling to place where exactly. Even so, my stupid cock stirs in my pants. Not the most opportune time for that, given her vantage point of me from the ground.

Slowly, she starts to stand, albeit awkwardly because she can't roll onto her knees to help herself up and the pencil skirt she's wearing is restrictive around her thighs.

"That's not a good idea," I tell her. "You're bleeding. Your shoe is broken. Not to mention, you just admitted you're not sure if you're okay."

"I'm fine." She hisses out a shocked breath as her knee scrapes the ground. "I can't exactly live here and besides, I don't want to be late on my first day."

"I'm sure they'll understand when they see you."

She rolls onto her side, attempting to use her elbows, and this is just ridiculous.

"I don't know what that move is, but you're only going to hurt yourself more," I admonish. "Was your purse really worth this? Here, take my hand."

"No, thanks." She shoves my proffered hand away, her pride getting the better of her.

*Or maybe it's because you're being a dick to her after she was just attacked.* I push that thought away.

"Do you know who I am?" I ask coolly, annoyed she's brushing me off when I helped her with the mugger and am offering to help her again.

She strikes me with a look. "You mean other than the jerk standing over me, making fun of me? Yes, I know who you are."

"Then I'm shocked you're still speaking to me like this." She's an intern. That means she works for me whether directly or not. So her talking back to me like this?

"Me too. Must be all the blood loss and adrenaline making me loopy. I take it no one talks back or insults you?"

"Not if they have any sort of natural self-preservation instincts, which I think we already established you don't."

"Wow," she mocks. "You're a real prince amongst mortals, there, *Zaxton*." She snorts. "What kind of name is Zaxton anyway? Paxton, Jaxson, Saxton even, but I've never heard of a Zaxton."

My eyes narrow into menacing slits. I can be terrifying when motivated. "A none of your business, *intern*, name. Speaking of names..." I raise my eyebrow expectantly at her.

"Nuh-uh. I'll be fired for sure if you know who I am."

I have no idea what that means, but I don't care enough right now to fish for more answers. I can't stand watching her flounder about another second whether she wants my help or not. Bending down, I loop my arm around her hips, pulling the majority of her weight up to spare her knees. I do my best to ignore the way her body feels against mine. And how good she smells. Perfume, shampoo, body wash, or her natural fragrance—whatever it is, if I could bottle it up and sell it, I'd be richer than I already am.

Once she's upright, albeit a bit wobbly, I take a step back, releasing her as fast as I can without her falling back to the ground.

"Thank you," she murmurs. "And thank you for saving my purse. Maybe I shouldn't have tried to fight him for it, but I've had enough of people taking from me and walking all over me to let it happen with some kid." Turning away from me, she starts hobbling one-heeled up the steps, anxious to get inside and away from me. Is she for real?

"You're dripping blood everywhere," I call after her, hating how quick she was to dismiss me. Hating how I want her eyes back on mine. "Will you stop? You can barely walk like this."

She emits an exasperated sigh because she knows I'm right. Blood is running all down her legs and across her heelless foot and even into the other remaining good shoe.

I'm fed up with this game.

"I don't remember asking for your—ah!" She belts out a half-scream as her legs are swooped out from beneath her and I lift her body into my arms. "What are you doing?"

"Carrying you in. You're bleeding all over my steps and were just attacked. I have to make sure you're okay."

I hold her tightly against me while I carry her bride-style up the steps. She's tall and thin, but with perfect fucking curves in all the right places. Her hair kicks up in my face as I adjust her, assaulting me with her delicious scent. I pull her in closer, liking the way she feels against me a little too much. What is that fragrance? A goddamn summer afternoon in the country with wind, wildflowers, and sun? It's killing me not to bury my nose in her silky hair and breathe it in deeper.

"I can walk," she protests, completely oblivious to what she's doing to me.

"I beg to differ. Stop squirming."

"I'd stop squirming if you put me down."

"We're almost there. Now stop. Squirming." My hand on her thigh clenches in warning, and she gives up the protest.

"I'm trying not to get your suit sleeve covered in my blood."

"Appreciated, but I'm going to be changing suits in a few minutes anyway."

She laughs bitterly at that. "That your standard practice, Mr. Monroe? Just how many wardrobe changes a day do you have?"

My head tilts down. My eyes, dark and hooded, lock with hers. I smirk at how brazen she is with me. "You've got quite the mouth on you for an intern speaking to her boss on her first day."

She shrugs against me, trying to keep her face hidden since people are absolutely staring at us. I can't exactly blame them either. Of the many, many things I'm known for, carrying damsels in distress up the steps and into my building isn't one of them.

The door opens, a blast of frigid air making her shiver when it hits the blood on her skin. I press her tighter. "You all right there?"

"I'm fine. Totally great. I mean, considering it's my first day and I was nearly mugged, the heel of my shoe snapped, and I'm bleeding like a bad bitch out of hell. Oh, and I'm swearing at my boss, who just so happens to be you of all people." She claps a hand over her mouth, murmuring, "Sorry," through her fingers. "I just." A heavy sigh. "I didn't want to see you like this. I didn't think I'd ever have to see you at all. That's what he said and then you swoop in to save the day and I... I'm done talking now."

I'm not sure I understand anything she's saying. My confusion must be evident because she gnaws on her lip and shakes her head, indicating to me she's not going to clarify.

"Mr. Monroe, what happened?" The lobby security guard walks briskly by our side as I carry her over to a bank of seats along the wall between the elevators and floor-to-ceiling windows.

"She got hurt outside on the steps. Do we have a first aid kit down here, George?"

"Of course, sir. I'll go fetch it right away."

George scurries off just as I place her upright on the cushioned leather. Then I'm kneeling before her, tugging my white silk handkerchief from my breast pocket and pressing it against the cut that's bleeding the most.

I know it has to burn. Her chin wobbles and she sucks in a sharp breath as her pretty blue eyes glass over.

"You know his name." It's a half whisper as she stares down at her knees, refusing to meet my eyes.

"Yes. I know his name." My tone is terse. "I know his wife's name as well as his children's names. He's been working here since I was a kid and he's a good man."

Her head bobs up and down. "Didn't mean for that to come out as judgmental as it sounded." She tilts her head. "Or maybe I did. Sorry." She touches the sleeve of my suit coat. "My blood is on you."

My eyes stay locked on her pretty face. "Should that bother me?"

"Doesn't it?"

Does it? It feels like it should be gross, yet it's erotic in some strange way.

"No."

She peeks up at me through her long lashes, a coy smile curving up her lips, and the air leaves my lungs like someone just drove a knife right through my chest. She's easily the most stunning heart-breaker I've ever encountered.

"Does everyone hop to do your bidding the second you snap your fingers?" she asks, ignoring everything but my sour attitude while dropping her broken shoe to the floor and checking her watch. She's late or getting there. So am I, for that matter, but I don't care all that much right now.

I like her attitude. I like that she fought back even though it cost her her shoe and knees. I like her snapping at me and calling me out on my shit while asking me bold questions no one ever has the balls to ask.

"Yes," I answer flatly, still crouched before her, unable to so much as shift away from her.

"You're quite the intimidating man."

I grunt in dismay at her cheeky tone and mockingly flirty expression.

"No, I mean it," she insists. "You are. I bet you can feel it every time you touch me."

My eyebrows bounce in surprise and my grip on her calf tightens while my other still presses in on her wound. I intimidate her, but she's not afraid of me.

"What exactly does my touch do to you?" Thumbs on both hands brush back and forth along her skin and goose bumps erupt in their wake, her pupils expanding ever so slightly.

Fuck.

That's what my touch does to her. I'm not the only one feeling this. I shouldn't be reacting to her—she is an intern, and this is *not* what I do—but it's as if my brain and body are on disconnect. Because I recognize her elegantly radiant face. I never catalog a woman's features anymore. Not beyond the scope of professionalism and necessity of business.

But I know her face from somewhere.

"Repulses me," she whispers, still half-smiling at me.

"Is that so?" My thumbs brush again, dragging a longer trail on her skin, and her breath skitters in a sharp hiccup. I smirk arrogantly. "Are you always this much of a brat to people who help you?"

"I think it's just with you. You seem to have a strange effect on me."

"What if I like having this effect on you?" Not words I should be saying to her, but again, I want to see how she reacts to me if for no other reason than my own perverse need.

Mercifully and before this can go any further, George returns, proudly carrying the first aid kit. "Sir, you're needed upstairs."

"Tell them—"

"I can take it from here," she interrupts, snatching the kit out of George's hand. Swinging her legs out of my grip, she places them up on the seat and pops open the white top of the large box, effectively dismissing me.

I stand, pocketing the blood-soaked handkerchief when I should throw it away.

"Thank you for your help," she tells me, forcing a weak smile that doesn't reach her eyes. "I'm sorry if I was short or even insubordinate with you. It's obviously already been a day for me and hopefully, you can pretend I was nothing but respectful and polite."

I scowl, annoyed with everything. Her. Me. The way I want to clean her wounds and bandage her up. How I want more time with her when I shouldn't.

Without another word, I'm gone. The tap of my perfect, nonbroken shoes on the marble floors echoes through the lobby that is progressively growing more and more crowded as the official start of the day approaches. The elevator is already there waiting, but before I step on, I glance back in her direction.

Our eyes lock for the briefest of seconds, my pulse jumps, and then I'm on the elevator alone. No one else dares to step on while I'm in here. I press the button for the top floor and curse under my breath as the doors close. What the fuck did I just do with that girl and why do I want to do it all over again?

I scrub my hands up my face. I never should have gotten out of bed this morning.

Want to find out what happens next with Zax and Aurelia? Grab your copy of this grumpy/sunshine, enemies to lovers romance today!

# END OF BOOK NOTE

Hello lovely reader. Thank you so much for taking the time to read Wynter and Asher's story. I hope you loved it as much as I do. When I originally sat down to write Asher's story, I knew I wanted to do something I hadn't done before (other than sports romance). The idea for a surprise baby came naturally since I had already built up in previous books his horrible one-nighter with the woman of his dreams. In the end, it was SO much fun to write and I just fell in love with Asher as both a lover and a father.

I want to thank a few people for their help with this story. My family, first and always. I have the most incredibly loving and supportive husband and I couldn't do any of this without him. He is the hero of my everyday romance story. Thank you to my amazing girls for dealing with their money who likely spends too much time in front of a screen writing. But with out their love, laughter, smiles, hugs, and endless fun, I'd be lost.

I want to thank my team of Patricia, Kelly, Danielle, and Joy. I am eternally grateful for all that you do for me! You're the absolute best! And to my author bestie Lisa who keeps me on tasks, listens when I need to vent, and cracks the whip when I need it most. Thank you!!

If you're new to me, feel free to check out my website for more information. www.jsamanbooks.com.

Thank you!

XO,

J. Saman